KING'S CAGE

Also by Victoria Aveyard

Realm Breaker

Red Queen

Glass Sword

War Storm

Broken Throne: A Red Queen Collection

Red Queen: The Official Coloring Book

Digital Novellas

Queen Song

Steel Scars

Novella Collection

Cruel Crown

KING'S CAGE

VICTORIA AVEYARD

An Imprint of HarperCollinsPublishers

HarperTeen is an imprint of HarperCollins Publishers.

King's Cage
Copyright © 2017 by Victoria Aveyard
Endpapers and map © & ™ 2017 Victoria Aveyard. All rights reserved.
Endpapers and map illustrated by Amanda Persky

Library of Congress Control Number: 2018960534
ISBN 978-0-06-231070-5

Typography by Torborg Davern
22 23 24 25 26 LBC 16 15 14 13 12

First paperback edition, 2019

Never doubt that you are valuable and powerful and deserving of every chance and opportunity in the world to pursue and achieve your own dreams.
—HRC

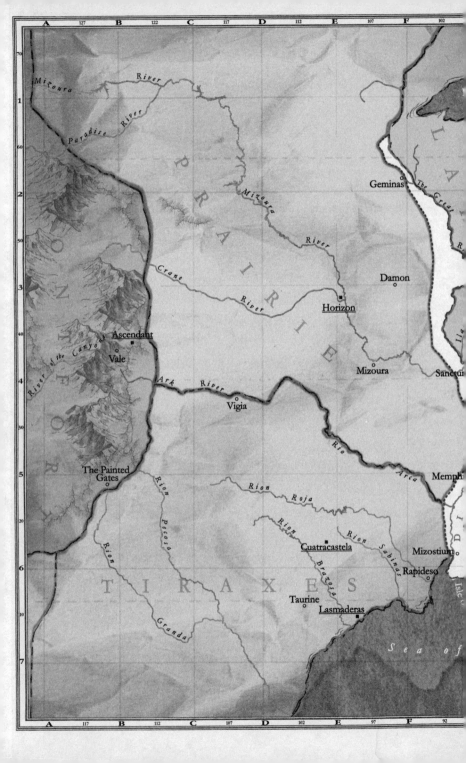

KING'S CAGE

ONE
Mare

I rise to my feet when he lets me.

The chain jerks me up, pulling on the thorned collar at my throat. Its points dig in, not enough to draw blood—not yet. But I'm already bleeding from the wrists. Slow wounds, worn from days of unconscious captivity in rough, ripping manacles. The color stains my white sleeves dark crimson and bright scarlet, fading from old blood to new in a testament to my ordeal. To show Maven's court how much I've suffered already.

He stands over me, his expression unreadable. The tips of his father's crown make him seem taller, as if the iron is growing out of his skull. It gleams, each point a curling flame of black metal shot with bronze and silver. I focus on the bitterly familiar thing so I don't have to look into Maven's eyes. He draws me in anyway, tugging on another chain I can't see. Only feel.

One white hand circles my wounded wrist, somehow gentle. In spite of myself, my eyes snap to his face, unable to stay away. His smile is anything but kind. Slim and sharp as a razor, biting at me with every tooth. And his eyes are worst of all. Her eyes, Elara's eyes. Once I thought them cold, made of living ice. Now I know better. The hottest fires burn blue, and his eyes are no exception.

The shadow of the flame. He is certainly ablaze, but darkness eats at his edges. Bruise-like splotches of black and blue surround eyes bloodshot with silver veins. He has not slept. He's thinner than I remember, leaner, crueler. His hair, black as a void, has reached his ears, curling at the ends, and his cheeks are still smooth. Sometimes I forget how young he is. How young we both are. Beneath my shift dress, the *M* brand on my collarbone stings.

Maven turns quickly, my chain tight in his fist, forcing me to move with him. A moon circling a planet.

"Bear witness to this prisoner, this victory," he says, squaring his shoulders to the vast audience before us. Three hundred Silvers at least, nobles and civilians, guards and officers. I'm painfully aware of the Sentinels on the edge of my vision, their fiery robes a constant reminder of my quickly shrinking cage. My Arven guards are never out of sight either, their white uniforms blinding, their silencing ability suffocating. I might choke on the pressure of their presence.

The king's voice echoes across the opulent stretches of Caesar's Square, reverberating through a crowd that responds in kind. There must be microphones and speakers somewhere, to carry the king's bitter words throughout the city, and no doubt the rest of the kingdom.

"Here is the leader of the Scarlet Guard, Mare Barrow." In spite of my predicament, I almost snort. *Leader.* His mother's death has not stemmed his lies. "A murderer, a terrorist, a great enemy to our kingdom. And now she kneels before us, bare to her blood."

The chain jerks again, sending me scuttling forward, arms outstretched to catch my balance. I react dully, eyes downcast. So much pageantry. Anger and shame curl through me as I realize the amount of damage this simple act will do to the Scarlet Guard. Reds across Norta will watch me dance on Maven's strings and think us weak, defeated, unworthy of their attention, effort, or hope. Nothing could be further from the truth. But there isn't anything I can do, not now, not here, standing on the knife edge of Maven's mercy. I wonder about Corvium, the military city we saw burning on our way to the Choke. There was rioting after my broadcast message. Was it the first gasp of revolution—or the last? I have no way of knowing. And I doubt anyone will bother to bring me a newspaper.

Cal warned me against the threat of civil war a long time ago, before his father died, before he was left with nothing but a tempestuous lightning girl. *Rebellion on both sides,* he said. But standing here, leashed before Maven's court and his Silver kingdom, I see no division. Even though I showed them, told them of Maven's prison, of their loved ones taken away, of their trust betrayed by a king and his mother—I am still the enemy here. It makes me want to scream, but I know better. Maven's voice will always be louder than mine.

Are Mom and Dad watching? The thought of it brings a fresh wave of sorrow, and I bite hard against my lip to keep more tears at bay. I know there are video cameras nearby, focused on my face. Even if I can't feel them anymore, I know. Maven would not miss the opportunity to immortalize my downfall.

Are they about to see me die?

The collar tells me no. Why bother with this spectacle if he's just going to kill me? Another might feel relieved, but my insides turn cold with fear. He will not kill me. Not Maven. I feel it in his touch. His long, pale fingers still cling to my wrist, while his other hand still holds my leash. Even now, when I am painfully his, he won't let go. I would prefer death to this cage, to the twisted obsession of a mad boy king.

I remember his notes, each one ending with the same strange lament.

Until we meet again.

He continues speaking, but his voice dulls in my head, the whine of a hornet coming too close, making every nerve stand on edge. I look over my shoulder. My eyes drift through the crowd of courtiers behind us. All of them stand proud and vile in their mourning black. Lord Volo of House Samos and his son, Ptolemus, are splendid in polished, ebony armor with scaled silver sashes from hip to shoulder. At the sight of the latter, I see scarlet, raging red. I fight the urge to lunge and rip the skin from Ptolemus's face. To stab him through his heart the way he did my brother Shade. The desire shows, and he has the spine to smirk at me. If not for the collar and the silent guards restricting everything I am, I would turn his bones to smoking glass.

Somehow his sister, an enemy of so many months ago, isn't looking at me. Evangeline, her gown spiked with black crystal, is ever the glittering star of such a violent constellation. I suppose she'll be queen soon, having suffered her betrothal to Maven long enough. Her gaze is on the king's back, dark eyes fixed with burning focus on the nape of his neck. A breeze picks up, stirring her glossy curtain of silver hair, blowing it back from her shoulders, but she doesn't blink. Only after a long moment does she seem to notice me staring. And even then, her eyes barely flick to mine. They are empty of feeling. I am no longer worthy of her attention.

"Mare Barrow is a prisoner of the crown, and she will face the crown and council's judgment. Her many crimes must be answered for."

With what? I wonder.

The crowd roars in response, cheering his decree. They are Silvers, but "common," not of noble descent. While they revel in Maven's words, his court does not react. In fact, some of them turn gray, angry, stone-faced. None more so than House Merandus, their mourning garb slashed with the dark blue of the dead queen's wretched colors. While Evangeline did not notice me, they fix on my face with startling intensity. Eyes of burning blue from every direction. I expect to hear their whispers in my head, a dozen voices burrowing like worms through a rotten apple. Instead, there is only silence. Perhaps the Arven officers flanking me are not just jailers, but protectors as well, smothering my ability as well as the abilities of anyone who would use them against me. Maven's orders, I assume. No one else may hurt me here.

No one but him.

But everything hurts already. It hurts to stand, hurts to move, hurts to think. From the jet crash, from the sounder, from the crushing weight of the silencing guards. And those are only physical wounds. Bruises. Fractures. Pains that will heal if given the time. The same cannot be said of the rest. My brother is dead. I am a prisoner. And I don't know what really happened to my friends however many days ago when I struck this devil's bargain. Cal, Kilorn, Cameron, my brothers Bree and Tramy. We left them behind in the clearing, but they were wounded, immobilized, vulnerable. Maven could have sent any number of assassins back to finish what he started. I traded myself for them all, and I don't even know if it worked.

Maven would tell me if I asked him. I can see it in his face. His eyes dart to mine after every vile sentence, punctuating every lie performed for his adoring subjects. To make sure I'm watching, paying attention, looking at him. Like the child he is.

I will not beg him. Not here. Not like this. I have pride enough for that.

"My mother and father died fighting these animals," he rails on. "They gave their lives to keep this kingdom whole, to keep you safe."

Defeated as I am, I can't help but glare at Maven, meeting his fire with a hiss of my own. We both remember his father's death. His murder. Queen Elara whispered her way into Cal's brain, turning the king's beloved heir into a deadly weapon. Maven and I watched as Cal was forced to become his father's killer, cutting off the king's head and any chance Cal had of ruling. I have seen many horrible things since then, and still the memory haunts me.

I don't remember much of what happened to the queen outside the walls of Corros Prison. The state of her body afterward was testament enough to what unbridled lightning can do to human flesh. I know I killed her without question, without remorse, without regret. My ravaging storm fed by Shade's sudden death. The last clear image I have of the Corros battle is of him falling, his heart pierced by Ptolemus's needle of cold, unforgiving steel. Somehow Ptolemus escaped my blind rage, but the queen did not. At least the Colonel and I made sure the world knew what happened to her, displaying her corpse during our broadcast.

I wish Maven had some of her ability, so he could look into my head and see exactly what kind of ending I gave his mother. I want him to feel the pain of loss as terribly as I do.

His eyes are on me as he finishes his memorized speech, one hand outstretched to better display the chain binding me to him. Everything he does is methodical, performed for an image.

"I pledge myself to do the same, to end the Scarlet Guard and the monsters like Mare Barrow, or die in the attempt."

Die, then, I want to scream.

The roar of the crowd drowns out my thoughts. Hundreds cheer on their king and his tyranny. I cried on the walk across the bridge, in the face of so many blaming me for their loved ones' deaths. I can still feel the tears drying on my cheeks. Now I want to weep again, not in sadness, but anger. How can they believe this? How can they stomach these lies?

Like a doll, I am turned from the sight. With the last of my strength, I crane my neck over one shoulder, hunting for the cameras, the eyes of the world. *See me,* I beg. *See how he lies.* My jaw tightens, my eyes narrow, painting what I pray is a picture of resilience, rebellion, and rage. *I am the lightning girl. I am a storm.* It feels like a lie. The lightning girl is dead.

But it is the last thing I can do for the cause, and for the people I love still out there. They will not see me stumble in this final moment. No, I will stand. And though I have no idea how, I have to keep fighting, even here in the belly of the beast.

Another tug forces me to spin around to face the court. Cold Silvers stare back, their skin undertoned by blue and black and purple and gray, leached of life, with veins of steel and diamond rather than blood. They focus not on me, but on Maven himself. In them I find my answer. In them I see hunger.

For a split second, I pity the boy king alone on his throne. Then, deep down, I feel the teasing breath of hope.

Oh, Maven. What a mess you're in.

I can only wonder who will strike first.

The Scarlet Guard—or the lords and ladies ready to slit Maven's throat and take everything his mother died for.

He hands my leash over to one of the Arvens as soon as we flee the Whitefire steps, retreating into the yawning entrance hall of the palace.

Strange. He was so fixated on getting me back, on putting me into his cage, but he tosses my chains away without so much as a glance. *Coward,* I tell myself. He can't bring himself to look at me when it isn't for spectacle.

"Did you keep your promise?" I demand, breathless. My voice sounds raspy from days of disuse. "Are you a man of your word?"

He doesn't answer.

The rest of the court falls in behind us. Their lines and rows are well practiced, based on the complicated intricacies of status and rank. Only I am out of place, the first one to follow the king, walking a few steps behind where a queen should be. I could not be further from the title.

I glance at the larger of my jailers, hoping to see something besides blind loyalty in him. He wears a white uniform, thick, bulletproof, zipped tight up his throat. Gloves, gleaming. Not silk, but plastic— rubber. I flinch at the sight. Despite their silencing ability, the Arvens won't take any chances with me. Even if I manage to slip a spark past their continuous onslaught, the gloves will protect their hands and allow them to keep me collared, chained, caged. The big Arven doesn't meet my gaze, his eyes focused ahead while his lips purse in concentration. The other is just the same, flanking me in perfect step with his brother or cousin. Their naked scalps gleam, and I'm reminded of Lucas Samos. My kind guard, my friend, who was executed because I existed, and because I used him. I was lucky then, that Cal gave me such a decent Silver to keep me prisoner. And, I realize, I am lucky now. Indifferent guards will be easier for me to kill.

Because they must die. Somehow. Some way. If I am to escape, if I want to reclaim my lightning, they are the first obstacles. The rest are easy to guess. Maven's Sentinels, the other guards and officers posted throughout the palace, and of course Maven himself. I'm not leaving this place unless I leave behind his corpse—or mine.

I think about killing him. Wrapping my chain around his neck and squeezing the life from his body. It helps me ignore the fact that every step takes me deeper into the palace, over white marble, past gilded, soaring walls, beneath a dozen chandeliers with crystal lights carved of flame. As beautiful and cold as I remember. A prison of golden locks and diamond bars. At least I won't have to face its most violent and dangerous warden. The old queen is dead. Still, I shiver at the thought of her. Elara Merandus. Her shadow ghosts through my head. Once she tore through my memories. Now she's one of them.

An armored figure cuts through my glare, sidling around my guards to plant himself between the king and me. He keeps pace with us, a dogged guardian even though he doesn't wear the robes or mask of a Sentinel. I suppose he knows I'm thinking about strangling Maven. I bite my lip, bracing myself for the sharp sting of a whisper's assault.

But no, he is not of House Merandus. His armor is obsidian dark, his hair silver, his skin moon white. And his eyes, when he looks over his shoulder at me—his eyes are empty and black.

Ptolemus.

I lunge teeth first, not knowing what I'm doing, not caring. So long as I leave my mark. I wonder if Silver blood tastes different from Red.

I never find out.

My collar snaps backward, pulling me so violently my spine arches and I crash to the floor. A bit harder and I would've broken my neck. The crack of marble on skull makes the world spin, but not enough to keep me down. I scramble, my sight narrowing to Ptolemus's armored legs, now turning to face me. Again I lurch for them, and again the collar pulls me back.

"Enough of this," Maven hisses.

He stands over me, halting to watch my poor attempts to repay Ptolemus. The rest of the procession has stopped too, many crowding forward to see the twisted Red rat fight in vain.

The collar seems to tighten, and I gulp against it, reaching for my throat.

Maven keeps his eyes on the metal as it shrinks. "Evangeline, I said enough."

Despite the pain, I turn to see her at my back, one fist clenched at her side. Like him, she stares at my collar. It pulses as it moves. It must match her heartbeat.

"Let me loose her," she says, and I wonder if I misheard. "Let me loose her right here. Dismiss her guards, and I'll kill her, lightning and all."

I snarl back at her, every inch the beast they think I am. "Try it," I tell her, wishing with all my heart that Maven would agree. Even with my wounds, my days of silence, and my years of inferiority to the magnetron girl, I want what she offers. I beat her before. I can do it again. It is a chance, at least. A better chance than I could ever hope for.

Maven's eyes snap from my collar to his betrothed, his face falling into a tight, searing scowl. I see so much of his mother in him. "Are you questioning the orders of your king, Lady Evangeline?"

Her teeth flash between lips painted purple. Her shroud of courtly manner threatens to fall away, but before she can say something truly damning, her father shifts just so, his arm brushing her own. His message is clear: *Obey*.

"No," she growls, meaning *yes*. Her neck bends, inclining her head. "Your Majesty."

The collar releases, widening back to size around my neck. It might even be looser than before. Small blessing that Evangeline is not so meticulous as she strives to appear.

"Mare Barrow is a prisoner of the crown, and the crown will do with her as it sees fit," Maven says, his voice carrying past his volatile bride. His eyes sweep through the rest of the court, making his intentions clear. "Death is too good for her."

A low murmur ripples through the nobles. I hear tones of opposition, but even more agreement. *Strange.* I thought all of them would want me executed in the worst way, strung up to feed vultures and bleed away whatever ground the Scarlet Guard has gained. But I suppose they want worse fates for me.

Worse fates.

That's what Jon said before. When he saw what my future held, where my path led. He knew this was coming. Knew, and told the king. Bought a place at Maven's side with my brother's life and my freedom.

I find Jon standing in the crowd, given a wide berth by the others. His eyes are red, livid; his hair prematurely gray and tied into a neat tail. Another newblood pet for Maven Calore, but this one wears no chains that I can see. Because he helped Maven stop our mission to save a legion of children before it could even begin. Told Maven our paths and our future. Gift-wrapped me for the boy king. Betrayed us all.

Jon is already staring at me, of course. I don't expect an apology for what he did, and do not receive one.

"What about interrogation?"

A voice I do not recognize sounds to my left. Still, I know his face.

Samson Merandus. An arena fighter, a savage whisper, a cousin to the dead queen. He shoulders his way toward me, and I can't help but flinch. In another life I saw him make his arena opponent stab himself to death. Kilorn sat by my side and watched, cheering, enjoying the last hours of his freedom. Then his master died, and our entire world shifted. Our paths changed. And now I sprawl across flawless marble, cold and bleeding, less than a dog at the feet of a king.

"Is she too good for interrogation, Your Majesty?" Samson continues, pointing one white hand in my direction. He catches me beneath the chin, forcing me to look up. I fight the urge to bite him. I don't need to give Evangeline another excuse to choke me. "Think of what she's seen. What she knows. She's their leader—and the key to unraveling her wretched kind."

He's wrong, but still my heartbeat thrums in my chest. I know enough to be of great damage. Tuck flashes before my eyes, as well as the Colonel and the twins from Montfort. The infiltration of the legions. The cities. The Whistles across the country, now ferrying refugees to safety. Precious secrets carefully kept, and soon to be revealed. How many will my knowledge put in danger? How many will die when they crack me open?

And that's just military intelligence. Worse still are the dark parts of my own mind. The corners where I keep my worst demons. Maven is one of them. The prince I remembered and loved and wished were real. Then there's Cal. What I've done to keep him, what I've ignored, and what lies I tell myself about his allegiances. My shame and my mistakes eat away, gnawing on my roots. I can't let Samson—or Maven—see such things inside me.

Please, I want to beg. My lips do not move. As much as I hate Maven, as much as I want to see him suffer, I know he's the best chance I have. But pleading for mercy before his strongest allies and worst enemies will only weaken an already-weak king. So I keep quiet, trying to ignore Samson's grip on my jaw, focusing only on Maven's face.

His eyes find mine for the longest and shortest of moments.

"You have your orders," he says brusquely, nodding to my guards.

Their grip is firm but not bruising as they lift me to my feet, using hands and chains to guide me out of the crowd. I leave them all behind. Evangeline, Ptolemus, Samson, and Maven.

He turns on his heel, heading in the opposite direction, toward the only thing he has left to keep him warm.

A throne of frozen flames.

TWO
Mare

I am never alone.

The jailers do not leave. Always two, always watching, always keeping what I am silent and suppressed. They don't need anything more than a locked door to make me a prisoner. Not that I can even get close to the door without being manhandled back to the center of my bedchamber. They're stronger than I am, and forever vigilant. My only escape from their eyes is the small bathroom, a chamber of white tile and golden fixings, with a forbidding line of Silent Stone along the floor. There are enough of the pearly gray slabs to make my head pound and my throat constrict. I have to be quick in there, and make use of every strangling second. The sensation reminds me of Cameron and her ability. She can kill someone with the strength of her silence. As much as I hate my guards' constant vigil, I will not risk suffocating on a bathroom floor for a few extra minutes of peace.

Funny, I used to think my greatest fear was being left alone. Now I am anything but, and I've never been more terrified.

I have not felt my lightning in four days.

Five.

Six.

Seventeen.

Thirty-one.

I notch each day in the baseboard next to the bed, using a fork to dig the passing time. It feels good to leave my mark, to inflict my own small injury on the prison of Whitefire Palace. The Arvens don't mind. They ignore me for the most part, focused only on total and absolute silence. They keep to their places by the door, seated like statues with living eyes.

This is not the same room I slept in the last time I was at Whitefire. Obviously it wouldn't be proper to house a royal prisoner in the same place as a royal bride. But I'm not in a cell either. My cage is comfortable and well furnished, with a plush bed, a bookshelf stocked with boring tomes, a few chairs, a table to eat at, even fine curtains, all in neutral shades of gray, brown, and white. Leached of color, as the Arvens leach power from me.

I slowly get used to sleeping alone, but nightmares plague me without Cal to keep them away. Without someone who cares for me. Every time I wake up, I touch the earrings dotting my ear, naming each stone. Bree, Tramy, Shade, Kilorn. Brothers in blood and bond. Three living, one a ghost. I wish I had an earring to match the one I gave Gisa, so I could have a piece of her too. I dream of her sometimes. Nothing concrete, but flashes of her face, her hair red and dark as spilled blood. Her words haunt me like nothing else. *One day people are going to come and take everything you have.* She was right.

There are no mirrors, not even in the bathroom. But I know what this place is doing to me. Despite the hearty meals and the lack of exercise, my face feels thinner. My bones cut beneath skin, sharper than ever as I waste. There isn't much more to do than sleep or read one of the volumes on Nortan tax code, but still, exhaustion set in days ago. Bruises blossom from every touch. And the collar feels hot even though I spend my days cold, shivering. It could be a fever. I could be dying.

Not that I have anyone to tell. I barely even speak through the days. The door opens for food and water, for the change in my jailers, and nothing more. I never see a Red maid or servant, though they must exist. Instead, the Arvens retrieve meals, linens, and clothes deposited outside, bringing them in for me to use. They clean up as well, grimacing as they perform such a lowly task. I suppose letting a Red in my room is too dangerous. The thought makes me smile. So the Scarlet Guard is still a threat, enough to warrant such rigid protocol that even servants aren't allowed near me.

But then, it seems no one else is either. No one comes to gawk or gloat over the lightning girl. Not even Maven.

The Arvens do not talk to me. They don't tell me their names. So I give them some of my own. Kitten, the older woman smaller than me, with a tiny face and keen, sharp eyes. Egg, his head round, white, and bald like the rest of his guardian kin. Trio has three lines tattooed down his neck, like the dragging of perfect claws. And green-eyed Clover, a girl near my age, unwavering in her duties. She is the only one who dares look me in the eye.

When I first realized Maven wanted me back, I expected pain, or darkness, or both. Most of all I expected to see him and endure my torment under his blazing eyes. But I receive nothing. Not since the day I arrived and was forced to kneel. He told me then he would put my body on display. But no executioners have come. Neither have the whispers, men like Samson Merandus and the dead queen, to pry my head open and unspool my thoughts. If this is my punishment, it is a boring one. Maven has no imagination.

There are still the voices in my head, and so many, too many memories. They cut with a blade's edge. I try to dull the pain with even duller books, but the words swim before my eyes, letters rearranging until all I see are the names of the people I left behind. The living and the dead. And always, everywhere, Shade.

Ptolemus might have killed my brother, but I was the one to put Shade in his path. Because I was selfish, thinking myself some kind of savior. Because, once again, I put my trust in someone I shouldn't have and traded lives as a gambler does playing cards. *But you liberated a prison. You freed so many people—and you saved Julian.*

A weak thought, an even weaker consolation. I know now what the cost of Corros Prison was. And every day I come to terms with the fact that, if given the choice, I would not pay it again. Not for Julian, not for a hundred living newbloods. I wouldn't save any of them with Shade's life.

And it was all the same in the end. Maven had asked me to return for months, begging with every bloodstained note. He had hoped to buy me with corpses, with the bodies of the dead. But I'd thought there was no trade I would make, not even for a thousand innocent lives. Now I wish I'd done as he asked long ago. Before he thought to come for the ones I truly care for, knowing I would save them. Knowing that Cal, Kilorn, my family—they were the only bargain I was willing to make. For their lives, I gave everything.

I guess he knows better than to torture me. Even with the sounder, a machine made to use my lightning against me, to split me apart, nerve by nerve.

My agony is useless to him. His mother taught him well. My only comfort is knowing that the young king is without his vicious puppeteer. While I am kept here, watched day and night, he is alone at the head of a kingdom, without Elara Merandus to guide his hand and protect his back.

It's been a month since I've tasted fresh air, and almost as long since I saw anything but the inside of my room and the narrow view my single window affords.

The window looks out over a courtyard garden, well past dead at the end of autumn. Its grove of trees is twisted by greenwarden hands. In leaf, they must look marvelous: a verdant crown of blossoms with spiraling, impossible branches. But bare, the gnarled oaks, elms, and beeches curl into talons; their dry, dead fingers scraping against one another like bones. The courtyard is abandoned, forgotten. Just like me.

No, I growl to myself.

The others will come for me.

I dare to hope. My stomach lurches every time the door opens. For a moment, I expect to see Cal or Kilorn or Farley, perhaps Nanny wearing another person's face. The Colonel, even. Now I would weep to see his scarlet eye. But no one comes for me. No one is coming for me.

It's cruel to give hope where none should be.

And Maven knows it.

As the sun sets on the thirty-first day, I understand what he means to do.

He wants me to rot. To fade. To be forgotten.

Outside in the courtyard of bones, early snow drifts in flurries born of an iron-gray sky. The glass is cold to the touch, but it refuses to freeze.

So will I.

The snow outside is perfect in the morning light, a crust of white gilding barer trees. It'll melt by afternoon. By my count, it's December 11. A cold, gray, dead time in the echo between autumn and winter. The true snows won't set in until next month.

Back home we used to jump off the porch into snowdrifts, even after Bree broke his leg when he landed on a buried pile of firewood. Cost Gisa a month's wages to get him fixed up, and I had to steal most of the supplies our so-called doctor needed. That was the winter before Bree was conscripted, the last time our entire family was together. The last time. Forever. We'll never be whole again.

Mom and Dad are with the Guard. Gisa and my living brothers too. *They're safe. They're safe. They're safe.* I repeat the words as I do every morning. They are a comfort, even if they might not be true.

Slowly, I push away my plate of breakfast. The now-familiar spread of sugary oatmeal, fruit, and toast holds no comfort for me.

"Finished," I say out of habit, knowing no one will reply.

Kitten is already at my side, sneering at the half-eaten food. She picks up the plate as one would a bug, holding it at arm's length to carry it to the door. I raise my eyes quickly, hoping for a single glimpse of the antechamber outside my room. Like always, it's empty, and my heart sinks. She drops the plate on the floor with a clatter, maybe breaking it, but that's not her concern. Some servant will clean it up. The door shuts behind her, and Kitten returns to her seat. Trio occupies the other chair, his arms crossed, eyes unblinking as he stares at my torso. I can feel his ability and hers. They feel like a blanket wrapped too tight, keeping my lightning pinned and hidden, far away in a place where I cannot even begin to go. It makes me want to tear my skin off.

I hate it. I hate it.

I. Hate. It.

Smash.

I throw my water glass against the opposite wall, letting it splatter and splinter against horrible gray paint. Neither of my guards flinches. I do this a lot.

And it helps. For a minute. Maybe.

I follow the usual schedule, the one I've developed over the last month of captivity. Wake up. Immediately regret it. Receive breakfast. Lose appetite. Have food taken away. Immediately regret it. Throw water. Immediately regret it. Strip bed linens. Maybe rip up the sheets, sometimes while shouting. Immediately regret it. Attempt to read a book. Stare out window. Stare out window. Stare out window. Receive lunch. Repeat.

I'm a very busy girl.

Or I guess I should say woman.

Eighteen is the arbitrary divide between child and adult. And I turned eighteen weeks ago. November 17. Not that anyone knew or noticed. I doubt the Arvens care that their charge is another year older. Only one person in this prison palace would. And he did not visit, to my relief. It's the single blessing to my captivity. While I am held here, surrounded by the worst people I'll ever know, I don't have to suffer his presence.

Until today.

The utter silence around me shatters, not with an explosion, but with a click. The familiar turn of the door lock. Off schedule, without warrant. My head snaps to the sound, as do the Arvens', their concentration breaking in surprise. Adrenaline bleeds into my veins, driven by my suddenly thrumming heart. In the split second, I dare to hope again. I dream of who could be on the other side of the door.

My brothers. Farley. Kilorn.

Cal.

I want it to be Cal. I want his fire to consume this place and all these people whole.

But the man standing on the other side is no one I recognize. Only his clothes are familiar—black uniform, silver detailing. A Security officer, nameless and unimportant. He steps into my prison, holding the door open with his back. More of his like gather outside the doorway, darkening the antechamber with their presence.

The Arvens jump to their feet, just as surprised as I am.

"What are you doing?" Trio sneers. It's the first time I've ever heard his voice.

Kitten does as she is trained to do, stepping between me and the officer. Another burst of silence knocks into me, fed by her fear and confusion. It crashes like a wave, eating at the little bits of strength I still have left. I stay rooted in my chair, loath to fall down in front of other people.

The Security officer says nothing, staring at the floor. Waiting.

She enters in reply, in a gown made of needles. Her silver hair has been combed and braided with gems in the fashion of the crown she hungers to wear. I shudder at the sight of her, perfect and cold and sharp, a queen in bearing if not yet title. Because she's still not a queen. I can tell.

"Evangeline," I murmur, trying to hide the tremors in my voice,

both from fear and disuse. Her black eyes pass over me with all the ten-
derness of a cracking whip. Head to toe and back again, noting every
imperfection, every weakness. I know there are many. Finally her gaze
lands on my collar, taking in the pointed metal edges. Her lip curls in
disgust, and also hunger. How easy it would be for her to squeeze, to
drive the points of the collar into my throat and bleed me bone-dry.

"Lady Samos, you are not permitted to be here," Kitten says, still
standing between us. I'm surprised by her boldness.

Evangeline's eyes flicker to my guard, her sneer spreading. "You
think I would disobey the king, my betrothed?" She forces a cold laugh.
"I am here on his orders. He commands the presence of the prisoner at
court. Now."

Each word stings. A month of imprisonment suddenly seems far
too short. Part of me wants to grab on to the table and force Evangeline
to drag me out of my cage. But even isolation has not broken my pride.
Not yet.

Not ever, I remind myself. So I stand on weak limbs, joints aching,
hands quivering. A month ago I attacked Evangeline's brother with little more than my teeth. I try to summon as much of that fire as I can, if
only to stand up straight.

Kitten keeps her ground, unmoving. Her head tips to Trio, locking
eyes with her cousin. "We had no word. This is not protocol."

Again Evangeline laughs, showing white, gleaming teeth. Her
smile is beautiful and violent as a blade. "Are you refusing me, Guard
Arven?" As she speaks, her hands wander to her dress, running perfect
white skin through the forest of needles. Bits of it stick to her like a
magnet, and she comes away with a handful of spikes. She palms the
clinging slivers of metal, patient, waiting, one eyebrow raised. The
Arvens know better than to extend their crushing silence to a Samos

daughter, let alone the future queen.

The pair of them exchange wordless glances, clearly coming down on either side of Evangeline's question. Trio furrows his brow, glaring, and finally Kitten sighs aloud. She steps away. She backs down.

"A choice I'll not forget," Evangeline murmurs.

I feel exposed before her, alone in front of her piercing eyes despite the other guards and officers looking on. Evangeline knows me, knows what I am, what I can do. I almost killed her in the Bowl of Bones, but she ran, afraid of me and my lightning. She is certainly not afraid now.

Deliberate, I take a step forward. Toward her. Toward the blissful emptiness that surrounds her, allowing her ability. Another step. Into the free air, into electricity. Will I feel it immediately? Will it come rushing back? It must. It has to.

But her sneer bleeds into a smile. She matches my pace, moving back, and I almost snarl. "Not so fast, Barrow."

It's the first time she's ever said my real name.

She snaps her fingers, pointing at Kitten. "Bring her along."

They drag me like they did the first day I arrived, chained at the collar, my leash tightly grasped in Kitten's fist. Her silence and Trio's continue, beating like a drum in my skull. The long walk through Whitefire feels like sprinting miles, though we move at an easy pace. As before, I am not blindfolded. They don't bother to try to confuse me.

I recognize more and more as we get closer to our destination, cutting down passages and galleries I explored freely a lifetime ago. Back then I didn't feel the need to sort them. Now I do my best to map the palace in my head. I'll certainly need to know its layout if I ever plan to get out of here alive. My bedchamber faces east, and it is on the fifth floor; that much I know from counting windows. I remember

Whitefire is shaped like interlocking squares, with each wing surrounding a courtyard like the one my room looks out on. The view out the tall, arched windows changes with every new passageway. A courtyard garden, Caesar's Square, the long stretches of the training yard where Cal drilled with his soldiers, the distant walls and the rebuilt Bridge of Archeon beyond. Thankfully we never pass through the residences where I found Julian's journal, where I watched Cal rage and Maven quietly scheme. I'm surprised by how many memories the rest of the palace holds, despite my short time here.

We pass a block of windows on a landing, looking west across the barracks to the Capital River and the other half of the city beyond it. The Bowl of Bones nestles among the buildings, its hulking form too familiar. I know this view. I stood in front of these windows with Cal. I lied to him, knowing an attack would come that night. But I didn't know what it would do to either of us. Cal whispered then that he wished things were different. I share the lament.

Cameras must follow our progress, though I can no longer feel them. Evangeline says nothing as we descend to the main floor of the palace with her officers in tow, a flocking troop of blackbirds around a metal swan. Music echoes from somewhere. It pulses like a swollen and heavy heart. I've never heard such music before, not even at the ball I attended or during Cal's dancing lessons. It has a life of its own, something dark and twisting and oddly inviting. Ahead of me, Evangeline's shoulders stiffen at the sound.

The court level is oddly empty, with only a few guards posted along the passages. Guards, not Sentinels, who will be with Maven. Evangeline doesn't turn right, as I expect, to enter the throne room through the grand, arching doors. Instead, she surges forward, all of us in tow, pushing into another room I know all too well.

The council chamber. A perfect circle of marble and polished, gleaming wood. Seats ring the walls, and the seal of Norta, the Burning Crown, dominates the ornate floor. Red and black and royal silver, with points of bursting flame. I almost stumble at the sight of it, and I have to shut my eyes. Kitten will pull me through the room, I have no doubt of that. I'll gladly let her drag me if it means I don't have to see any more of this place. Walsh died here, I remember. Her face flashes behind my eyelids. She was hunted down like a rabbit. And it was wolves that caught her—Evangeline, Ptolemus, Cal. They captured her in the tunnels beneath Archeon, following her orders from the Scarlet Guard. They found her, dragged her here, and presented her to Queen Elara for interrogation. It never got that far. Because Walsh killed herself. She swallowed a murderous pill in front of us all, to protect the secrets of the Scarlet Guard. To protect me.

When the music triples in volume, I open my eyes again.

The council chamber is gone, but the sight before me is somehow worse.

THREE
Mare

Music dances on the air, undercut with the sweet and sickening bite of alcohol as it permeates every inch of the magnificent throne room. We step out onto a landing elevated a few feet above the chamber floor, allowing a grand view of the raucous party—and a few moments before anyone realizes we're here.

My eyes dart back and forth, on edge, on defense, searching every face and every shadow for opportunity, or danger. Silk and gemstones and beautiful armor wink beneath the light of a dozen chandeliers, creating a human constellation that surges and twists on the marble floor. After a month of imprisonment, the sight is an assault on my senses, but I gulp it in, a girl starved. So many colors, so many voices, so many familiar lords and ladies. For now they take no notice of me. Their eyes do not follow. Their focus is on one another, their cups of wine and multicolored liquor, the harried rhythm, the fragrant smoke curling through the air. This must be a celebration, a wild one, but for what, I have no idea.

Naturally, my mind flies. Have they won another victory? Against

Cal, against the Scarlet Guard? Or are they still cheering my capture?

One look at Evangeline is answer enough. I've never seen her scowl this way, not even at me. Her catlike sneer turns ugly, angry, full of rage like I can't imagine. Her eyes darken, shifting over the display. They are black like a void, swallowing up the sight of her people in a state of ultimate bliss.

Or, I realize, ignorance.

At someone's command, a flurry of Red servants push off the far wall and move through the chamber in practiced formation. They carry trays of crystal goblets with liquid like ruby, gold, and diamond starlight. By the time they reach the opposite side of the crowd, their trays are empty and are quickly refilled. Another pass, and the trays empty again. How some of the Silvers are still standing, I have no idea. They continue in their revelry, talking or dancing with hands clawed around their glasses. A few puff on intricate pipes, blowing oddly colored smoke into the air. It doesn't smell like tobacco, which many of the elders in the Stilts jealously hoard. I watch sparks in their pipes with envy, each one a pinprick of light.

Worse is the sight of the servants, the Reds. They make me ache. What I would give to take their place. To be only a servant instead of a prisoner. *Stupid,* I scold myself. *They are imprisoned same as you. Just like all of your kind. Trapped beneath a Silver boot, though some have more room to breathe.*

Because of him.

Evangeline descends from the landing, and the Arvens force me to follow. The stairs lead us directly to the dais, another elevated platform high enough to denote its ultimate importance. And of course a dozen Sentinels stand upon it, masked and armed, terrifying in every inch.

I expect the thrones I remember. Diamondglass flames for the king's seat, sapphire and polished white gold for the queen's. Instead, Maven sits upon the same kind of throne I saw him rise from a month ago, when he held me chained in front of the world.

No gems, no precious metals. Just slabs of gray stone swirled with something shiny, flat-edged, and brutally absent of insignia. It looks cold to the touch and uncomfortable, not to mention terribly heavy. It dwarfs him, making him seem younger and smaller than ever. To look powerful is to be powerful. A lesson I learned from Elara, though somehow Maven didn't. He seems the boy he is, sharply pale against his black uniform, the only color on him the bloodred lining of his cape, a silver riot of medals, and the shivering blue of his eyes.

King Maven of House Calore meets my gaze the moment he knows I'm here.

The instant hangs, suspended on a thread of time. A canyon of distractions yawns between us, filled with so much noise and graceful chaos, but the room might as well be empty.

I wonder if he notices the difference in me. The sickness, the pain, the torture my quiet prison has put me through. He must. His eyes slide over my pronounced cheekbones to my collar, down to the white shift they dress me in. I'm not bleeding this time, but I wish I were. To show everyone what I am, what I've always been. Red. Wounded. But alive. As I did before the court, before Evangeline a few minutes ago, I straighten my spine, and stare with all the strength and accusation I have to give. I take him in, looking for the cracks only I can see. Shadowed eyes, twitching hands, posture so rigid his spine might shatter.

You are a murderer, Maven Calore, a coward, a weakness.

It works. He tears his eyes away from me and springs to his feet, both hands still gripping the arms of his throne. His rage falls like the blow from a hammer.

"Explain yourself, Guard Arven!" he erupts at my closest jailer.

Trio jumps in his boots.

The outburst stops the music, the dancing, and the drinking in the span of a heartbeat.

"S-Sir—" Trio sputters, and one of his gloved hands grips my arm. It bleeds silence, enough to make my heartbeat slow. He tries to find an explanation that doesn't place blame on himself, or the future queen, but comes up short.

My chain trembles in Kitten's hand, but her grip is still tight.

Only Evangeline is unaffected by the king's wrath. She expected this response.

He didn't order her to bring me. There was no summons at all.

Maven is not a fool. He waves a hand at Trio, ending his mumbling with a single motion. "Your feeble attempt is answer enough," he says. "What do you have to say for yourself, Evangeline?"

In the crowd, her father stands tall, watching with wide, stern eyes. Another might call him afraid, but I don't think Volo Samos has the power to feel emotion. He simply strokes his pointed silver beard, his expression unreadable. Ptolemus is not so gifted at hiding his thoughts. He stands on the dais with the Sentinels, the only one without fiery robes or a mask. Though his body is still, his eyes dart between the king and his sister, and one fist clenches slowly. *Good. Fear for her as I feared for my brother. Watch her suffer as I watched him die.*

Because what else can Maven do now? Evangeline has deliberately disobeyed his orders, leaping past the allowances their betrothal allows. If I know anything, I know that to cross the king is to be punished. And to do it here, in front of the entire court? He might just execute her on the spot.

If Evangeline thinks she's risking death, she doesn't show it. Her voice never cracks or wavers. "You ordered the terrorist to be imprisoned, shut away like a useless bottle of wine, and after a month of council deliberation, there has been no agreement on what is to be done with her. Her crimes are many, worthy of a dozen deaths, a thousand lifetimes in our worst jails. She killed or maimed hundreds of your subjects since she was discovered, your own parents included, and still she rests in a comfortable bedchamber, eating, breathing—alive without the punishment she deserves."

Maven is his mother's son, and his court facade is nearly perfect. Evangeline's words don't seem to bother him in the slightest.

"The punishment she deserves," he repeats. Then he looks to the room, one corner of his chin raised. "So you brought her here. Really, are my parties that bad?"

A thrum of laughter, both genuine and forced, ripples through the rapt crowd. Most of them are drunk, but there are enough clear heads to know what's going on. What Evangeline has done.

Evangeline pulls a courtly smile that looks so painful I expect her lips to start bleeding at the corners. "I know you are grieving for your mother, Your Majesty," she says without a hint of sympathy. "As we all are. But your father would not act this way. The time for tears is over."

Those last are not her words, but the words of Tiberias the Sixth. Maven's father, Maven's ghost. His mask threatens to slip for a moment, and his eyes flash with equal parts dread and anger. I remember those words as well as he does. Spoken before a crowd just like this, in the wake of the Scarlet Guard's execution of political targets. Targets chosen by Maven, fed to him by his mother. We did their dirty work, while they added to the body count with an atrocious attack of their own. They used me, used the Guard to eliminate some of their enemies and demonize others in one fell swoop. They destroyed more, killed more than any of us ever wanted.

I can still smell the blood and smoke. I can still hear a mother weeping over her dead children. I can still hear the words framing the rebellion for it all.

"Strength, power, death," Maven murmurs, his teeth clicking. The words scared me then, and they terrify me now. "What do you suggest, my lady? A beheading? A firing squad? Do we take her apart, piece by piece?"

My heart gallops in my chest. Would Maven allow such a thing? I don't know. I don't know what he would do. I have to remind myself, I don't even know *him*. The boy I thought him to be was an illusion. But the notes, brutally left, but full of pleas for me to return? The month of quiet, gentle captivity? Perhaps those were false too, another trick to ensnare me. Another kind of torture.

"We do as the law requires. As your father would have done."

The way she says *father*, using the word as brutally as she would any knife, is confirmation enough. Like so many people in this room, she knows Tiberias the Sixth did not end the way the stories say.

Still, Maven grips his throne, white-knuckling the gray slabs. He glances at the court, feeling their eyes upon him, before sneering back at Evangeline. "Not only are you not a member of my council, but you did not know my father well enough to know his mind. I am a king as he was, and I understand the things that must be done for victory. Our laws are sacred, but we are fighting two wars now."

Two wars.

Adrenaline pulses through me so quickly I think my lightning has returned. No, not lightning. Hope. I bite my lip to keep from grinning.

Weeks into my captivity the Scarlet Guard continues, and thrives. Not only are they still fighting, but Maven admits it openly. They are impossible to hide or dismiss now.

Despite the need to know more, I keep my mouth shut.

Maven burns a stare through Evangeline. "No enemy prisoner, especially not one as valuable as Mare Barrow, should be wasted on common execution."

"You waste her still!" Evangeline argues, firing back so quickly I know she must have practiced for this argument. She takes a few more steps forward, closing the distance between herself and Maven. It all seems a show, an act, something played out on the platform for the court to witness. But for whose benefit? "She sits collecting dust, doing nothing, giving us nothing, while Corvium burns!"

Another jewel of information to keep close. *More, Evangeline. Give me more.*

I saw the fortress city, the heart of the Nortan military, erupt in riots with my own eyes a month ago. It's still happening. Mention of Corvium sobers the crowd. Maven does not miss it, and he fights to keep his calm.

"The council is days away from a decision, my lady," he says through gritted teeth.

"Forgive my boldness, Your Majesty. I know you wish to honor your council as best you can, even the weakest parts of it. Even the cowards who cannot do what must be done." Another step closer, and her voice softens to a purr. "But you are the king. The decision is yours."

Masterful, I realize. Evangeline is just as adept at manipulation as any other. In a few words, she's not only saved Maven from appearing weak, but also forced him to follow her will to maintain an image of strength. In spite of myself, I draw in a harried breath. Will he do as she bids? Or will he refuse, throwing fuel on the fire of insurrection already blazing through the High Houses?

Maven is no fool. He understands what Evangeline is doing, and he keeps his focus on her. They hold each other's gaze, communicating with forced smiles and sharp eyes.

"Queenstrial certainly did bring forth the most talented daughter," he says, taking her hand. Both of them look disgusted by the action. His head snaps to the crowd, looking to a lean man in dark blue. "Cousin! Your petition of interrogation is granted."

Samson Merandus snaps to attention and emerges from the crowd, clear-eyed. He bows, almost grinning. Blue robes billow, dark as smoke. "Thank you, Your Majesty."

"No."

The word wrenches itself from me.

"No, Maven!"

Samson moves quickly, ascending the platform with controlled fury. He closes the distance between us in a few determined strides, until his eyes are the only thing in my world. Blue eyes, Elara's eyes, Maven's eyes.

"Maven!" I gasp again, begging even though it will do nothing. Begging even though it burns my pride to think I'm asking him for anything. But what else is there to do? Samson is a whisper. He'll destroy me from the inside out, search everything I am, everything I know. How many people will die because of what I've seen? "Maven, please! Don't let him do this!"

I'm not strong enough to break Kitten's grasp on my chain, or even struggle much when Trio seizes my shoulders. Both of them hold me in place with ease. My eyes flash from Samson to Maven. One hand on his throne, one hand in Evangeline's. *I miss you,* his notes said. He is unreadable, but at least he's looking.

Good. If he won't save me from this nightmare, I want him to see it happen.

"Maven," I whisper one last time, trying to sound like myself. Not the lightning girl, not Mareena the lost princess, but Mare. The girl he watched through the bars of a cell and pledged to save. But that girl isn't enough. He drops his eyes. He looks away.

I am alone.

Samson takes my throat in his hand, squeezing above the metal collar, forcing me to look into his wretched, familiar eyes. Blue as ice, and just as unforgiving.

"You were wrong to kill Elara," he says, not bothering to temper his words. "She was a surgeon with minds."

He leans in, hungry, a starving man about to devour a meal.

"I am a butcher."

When the sounder device leveled me, I wallowed in agony for three long days. A storm of radio waves turned my own electricity against me. It resounded in my skin, rattling between my nerves like bolts in a jar. It left scars. Jagged lines of white flesh down my neck and spine, ugly things that I'm still not used to. They twinge and tug at odd angles, making benign movements painful. Even my smiles are tainted, smaller in the wake of what was done to me.

Now I would beg for it if I could.

The screeching click of a sounder as it peels me apart would be a heaven, a bliss, a mercy. I would rather be broken in bone and muscle, shattered down to teeth and fingernails, obliterated in every inch, than suffer another second of Samson's whispers.

I can feel him. His mind. Filling up my corners like a corruption or a rot or a cancer. He scrapes inside my head with sharp skin and even sharper intentions. Any part of me not taken by his poison writhes in pain. He enjoys doing this to me. This is his revenge, after all. For what I did to Elara, his blood and his queen.

She was the first memory he tore from me. My lack of remorse incensed him, and I regret it now. I wish I could've forced some sympathy, but the image of her death was too frightening for much more than shock. I remember it now. He forces me to.

In an instant of blinding pain, sucking me backward through my memories, I find myself back in the moment I killed her. My ability draws lightning out of the sky in ragged lines of purple-white. One strikes her head-on, cascading into her eyes and mouth, down her neck and arms, from fingers to toes and back again. The sweat on her skin boils to steam, her flesh chars until it smokes, and the buttons on her jacket turn red hot, burning through cloth and skin. She jerks, tearing at herself, trying to be rid of my electric rage. Her fingertips rip clean, exposing bone, while the muscles of her beautiful face go slack, drooping from the relentless pull of jumping currents. Ash-white hair burns black and smolders, disintegrating. And the smell. The sound. She screams until her vocal cords pull apart. Samson makes sure the scene passes slowly, his ability manipulating the forgotten memory until every second brands itself into my conscience. A butcher indeed.

His rage sends me spinning with nothing to cling to, caught in a storm I cannot control. All I can do is pray not to see what Samson is searching for. I try to keep Shade's name from my thoughts. But the walls I put up are little more than paper. Samson rips through them gleefully. I feel each one being torn away, another part of me mangled. He knows what I'm trying to keep from him, to never live through again. He chases through my thoughts, faster than my brain, outrunning every weak attempt to stop him. I try to scream or beg, but no sound comes from my mouth or mind. He holds everything in the palm of his hand.

"Too easy." His voice echoes in me, around me.

Like Elara's ending, Shade's death is captured in perfect, painful detail. I must relive every awful second in my own body, unable to do anything but watch, trapped inside myself. Radiation tangs the air. Corros Prison is on the edge of the Wash, close to the nuclear wasteland forming our southern border. Cold mist shrouds morning against a gray dawn. For a moment, all is still, suspended in balance. I stare out, unmoving, frozen midstep. The prison yawns at my back, still shuddering with the riot we began. Prisoners and pursuers bleed from its gates. Following us to freedom, or something like it. Cal is already gone, his familiar form a hundred yards away. I made Shade jump him first, to protect one of our only pilots, and our only manner of escape. Kilorn is still with me, frozen as I am, his rifle tucked against his shoulder. He aims behind us, at Queen Elara, her guards, and Ptolemus Samos. A bullet explodes from the muzzle, born of sparks and gunpowder. It, too, hangs in midair, waiting for Samson to release his grip on my mind. Overhead, the sky swirls, heavy with electricity. My own power. The feel of it would make me cry if I could.

The memory begins to move, slowly at first.

Ptolemus forges himself a long, gleaming needle in addition to the many weapons already at hand. The perfect edge glitters with Red and Silver blood, each droplet a gemstone warbling through the air. Despite her ability, Ara Iral is not fast enough to dodge its lethal arc. It slices through her neck in one lingering second. She falls a few feet away from me, sluggishly, as if through water. Ptolemus means to kill me in the same motion, using the momentum of his blow to turn the needle on my heart. Instead, he finds my brother in the way.

Shade jumps back to us, to teleport me to safety. His body materializes from thin air: first his chest and head, then his extremities paint into existence. Hands outstretched, eyes focused, his attention only on me. He doesn't see the needle. He doesn't know he's about to die.

It was not Ptolemus's intent to kill Shade, but he doesn't mind doing it. Another enemy dead makes no difference to him. Just another obstacle in his war, another body with no name and no face. How many times have I done the same thing?

He probably doesn't even know who Shade is.

Was.

I know what comes next, but no matter how hard I try, Samson won't let me shut my eyes. The needle pierces my brother with clean grace, through muscle and organ, blood and heart.

Something in me erupts and the sky responds. As my brother falls, so does my rage. But I never feel the bittersweet release of it. The lightning never strikes the earth, killing Elara and scattering her guards as it should. Samson never allows me that small mercy. Instead, he pulls the scene backward. Again it plays. Again my brother dies.

Again.

Again.

Each time he forces me to see something else. A mistake. A misstep. A choice I could've made to save him. Small decisions. Step here, turn there, run a bit faster. It is torture of the worst kind.

Look what you did. Look what you did. Look what you did.

His voice ripples, all around me.

Other memories splinter through Shade's death, visions bleeding into one another. Each plays on a different fear or weakness. There's the tiny corpse I found in Templyn, a Red baby murdered by Maven's newblood hunters at Maven's command. In another instant, Farley's fist connects with my face. She screams horrible things, blaming me for Shade's death while her own anguish threatens to consume her. Steaming tears run down Cal's cheeks as a sword trembles in his hand, the blade edged against his father's neck. Shade's meager grave on Tuck, alone beneath the autumn sky. The Silver officers I electrocuted in Corros, in Harbor Bay, men and women who were only following orders. They had no choice. No choice.

I remember all the death. All the heartache. The look on my sister's face when an officer broke her hand. Kilorn's bleeding knuckles when he found out he was going to be conscripted. My brothers taken to war. My father returning from the front half a man in mind and body, exiling himself to a rickety wheelchair—and a life apart from us. My mother's sad eyes when she told me she was proud of me. A lie. A lie now. And finally the sick ache, the hollow truth that dogged every moment of my old life—that I was ultimately doomed.

I still am.

Samson sweeps through it all with abandon. He pulls me through useless memories, drawn up only to subject me to more pain. Shadows jump through the thoughts. Moving images behind every painful moment. Samson spools through them, too fast for me to truly grasp. But I gather enough. The Colonel's face, his scarlet eye, his lips forming words I can't hear. But surely Samson can. This is what he's looking for. Intelligence. Secrets he can use to crush the rebellion. I feel like an egg with a cracked shell, slowly seeping my innards. He pulls whatever he wants from me. I don't even have the ability to feel ashamed at what else he finds.

Nights spent curled against Cal. Forcing Cameron to join our cause. Stolen moments rereading Maven's sickening notes. Memories of who I thought the forgotten prince was. My cowardice. My nightmares. My mistakes. Every selfish step I took that led me here.

Look what you did. Look what you did. Look what you did.

Maven will know it all soon enough.

This was always what he wanted.

The words, scrawled in his looping hand, burn through my thoughts.

I miss you.

Until we meet again.

FOUR
Cameron

I still can't believe we survived. I dream about it sometimes. Watching them drag Mare away, her body held tightly between a pair of gigantic strongarms. They were gloved against her lightning, not that she tried to use it after she made her bargain. Her life for ours. I didn't expect King Maven to follow through. Not with his exiled brother on the line. But he kept his deal. He wanted her more than the rest.

Still, I wake up from the usual nightmares, afraid he and his hunters have returned to kill us. The snores from the rest of my bunk room chase the thoughts away.

They told me the new headquarters was a bleeding ruin, but I expected something more like Tuck. A once-abandoned facility, isolated but functional, rebuilt in secret with all the amenities a burgeoning rebellion might need. I hated Tuck on sight. The block barracks and guard-like soldiers, even if they were Red, reminded me too much of Corros Prison. I saw the island as another jail. Another cell I was being forced into, this time by Mare Barrow instead of a Silver officer. But at least on Tuck I had the sky above me. A clean breeze in my lungs.

Compared to Corros, compared to New Town, compared to this, Tuck was a reprieve.

Now I shiver with the rest in the concrete tunnels of Irabelle, a Scarlet Guard stronghold on the outskirts of the Lakelander city of Trial. The walls feel frozen to the touch, and icicles dangle from rooms without a heat source. A few of the Guard officers have taken to following Cal around, if only to take advantage of his radiating warmth. I do the opposite, avoiding his lumbering presence as best I can. I have no use for the Silver prince, who looks at me with nothing but accusation.

As if I could have saved her.

My barely trained ability was nowhere near enough. *And you weren't enough either, Your Bleeding Highness,* I want to snap at him every time we cross paths. His flame was no match for the king and his hunters. Besides, Mare offered the trade and made her choice. If he's angry at anyone, it should be her.

The lightning girl did it to save us, and for that I am always thankful. Even if she was a self-centered hypocrite, she doesn't deserve what's happening to her.

The Colonel gave the order to evacuate Tuck the moment we were able to radio back to him. He knew any interrogation of Mare Barrow would lead directly to the island. Farley was able to get everyone to safety, either in boats or the massive cargo jet stolen from the prison. We were forced to travel overland ourselves, hightailing from the crash site to rendezvous with the Colonel across the border. I say *forced* because, once again, I was told what to do and where to go. We had been flying to the Choke in an attempt to rescue a legion of child soldiers. My brother was one of them. But our mission had to be abandoned. *For now,* they told me every time I got enough courage to refuse another step away from the war front.

The memory makes my cheeks burn. I should've kept going. They wouldn't have stopped me. Couldn't have stopped me. But I was afraid. So close to the trench line, I realized what it meant to march alone. I would have died in vain. Still, I can't shake the shame of that choice. I walked away and left my brother yet again.

It took weeks for everyone to reunite. Farley and her officers arrived last of all. I think her father, the Colonel, spent every day she was gone pacing the frigid halls of our new base.

At the very least, Barrow's making her imprisonment useful. The distraction of such a prisoner, not to mention the boiling mess of Corvium, has stalled any troop movements around the Choke. My brother is safe. Well, as safe as a fifteen-year-old can possibly be with a gun and a uniform. Safer than Mare certainly is.

I don't know how many times I've seen King Maven's address. Cal took over a corner of the control room to play it again and again once we arrived. The first time we saw it, I don't think any of us dared to breathe. We all feared the worst. We thought we were about to watch Mare lose her head. Her brothers were beside themselves, fighting tears, and Kilorn couldn't even look, hiding his face in his hands. When Maven declared execution was too good for her, I think Bree actually fainted in relief. But Cal looked on in deafening silence, his brows knit together in focus. Deep down he knew, like we all did, that something much worse than death waited for Mare Barrow.

She knelt before a Silver king and stood still while he put a collar around her throat. Said nothing, did nothing. Let him call her a terrorist and murderer before the eyes of our entire nation. Part of me wishes she'd snapped, but I know she couldn't put a toe out of line. She just glared at everyone around her, eyes sweeping back and forth between the Silvers crowding her platform. They all wanted to get close to her. Hunters around a trophy kill.

In spite of the crown, Maven didn't look so kingly. Tired, maybe sick, definitely angry. Probably because the girl next to him had just murdered his mother. He tugged at Mare's collar, forced her to walk inside. She managed one last look over her shoulder, eyes wide and searching. But another tug turned her around for good, and we haven't seen her face since.

She's been there, and I've been here, rotting, freezing, spending my days rewiring equipment older than I am. All of it a bleeding waste.

I steal one last minute in my bunk to think about my brother, where he might be, what he's doing. Morrey. My twin in nothing but appearance. He was a soft boy in the hard alleys of New Town, constantly sick from the factory smoke. I don't want to imagine what military training has done to him. Depending on who you ask, techie workers were either too valuable or too weak for the army. Until the Scarlet Guard started their meddling, killed a few Silvers, and forced the old king into some meddling of his own. We were both conscripted, even though we had jobs. Even though we were only fifteen. The bloody Measures enacted by Cal's own father changed everything. We were selected, told to be soldiers, and we were marched away from our parents.

They split us up almost immediately. My name was on some list and his wasn't. Once, I was grateful I was the one sent to Corros. Morrey would have never survived the cells. Now I wish we could trade places. Him free, and me on the lines. But no matter how many times I petition the Colonel for another attempt at the Little Legion, he always turns me away.

So I might as well ask again.

The tool belt is a familiar weight around my hips, thunking with every step. I walk with purpose, enough to deter anyone who might bother to stop me. But for the most part, the halls are empty. No one is around to watch me stalk past, gnawing on a breakfast roll. More captains and their units must be out on patrol again, scouting Trial and the border. Looking for Reds, I think, the ones lucky enough to make it north. Some come here to join up, but they're always of military age or workers with skills useful to the cause. I don't know where the families are sent: the orphans, the widows, the widowers. The ones who would only be in the way.

Like me. But I get underfoot on purpose. It's the only way to get any kind of attention.

The Colonel's broom closet—I mean office—is one floor above the bunk rooms. I don't bother to knock, trying the doorknob instead. It turns easily, opening into a grim, cramped room with concrete walls, a few locked cabinets, and a currently occupied desk.

"He's over in control," Farley says, not looking up from her papers. Her hands are ink-stained, and there are even smudges on her nose and under her bloodshot eyes. She pores over what look like Guard communications, coded messages and orders. From Command, I know, remembering the constant whispers about the upper levels of the Scarlet Guard. No one knows much about them, least of all me. Nobody tells me anything unless I ask a dozen times.

I frown at her appearance. Despite the table hiding her stomach, her condition has begun to show. Her face and fingers look swollen. Not to mention the three plates piled with food scraps.

"Probably a good idea to sleep now and then, Farley."

"Probably." She seems annoyed by my concern.

Fine, don't listen. With a low sigh, I turn back to the doorway, putting her behind me.

"Let him know Corvium is on the edge," Farley adds, her voice strong and cutting. An order but also something else.

I glance over my shoulder at her, an eyebrow raised. "Edge of what?"

"There have been riots, sporadic reports of Silver officers turning up dead, and ammunition depots have developed a nasty habit of exploding." She almost smirks at that. Almost. I haven't seen her smile since Shade Barrow died.

"Sounds like familiar work. Is the Scarlet Guard in the city?"

Finally she looks up. "Not to our knowledge."

"Then the legions are turning." Hope flares sharp and raw in my chest. "The Red soldiers—"

"There's thousands of them stationed at Corvium. And more than a few have realized they substantially outnumber their Silver officers. Four to one, at least."

Four to one. Just like that, my hope sours. I've seen what Silvers are and what they can do firsthand. I've been their prisoner and their opponent, able to fight only because of my own ability. Four Reds against a single Silver is still suicide. Still an outright loss. But Farley doesn't seem to agree.

She senses my unease and softens as best she can. Like a razor turning into a knife. "Your brother isn't in the city. The Dagger Legion is still behind the lines of the Choke."

Stuck between a minefield and a city on fire. Fantastic.

"It's not Morrey that I'm worried about." *At the moment.* "I just don't see how they can expect to take the city. They might have the numbers, but the Silvers are . . . well, they're Silvers. A few dozen magnetrons could kill hundreds without blinking."

I picture Corvium in my head. I've only seen it in brief videos, snippets taken from Silver broadcasts or report footage filtered down through the Scarlet Guard. It's more fortress than city, walled with foreboding black stone, a monolith looking north to the barren wastes of war. Something about it reminds me of the place I reluctantly called home. New Town had walls of its own, and so many officers overseeing our lives. We were thousands too, but our only rebellions were being late to shift or sneaking out after curfew. There was nothing to be done. Our lives were weak and meaningless as smoke.

Farley turns back to her work. "Just tell him what I said. He'll know what to do."

I can only nod, shutting the door as she tries and fails to hide a yawn.

"Have to recalibrate the video receivers, Captain Farley's orders—"

The two Guardsmen flanking the door to central control step back before I even finish my sentence, my usual lie. Both look away, avoiding my gaze, and I feel my face burn with an ashamed flush.

Newbloods scare people as much as Silvers do, if not more so. Reds with abilities are just as unpredictable, just as powerful, just as dangerous, in their eyes.

After we first got here and more soldiers arrived, the whispers about me and the others spread like disease. *The old woman can change her face. The twitchy one can surround you with illusions. The techie girl can kill you with thought alone.* It feels terrible to be feared. And worst of all, I can't blame anyone for it. We are different and strange, with powers not even Silvers can claim. We are frayed wires and glitching machines, still learning ourselves and our abilities. Who knows what we might become?

I swallow the familiar discomfort and step into the next room.

Central control usually buzzes with screens and communication equipment, but for now the room is oddly quiet. Only a single broadcaster whirs, spitting out a long strip of correspondence paper printed with a decrypted message. The Colonel stands over the machine, reading as the strip lengthens. His usual ghosts, Mare's brothers, sit close by, both of them jumpy as rabbits. And the fourth occupant of the room is all I need to know about whatever report is coming in.

This is news of Mare Barrow.

Why else would Cal be here too?

He broods, as usual, his chin resting on interlocked fingers. Long days underground have taken their toll, paling his already-pale skin. For a prince, he really lets himself go in times of crisis. Right now he looks like he needs a shower and a shave, not to mention a few well-aimed slaps to wake him out of his stupor. But he's a soldier still. His eyes snap to mine before the others'.

"Cameron," he says, doing his best not to growl.

"Calore." He's an exiled prince at best. No need for titles. Unless I really want to piss him off.

Like father, like daughter. Colonel Farley doesn't look up from the communication, but he acknowledges me with a dramatic sigh. "Let's save ourselves some time, Cameron. I have neither the manpower nor the opportunity to attempt rescuing an entire legion."

I mouth the words along with him. He says them to me almost every day.

"A legion of barely trained children who Maven will slaughter once given the opportunity," I counter.

"So you keep reminding me."

"Because you need to be reminded! Sir," I add, almost wincing at the word. *Sir*. I'm not oathed to the Guard, no matter how much they treat me like a member of their club.

The Colonel's eyes narrow in on part of the message. "She's been interrogated."

Cal stands so quickly he knocks over his chair. "Merandus?"

A tremor of heat pulses through the room, and I feel a ripple of sickness in me. Not because of Cal, but because of Mare. Because of the horrors happening to her. Upset, I knit my hands together behind my head, pulling the curly dark hair at the nape of my neck.

"Yes," the Colonel replies. "A man named Samson."

The prince curses quite colorfully for a royal.

"What does that mean?" Bree, Mare's burly eldest brother, dares to ask.

Tramy, the other surviving Barrow son, frowns deeply. "Merandus is the queen's house. Whispers—mind readers. They'll pull her apart to find us."

"And for sport," Cal murmurs with a low rumble. Both Barrow brothers flush red at the implication. Bree blinks back fierce, sudden tears. I want to take his arm, but I stay still. I've seen enough people flinch away from my touch.

"Which is why Mare knows nothing of our operations outside Tuck, and Tuck has been thoroughly left behind," the Colonel says quickly. It's true. They abandoned Tuck with blinding speed, casting off anything that Mare Barrow knew of. Even the Silvers we captured from Corros—or rescued, depending on who you ask—were left at the coast. Too dangerous to keep hold of, too many to control.

I've only been with the Scarlet Guard a month, but I already know their words by heart. *Rise, red as the dawn*, of course, and *know only what you need*. The first is a battle cry, the second a warning.

"Whatever she gives them will be peripheral at best," he adds. "Nothing important about Command, and little about our dealings outside Norta."

No one cares, Colonel. I bite my tongue to keep from snapping at him.

Mare is a prisoner. So what if they don't get anything about the Lakelands, Piedmont, or Montfort?

Montfort. The distant nation ruled by a so-called democracy, an equal balance of Reds, Silvers, and newbloods. A paradise? Maybe, but I have long since learned that paradise does not exist in this world. I probably know more about the country than Mare now, what with the twins, Rash and Tahir, always squawking about Montfort's merits. I'm not stupid enough to trust their word. Not to mention it's pure torture holding a conversation with them, always finishing each other's thoughts and sentences. Sometimes I want to use my silence on them both, to sever the ability that binds their thoughts into one. But that would be cruel, not to mention idiotic. People are already wary of us without watching newbloods ability-bicker.

"Does what they get out of her really matter right now?" I force through gritted teeth. Hopefully the Colonel understands what I'm trying to say. *At least spare her brothers this, Colonel. Have some shame.*

He just blinks, one good eye and one destroyed. "If you can't stomach intelligence, then don't come to control. We need to know what they got out of her in interrogation."

"Samson Merandus is an arena fighter, though he has no reason to be," Cal says in a low voice. Trying to be gentle. "He enjoys using his ability to inflict pain. If he is the one to interrogate Mare, then . . ." He stumbles over the words, reluctant to speak. "It'll be torture, plain and simple. Maven has given her to a torturer."

Even the Colonel looks disturbed by the thought.

Cal stares at the floor, silent for a long, stoic moment. "I never thought Maven would do that to her," he mutters finally. "She probably didn't either."

Then you're both stupid, my brain screams. *How many times does one wicked boy have to betray you people before you learn?*

"Did you need something else, Cameron?" Colonel Farley asks. He rolls up the message, spooling it like a circle of thread. The rest is clearly not for my ears.

"It's about Corvium. Farley says it's on the edge."

The Colonel blinks. "Those were her words?"

"That's what I said."

Suddenly I'm no longer the focus of his attention. Instead, his eyes sweep to Cal.

"Then it's time to push."

The Colonel looks eager, but Cal could not seem more reluctant. He keeps still, knowing that any twitch might betray his true feelings. The lack of movement is just as damning. "I'll see what I can come up with," he finally forces out. That seems to be enough for the Colonel. He ducks his chin in a nod before turning his attention to Mare's brothers.

"Best let your family know," he says, putting on a show of being gentle. "And Kilorn."

I shift, uncomfortable watching them digest the painful news of their sister and accept the burden of carrying it to the rest of their family. Bree's words stick, but Tramy has strength enough to speak for his older brother. "Yes, sir," he replies. "Though I don't know where Warren gets to these days."

"Try the newblood barracks," I offer. "He's there more often than not."

Indeed, Kilorn spends most of his time with Ada. After Ketha died, Ada took on the arduous task of teaching him to read and write. Though I suspect he sticks with us because he has no one else. The Barrows are the closest thing he has to family, and they are a family of ghosts now, haunted by memories. I've never even seen her parents. They keep to themselves, deep in the tunnels.

We take our leave of the Colonel together, four of us trooping out of the control room in awkward, stilted single file. Bree and Tramy peel away quickly, stomping their way toward their family's quarters on the other side of the base. I do not envy them. I remember how my mother screamed when my brother and I were taken away. I wonder what hurts more—to hear nothing of your children, knowing they are in danger, or to be fed news of their pain piece by piece.

Not that I'll ever find out. There is no place for children, especially children of mine, in this stupid, ruined world.

I give Cal space, but quickly think better of it. We're nearly the same height, and catching up to his harried stride is no problem.

"If your heart's not in this, you're going to get a lot of people killed."

He whirls, almost knocking me on my ass with the speed and force of his movement. I have seen his fire firsthand, but never so strongly as the flame blazing in his eyes.

"Cameron, my heart is quite literally in this," he hisses through gritted teeth.

Swooning words. A romantic declaration. I can barely stop my eyes from rolling.

"Save it for when we get her back," I grumble. *When*, not *if*. He nearly set the control room on fire when the Colonel denied his request to explore ways to get messages to Mare within the palace. I don't need him melting the hallway over a poor choice of words.

He starts walking again, his pace doubled, but I'm not as easily left behind as the lightning girl.

"I just mean to say that the Colonel has strategists of his own . . . people at Command . . . Scarlet Guard officers who don't have"—I search for the proper term—"conflicting allegiances."

Cal huffs loudly, his broad shoulders rising and falling. Clearly any etiquette lessons he may have had took a backseat to military training.

"Show me an officer who knows as much as I do about Silver protocols and the Corvium defense system and I'll gladly step back from this mess."

"I'm sure there's someone, Calore."

"Who's fought with newbloods? Knows your abilities? Knows how best to use you in a fight?"

I bristle at his tone. "'Use,'" I spit. *Use* indeed. I remember those of us who didn't survive Corros. Newbloods recruited by Mare Barrow, newbloods she promised to protect. Instead, Mare and Cal threw us into a battle we were not prepared for, and it became clear Mare couldn't even protect herself. Nix, Gareth, Ketha, and others from the prison I didn't even know. Dozens dead, discarded like pieces on a game board.

That's how it's always worked with the Silver masters, and that's how Cal was taught to fight. Win at all costs. Pay for every inch in Red blood.

"You know what I mean."

I snort. "Maybe that's why I'm not exactly confident."

Harsh, Cameron.

"Listen," I continue, switching tactics. "I know I'd burn everyone here if it meant getting my brother back. And luckily, that's not a decision I have to make. But you—you actually have that option. I want to make sure you don't take it."

It's true. We're here for the same reason. Not blind obedience to the Scarlet Guard, but because they are our only hope of saving the ones we love and lost.

Cal quirks a crooked smile, the same one I've seen Mare moon over. It makes him look like more of a fool. "Don't try to sweet-talk me, Cameron. I'm doing everything I can to keep us out of another massacre. Everything." His expression turns harsh. "You think it's just Silvers who care only about victory?" he mutters. "I've seen the Colonel's reports. I've seen correspondence with Command. I've heard things. You're embedded with people who think exactly the same way. They'll burn all of us to get what they want."

Maybe true, I think, *but at least what they want is justice.*

I think of Farley, the Colonel, the oathed soldiers of the Scarlet Guard, and the Red refugees they protect. I've seen them ferry people across the border with my own eyes. I sat on one of their airjets as it screamed toward the Choke, intent on rescuing a legion of child soldiers. They have objectives with high costs, but they are not Silver. They kill, but not without reason.

The Scarlet Guard are not peaceful, but peace has no place in this conflict. No matter what Cal might think of their methods and their secrecy, theirs is the only way anyone can hope to fight Silvers and win. Cal's people brought this upon themselves.

"If you're so worried about Corvium, don't go," he says with a forced shrug.

"And miss the chance to paint my hands in Silver blood?" I snap at him. I don't know if I'm making a poor attempt to joke or threatening him outright. My patience has worn through yet again. I already had to deal with the whining of a walking lightning rod. I'm not going to tolerate the attitude of a mopey matchstick prince.

Again his eyes blaze with anger and heat. I wonder if I'm fast enough with my ability to incapacitate him. What a fight that would be. Fire against silence. Would he burn or would I?

"Funny thing, you telling me not to be careless with human life. I remember you doing everything you could to kill back in the prison."

A prison where I was kept. Starved, neglected, forced to watch the people around me wither and die because they were born . . . wrong. And even before I entered Corros, I was a prisoner of another jail. I am a daughter of New Town, conscripted to a different army since the day I was born, doomed to live my life in shadow and ash, at the mercy of the shift whistle and the factory schedule. Of course I tried to kill the ones who held me captive. I would do it again if given the choice.

"Proud of it," I tell him, setting my jaw.

He despairs of me. That much is clear. Good. There's no amount of speechmaking that will ever sway me to his thinking. I doubt anyone else will listen much either. Cal is a prince of Norta. Exiled, yes, but different from us in every way. His ability is to be used as much as mine, but he is a barely tolerated weapon. His words can only travel so far. And even then they fall on deaf ears. Mine especially.

Without warning, he sets off down a smaller passage, one of the many burrowing through the warren of Irabelle. It branches off from the wider hall, angling upward to the surface in a gentle slope. I let him go, puzzled. There's nothing in that direction. Just empty passages, abandoned, unused.

Yet something tugs. *I've heard things,* he said. Suspicion flares in my chest as he walks away, his broad form getting smaller by the second.

For a moment, I hesitate. Cal is not my friend. We're barely on the same side.

But he is nothing if not annoyingly noble. He won't hurt me.

So I follow.

The corridor is obviously unused, cluttered with scraps and dark in places where the lightbulbs are burned out. Even from a distance, Cal's presence warms the close air with every passing second. It's actually a comfortable temperature, and I make a mental note to speak with a few other escaped techies. Maybe we can figure out a way to warm up the lower passages using pressurized air.

My eyes trail the cabled wires along the ceiling, counting them. More there than there should be, to feed a few lightbulbs.

I hang back, watching as Cal shoulders some wood pallets and scrap metal from a wall. He reveals a door beneath, with the cables running overhead and into whatever room it hides. When he disappears, pulling the door shut behind him, I dare to get a little closer.

The tangle of cables comes into sharper focus. Radio array. Now I see it, clear as the nose on my bleeding face. The telltale braid of black wires that means the room inside has the ability to communicate beyond the walls of Irabelle.

But who could he possibly be communicating with?

My first instinct is to tell Farley or Kilorn.

But then . . . if Cal thinks that whatever he's doing will keep me and a thousand others from a suicide attack on Corvium, I should let him continue.

And hope I don't regret it.

FIVE
Mare

I drift on a dark sea, and shadows drift with me.

They could be memories. They could be dreams. Familiar but strange, and something wrong with each. Cal's eyes are shot with silver, bleeding hot, smoking blood. My brother's face looks more skeleton than flesh. Dad gets out of his wheelchair, but his new legs are spindle thin, knobbled, ready to splinter with every shaking step. Gisa has metal pins in both hands, and her mouth is sewn shut. Kilorn drowns in the river, tangled in his perfect nets. Red rags spill from Farley's slit throat. Cameron claws at her own neck, struggling to speak, trapped in a silence of her own making. Metal scales shudder over Evangeline's skin, swallowing her whole. And Maven slumps on his odd throne, letting it tighten and consume him until he is stone himself, a seated statue with sapphire eyes and diamond tears.

Purple eats at the edge of my vision. I try to turn in to its embrace, knowing what it holds. My lightning is so close. If only I could find the memory of it and taste one last drop of power before plunging back into darkness. But it fades like the rest, ebbing away. I expect to feel cold as the darkness presses in. Instead, heat rises.

Maven is suddenly too close to bear. Blue eyes, black hair, pale as a dead man. His hand hovers inches from my cheek. It trembles, wanting to touch, wanting to pull away. I don't know which I would prefer.

I think I sleep. Darkness and light trade places, stretching back and forth. I try to move, but my limbs are too heavy. The work of manacles or guards or both. They weigh me down worse than before, and the terrible visions are the only escape. I chase what matters most—Shade, Gisa, the rest of my family, Cal, Kilorn, lightning. But they always dance out of my grip or flicker to nothing when I reach them. Another torture, I suppose—Samson's way of running me ragged even as I sleep. Maven is there too, but I never go to him, and he never moves. Always sitting, always staring, one hand on his temple, massaging an ache. I never see him blink.

Years or seconds pass. The pressure dulls. My mind sharpens. Whatever fog held me captive recedes, burning off. I am allowed to wake up.

I feel thirsty, bled dry by bitter tears I do not remember shedding. The crushing weight of silence hangs heavy as always. For a moment it's too difficult to breathe, and I wonder if this is how I die. Drowned in this bed of silk, burned by a king's obsession, smothered by open air.

I'm back in my prison bedchamber. Maybe I've been here the entire time. The white light streaming from the windows tells me it has snowed again, and the world outside is bright winter. When my sight adjusts to it, letting the room come into clearer focus, I risk looking around. Flashing my eyes left and right, not moving more than I have to. Not that it matters.

The Arvens stand guard at the four corners of my bed, each one staring down. Kitten, Clover, Trio, and Egg. They exchange glances with one another as I blink up at them.

Samson is nowhere I can see, though I expect him to loom over me with a malicious smile and a snappy welcome. Instead, a small woman in plain clothes, with flawless blue-black skin like a polished gem, stands at the foot of my bed. I don't know her face, but there's something familiar about her features. Then I realize what I thought were manacles were actually hands. Hers. Each one tight around an ankle, soothing against my skin and the bones beneath.

I recognize her colors. Red and silver crossed on her shoulders, representing both kinds of blood. Healer. Skin healer. She's of House Skonos. The sensation I feel from her touch is healing me—or at least keeping me alive against the onslaught of four pillars of silence. Their pressure must be enough to kill me, if not for a healer. A delicate balance to be sure. She must be very talented. She has the same eyes as Sara. Bright, dark gray, expressive.

But she isn't looking at me. Her eyes, instead, are on something to my right.

I flinch when I follow her gaze.

Maven sits as I dreamed him. Still, focused, one hand on his temple. The other hand waves in silent order.

And then there really are manacles. The guards move quickly, fastening strange braided metal studded with smoothly polished orbs around my ankles and wrists. They lock each one with a single key. I try to follow the key's path, but in my daze, it flickers in and out of focus. Only the manacles stand out. They feel heavy and cold. I expect one more, a new collar to mark my neck, but my neck is left blissfully bare. The jeweled thorns don't come back.

To my eternal surprise, the healer and the guards take their leave of me, walking from the room. I watch them go in confusion, trying to hide the sudden leap of excitement sending my pulse into overdrive.

Is everyone really this stupid? Will they leave me alone with Maven? Does he think I won't try to kill him in a heartbeat?

I turn to him, trying to get out of bed, trying to move. But anything faster than sitting up feels impossible, as if my very blood has turned to lead. I quickly understand why.

"I'm quite aware of what you'd like to do to me," he says, his voice barely a whisper.

My fists clench, fingers twitching. I reach for what still won't respond. What can't respond. "More Silent Stone," I mumble, saying the words like a curse. The polished orbs of my wearable prison gleam. "You must be running low by now."

"Thank you for your concern, but the supply is well in order."

As I did in the cells beneath the Bowl of Bones, I spit in his direction. It lands harmlessly at his feet. He doesn't seem to mind. In fact, he smiles.

"Get it out of your system now. The court will not take kindly to such behavior."

"As if I— Court?" The last word sputters out.

His smile spreads. "I did not misspeak."

My insides cringe at the sight of his grin. "Lovely," I say. "You're tired of keeping me caged up where you can't see me."

"Actually, I find it difficult being this close to you." His eyes flicker over me with an emotion I don't want to place.

"The feeling is mutual," I snarl, if only to kill the strange softness in him. I would rather face his fire, his rage, than any quiet word.

He doesn't rise to the bait. "I doubt that."

"Where's my leash, then? Do I get a new one?"

"No leash, no collar." He angles his chin at my manacles. "Nothing but those now."

What he's getting at, I cannot begin to fathom. But I've long stopped trying to understand Maven Calore and the twists of his labyrinthine brain. So I let him keep talking. He always tells me what I need, in the end.

"Your interrogation was very fruitful. So much to learn about you, about the terrorists calling themselves the Scarlet Guard." My breath catches in my throat. What did they find? What did I miss? I try to remember the most important pieces of my knowledge, to figure out which will be the most harmful to my friends. Tuck, the Montfort twins, the newblood abilities?

"Cruel people, aren't they?" he continues. "Bent on destroying everything and everyone who is not like them."

"What are you talking about?" The Colonel locked me up, yes, and fears me still, but we are allies now. What could that mean to Maven?

"Newbloods, of course."

I still don't understand. There's no reason for him to care about Reds with abilities beyond what he must do to get rid of us. First he denied we existed, calling me a trick. Now we are freaks, threats. Things to be feared and eradicated.

"It's such a shame, to know you were treated so badly you felt the need to run from that old man calling himself a colonel." Maven enjoys this, explaining his plan in slivers, waiting for me to piece it together. My head is still foggy, my body weak, and I try my best to figure out what he means. "Worse still, that he debated shipping you off to the mountains, discarding you all like garbage." Montfort. But that wasn't what happened. That wasn't what was offered to us. "And of course I was very upset to learn the true intentions of the Scarlet Guard. To make a Red world, a Red dawn, with room for nothing else. No one else."

"Maven." The word quivers with all the rage I have strength to call. If not for my manacles, I would explode. "You can't—"

"Can't what? Tell the truth? Tell my country the Scarlet Guard is luring newbloods to its side only to kill them? To make a genocide of them—of you—as well as us? That the infamous rebel Mare Barrow came back to me willingly, and that this was discovered during an interrogation where the truth is impossible to hide?" He leans forward, well within striking distance. But he knows I can barely lift a finger. "That you are on our side now, because you have seen what the Scarlet Guard truly is? Because you and your newbloods are feared as we are, blessed as we are, Silver as we are, in everything but the color of blood?"

My jaw works, opening and closing my mouth. But I can't find the words to match my horror. All this done without Queen Elara's whispers. All this with her dead and cold.

"You're a monster" is all I can say. A monster, all on his own.

He draws back, still smiling. "Never tell me what I cannot do. And never underestimate what I will do—for my kingdom."

His hand falls on my wrist, drawing one finger down the manacle of Silent Stone keeping me prisoner. I tremble out of fear, but so does he.

With his eyes on my hand, I'm given time to study him. His casual clothes, black as always, are rumpled, and he does not stand on ceremony. No crown, no badges. An evil boy, but a boy still.

One I must figure out how to fight. But how? I'm weak, my lightning is gone, and anything I might say will be twisted beyond my control. I can barely walk, let alone escape unaided. Rescue is all but impossible, a hopeless dream that I can't waste any more time on. I'm stuck here, trapped by a lethal, conniving king. He dogged me over months, haunting me from afar in everything from broadcasts to his deadly notes.

I miss you. Until we meet again.

He said he was a man of his word. Perhaps, in this alone, he is.

With a deep breath, I poke at the only weakness I suspect he might still have.

"Were you here?"

Blue eyes snap to mine. It's his turn to look confused.

"Through this." I glance at the bed, and then far away. It's painful to remember Samson's torture, and I hope it shows. "I dreamed you were here."

The warmth of him recedes, drawing back to leave the room cold with oncoming winter. His eyelids flutter, dark lashes against white skin. For a second, I remember the Maven I thought he was. I see him again, a dream or a ghost.

"Every second," he answers.

When a gray flush spreads across his cheeks, I know it's the truth.

And now I know how to hurt him.

The manacles make it too easy to fall asleep, so merely pretending to do so is difficult. Beneath the blanket, I clench a fist, digging my nails into my palm. I count the seconds. I count Maven's breaths. Finally, his chair creaks. He stands. He hesitates. I can almost feel his eyes, their touch burning against my still face. And then he goes, footsteps light against the wood floor, sweeping through my bedroom with the grace and quiet of a cat. The door shuts softly behind him.

So easy to sleep.

I wait instead.

Two minutes pass, but the Arven guards don't return.

I suppose they think the manacles are enough to keep me here.

They are wrong.

My legs wobble when they hit the floor, bare feet against cold wood in parquet designs. If there are cameras watching, I don't care. They can't stop me from walking. Or trying to walk.

I don't like doing things slowly. Especially now, when every moment counts. Every second could mean another person I love dead. So I shove off the bed, forcing myself to stand on weak, trembling legs. An odd sensation, with Silent Stone weighing down my wrists and ankles, leaching what little strength my anger gives me. It takes a long moment to bear the pressure. I doubt I'll ever get used to it. But I can get past it.

The first step is the easiest. A lunge to the little table where I take my meals. The second is more difficult, now that I know how much effort it takes. I walk like a man drunk or hobbled. For a split second, I envy my father's wheelchair. The shame of such thoughts fuels my next steps, across the length of the room. Panting, I reach the other side, almost collapsing against the wall. The burn in my legs is pure fire, sending a prickle of sweat down my spine. A familiar feeling, like I've just run a mile. The nausea in the pit of my stomach is different, though. Another side effect of the Stone. It makes every beat of my heart feel heavier, and wrong somehow. It tries to empty me out.

My forehead touches the paneled wall, letting the cold soothe. "Again," I force out.

I turn and stumble across the room.

Again.

Again.

Again.

By the time Kitten and Trio deliver my lunch, I'm drenched with sweat and I have to eat lying on the floor. Kitten doesn't seem to care, toeing the plate of evenly balanced meat and vegetables toward me. Whatever's going on outside the city walls, it doesn't seem to have any effect on food supply. A bad sign. Trio leaves something else on my bed, but I focus on eating first. I force down every single bite.

Getting up is a bit easier. My muscles are already responding, adjusting to the manacles. There's a small blessing in them. The Arvens are living Silvers, their ability fluctuating with their own concentration, as changing as crashing waves. Their silence is much harder to adapt to than the constant press of the Stone.

I rip open the parcel on my bed, discarding the thick, luxurious wrapping. The gown slithers out, falling against my blankets. I take a step back slowly, my body going cold as I'm seized by the familiar urge to jump out the window. For a second I shut my eyes, trying to will the dress away.

Not because it's ugly. The dress is shockingly beautiful, a gleam of silk and jewels. But it forces me to realize a terrible truth. Before the dress, I was able to ignore Maven's words, his plan, and what he means to do. Now it stares me in the face, a mocking piece of artistry. The fabric is red. *As the dawn,* my mind whispers. But that is wrong too. This is not the color of the Scarlet Guard. Ours is a lurid, bright, angry red, something to be seen and recognized, almost shocking to the eye. This gown is different. Worked in darker shades, crimson and scarlet, beaded with chips of gemstones, woven with intricate embroidery. It shimmers in the darkest way, catching the light overhead like a pool of red oil.

Like a pool of red blood.

The dress will make me—and what I am—impossible to forget.

I laugh bitterly to myself. It's almost funny. My days as Maven's betrothed were spent hiding, pretending to be Silver. At least now I won't have to be painted into one of them. A very, very small mercy in the light of all else.

So, I am going before his court, and the world, the color of my blood bare for all to see. I wonder if the kingdom will realize I am nothing more than a lure hiding a steel-sharp hook.

He doesn't come back until the next morning. When he enters, he frowns at the dress, balled up in the corner. I couldn't stand to look at it. I can't really look at him either, so I keep at my exercises: currently a very stunted, slow version of sit-ups. I feel like a clumsy toddler, my arms heavier than usual, but I force through it. He takes a few steps closer, and I clench a fist, willing myself to send a spark in his direction. Nothing happens, just as nothing happened the last dozen times I tried to use my electricity.

"Good to know they got the balance right," he muses, settling into his seat at the table. Today he looks polished, with his badges bright and shining on his chest. He must've come from outside. There's snow in his hair, and he removes his leather gloves with his teeth.

"Oh yes, these bracelets are just lovely," I bite back at him, waving one heavy hand in his direction. The manacles are loose enough to spin, but tight enough that I could never pull them off, even if I dislocated a thumb. I considered it, until I realized it would be pointless.

"I'll give Evangeline your compliments."

"Of course she made them," I scoff. She must be so pleased to know she is the literal creator of my cage. "Surprised she has the time, though. She must be spending every second making crowns and tiaras to wear. Dresses too. I bet you cut yourself every time you have to hold her hand."

A muscle in his cheek ticks. Maven has no feelings for Evangeline, something I've always known. Something I can easily exploit.

"Have you set a date?" I ask, sitting up.

Blue eyes flash to mine. "What?"

"I doubt a royal wedding is something you can do on short notice. I assume you know exactly when you're marrying Samos."

"Oh, that." He shrugs, brushing it off with a wave. "Planning the wedding is her business."

I hold his gaze. "If it were her business, she'd have been queen months ago." When he doesn't reply, I push harder. "You don't want to marry her."

Instead of crumbling, his facade strengthens. He even chuckles, projecting an image of abject disinterest. "That's not why Silvers get married, as well you know."

I try a different tactic, playing on the pieces of him I used to know. The pieces I hope are still real. "Well, I don't blame you for stalling—"

"It isn't stalling to postpone a wedding in wartime."

"She's not who you would've chosen—"

"As if there's choice in the matter."

"Not to mention the fact that she was Cal's before she was yours."

The mention of his brother stills his lazy protesting. I can almost see the muscles tighten beneath his skin, and one hand flicks the bracelet at his wrist. Every gentle ting of the metal rings as loud as a warning bell. One spark from it and he will burn.

But fire doesn't scare me anymore.

"Based on your progress, it should take another day or so for you to learn how to walk properly with those." His words are measured, forced, calculated. He probably rehearsed them before he came in here. "And then you'll finally be of some use to me."

As I do every day, I glance around the room, looking for cameras. I still don't see them, but they must be there. "Do you spend all day spying on me, or does a Security officer give you a summary? Some kind of written report?"

Maven lets the remark glance off. "Tomorrow you will stand up and say exactly what I tell you to."

"Or what?" I force myself to my feet without any of the grace or agility I used to claim. He watches every inch. I let him. "I'm already your prisoner. You can kill me whenever you like. And quite frankly, I'd prefer that to luring newbloods into your net to die."

"I'm not going to kill you, Mare." Even though he's still sitting, I feel like he towers over me. "And I don't want to kill them either."

I understand what the words mean, but not when they come from Maven's mouth. It makes no sense. No sense at all. "Why?"

"You'll never fight for us, I know that. But your kind . . . they're strong, stronger than many Silvers could ever be. Imagine what we will do with an army of them, combined with an army of mine. When they hear your voice, they'll come. How they are treated once they arrive depends on your behavior, of course. And your compliance." Finally, he stands. He's grown in the past few months. Taller and leaner, taking after his mother, as he does in most things. "So I have two choices, and you get to pick which one I follow. Either you bring me newbloods, and they join with us, or I continue finding them on my own, and killing them."

My slap lands weakly, barely moving his jaw at all. My other hand smacks against his chest, just as inconsequential. He almost rolls his eyes at the effort. He might even enjoy it.

I feel my face turn bright red, flushing both in anger and helpless sorrow. "How can you be like this?" I curse, wishing I could tear him apart. If not for the manacles, my lightning would be everywhere. Instead, words pour out of me. Words I can barely think about before they rage from me. "How can you still be like this? She's dead. I killed her. You are free from her. You—you shouldn't be her son anymore."

His hand grips my chin hard, shocking me into silence. The force of it makes me bend, lean backward, almost lose balance. I wish I would. I wish I could fall out of his hands, hit the floor, and splinter into a thousand pieces.

Back at the Notch, in the warmth of the cot I shared with Cal, deep in the night, I thought of moments like this. Being alone with Maven again. Getting the chance to see what he truly was beneath the mask I remembered and the person his mother forced him to be. In that strange place between sleep and waking, his eyes followed me. Always the same color, but somehow changing. His eyes, her eyes, eyes I knew and eyes I could never know. They look the same now, burning with a cold fire, threatening to consume me.

Knowing it's what he wants to see, I let the tears of frustration overwhelm me and fall. He tracks their paths with hunger.

Then he shoves me away. I stagger to a knee.

"I am what she made me," he whispers, leaving me behind.

Before the door shuts behind him, I notice guards on either side. Clover and Egg this time. So the Arvens are not far away, even if I somehow manage to free myself.

I sink slowly to the floor and sit back on my heels. I put one hand over my face, hiding the fact that my eyes are suddenly dry. As much as I wished Elara's death would change him, I knew it would not. I'm not that stupid. I cannot trust anything where Maven is concerned.

The smallest of his ceremonial badges bites in my other hand, hidden by my curling fingers. Even Silent Stone cannot take away a thief's instincts. The badge's metal pin digs into skin. I'm tempted to let it break through, to bleed crimson and scarlet, to remind myself and anyone watching what I am, and what I am capable of.

Under the guise of straightening up, I slip the badge under my mattress. Along with the rest of my plunder: hairpins, broken fork tines, shards of shattered glass and porcelain plates. My arsenal, humble as it is, will have to do.

I glare at the dress in the corner, as if the dress is somehow at fault for this.

Tomorrow, he said.

I return to my sit-ups.

SIX
Mare

The cards are carefully typed, outlining what I must say. I can't even look
at them, and leave them lying on my bedside table.

I very much doubt I'll get the benefit of maids to make me up into
whatever Maven imagines presenting to the court. It looks like an
arduous task, buttoning and zipping myself into the scarlet gown. It
has a high collar, trailing hem, and long sleeves to hide not just Maven's
brand on my collarbone but the manacles still attached to my wrists and
ankles.

No matter how many times I escape this elegant pageantry, I seem
doomed to play a role in it. The dress will be too big when I finally
get it on, loose around the arms and waist. I'm thinner here, no matter
how much I force myself to eat. Based on what I can glean from my
reflection in the window, my hair and skin have also suffered under
the weight of silence. My face is yellowed and sunken, sickly-looking,
while red rims my eyes. And my dark brown hair, still tinged by the
slow creep of gray at the ends, is rattier than ever, tangled to the root. I
braid it back hastily, working the knotted strands.

No amount of silk can change what I look like beneath Maven's costume. But it's no matter. I'll never wear it, if all goes to plan.

The next step in my preparation makes my heart pound. I do my best to look calm, for the cameras in my bedroom at least. They cannot know what I'm about to do, not if it's going to work. And even if I manage to fool my guards, there's another rather large obstacle.

This could kill me.

Maven did not put cameras in my bathroom. Not to protect my privacy, but to placate his own jealousy. I know enough of him to realize he won't let another person see my body. The added weight of Silent Stone, the slabs set into walls, is confirmation. Maven made sure guards would never have a reason to escort me in here. My heart beats sluggishly in my chest, but I push through it. I have to.

The shower hisses and steams, scalding hot as soon as I turn it on to full blast. If not for the bathroom Stone, I would have spent many days enjoying the singular comfort of a hot wash. I must work quickly, or let myself be smothered.

Back at the Notch we were lucky to bathe in cold rivers, while on Tuck the showers were timed and lukewarm. I laugh at the thought of what passed for bathing at home. A tub filled from the kitchen faucet, warm in the summer, cold in the winter, with stolen soap to clean with. I still don't envy my mother's job of helping my father wash.

With any luck—lots of luck—I'll see them again soon.

I push the showerhead, angling it away from the basin and onto the floor of the bathroom. The water pelts against white tile, drenching it. The spray hits my bare feet, and the heat shivers my skin, gentle and inviting as a warm blanket.

As water seeps out beneath the bathroom door, I work quickly. First I put the long shard of glass on the counter, well within arm's length.

Then I reach for the true weapon.

Whitefire Palace is a marvel in every inch, and my bathroom is no exception. It's lit by a modest chandelier, if there is such a thing: worked in silver, with curling arms like tree branches giving bud to a dozen lightbulbs. I have to stand on the sink, precariously balanced, to get at it. A few forceful but focused tugs pull the dangling fixture forward, its wiring peeling through the ceiling. Once I have enough slack, I crouch, the still-lit chandelier in hand. I brace it on the sink to wait.

The pounding starts a few minutes later. Whoever is watching my room has noticed the water spilling out from underneath my bathroom door. Ten seconds later, two sets of feet troop into my bedroom. Which Arvens, I'm not sure, but it doesn't really matter.

"Barrow!" a man's voice calls, accompanied by a fist knocking on the bathroom door.

They waste no time when I don't respond, and neither do I.

Egg pushes the door in, his white face almost blending into the tiled walls as he steps inside, sloshing through. Clover does not follow, but stands with one foot in the bathroom, the other in my bedchamber. It doesn't matter. Both her feet are in the puddle of steaming water.

"Barrow . . . ?" Egg says, slack-jawed at the sight of me.

It doesn't take much to let the chandelier drop, but the action feels heavy all the same.

It smashes against the wet tile. When the electricity hits the water, a surge pulses through the room, shorting out not just the other bathroom lights, but the lights in my bedroom. Probably this entire wing of the palace.

Both Arvens jump and twitch as the sparks dance through their flesh. They crumple quickly, muscles seizing.

I vault over the water and their bodies, almost gasping as the weight of the bathroom's Silent Stone melts away. The manacles still weigh on my limbs, and I waste no time searching the Arvens, careful to keep out of the water. I turn out their pockets as quickly as I can, searching for the key that haunts my waking moments. Shaking, I feel a curl of metal beneath Egg's collar, lying flush to his breastbone. With trembling hands, I yank it free and set to loosening my manacles one by one. As they drop away, the silence lifts, bit by bit. I gasp down air, trying to force lightning into myself. It's coming back. It must.

But I still feel numb.

Egg's body is at my mercy, warm and alive beneath my hands. I could cut his throat and Clover's, slice their jugulars with any one of the jagged bits of glass I keep well hidden. *I should do it,* I tell myself. But I've already wasted too much time. I leave them living.

As expected, the Arvens are trained enough in their duties to have locked my bedroom door behind them. No matter. A hairpin is just as good as a key. I pop the lock in a second.

It's been a few days since I stepped outside my prison, and then I was leashed to Evangeline, guarded on all sides. Now the hallway is empty. Dead lightbulbs march down the hall overhead, taunting in their emptiness. My electrical sense is weak, barely a spark across the darkness. It has to come back. This won't work if it doesn't come back. I fight a swell of panic—what if it's gone for good? What if Maven took my lightning from me?

I sprint as fast as I can, holding on to what I know of Whitefire. Evangeline took me left, to the ballrooms and the great halls and the throne room. Those places will be crawling with guards and officers, not to mention the nobility of Norta, dangerous on their own. So I go right.

Cameras follow, of course. I spot them at every corner. I wonder if they shorted out too, or if I'm entertainment for a few officers. They might be making bets on how far I get. The doomed endeavor of a doomed girl.

A service stair takes me down a landing, and I almost knock over a servant in my haste.

My heart leaps at the sight of him. A boy, my age, maybe, his face already flushing as he holds on to his tea tray. Flushing red.

"It's a trick!" I shout at him. "What they're going to make me do, it's a trick!"

At the top of the stairs, and the bottom, a pair of doors bang open in succession. Cornered again. A bad habit I've developed.

"Mare—" the boy says, my name trembling on his lips. I frighten him.

"Find a way; tell the Scarlet Guard. Tell whoever you can. It's another lie!"

Someone seizes me around my middle, pulling me backward, up and away. I keep my focus on the serving boy. The uniformed officers ascending from below shove him away, pressing him up against the wall without thought. His tray clatters to the floor, spilling tea.

"It's all a lie!" I manage to get out before a hand clamps over my mouth.

I try to spark, reaching for lightning that I still barely feel. Nothing happens, so I bite down hard enough to taste blood.

The Security officer drops his hand, swearing, while another comes up in front of me, deftly grabbing my kicking legs. I spit blood in her face.

When she backhands me, the action full of deadly grace, I recognize her.

"Good to see you, Sonya," I hiss. I try to kick her in the stomach, but she dodges with boredom.

Please, I beg in my mind, as if the electricity can hear me. Nothing responds, and I choke back a sob. I'm too weak. It's been too long.

Sonya is a silk, too swift and agile to be bothered with the resistance of a weak girl. I glance at her uniform. Black piped with silver, with the blue and red of House Iral on her shoulders. Judging by the badges on her chest and the pins on her collar, she's a ranking officer of Security now. "Congratulations on the promotion," I growl in frustration, lashing out because it's all I can do. "Done with Training so soon?"

She tightens her grip on my feet, her hands like pincers.

"Too bad you never finished Protocol." Still carrying my legs, she rubs her face on her shoulder, trying to wipe away the silver blood on her cheek. "You could use some manners."

It's only been a few months since I last saw her. Standing with her grandmother Ara and Evangeline, dressed in mourning black for the king. She was one of many who watched me in the Bowl of Bones, who wanted to see me die. Her house is famed for their skill not just in body, but in mind. Spies all, trained to discover secrets. I doubt she believed Maven when he told everyone I was a trick, a Scarlet Guard creation sent to infiltrate the palace. And I doubt she'll believe what's about to happen.

"I saw your grandmother," I tell her. A daring card to play.

Her flawless composure does not change, but I feel her grip on my legs weaken, if only a little. Then she dips her chin. *Continue,* she's trying to say.

"In Corros Prison. Starved, weakened by Silent Stone." *Like I am now.* "I helped free her."

Another might call me a liar. But Sonya remains quiet, her eyes anywhere but me. To anyone else, she looks disinterested.

"I don't know how long she spent in there, but she put up more of a fight than anyone else." I remember her now, flashing across my memories. An old woman with the vicious strength of her namesake, the Panther. She even saved my life, plucking a razor-sharp wheel out of the air before it could take my head. "Ptolemus got her in the end, though. Right before he killed my brother."

Her gaze falls to the floor, brow furrowed slightly. Every inch of her tightens. For a second I think she might cry, but the threatening tears never spill. "How?" I barely hear her.

"Through the neck. Quickly."

Her next slap is well aimed, but without much strength behind it. A show, like everything else in this hellish place.

"Keep your filthy lies to yourself, Barrow," she hisses, ending our conversation.

I end up in a heap on my bedroom floor, both cheeks stinging, with the crushing weight of four Arven guards washing over me. Egg and Clover look a bit rumpled, but healers have already seen to their injuries, whatever they were. Pity I didn't kill them.

"Shocked to see me?" I drawl at them, chuckling at the horrific joke.

In response, Kitten forces me into the scarlet gown, making me strip in front of them all. She takes her time in the humiliation. The dress smarts as it pulls across my brand. *M* for *Maven*, *M* for *monster*, *M* for *murder*.

I can still taste the Security officer's blood when Kitten shoves the speech cards into my chest.

* * *

The full strength of the Silver court has been summoned to the throne room. The High Houses press together in their usual riot. Every color is an assault, a firework of gems and brocade. I join the chaos, adding blood red to the collection. The doors to the throne room seal shut behind me, caging me in with the worst of them. The houses part to let me pass, forming a long corridor from the entrance to the throne. They whisper as I go, noting every imperfection and every rumor. I catch snippets. Of course they all know about my little adventure this morning. The Arven guards, two in front, two behind, are confirmation enough of my continued status as prisoner.

So Maven's newest lie is not for them this time. I try to puzzle out his motives, the turns of his labyrinthine manipulations. He must have weighed the costs of what to tell them—and decided bringing his closest nobles in on such a delicious secret was worth the risk. They won't mind his lies if he isn't lying to them.

As before, he sits on his throne of gray stone slabs, both hands clawed to the armrests. Sentinels have his back, lining the wall behind him, while Evangeline takes his left, standing proud. She glitters, a lethal star, with a cape and slashed gown of intricate silver scales. Her brother, Ptolemus, matches in a new suit of armor, close as a guardian for both his sister and the king. Another bitterly familiar face holds Maven's right. He does not wear armor. He does not need armor. His mind is weapon and shield enough.

Samson Merandus grins at me, a vision in dark blue and white lace, colors I hate above all others. Even silver. *I am a butcher,* he warned me before my interrogation. He was not lying. I will never fully recover from the way he carved me up: a pig on a hook, bled dry.

Maven notes my appearance, pleased with it. The same Skonos healer attempted to do something with my hair, pulling it back into a neat tail while swiping a bit of makeup across my frazzled features. She didn't take long, but I wish she'd lingered. Her touch was cool and soothing, fixing up whatever bruises I earned in my doomed escape.

I feel no fear as I approach, walking before the eyes of dozens of Silvers. There are far worse things to be afraid of. Like the cameras ahead, for example. They aren't trained on me yet, but they will be soon. I can hardly stomach the thought.

Maven stops us short with a single gesture, holding up his palm. The Arvens know what it means and peel away, leaving me to walk the last few yards by myself. That's when the cameras switch on. To show me walking alone, unguarded, unleashed, a free Red standing with Silvers. The image will be broadcast everywhere, to everyone I love, and anyone I could ever hope to protect. This simple action might be enough to doom dozens of newbloods, and strike a heavy blow against the Scarlet Guard.

"Come forward, Mare."

That is Maven's voice. Not Maven, but Maven. The boy I thought I knew. Gentle, tender. He keeps that voice stored away, ready to be drawn and used against me like a sword. It strikes me to my core, as he knows it will. In spite of myself, I feel the familiar longing for a boy who does not exist.

My footsteps echo on the marble. In Protocol, the late Lady Blonos tried to teach me how to hold my face at court. Her ideal expression was cold, emotionless, beyond unfeeling. I am none of those things, and I fight the urge to slip behind such a mask. Instead, I try to school my features into something that will both satisfy Maven and somehow let the country know this is not my choice at all. A hard line to walk.

Still grinning, Samson takes a step sideways, leaving space next to the throne. I shiver at the intention, but do as I must. I take Maven's right side.

What a picture this must be. Evangeline in silver, me in red, with the king in black between.

SEVEN
Cameron

The so-called "lightning alert" echoes through the main floor of Irabelle, up and down the scaffolded landings, back and forth between passages. Runners go out, seeking those of us deemed important enough to get updates on Mare. Usually I'm not a priority. No one drags me down to be debriefed with the rest of her club. The kids find me later on, at work, and hand me a paper detailing whatever snippets the Guard spies gathered on precious Barrow's cell time. Useless stuff. What she ate, her guard rotation, that kind of thing. But today the runner, a little girl with slick, straight black hair and russet skin, tugs on my arm.

"Lightning alert, Miss Cole. Come with me," she says, adamant and cloying.

I want to snap that my priority is to get the heat working in my barracks, not find out how many times Mare used the bathroom today, but her sweet face stops the impulse. Farley must've sent the cutest bleeding kid in the base. *Damn her.*

"All right, I'll go," I huff, tossing my tools back into their case. When she takes my hand, I'm reminded of Morrey. He's shorter than I am, and back when we were kids working the assembly line, he used to hold my hand when the noisy machines frightened him. But this little girl shows no signs of fear.

She pulls me through curling passages, proud of herself for knowing which way to go. I frown at the red scrap tied around her wrist. She's too young to be oathed to rebels, let alone living in their tactical headquarters. But then, I was sent to work when I was five, sorting scrap from the junk piles. She's twice that age.

I open my mouth to ask what brought her here, but think better of it. Her parents, obviously, either by their life's choices or their life's ending. I wonder where they might be. Just like I wonder about mine.

Passages 4 and 5 and Sub 7 need wire stripping. Barracks A needs heat. I repeat the always-growing list of tasks to dull the sudden pain. My own parents fade from my thoughts as I push away their faces. Daddy driving a transport truck, his hands sure as ever on the wheel. Mama in the factory alongside me, quicker than I'll ever be. She was sick when we left, her hair thinning while her dark skin seemed to gray. I almost choke on the memory. Both of them are out of my reach. But Morrey isn't. Morrey I can get to.

Passages 4 and 5 and Sub 7 need wire stripping. Barracks A needs heat. Morrey Cole needs to be saved.

We reach the passage to central control the same time Kilorn does. His own runner trails behind, sprinting to keep up with the lanky boy tearing around the corner. Kilorn must have been topside, out in the frozen air of oncoming winter. His cheeks bloom red from the cold. As he walks, he pulls off a knit hat, upending uneven tawny locks.

"Cam." He nods at me, stopping where our paths cross. He vibrates with fear, eyes vividly green in the fluorescent lights of the passage. "Any ideas?"

I shrug. I know less than anyone where Mare is concerned. I don't even know why they bother to keep me in the loop. Probably to make me feel included. Everyone knows I don't want to be here, but I have nowhere else to go. Not back to New Town, not to the Choke. I'm stuck.

"None," I reply.

Kilorn glances back at his runner, offering a smile. "Thanks," he says, kindly dismissive. The kid takes a hint, turning away with relief. I do the same to mine, gesturing with a bob of my head and a grateful smile. She takes off in the other direction, disappearing around a bend.

"Starting them young," I can't help but whisper under my breath.

"Not as young as we were," Kilorn replies.

I frown. "True."

In the past month or so, I've learned enough about Kilorn to know I can trust him as much anyone down here. Our lives are similar. He started apprenticing at a young age, and, like me, he had the luxury of a job to keep him from conscription. Until the rules changed on us both, and we ended up pulled into the lightning girl's orbit. Kilorn would argue that his presence here is by choice, but I know better. He was Mare's best friend, and he followed her into the Scarlet Guard. Now blind stubbornness—not to mention his fugitive status—keeps him here.

"But we weren't indoctrinated into something, Kilorn," I continue, hesitating to take the next few steps. The control-room guards wait a few yards away, silent in their duties at the door. They're watching us both. I don't like the feeling.

Kilorn offers a strange, sad twitch of a smile. His eyes lower to my tattooed neck, where I am permanently marked with my profession and place. The black ink stands out, even against my dark skin. "Yes, we were, Cam," he says quietly. "Come on."

He slips an arm around my shoulders, moving us both forward. The guards stand aside, letting us pass through the door.

This time, the control room is more crowded than I've ever seen. Every technician sits in rapt attention, their focus on the several screens at the front of the room. Each displays the same thing: the Burning Crown, the emblem of Norta, its flames of red, black, and silver. Usually the symbol bookends official broadcasts, and I assume I'm about to be subjected to the latest message from King Maven's regime. I'm not the only one to think so.

"We might see her," Kilorn breathes, his voice tempered by equal parts longing and fear. On-screen, the image jumps a little. Frozen, paused. "What are we waiting for?"

"More like who," I reply, casting a look about the room. As far as I can see, Cal is here already, stoically folded at the back of the room, keeping his distance from everyone. He feels me watching, but doesn't do much more than nod.

To my dismay, Kilorn waves him over. After a second of hesitation, Cal complies, moving gently through the room as it crowds full. For whatever reason, this lightning alert has drawn many to control, all of them as on edge as Kilorn. Most of them I don't recognize, but a few newbloods join the mix. I spot Rash and Tahir at their usual position, seated with their radio equipment, while Nanny and Ada stick close together. Like Cal, they occupy the back wall, reluctant to draw any attention to themselves. As the prince gets closer, Red officers all but jump out of his way. He pretends to ignore it.

Cal and Kilorn trade weak smiles. Their usual rivalry is long gone, but replaced by trepidation.

"Wish the Colonel would move his ass a little faster," a voice says on my right.

I turn to see Farley sidle up to us, doing her best to remain inconspicuous despite her belly. It's mostly hidden by her large jacket, but it's hard to keep secrets in a place like this. She's close to four months and doesn't care who knows. Even now, she balances a plate of fried potatoes in one hand, a fork in the other.

"Cameron, boys," she adds, nodding at us in turn. I do the same, as does Kilorn. She gives Cal a mock salute with her fork, and he barely grunts a response. His jaw clenches so tightly his teeth might shatter.

"Thought the Colonel slept in here," I reply, fixing my gaze on the screen. "Typical. The one time we need him around."

Any other day, I would wonder if his absence was a ploy. Maybe to let us know who's in charge. As if any of us could forget. Even next to Cal, a Silver prince and general, or a host of newbloods with a terrifying array of abilities, he somehow manages to hold all the cards. Because here, in the Scarlet Guard, in this world, information is more important than anything, and he's the only one who knows enough to keep control of us all.

I can respect that. Parts of a machine don't need to know what the other pieces are doing. But I'm not just a gear. Not anymore.

The Colonel enters, flanked by Mare's brothers. Still no sign of her parents, who remain stowed away somewhere, alongside her sister with the dark red hair. I thought I saw her once, a smart, quick thing darting through the mess hall, but I never got close enough to ask. I've heard rumors, of course. Whispers from the other technicians and soldiers. A Security officer crushed the girl's foot, forcing Mare to beg at the summer palace. Or something like that. I have a feeling that asking Kilorn for the real story would be inconsiderate.

The control center turns to watch for the Colonel, eager for him to start whatever we're here to see. So we react together, stifling gasps or surprised expressions when another Silver follows the Colonel into the already-crowded room.

Every time I see him, I want to hate him. He was the reason Mare forced me to join her, forced me to return to my prison, forced me to kill, forced others to die so this insignificant dry twig of a man could live. But those choices weren't his. He was a prisoner as much as I was, doomed to the cells of Corros and the slow, crushing death of Silent Stone. It's not his fault the lightning girl loves him, and he must bear the curse that love brings with it.

Julian Jacos does not shrink against the back wall with the new-bloods, and he doesn't take the spot next to his nephew Cal either. Instead, he keeps close to the Colonel, allowing the crowd to part so that he might see this broadcast as best he can. I focus on his shoulders as he settles into place. His posture reeks of Silver decadence. Straight-backed, perfect. Even in the hand-me-down uniform, faded by use, with gray in his hair and the pallid, cold look we all take on underground, there's no denying what he is. Others share my sentiments. The soldiers around him touch their holstered guns, keeping one eye on the Silver man. The rumors are more pointed where is he concerned. He's Cal's uncle, a dead queen's brother, Mare's old tutor. Woven into our ranks like a thread of steel among wool. Embedded, but dangerous and easily pulled free.

They say he can control a man with his voice and his eyes. Like the queen could. Like many still can.

One more person I will never, ever turn my back on. It's a long list.

"Let's see it," the Colonel barks, cutting off the low murmur born of Julian's presence. The screens respond in kind, jittering into motion.

No one speaks, and the sight of King Maven's face cuts through us all.

He beckons from that hulking throne, deep in the heart of the Silver court, eyes wide and inviting. I know he's a snake, so I can ignore his well-chosen disguise. But I imagine most of the country cannot see through the mask of a young boy called to greatness, dutifully doing what he can for a kingdom on the edge of chaos. He's good-looking. Not broad like Cal, but finely shaped, a sculpture of sweeping cheekbones and glossy black hair. Beautiful, not handsome. I hear someone scratching notes, probably recording everything on-screen. Allowing the rest of us to watch unfettered, focused only on what horror Maven is about to perform.

He leans forward, one hand extended, as he stands to call someone to him.

"Come forward, Mare."

The cameras turn, revolving smoothly to show Mare standing before the king. I expected rags, but instead she wears finery I could never dream of. Every inch of her is covered in bloodred gemstones and embroidered silk. It all shimmers as she walks down a grand aisle parting the crowd of Silvers assembled for whatever this is. No more collar, no more leash. Again I see through the mask. Again I hope the kingdom does too—but how can they? They don't know her like we do. They don't see the shadows in her dark eyes, flickering with every step. Her hollow cheeks. The purse of her lips. The twitching fingers. A tightening jaw. And that's only what I notice. Who knows what Cal or Kilorn or her brothers can see in the lightning girl?

The dress covers her from just below her neck to wrist and ankle. Probably to hide bruises, scars, and the brand she bears from the king.

It's not a dress at all, but a costume.

I'm not the only one to suck in a breath of fear when she reaches the king. He takes her hand in his, and she hesitates to close her fingers. Only a fraction of a second, but enough to cement what we already know. This is not her choice. Or if it is, the alternative was much, much worse.

A current of heat ripples on the air. Kilorn does his best to sidle away from Cal without drawing attention, bumping into me. I make room as best I can. No one wants to be too close to the fire prince if things go south.

Maven does not have to gesture. Mare knows him and his schemes well enough to understand what he wants from her. The camera image pulls back as she moves to the right of his throne. What we see now is a display of ultimate strength. Evangeline Samos, the king's betrothed, a future queen in power and appearance, on one side, with the lightning girl on the other. Silver and Red.

Other nobles, the greatest of the High Houses, stand in assembly on the dais. Names and faces I don't know, but I'm sure many here do. Generals, diplomats, warriors, advisers. Every one of them dedicated to our complete annihilation.

The king takes his throne again, slowly, eyes locked deep into the camera, and so into us.

"Before I say anything else, before I begin this speech"—he gestures, confident and almost charming—"I want to thank the fighting men and women, Silver and Red, who serve to protect our borders, who are currently defending us from enemies outside this nation, and the enemies within. To the soldiers of Corvium, the loyal warriors resisting the constant and deplorable terrorist attacks of the Scarlet Guard, I salute you, and I am with you."

"Liar," someone snarls in the room, but they're quickly hushed.

On-screen, Mare looks like she shares the sentiment. She does her best not to twitch or let her face betray her emotions. It works. Almost. A flush creeps up her neck, partially hidden by her high collar. Not high enough. Maven would have to put a bag over her head to hide her feelings.

"In recent days, after much deliberation with my council and the courts of Norta, Mare Barrow of the Stilts was sentenced for her crimes against this kingdom. She stood accused of murder and terrorism, and we believed her to be the worst of the rats gnawing at our roots." Maven glances up at her, face still and focused. How many times he's practiced this, I don't want to know. "Her punishment was to face a lifetime in prison, after first being interrogated by my own cousins of House Merandus."

At the king's bidding, a man in dark blue steps forward. He comes within inches of Mare, close enough to brush a hand against whatever part of her he chose. She freezes in place, snapping every centimeter still to keep from flinching.

"I am Samson of House Merandus, and I performed the interrogation of Mare Barrow."

Ahead of me, Julian raises a hand to his mouth. The only indication of how affected he is.

"As a whisper, my ability allows me to bypass the usual lies and twists of speech that most prisoners rely on. So when Mare Barrow told us the truth of the Scarlet Guard and its horrors, I confess I did not believe her. I testify here, on record, that I was wrong to doubt her. What I saw in her memories was painful and chilling."

Another round of whispers through the room, another round of hushing. The tension is still palpable, though, as well as the confusion.

The Colonel straightens, arms crossed. I'm sure they're all thinking on their sins, and what this Samson fool could be rattling on about. On one side, Farley taps her fork against her lip, eyes narrowed. She curses under her breath, but I can't ask why.

Mare lifts her chin, looking like she might vomit on the king's boots. I bet she wants to.

"I went to the Scarlet Guard willingly," she says. "They told me my brother had been executed while serving in the legions, for a crime he did not commit." Her voice cracks at the mention of Shade. Next to me, Farley's breath quickens and her hand curls over her stomach. "They asked if I wanted vengeance for his death. I did. So I swore my allegiance to their cause, and I was placed as a servant inside the royal residence at the Hall of the Sun.

"I came to the palace as a Red spy, but even I did not know I was something else entirely. During the right of Queenstrial, I discovered I somehow possessed electrical ability. After consultation, the late King Tiberias and Queen Elara decided to take me in, to quietly study what I was and, hopefully, teach me what my ability could become. They disguised me as a Silver to protect me. They rightfully knew that a Red with an ability would be considered a freak at best, an abomination at worst, and they hid my identity to keep me safe from the prejudices of both Red and Silver. My blood status was known to a few, Maven included, as well as Ca—Prince Tiberias.

"But the Scarlet Guard discovered what I was. They threatened to expose me publicly, both to ruin the credibility of the king and to put me in danger. I was forced to serve them as a spy, to follow their orders, and to facilitate their infiltration of the king's court."

The next outcry from the room is louder, and not easily put down.

"This is some impressive bullshit," Kilorn growls.

"My ultimate mission was to gain Silver allies for the Scarlet Guard. I was instructed to target Prince Tiberias, a cunning warrior and the heir to the throne of Norta. He was . . ." She hesitates, her eyes boring into ours. They shift back and forth, searching. Out of the corner of my eye, I see Cal lower his head. "He was easily convinced. Once I figured out how to convince him, I also aided the Scarlet Guard in their plans for the Sun Shooting, which left eleven dead, and the bombing of the Bridge of Archeon.

"When Prince Tiberias killed his father, King Maven acted swiftly, making the only choice he thought he could," her voice warbles. Next to her, Maven does his best to look sad at the mention of his murdered father. "He was grieving, and we were sentenced to execution in the arena. We escaped with our lives only because of the Scarlet Guard. They took us both to an island stronghold off the Nortan coast.

"I was held prisoner there, as were Prince Tiberias and, I discovered, the brother I thought I'd lost. Like me, he had an ability, and like me, he was feared by the Scarlet Guard. They intended to kill us, the ones they call newbloods. When I discovered that others like me existed, and the Scarlet Guard was hunting them down to exterminate them, I managed to escape with my brother and a few others. Prince Tiberias came with us. I know now that he intended to build himself an army to challenge his brother. After a few months, the Scarlet Guard caught up with us all, and they killed the few abilitied Reds we were able to find. My brother was murdered in the conflict, but I escaped alone."

For once, the heat in the room isn't coming from Cal. Everyone boils with rage. This isn't Mare. These aren't her words. But still I feel anger as much as the rest. How can she even let this out of her mouth? I'd spit blood before speaking Maven's lies. But what choice does she have?

"With nowhere else to go, I turned myself in to King Maven and whatever justice he saw to give me." Her resolve breaks piece by piece, until tears course down her cheeks. I'm ashamed to say they help her little speech more than anything else. "I stand here now a willing prisoner. I am sorry for what I've done, but I am ready to do whatever I can to stop the Scarlet Guard and their terrifying hope for the future. They stand for no one but themselves and the people they can control. They kill everyone else, everyone who stands in their way. Everyone who is different."

The last words stick, refusing to come out. On the throne, Maven sits still, but his throat works a little. Emitting a noise the camera cannot hear, urging her to finish as he demands.

Mare Barrow raises her chin and glares forward. Her eyes seem black with rage. "We, the newbloods, are not fit for their dawn."

Shouts and protests erupt through the room, hurling obscenities at Maven, at the Merandus whisper, even at the lightning girl for speaking the words.

"—vile beast of a king—"

"—would rather kill myself than say—"

"—barely a puppet—"

"—traitor, plain and simple—"

"—not her first time singing their song—"

Kilorn is the first to break, both hands curling into fists. "You think she wanted to do this?" he says, his voice loud enough to carry, but not harsh. His face reddens with frustration, and Cal puts a hand on his shoulder, standing with him. It silences more than a few, particularly the younger officers. They look embarrassed, apologetic, even, shamed by the reprimand of an eighteen-year-old boy.

"Quiet, all of you!" the Colonel rumbles, shutting up the rest. He turns once to glare with his mismatched eyes. "The brat is still speaking."

"Colonel . . . ," Cal growls. His tone is a threat plain as day.

In reply, the Colonel points on-screen. At Maven, not Mare.

". . . offer refuge to any fleeing the terror of the Scarlet Guard. And to the newbloods among you, hiding from what seems to be little more than genocide, my own doors are open. I have instructed the royal palaces of Archeon, Harbor Bay, Delphie, and Summerton, as well as the military forts of Norta, to protect your kind from slaughter. You will have food, shelter, and, if you wish it, training for your abilities. You are my subjects to protect, and I will do it with every resource I have to give. Mare Barrow is not the first of you to join us, and she will not be the last." He has the smug audacity to lay a hand on her arm.

So this is how barely more than a boy becomes a king. He's not only ruthless and remorseless, but just plain brilliant. If not for the rage curling in me, I would be impressed. His ploy will cause problems for the Guard, of course. Personally, I'm more concerned with the newbloods still out there. We were recruited to Mare and her rebellion with little choice in the matter. Now there's even less. The Guard or the King. Both see us as weapons. Both will get us killed. But only one will keep us in chains.

I glance over my shoulder, seeking out Ada. Her eyes are glued to the screen, effortlessly memorizing every tick and inflection to be scrutinized later. Like me, she frowns, thinking about the deeper worry no member of the Scarlet Guard has yet. What will happen to the people like us?

"To the Scarlet Guard, I say only this," Maven adds, standing up from his throne. "Your dawn is little more than darkness, and it will never take this country. We fight to the last. Strength and power."

On the dais, and across the rest of the throne room, the chant echoes from every mouth. Including Mare's. "Strength and power."

The image holds for a second, burning the sight into every brain. Red and Silver, the lightning girl and King Maven, united against the great evil they've made us out to be. I know it isn't Mare's choice, but it is her fault. Didn't she realize he would use her if he didn't kill her?

She didn't think he would do it. Cal said that before, about her interrogation. They are both weak where Maven is concerned, and that weakness continues to plague us all.

Back at the Notch, Mare did her best to school me in my ability. I practice here when I can, together with the other newbloods learning their limits. Cal and Julian Jacos attempt to help, but I and many others are loath to trust their tutelage. Besides, I've found someone else to help me.

I know my ability has grown in strength, if not control. I feel it now, prodding beneath my skin, a blissful emptiness to still the chaos around me. It begs, and I clench a fist against it, keeping the silence back. I can't turn my anger on the people in this room. They aren't the enemy.

When the screen cuts to black, signaling the end of the address, a dozen voices sound at once. Cal's palm slams against the desk in front of him, and he turns, muttering to himself.

"I've seen enough," I think he says before he pushes his way out of the room. *Stupid.* He knows his own brother. He can dissect Maven's words better than any of us.

The Colonel knows it too. "Get him back here," he says under his breath, leaning in to speak to Julian. The Silver nods, moving smoothly to retrieve his nephew. Many stop talking to watch him go.

"Captain Farley, your thoughts?" the Colonel says, his sharp voice drawing attention back where it belongs. He crosses his arms and turns to face his daughter.

Farley snaps to focus, seemingly unaffected by the speech. She swallows a bite of potato. "The natural response would be a broadcast of our own. Refuting Maven's claims, showing the country who we saved."

Using us as propaganda. Doing exactly what Maven is doing to Mare. My stomach tightens at the thought of being shoved in front of a camera, forced to sing the praises of the people I barely tolerate and cannot fully trust.

Her father nods. "I agree—"

"But I don't think that's the right course of action."

The Colonel raises the brow of his ruined eye.

She takes it as an invitation to continue. "It'll just be words. Nothing of use in the end, in the scheme of what's going on." Her fingers tap against her lips, and I can almost see the wheels turning in her head. "I think we keep Maven talking, while we keep on doing. Already our infiltration of Corvium is placing strain on the king. See how he singled out the city? Its military? He's bolstering morale. Why do that if they don't need it?"

At the back of the room, Julian returns, one hand on Cal's shoulder. They're of the same height, though Cal looks about fifty pounds heavier than his uncle. Corros Prison certainly took as much of a toll on Julian as it did the rest of us.

"We have a good deal of information regarding Corvium," Farley adds. "And its importance to Nortan military, not to mention Silver morale, makes it the perfect place."

"For what?" I hear myself ask, surprising everyone in the room, myself included.

Farley is good enough to address me directly. "The first assault. The Scarlet Guard's official declaration of war against the king of Norta."

A strangled sort of yelp erupts from Cal, not the kind anyone would expect from a prince and soldier. His face pales, eyes wide with what can only be fear. "Corvium is a fortress. A city built with the sole purpose of surviving a war. There are a thousand Silver officers in there, soldiers trained to—"

"To organize. To fight Lakelanders. To stand behind a trench and mark places on a map," Farley fires back. "Tell me I'm wrong, Cal. Tell me your kind is prepared to fight inside its own walls."

The glare he levels at her would cut through anyone else, but Farley stands firm. If anything, she strengthens in her opposition.

"It's suicide, for you and for anyone in your way," he tells her. She laughs at the blatant dodge, inciting him further. He controls himself well, a fire prince reluctant to burn. "I'm not part of this," he snarls. "Good luck assaulting Corvium without whatever intelligence you counted on from me."

Farley's emotions are not so hindered by a Silver ability. The room will not burn with her, no matter how red her face flushes. "Thanks to Shade Barrow, I already have everything I need!"

The name usually has a sobering effect. To remember Shade is to remember how he died, and what it did to the people he loved. For Mare, it turned her cold, empty, into the person willing to trade herself to keep her friends and family from the same fate. For Farley, it left her alone, singular in her pursuits, focused only on the Scarlet Guard and nothing else. I didn't know either of them for very long before Shade died, but even I lament who they were. The loss changed them both, and not for the better.

She forces herself through the pain Shade's memory brings, if only to shove Cal's nose in it. "Before we faked his execution, Shade was our key operative in Corvium. He used his ability to feed us as much information as he could give. Don't think for one second you are our only card to play in this," Farley says evenly. Then she turns back to the Colonel. "I advise a full assault, utilizing newbloods in conjunction with Red soldiers and our infiltrators already inside the city."

Utilizing newbloods. The words sting, stab, and burn, leaving a bitter taste in my mouth.

I guess it's my turn to storm from the room.

Cal watches me go, mouth pressed into a grim, firm line.

You're not the only one who can be dramatic, I think as I leave him behind.

EIGHT
Mare

I make it easy for the Arvens to remove me from the dais. Egg and Trio take my arms, leaving Kitten and Clover behind. My body goes numb as they escort me out of sight. *What have I done?* I wonder. *What will this do?*

Somewhere the others watched. Cal, Kilorn, Farley, my family. They saw that. The shame almost makes me vomit all over my wretched, magnificent gown. I feel worse than when I read the Measures of Maven's father, dooming so many to conscription in payment for the Scarlet Guard's action. But then, everyone knew the Measures were not my doing. I was only the messenger.

The Arvens push me forward. Not back the way I came, but behind the throne, through a doorway, to rooms I've never seen.

The first is clearly another council chamber, with a long table topped in marble, surrounded by more than a dozen plush chairs. One seat is stonework, a cold construction of gray. For Maven. The room is brightly lit, flooded by the setting sun on one side. The windows face west, away from the river, looking over the palace walls and the gently sloping hills covered in snowy forest.

Last year Kilorn and I cut river ice for spare coins, risking frostbite in favor of honest work. That lasted about a week, until I realized coppers for breaking up ice that would only refreeze was a poor use of our time. How strange, to know that was only a year ago, and a lifetime away.

"Your pardon," a soft voice says, sounding from the only seat in shadow. I turn to it and watch Jon unfold himself from his chair, a book in one hand.

The seer. His red eyes glow with some inner light I can't name. I thought he was an ally, a newblood with an ability as strange as mine. He is more powerful than an eye, able to see farther into the future than any Silver can. Now he stands before me as an enemy, having betrayed us to Maven. His stare feels like hot needles pricking skin.

He is the reason I led my friends to Corros Prison, and the reason my brother is dead. The sight of him chases the icy numbness away, replacing all that emptiness with livid, electric heat. I want nothing more than to beat him across the face with whatever I can. I settle for snarling at him.

"Good to see Maven doesn't keep all his pets on a leash."

Jon just blinks at me. "Good to see you are not so blind as you once were," he replies as I pass him.

When we first met him, Cal warned us that people go mad puzzling out riddles of the future. He was absolutely right, and I won't fall into that trap again. I turn away, resisting the urge to dissect his carefully chosen words.

"Ignore me all you want, Miss Barrow. I'm not your concern," he adds. "Only one person here is."

I glance over my shoulder, my muscles moving before my brain can react. Of course Jon speaks before I do, stealing the words from my throat.

"No, Mare, I don't mean yourself."

We leave him behind, continuing on to wherever I am being led. The silence is a torture as much as Jon, giving me nothing to focus on except his words. He means Maven, I realize. And it's not difficult to guess the implication. And the warning.

There are pieces of me, small pieces, still in love with a fiction. A ghost inside a living boy I cannot begin to fathom. The ghost who sat by my bed while I dreamed in pain. The ghost who kept Samson from my mind as long as he could, I know, delaying an inevitable torture.

The ghost who loves me, in what poisoned way he can.

And I feel that poison working in me.

As I suspect, the Arvens don't take me back to my prison of a bedroom. I try to memorize our path, noting doors and passages branching off the many council chambers and salons in this wing of the palace. The royal apartments, every inch more decorated than the last. But I'm more interested in the colors dominating the rooms rather than the furniture itself. Red, black, and royal silver—that's easy to understand. The colors of reigning House Calore. There's navy as well. The shade gives me a sick feeling in my stomach. It stands for Elara. Dead, but still here.

We finally stop in a small but well-stocked library. Sunset angles through the heavy curtains, drawn against the light. Dust motes dance in the red beams, ash above a dying fire. I feel like I am inside a heart, surrounded by bloody red. This is Maven's study, I realize. I fight the urge to take the leather seat behind a lacquered desk. To claim something of his as my own. It might make me feel better, but only for a moment.

Instead, I observe what I can, looking around with wide, absorbing eyes. Scarlet tapestries worked with black and glinting silver thread hang between portraits and photographs of Calore ancestors. House Merandus is not so evident here, represented only by a flag of blue and white hanging from the vaulted ceiling. The colors of other queens are there too, some bright, some faded, some forgotten. Except for the golden yellow of House Jacos. It isn't there at all.

Coriane, Cal's mother, has been erased from this place.

I search the pictures quickly, though I don't really know what I'm searching for. None of the faces look familiar, except for Maven's father. His painting, larger than the rest, glowering over the empty fireplace, is difficult to ignore. Still draped in black, a sign of mourning. He's been dead only a few months.

I see Cal in his face, and Maven too. The same straight nose, high cheekbones, and thick, glossy black hair. Family traits, judging by the other pictures of Calore kings. The one labeled Tiberias the Fifth is particularly good-looking, almost startlingly so. But then, painters are not paid to make their subjects look ugly.

I'm not surprised to see Cal isn't represented. Like his mother, he has been removed. A few spaces are conspicuously empty, and I suppose he used to occupy them. Why wouldn't he? Cal was his father's first-born, his favorite son. It's no wonder Maven took down his brother's pictures. No doubt he burned them.

"How's the head?" I ask Egg, offering a sly, empty smile.

He responds with a glare, and my smile spreads. I'll treasure the memory of him flat on his back, electrocuted into unconsciousness.

"No more shakes?" I press on, fluttering a hand the way his body flopped. Again no response, but his neck colors blue-gray in an angry flush. That's entertainment enough for me. "Damn, those skin healers are good."

"Having fun?"

Maven enters alone, his presence oddly small in comparison to the figure he cuts on the throne. His Sentinels must be close, though, just outside the study. He's not foolish enough to go anywhere without them. With one hand he gestures, sweeping the Arvens from the room. They go swiftly, quiet as mice.

"I don't have much else for amusement," I say when they disappear. For the thousandth time today, I curse the presence of the manacles. Without them, Maven would be as dead as his mother. Instead, they force me to tolerate him in all his disgusting glory.

He grins at me, enjoying the dark joke. "Good to see not even I can change you."

To that I have no response at all. I can't count the ways Maven has changed me, and destroyed the girl I used to be.

As I suspected, he flounces to the desk and sits with a cool, practiced grace. "I must apologize for my rudeness, Mare." I think my eyes bug out of my head, because he laughs. "Your birthday was more than a month ago, and I didn't get you anything." As with the Arvens, he gestures, motioning for me to take a seat in front of him.

Surprised, shaken, still numb from my little performance, I do as he commands. "Trust me," I mutter, "I'm fine without whatever new horror you plan to gift to me."

His smile widens. "You'll like this, I promise."

"Somehow I don't believe that."

Grinning, he reaches into a drawer of his desk. Without ceremony, he tosses me a scrap of silk. Black, one half of it embroidered with red and gold flowers. I snatch it up greedily. Gisa's handiwork. I run it between my fingers. It still feels smooth and cool, though I expect something slimy, corrupted, poisoned by Maven's possession. But every twist of thread is a piece of her. Perfect in its fierce beauty, flawless, a reminder of my sister and our family.

He watches me turn the silk over and over. "We took it off you when we first apprehended you. While you were unconscious."

Unconscious. Imprisoned in my own body, tortured by the weight of the sounder.

"Thank you," I force out stiffly. As if I have any reason to thank him for anything.

"And—"

"And?"

"I offer you one question."

I blink at him, confused.

"You may ask one question, and I will answer it truthfully."

For a second, I don't believe him.

I'm a man of my word, when I want to be. He said that once, and stands by it. It really is a gift, if he holds to his promise.

The first question rises without thought. *Are they alive? Did you really leave them there, and let them get away?* It almost slips past my lips before I think better of wasting my question. Of course they got away. If Cal were dead, I would know it. Maven would still be gloating, or someone would have said something. And he is far too concerned with the Scarlet Guard. If the others had been captured after me, he would know more and fear less.

Maven tips his head, watching me think as a cat watches a mouse. He's enjoying this. It makes my skin crawl.

Why give me this? Why even let me ask? Another question almost wasted. Because I know the answer to this too. Maven is not who I thought he was, but that doesn't mean I don't know parts of him. I can guess what this is, as much as I want to be wrong. It's his version of an explanation. A way to make me understand what he's done and why he continues to do it. He knows what question I will eventually summon the courage to ask. He is a king, but a boy too, alone in a world of his own making.

"How much of it was her?"

He doesn't flinch. He knows me too well to be surprised. A more foolish girl would dare to hope—would believe him a puppet to an evil woman, now abandoned, now adrift. Continuing on a course he has no idea how to change. Luckily, I'm not that stupid.

"I was slow to walk, you know." He isn't looking at me anymore, but at the blue flag above us. Adorned in white pearls and cloudy gems, a rich thing doomed to collect dust in Elara's memory. "The doctors, even Father, they told Mother I would be fine in my own time. It would happen one day. But 'one day' wasn't fast enough for her. She couldn't be the queen with the crippled, slow son. Not after Coriane gave the kingdom a prince like Cal, always smiling and talking and laughing and perfect. She had my nurse discarded, blamed her for my shortcomings, and took it upon herself to make me stand. I don't remember it, but she told me the story so many times. She thought it showed how much she loved me."

Dread pools in my stomach, though I don't understand why. Something warns me to get up, to walk from this room and into the waiting arms of my guards. *Another lie, another lie,* I tell myself. *Artfully woven, as only he can do.* Maven cannot look at me. I taste shame on the air.

His perfect eyes made of ice gloss over, but I've long hardened myself to his tears. The first gets stuck in his dark lashes, a wobbling drop of crystal.

"I was a baby, and she hammered her way into my head. She made my body stand, and walk, and fall. She did it every day, until I cried when she entered a room. Until I learned to do it myself. Out of fear. But that would not do either. A baby crying whenever his mother held him?" He shakes his head. "Eventually she took the fear away too." His eyes darken. "Like so many other things.

"You ask how much of it was me," he whispers. "Some. Enough."

But not all.

I can't stand this any longer. With unbalanced motions, tipped by the weight of my manacles and the sick clenching of my heart, I clamber from the chair.

"You can't still blame this on her, Maven," I hiss at him, stepping back. "Don't lie to me and say you're doing this because of a dead woman."

As fast as his tears came, they disappear. Wiped away, as if they never existed. The crack in his mask seals shut. *Good.* I have no desire to see the boy beneath.

"I'm not," he says slowly, sharply. "She is gone now. My choices are my own. Of that I am infinitely sure."

The throne. His seat in the council chamber. Plain things compared to the diamondglass artistry or velvet his father used to sit. Hewn of blocked stone, simple, without gems or precious metal. And now I understand why. "Silent Stone. You make all your decisions sitting there."

"Wouldn't you? With House Merandus leering so close?" He leans back, propping his chin on one hand. "I've had enough of the whispers they call guidance. Enough to last a lifetime."

"Good," I spit at him. "Now you have no one else to blame for your evil."

One side of his mouth lifts in a weak, patronizing smile. "You'd think that."

I fight the urge to seize whatever I can and bash his head in with it, erasing his smile from the face of the earth. "If only I could kill you and be done with this."

"How you wound me." He clucks his tongue, amused. "And then what? Run back to your Scarlet Guard? To my brother? Samson saw him many times in your thoughts. Dreams. Memories."

"Still fixated on Cal, even now, when you've won?" It's an easy card to play. His grins annoy me, but my smirk vexes him just as much. We know how to needle each other. "Strange, then, that you're trying so hard to be like him."

It's Maven's turn to stand, his hands landing hard on the desk as he rises up to meet my eye. A corner of his mouth twitches, pulling his face into a bitter sneer. "I'm doing what my brother never could. Cal follows orders, but he can't make choices. You know that as well as I do." His eyes flicker, finding an empty spot on the wall. Looking for Cal's face. "No matter how wonderful you might think he is, so gallant, brave, and perfect. He would make a worse king than I ever could."

I almost agree. I've spent too many months watching Cal walk the line between Scarlet Guard and Silver prince, refusing to kill but refusing to stop us, never leaning to one side or the other. Even though he's seen horror and injustice, he still won't take a stand. But he is not Maven. He is not one inch the evil that Maven is.

"I've only heard one person describe him as perfect. You," I tell him calmly. It only maddens him further. "I think you may have a bit of an obsession where Cal is concerned. Are you going to blame that on your mother too?"

It was meant to be a joke, but to Maven it is anything but. His gaze wavers, only for an instant. A shocking one. In spite of myself, I feel my eyes widen and my heart drop in my chest. He doesn't know. He truly doesn't know what parts of his mind are his own and what parts were made by her.

"Maven," I can't help but whisper, terrified by what I may have stumbled upon.

He draws one hand through dark hair, pulling at the strands until they stand on end. An odd silence stretches, one that exposes us both. I feel as though I have wandered somewhere I should not be, trespassed into a place I really don't want to go.

"Leave," he finally says, the word quivering.

I don't move, drinking in what I can. *For use later,* I tell myself. Not because I'm too numb to walk away. Not because I feel one more incredible surge of pity for the ghost prince.

"I said leave."

I'm used to Cal's anger heating up a room. Maven's anger freezes, and a chill runs down my spine.

"The longer you make them wait, the worse they'll be." Evangeline Samos has the best and worst timing.

She blazes through in her usual storm of metal and mirrors, her long cape trailing. It picks up the red color of the room, glinting crimson and scarlet, flashing with every step. As I watch her, heart hammering in my chest, the cape splits and re-forms before my eyes, each half wrapping around a muscled leg. She smirks, letting me watch, as her court dress becomes an imposing suit of armor. It, too, is lethally beautiful, worthy of any queen.

As before, I am not her problem, and she turns her attention from me. She doesn't miss the strange current of tension on the air, or Maven's harried manner. Her eyes narrow. Like me, she takes in the sight. Like me, she will use this to her advantage.

"Maven, did you hear me?" She takes a few bold steps, rounding the desk to stand alongside him. Maven angles his body, ghosting swiftly from one of her hands. "The governors are waiting, and my father himself—"

With a vicious will, Maven grabs a sheet of paper from his desk. Judging by the florid signatures at the bottom, it must be some kind of petition. He glares at Evangeline, holding the paper away from his body as he flicks his wrist, drawing sparks from his bracelet. They light into twin arcs of flame, dancing through the petition like hot knives through butter. It disintegrates into ash, dusting the gleaming floor.

"Tell your father and his puppets what I think of his proposition."

If she's surprised by his actions, she does not show it. Instead, she sniffs, inspects her nails. I watch her sidelong, well aware that she'll attack me if I so much as breathe too loudly. I keep quiet and wide-eyed, wishing I'd noticed the petition before. Wishing I knew what it said.

"Careful, my dear," Evangeline says, sounding anything but loving. "A king without supporters is no king at all."

He turns on her, moving quickly enough to catch her off guard. They're close to the same height, and they stand almost eye to eye. Fire and iron. I don't expect her to flinch, not for Maven, the boy, the prince she used to run laps around in our Training lessons. Maven is not Cal.

But her eyelids flicker, black lashes against silver-white skin, betraying a sliver of fear she wants to hide.

"Don't assume you know what kind of king I am, Evangeline."

I hear his mother in him, and it frightens us both.

Then he turns his eyes back on me. The confused boy of a moment ago is gone again, replaced by living stone and a frozen glare. *The same goes for you,* his expression says.

Even though I want nothing more than to run from the room, I stand rooted. He has taken everything from me, but I won't give him my fear or my dignity. I won't run away now. Especially not in front of Evangeline.

She looks at me again, eyes flitting over every inch of my appearance. Memorizing what I look like. She must see me beneath the healer's touch, the bruises earned in my escape attempt, the permanent shadows beneath my eyes. When she focuses on my collarbone, it takes me a moment to understand why. Her lips part, just a little, in what can only be surprise.

Angry, ashamed, I pull the collar of my dress back up over my brand. But I never look away from her as I do. She will not take my pride either.

"Guards," Maven finally says, pitching his voice at the door. As the Arvens answer, gloves outstretched to hurry me away, Maven points his chin at Evangeline. "You too."

She doesn't take well to that, of course.

"I am not some prisoner to be ordered around—"

I smile as the Arvens pull me away and out the door. It eases shut, but Evangeline's voice echoes behind us. *Good luck,* I think. *Maven cares even less about you than he does about me.*

My guards set a quick pace, forcing me to keep up. More easily said than done, in the restricting dress, but I manage. The scrap of Gisa's silk feels soft against my skin, clenched tightly in a fist. I fight the urge to smell the fabric, to chase any remnant of my sister. I steal a glance back, hoping to glimpse exactly who might be waiting for an audience with our wicked king. Instead, I see only Sentinels, black-masked and flame-robed, standing guard at the study door.

It wrenches open violently, quivering on jumping hinges before slamming closed with a smack. For a girl raised a noble, Evangeline has a difficult time controlling her temper. I wonder if my old etiquette instructor, Lady Blonos, ever tried to teach her otherwise. The image almost makes me laugh, bringing a rare smile to my lips. It stings, but I don't care.

"Save your smirks, lightning girl," Evangeline snarls, doubling her speed.

Her reaction only goads me on, despite the danger. I laugh outright as I turn back around. Neither of my guards says a word, but they quicken their pace a little. Even they don't want to test an irritable magnetron itching for a scuffle.

She catches us anyway, smoothly sidestepping Egg to plant herself in front of me. The guards stop short, holding me with them.

"In case you haven't noticed, I'm a bit busy," I tell her, gesturing to the guards holding both my arms. "There isn't really room for bickering in my schedule. Go bother someone who can fight back."

Her smile flashes, sharp and bright as the scales of her armor. "Don't sell yourself short. You've got plenty of fight left in you." Then she leans forward, stepping into my space as she did with Maven. An easy way to show she is unafraid. I stand firm, willing myself not to wince, even when she plucks a razored scale from her armor like a petal from a flower.

"At least I hope so," she says under her breath.

With a careful flick of her hand, she cuts the collar of my dress, stripping back a piece of embroidered scarlet. I fight the urge to cover the *M* brand on my skin, feeling a hot flush of embarrassment creep up my throat.

Her eyes linger, tracing the rough lines of Maven's mark. Again she seems surprised.

"That doesn't look like an accident."

"Any other wonderful observations you'd like to share?" I mutter through gritted teeth.

Grinning, she replaces the scale on her bodice. "Not with you." It is a reprieve when she pulls back, putting a few precious inches between us. "Elane?"

"Yes, Eve," a voice says. From nowhere.

I nearly jump out of my skin when Elane Haven materializes behind her, seemingly from thin air. A shadow, able to manipulate light, powerful enough to make herself invisible. I wonder how long she's been standing with us. Or if she was in the study, either with Evangeline or before she even walked in. She could've been watching the entire time. For all I know, Elane could've been my ghost since the moment I got here.

"Has anyone ever tried to put a bell on you?" I snap, if only to hide my own discomfort.

Elane offers a pretty, tight-lipped smile that does not reach her eyes. "Once or twice."

Like Sonya, Elane is familiar to me. We spent many days in Training together, always at odds. She is another of Evangeline's friends, girls smart enough to ally themselves to a future queen. As a lady of House Haven, her gown and jewelry are deepest black. Not in mourning, but in deference to her house colors. Her hair is as red as I remember, bright copper in contrast to dark, angled eyes and skin that seems blurred, perfected, and flawless. The light around her is carefully manipulated, giving her a heavenly glow.

"We're finished here," Evangeline says, turning her laser focus on Elane. "For now." She throws back one daggered glance to make her point clear.

NINE
Mare

Being a doll is an odd thing. I spend more time on the shelf than at play. But when I'm forced to, I dance at Maven's command—he upholds his bargain while I do. After all, he's a man of his word.

The first newblood seeks refuge at Ocean Hill, the Harbor Bay palace, and as Maven promised, he is given full protection from the so-called terror of the Scarlet Guard. A few days later the poor man, Morritan, is escorted to Archeon and introduced to Maven himself. It is well broadcast. Both his identity and his ability are now commonly known in court. To the surprise of many, Morritan is a burner like the scions of House Calore. But unlike Cal and Maven, he has no need for a flamemaker bracelet, or even a spark. His fire comes from ability and ability alone, same as my lightning.

I have to sit and watch, perched on a gilded chair with the rest of Maven's royal entourage. Jon, the seer, sits with me, red-eyed and quiet. As the first two newbloods to join with the Silver king, we are afforded places of great honor at Maven's side, second to Evangeline and Samson Merandus. But only Morritan pays us any attention. As he approaches, before the eyes of court and a dozen cameras, his gaze is always on me. He trembles, afraid, but something about my presence keeps him from running away, keeps him walking forward. Obviously he believes what Maven made me say. He believes the Scarlet Guard hunted us all. He even kneels and swears to join Maven's army, to train with Silver officers. To fight for his king and his country.

Keeping silent and still is the most difficult part. Despite Morritan's lanky limbs, golden skin, and hands callused by years of servant work, he looks like nothing more than a little rabbit scurrying directly into a trap. One wrong word from me and the trap will spring.

More follow.

Day after day, week after week. Sometimes one, sometimes a dozen. From every corner of the nation they come, fleeing to the supposed safety of their king. Most because they are afraid, but some because they are foolish enough to want a place here. To leave their lives of oppression behind and become the impossible. I can't blame them. After all, we've been told our entire lives that the Silvers are our masters, our betters, our gods. And now they are merciful enough to let us live in their heaven. Who wouldn't try to join them?

Maven plays his part well. He embraces them all as brothers and sisters, smiling broadly, showing no shame or fear in an act that most Silvers find repulsive. The court follows his lead, but I see their sneers and scowls hidden behind jeweled hands. Even though this is part of the charade, a well-aimed blow against the Scarlet Guard, they dislike it. What's more, they fear it. Many of the newbloods have untrained abilities more powerful than their own, or beyond Silver comprehension. They watch with wolf eyes and ready claws.

For once, I am not the center of attention. It is my only respite, not to mention an advantage. No one cares about the lightning girl without her lightning. I do what I can, which is little, but not inconsequential. I listen.

Evangeline is restless despite an iron-faced facade. Her fingers drum the arms of her seat, still only when Elane is near, whispering or touching her. But then she does not dare to relax. She remains on an edge as sharp as her knives. It's not hard to guess why. Even for a prisoner, I've heard very little talk of a royal wedding. And though she is certainly betrothed to the king, she is still not a queen. It scares her. I see it in her face, in her manner, in her constant parade of glittering outfits, each one more complicated and regal than the last. She wears a crown in all but name, yet the name is what she wants more than anything. Her father wants it too. Volo haunts her side, resplendent in black velvet and silver brocade. Unlike his daughter, he doesn't wear any metal that I can see. Not a chain or even a ring. He doesn't need to wear weaponry to seem dangerous. With his quiet manner and dark robes, he looks more like an executioner than a noble. I don't know how Maven can stand his presence, or the steady, focused hunger in his eyes. He reminds me of Elara. Always watching the throne, always waiting for a chance to take it.

Maven notices, and does not care. He gives Volo the respect he requires, but little more. And he leaves Evangeline to Elane's dazzling company, obviously glad that his future wife has no interest in him. His focus is decidedly elsewhere. Not on me, strangely, but on his cousin Samson. I also have a hard time ignoring the whisper who tortured the deepest parts of me. I am constantly aware of his presence, trying to feel out his whispers if I can, though I hardly have the strength to resist them. Maven doesn't have to worry about that, not with his chair of Silent Stone. It keeps him safe. It keeps him empty.

When I was first trained to be a princess, a laughable thing in itself,

I was engaged to the second prince, and I attended very few meetings of court. Balls, yes, feasts many, but nothing like this until my confinement. Now I've almost lost count of how many times I've been forced to sit like Maven's well-trained pet, listening to petitioners, politicians, and newbloods pledging allegiance.

Today looks to be more of the same. The governor of the Rift region, a lord of House Laris, finishes a well-rehearsed plea for Treasury funds to repair Samos-owned mines. Another one of Volo's puppets, his strings clearly visible. Maven defers him easily, with a wave and a promise to review his proposal. Though Maven is a man of his word with me, he is not at court. The governor's shoulders slump in dejection, knowing it will never be read.

My back already hurts from the stiff chair, not to mention the rigid posture I have to maintain in my latest court ensemble. Crystal and lace. Red, of course, as always. Maven loves me in red. He says it makes me look alive, even as life is leached from me with every passing day.

A full court is not required for the daily hearings, and today the throne room is half empty. The dais is still crowded, though. Those chosen to accompany the king, flanking his left and right, take great pride in their position, not to mention the opportunity to be featured in yet another national broadcast. When the cameras roll, I realize that more newbloods must be coming. I sigh, resigning myself to another day of guilt and shame.

My gut twists when the tall doors open. I lower my eyes, not wanting to remember their faces. Most will follow Morritan's damning example and join Maven's war in an attempt to understand their abilities.

Next to me, Jon twitches in his usual way. I focus on his fingers, long and thin, drawing lines against his pant leg. Sweeping back and forth, like a person riffling through pages of a book. He probably is, reading the tentative threads of the future as they form and change. I wonder what he sees. Not that I would ever ask. I will never forgive him for his betrayal. At least he doesn't try to talk to me, not since I passed him in the council chambers.

"Welcome all," Maven tells the newbloods. His voice is practiced and steady, carrying through the throne room. "Not to worry. You're safe now. I promise you all, the Scarlet Guard will never threaten you here."

Too bad.

I keep my head bowed, hiding my face from the cameras. The rush of blood roars in my ears, hammering in time with my heart. I feel nauseous; I feel sick. *Run!* I scream in my head, even though no newblood could escape the throne room now. I look anywhere but at Maven and the newbloods, anywhere but at the invisible cage drawing in around them. My eyes land on Evangeline, only to find her staring back at me. She isn't smirking for once. Her face is blank, empty. She has much more practice at this than I do.

My nails are ragged, cuticles picked raw during long nights of worry and longer days of this painless torture. The Skonos healer who makes me look healthy always forgets to check my hands. I hope anyone watching the broadcasts does not.

Next to me, the king keeps at this horrid display. "Well?"

Four newbloods present themselves, each one more nervous than the last. Their abilities are often met with astonished gasps or harried whispers. It feels like a grim mirror to Queenstrial. Instead of performing their abilities for a bridal crown, the newbloods are performing for their lives, to earn what they think is sanctuary at Maven's side. I try not to watch, but find my eyes straying out of pity and fear.

The first, a heavyset woman with biceps to rival Cal's, tentatively walks through a wall. Just straight through, as if the gilded wood and ornate molding were air. At Maven's fascinated encouragement, she then does the same to a Sentinel guard. He flinches, the only indication of humanity behind his black mask, but is otherwise unharmed. I have no idea how her ability works at all, and I think of Julian. He's with the Scarlet Guard too, and hopefully watching every one of these broadcasts. If the Colonel allows it, that is. He's not exactly a fan of my Silver friends.

Two old men follow the woman, white-haired veterans with faraway eyes and broad shoulders. Their abilities are familiar to me. The shorter one with missing teeth is like Ketha, one of the newbloods I recruited months ago. Though she could explode an object or person with thought alone, she did not survive our raid on Corros Prison. She hated her ability. It is bloody and violent. Even though the newblood man only destroys a chair, blinking it to splinters, he doesn't look happy about it either. His friend is soft-spoken, introducing himself as Terrance before telling us he can manipulate sound. Like Farrah. Another recruit of mine. She did not come to Corros. I hope she is still alive.

The last is another woman, probably my mother's age, her braided black hair streaked with gray. She is graceful in movement, approaching the king with the quiet, elegant strides of a well-trained servant. Like Ada, like Walsh, like me once. Like so many of us were and still are. When she bows, she bows low.

"Your Majesty," she murmurs, her voice soft and unassuming as a summer breeze. "I am Halley, a servant of House Eagrie."

Maven gestures for her to rise, donning his false smile. She does as commanded. "You were a servant of House Eagrie," he says gently. Then he nods over her shoulder, finding the commanding head of

Eagrie in the small crowd. "My thanks, Lady Mellina, for bringing her to safety."

The tall, bird-faced woman is already curtsying, knowing the words before he speaks them. As an eye, she can see the immediate future, and I assume she saw her servant's ability before her servant even realized what she was.

"Well, Halley?"

Her eyes flick to mine for a single moment. I hope I hold up under her scrutiny. But she isn't looking for my fear, or what I hide beneath my mask. Her eyes turn faraway, seeing through and seeing nothing at the same time.

"She can control and create electricity, great and small," Halley says. "You have no name for this ability."

Then she looks at Jon. The same look slides over her. "He sees fate. As far as its path goes, for as long as a person walks it. You have no name for this ability."

Maven narrows his eyes, wondering, and I loathe myself for feeling the same way he does.

But she keeps going, staring and speaking as she turns.

"She can control metal materials through the manipulation of magnetic fields. Magnetron."

"Whisper."

"Shadow."

"Magnetron."

"Magnetron."

Down she goes through the line of Maven's advisers, pointing and naming their abilities with little difficulty. Maven leans forward, quizzical, head tipped to one side in animal curiosity. He watches closely, barely blinking. Many think him stupid without his mother, not a military genius like his brother, so what is he good for? They forget that strategy is not only for the battlefield.

"Eye. Eye. Eye." She gestures to her former masters, naming them as well before dropping her hand to her side. Her fist clenches and unclenches, waiting for the inevitable disbelief.

"So your ability is to sense other abilities?" Maven finally says, one eyebrow raised.

"Yes, Your Majesty."

"An easy thing to play at."

"Yes, Your Majesty," she admits, even softer now.

It could be done without much difficulty, especially by someone in her position. She serves a High House, present at court more often than not these days. It would be easy for her to memorize what others can do—but even Jon? As far as I know, he is lauded as the first new-blood to join Maven, but I don't think many know his ability. Maven wouldn't want people to think he relies on someone with red blood to advise his decisions.

"Keep going." He raises dark eyebrows, goading her on. Perform.

She does as he commands, naming Osanos nymphs, Welle green-wardens, a lone Rhambos strongarm. One after another, but they're wearing colors, and she is a servant. She's supposed to know these things. Her ability is a parlor trick at best, a lie and a death sentence at the worst. I know she feels the sword hanging over her head, growing closer with every tick of Maven's jaw.

At the back, an Iral silk in red and blue gets to his feet, adjusting his coat as he walks. I only notice because his steps are strange, not as fluid as a silk's should be. Odd.

And Halley notices too. She trembles, only for a second.

It could be her life or his.

"She can change her face," she whispers, her finger quivering in the air. "You have no name for this ability."

The usual whispers of court end without an echo, snuffed out like a candle. Silence falls, broken only by the rising beat of my heart. *She can change her face.*

My body buzzes with adrenaline. *Run!* I want to yell. *Run!*

And when the Sentinels take the Iral lord by the arms, marching him forward, I beg to myself, *Please be wrong. Please be wrong. Please be wrong.*

"I am a son of House Iral," the man growls, trying to break the grip of the Sentinel soldiers. An Iral would be able to do it, twisting away with a smile. But whoever he or she is does not. My stomach drops to my feet. "You take the word of a lying Red slave above *mine*?"

Samson reacts before Maven can even ask, quick as a swift. He descends the steps of the dais, his electric-blue eyes crackling with hunger. I guess he hasn't had many brains to feed on since mine. With a yelp, the Iral son stumbles to his knees, head bowed. Samson slams into his mind.

And then his hair bleeds gray, shortens, recedes to a different head with a different face.

"Nanny," I hear myself gasp. The old woman dares look up, eyes wide and scared and familiar. I remember recruiting her, bringing her to the Notch, watching her wrangle the newblood kids and tell stories of her own grandchildren. Wrinkled as a walnut, older than any of us, and always up for a mission. I would run to embrace her if that were remotely possible.

Instead, I fall to my knees, my hands latching onto Maven's wrist. I beg like I have only once before, my lungs full of ash and cold air, my head still spinning from the controlled crash of a jet.

The dress rips along a seam. It is not meant for kneeling. Not like me.

"Please, Maven. Don't kill her," I ask him, gulping at air, grasping at whatever I can to save her life. "She can be used; she is valuable. Look what she can do—"

He pushes me away, his palm against my brand. "She is a spy in my court. Aren't you?"

Still I beg, speaking before Nanny's smart mouth can get her well and truly killed. And for once, I hope the cameras are still watching.

"She has been betrayed, lied to, misled by the Scarlet Guard. It's not her fault!"

The king does not condescend to stand, not even for a murder at his feet. Because he's afraid to leave his Silent Stone, to make a decision beyond its circle of empty comfort and safety. "The rules of war are clear. Spies are to be dealt with swiftly."

"When you are sick, who do you blame?" I demand. "Your body or the disease?"

He glares down at me and I feel hollow. "You blame the cure that didn't work."

"Maven, I am begging you . . ." I don't remember starting to cry, but of course I am. They are shameful tears, because I weep for myself as well as her. This was the beginning of a rescue. This was for me. Nanny was my chance.

My vision blurs, fogging the edge of my sight. Samson raises a hand, eager to dive into what she knows. I wonder how devastating this will be to the Scarlet Guard—and how stupid they were to do this. What a risk, what a waste.

"Rise. Red as the dawn," she mutters, spitting.

Then her face changes one last time. To a face we all recognize.

Samson falls back a half step, surprised, while Maven gives a strangled sort of cry.

Elara stares back at us from the floor, a living ghost. Her face is mangled, destroyed by lightning. One eye is gone, the other bloodshot with vile silver. Her mouth curls into an inhuman sneer. It triggers terror in the pit of my stomach, though I know she's dead. I know I killed her.

It's a clever ploy, buying her enough time to raise a hand to her lips, to swallow.

I've seen suicide pills before. Even though I shut my eyes, I know what happens next.

It's better than what Samson would have done. And her secrets stay secrets. Forever.

TEN
Mare

I tear apart every book on my shelf, rip them to shreds. The bindings snap, the pages tear, and I wish they would bleed. I wish I could bleed. She's dead because I'm not. Because I'm still here, bait in a trap, a lure to draw the Scarlet Guard out of their sanctuaries.

After a few hours of pointless destruction, I realize I'm wrong. The Scarlet Guard wouldn't do this. Not the Colonel, not Farley, not for me.

"Cal, you stupid, stupid bastard," I say to no one.

Because of course this was his idea. It's what he learned. Victory at any cost. I hope he doesn't continue to pay this impossible price for me.

Outside, it's snowing again. I feel none of its cold, only my own.

In the morning, I wake up on my bed, still in my dress, though I don't remember getting up from the floor. The ruined books are gone too, meticulously swept from my life. Even the smallest pieces of torn paper. But the shelves aren't empty. A dozen leather-bound books, new and old, occupy the spaces. The urge to ruin them too consumes me, and I stumble to my feet, lunging.

The first one I grab is ratty, its cover torn and aged. I think it used to be yellow, or maybe gold. It doesn't really matter to me. I flip it open, one hand grabbing for a sheaf of pages, ready to tear them to bits like the rest.

Familiar handwriting freezes me to the spot. My heart leaps in recognition.

Property of Julian Jacos.

My knees stop working beneath me. I land with a soft thud, bent over the most comforting thing I've seen in weeks. My fingers trace the lines of his name, wishing he would spring from them, wishing I could hear his voice somewhere other than in my head. I flip through the pages, looking for more evidence of him. The words skim by, each one echoing with his warmth. A history of Norta, her formation, and three hundred years of Silver kings and queens blaze past. Some pieces are underlined or annotated. Each new burst of Julian makes my chest constrict with happiness. In spite of my circumstances, my painful scars, I smile.

The other books are the same. All Julian's, pieces of his much larger collections. I paw through them like a girl starved. He favors the histories, but there are sciences too. Even a novel. That one has two names inside. *From Julian, to Coriane.* I stare at the letters, the only evidence of Cal's mother in this entire palace. I put that one back with care, my fingers lingering on its unbroken spine. She never read it. Maybe she didn't get the chance.

Deep down, I hate that these make me happy. I hate that Maven knows me well enough to know what to give me. Because these are certainly from him. The only kind of apology he can make, the only one I could possibly accept. But I don't. Of course I don't. As quick as it came, my smile fades. I can't let myself feel anything but hatred where the king is concerned. His manipulations aren't as perfect as his mother's, but I feel them still, and I won't let them pull me in.

For a second, I debate ripping the books apart like I did the others. Showing Maven what I think of his gift. But I just can't. My fingers linger on the pages, so easy to tear. And then I shelve them carefully, one by one.

I will not destroy the books, so I settle for the dress instead, ripping the ruby-encrusted fabric from my body.

Someone like Gisa probably made this dress. A Red servant with keen hands and an artist's eye, perfectly sewing something so beautiful and terrible that only a Silver could wear it. The thought should make me sad, but only anger bleeds through me. I have no more tears. Not after yesterday.

When the next outfit is delivered by silent, stone-faced Clover and Kitten, I pull it on without hesitation or complaint. The blouse is flecked with a treasure trove of ruby, garnet, and onyx, with long, trailing sleeves striped in black silk. The pants are a gift too, loose enough to pass for comfortable.

The Skonos healer comes next. She focuses her efforts on my eyes, healing both the puffiness and my throbbing headache from last night's frustrated tears. Like Sara, she is quiet and skilled, her blue-black fingers fluttering along my aches. She works quickly. So do I.

"Can you speak, or did Queen Elara cut your tongue out too?"

She knows what I'm talking about. Her gaze wavers, lashes fluttering in quick blinks of surprise. Still, she doesn't speak. She has been trained well.

"Good decision. Last time I saw Sara, I was rescuing her from a prison. Seems even losing her tongue wasn't enough punishment." I glance past her, to Clover and Kitten looking on. Like the healer, they concentrate on me. I feel the cold ripple of their ability, pulsing in time with the constant silence of my manacles. "There were hundreds of Silvers in there. Many from the High Houses. Have any friends go missing lately?"

I don't have many weapons in this place. But I have to try.

"Keep your mouth shut, Barrow," Clover growls.

Just getting her to speak is victory enough for me. I push on.

"I find it odd that no one seems to mind that the little king is a bloodthirsty tyrant. But then I'm Red. I don't understand you people at all."

I laugh as Clover shoves me away from the healer, fuming now. "That's enough healing for her," she hisses, pulling me from the room. Her green eyes spark with anger, but also confusion. Self-doubt. Little cracks I intend to wheedle my way through.

No one else should risk rescuing me. I have to do it myself.

"Ignore her," Kitten mutters back at her comrade, her voice high and breathy and dripping venom.

"What an honor it must be for you two." I keep talking as they lead me down long, familiar corridors. "Babysitting some Red brat. Cleaning up after her meals, tidying her room. All so Maven can have his doll around when he wants."

It only makes them angrier and rougher with me. They quicken their pace, forcing me to keep up. Suddenly we turn left instead of right, into another part of the palace I dimly remember. Residence halls, where the royals live. I lived here once too, if only for a little while.

My heartbeat quickens as we pass a statue in an alcove. I recognize it. My room—my old bedchamber—is a few doors away. Cal's room too, and Maven's.

"Not so talkative now," Clover says, her voice sounding faraway.

Light streams in through the windows, doubly bright from the sun on fresh snow. It does nothing to comfort me. I can handle Maven in the throne room, in his study, when I am on display. But alone—truly alone? Beneath my clothes, his brand smarts and burns.

When we stop at a door and push through to the salon inside, I realize my mistake. Relief washes over me. Maven is king now. His living chambers aren't here anymore.

But Evangeline's are.

She sits in the center of the oddly bare salon, surrounded by twisted pieces of metal. They vary in color and material—iron, bronze, copper. Her hands work diligently, shaping flowers from chrome, curling them into a braided silver and gold band. Another crown for her collection. Another crown she can't wear yet.

Two attendants wait on her. A man and a woman, plainly dressed, their clothes striped with the colors of House Samos. With a jolt, I realize they are Red.

"Make her presentable, please," Evangeline says, not bothering to look up.

The Reds descend, waving me to the single mirror in the room. As I stare into it, I realize Elane is here as well, lazing on a long couch in a beam of sunlight like a satisfied cat. She meets my gaze without question or fear, only disinterest.

"You may wait outside," Elane says when she breaks eye contact, turning back to my Arven guards. Her red hair catches the light, rippling like liquid fire. Even though I have an excuse for looking horrible,

I still feel self-conscious in her presence.

Evangeline nods, agreeing, and the Arvens file out. Both cast disgruntled glances in my direction. I greedily drink them in to treasure later.

"Anyone care to explain?" I ask the quiet room, expecting no answer.

The other two laugh together, exchanging pointed glances. I take the opportunity to assess the room and the situation. There's another door, probably leading to Evangeline's bedroom, while the windows are locked tight against the cold. Her room looks out on a familiar courtyard, and I realize my cell of a bedroom must face hers. The revelation shivers me.

To my surprise, Evangeline drops her work with a clatter. The crown shatters, unable to hold its shape without her ability. "It is the queen's duty to receive guests."

"Well, I'm not a guest and you're not a queen, so . . ."

"If only your brain were as quick as your mouth," she snaps back.

The Red woman blinks rapidly, flinching like our words might hurt her. Actually, they might, and I resolve to be less stupid. I bite my lip to keep more foolish thoughts from spilling out, letting the two Red servants work. The man attends to my hair, brushing it through and coiling it into a spiral, while she does up my face. No Silver paint, but she uses blush, a bit of black to line my eyes, and striking red for my lips. A garish sight.

"That will do," Elane says from her back. The Reds are quick to pull away, dropping their hands to their sides and bowing their heads. "We can't have her looking too well treated. The princes won't understand it."

My eyes widen. *Princes. Guests.* Who am I being paraded in front of now?

Evangeline notices. She huffs aloud, flicking a bronze flower at Elane. It embeds in the wall above her head, but Elane doesn't seem to mind. She only sighs dreamily.

"Mind what you say, Elane."

"She'll find out in a few moments, my dear. What's the harm?" She gets up from her pillows, extending long limbs that glow with her ability. Evangeline's eyes track her every movement, sharpening when Elane crosses the room to my side.

She joins me at the mirror, looking into my face. "You'll behave today, won't you?"

I wonder how quickly Evangeline would skin me if I slammed my elbow into Elane's perfect teeth.

"I'll behave."

"Good."

And then she disappears, wiped from sight but not sensation. I still feel her hand on my shoulder. A warning.

I look through where Elane's body was, back to Evangeline. She gets up from the floor, her dress pooling around her, fluid as mercury. It very well could be.

When she strides toward me, I can't help but recoil. But Elane's hand keeps me from moving, forcing me to stand up straight and allow Evangeline to lean over me. A corner of her mouth lifts. She likes seeing me afraid. When she raises a hand and I flinch, she smiles openly. But instead of striking me, she tucks a strand of hair behind my ear.

"Make no mistake, this is all for my benefit," she says. "Not yours."

I have no idea what she's talking about, but I nod along anyway.

Evangeline doesn't lead us to the throne room, but to Maven's private council chambers. The Sentinels guarding the doors look more imposing than usual. When I enter, I realize they're even manning the windows. An extra precaution after Nanny's infiltration.

The last time I passed through, the room was empty save for Jon. He's still here, quiet in the corner, unassuming next to the half-dozen others around the room. I shiver at the sight of Volo Samos, a quiet spider in black with his son, Ptolemus, at his side. Of course, Samson Merandus is here too. He leers at me and I lower my eyes, avoiding his gaze as if I can shield myself from the memory of him crawling into my brain.

I expect to see Maven seated alone at the far end of the marble table, but instead, two men flank him closely. Both are draped in heavy furs and soft suede, dressed to withstand arctic cold even though we are well sheltered from the winter. They have deep, blue-black skin like polished stone. The one on the right has bits of gold and turquoise beaded into the intricate whorls of his braids, while the one on the left settles for long, gleaming locks topped by a crown of blossoms hewn from white quartz. Royalty, clearly. But not ours. Not from Norta.

Maven raises a hand, gesturing to Evangeline as she approaches. In the light of a winter sun, she gleams. "My betrothed, Lady Evangeline of House Samos," he says. "She was integral to the capture of Mare Barrow, the lightning girl and the leader of the Scarlet Guard."

Evangeline plays her part, bowing before the two. They bow their heads in turn, their motions long and fluid.

"Our congratulations, Lady Evangeline," the one with the crown says. He even extends a hand, gesturing for her own. She lets him kiss her knuckles, beaming at the attention.

When she glares at me, I realize Evangeline means for me to join her. I do so reluctantly. I intrigue the two newcomers, and they watch me in fascination. I refuse to so much as nod my head.

"This is the lightning girl?" the other prince says. His teeth flash moon white against night-dark skin. "This is the one giving you so much trouble? And you let her live?"

"Of course he did," his compatriot crows. He gets to his feet, and I realize he must be almost seven feet tall. "She's marvelous bait. Though I'm surprised her terrorists haven't attempted a real rescue, if she's as important as you say."

Maven shrugs. He exudes an air of quiet satisfaction. "My court is well defended. Infiltration is all but impossible."

I glance at him, meeting his eyes. *Liar.* He almost smirks at me, like it's a private joke between us. I fight the familiar urge to spit at him.

"In Piedmont we would march her through the streets of every city," the prince with the quartz crown says. "Show our citizens what becomes of people like her."

Piedmont. The word rings like a bell in my head. So these are the Piedmont princes. I rack my brain, trying to remember what I know of their country. An ally of Norta, forming part of our southern border. Governed by a collection of princes. All that I know from Julian's lessons. But I know other things too. I remember finding shipments on Tuck, supplies stolen from Piedmont. And Farley herself hinted that the Scarlet Guard was expanding there, intent on spreading their rebellion through Norta's closest ally.

"Does she speak?" the prince continues, looking between Maven and Evangeline.

"Unfortunately," she replies with a pointed smirk.

Both princes laugh at that, as does Maven. The rest of the room follows suit, pandering to their lord and master.

"Well then, Prince Daraeus? Prince Alexandret?" Maven sweeps his gaze over each in turn. He proudly plays the part of king, despite the two royals twice his age and size. Somehow he measures up against them. Elara trained him so well. "You wanted to see the prisoner. And you've seen her."

Alexandret, already standing so close, takes my chin in soft hands. I wonder what his ability is. I wonder how afraid of him I should be. "Indeed, Your Majesty. We have a few questions, if you would be so kind as to allow it?"

Though he frames the words as a request, this is little more than a demand.

"Your Majesty, I've already told you what she knows." Samson speaks up from his chair, leaning across the table so he can gesture to me. "Nothing in Mare Barrow's mind escaped my search."

I would nod in agreement, but Alexandret's grip keeps me still. I stare up at him, trying to deduce exactly what he wants from me. His eyes are an abyss, unreadable. I don't know this man and find nothing in him I can use. My skin crawls at his touch and I wish for my lightning, to put a little distance between us. Over his shoulder, Daraeus shifts so he can see me better. His gold beading catches the winter light, filling his hair with dazzling brightness.

"King Maven, we would like to hear it from her own lips," Daraeus says, leaning in to Maven. Then he smiles, all ease and charisma. Daraeus is beautiful and uses his looks well. "Prince Bracken's request, you understand. We only need a few minutes."

Alexandret, Daraeus, Bracken. I commit the names to memory.

"Ask what you will." Maven's hands grip the edge of his seat.

Neither one stops smiling, and nothing has ever looked so false. "Right here."

After a long moment, Daraeus relents. He inclines his head in a deferential bow. "Very well, Your Majesty."

Then his body blurs, moving so quickly I barely see his movements. He is suddenly right beside me. Swift. Not as fast as my brother, but fast enough to send a shock of adrenaline coursing through me. I still don't know what Alexandret can do. I can only pray he isn't a whisper, that I won't have to face such torture again.

"Is the Scarlet Guard operating in Piedmont?" Alexandret asks as he looms over me, his deep eyes boring into mine. Unlike Daraeus, there is no smile in him.

I wait for the telltale sting of another mind crashing into my own. It never comes. The manacles—they won't allow an ability to penetrate my cocoon of silence.

My voice cracks. "What?"

"I want to hear what you know of the Scarlet Guard's operations in Piedmont."

Every interrogation I've been subjected to has been performed by a whisper. It's odd to have someone ask me questions freely, and trust my answers without splitting open my skull. I suppose Samson has already told the princes everything he learned from me, but they don't trust what he said. Smart, then, to see if my story matches up with his.

"The Scarlet Guard is good at keeping secrets," I reply, my thoughts a blur. Do I lie? Do I throw more fuel to the fire of distrust between Maven and Piedmont? "I wasn't allowed much information regarding their operations."

"Your operations." Alexandret furrows his brow, forming a deep crease in the center of his forehead. "You were their leader. I refuse to believe you can be so useless to us."

Useless. Two months ago I was the lightning girl, a storm in human form. But before that I was as he says. Useless to everyone and everything, even my enemies. Back in the Stilts I hated it. Now I'm glad. I'm a poor weapon for a Silver to wield.

"I am not their leader," I tell Alexandret. Behind me, I hear Maven shift, settling back into his seat. I hope he's squirming. "I never even met their leaders."

He doesn't believe me. But he doesn't believe what he's already been told either. "How many of your operatives are in Piedmont?"

"I don't know."

"Who is funding your endeavors?"

"I don't know."

It starts as a prickle in my fingers and toes. A tiny sensation. Not pleasant but not uncomfortable. Like when a limb goes numb. Alexandret never lets go of my jaw. The manacles, I tell myself. They will protect me from him. They must.

"Where are Prince Michael and Princess Charlotta?"

"I don't know who those people are."

Michael, Charlotta. More names to memorize. The prickling continues, now in my arms and legs. I draw hissing breath through my teeth.

His eyes narrow in concentration. I brace myself for an explosion of pain born of whatever ability he will subject me to. "Have you had any contact with the Free Republic of Montfort?"

Still the prickling is bearable. Only his tight grip on my jaw is truly painful.

"Yes," I bite out.

Then he pulls back, letting my chin go with a sneer. He glances at my wrists, then forcibly raises one sleeve to see my bindings. The buzzing in my arms and legs recedes as he scowls.

"Your Majesty, I wonder if I might question her without manacles of Silent Stone?" Another demand disguised as a request.

This time, Maven denies him. Without my manacles, his ability will be unbound. It must be enormous for it to have penetrated even a little through my cage of silence. I'll be tortured. Again.

"You may not, Your Highness. She is far too dangerous for that," Maven says with a curt shake of his head. In spite of all my hatred, I feel the smallest bloom of gratitude. "And, as you said, she's valuable. I can't have you breaking her."

Samson doesn't bother to hide his disgust. "Someone should."

"Is there anything else I can do for Your Highnesses, or for Prince Bracken?" Maven pushes on, speaking over his demonic cousin. He unfolds himself from his chair, using one hand to smooth his dress uniform studded with medals and badges of honor. But he keeps one hand on the seat, clawed around an arm of Silent Stone. It is his anchor and his shield.

Daraeus bows low enough for both princes, smiling again. "I did hear rumors of a feast."

"For once," Maven replies with a sharp grin in my direction, "the rumors are true."

Lady Blonos never taught me the protocol for entertaining royalty of an ally nation. I've seen feasts before, balls, a Queenstrial I inadvertently ruined, but never anything like this. Perhaps because Maven's father was not so concerned with appearance, but Maven is his mother's son in flesh and bone. *To look powerful is to be powerful,* she said once. Today he takes that lesson to heart. His advisers, his Piedmont guests, and I are seated at a long table where we can overlook all the rest.

I've never set foot in this ballroom before. It dwarfs the throne room, the galleries, and the feasting chambers of the rest of Whitefire. It fits the entire assembled court, all the lords and ladies and their extended families, with ease. The chamber is three stories tall, towering windows of crystal and colored glass, each one depicting the colors of the High Houses. The result is a dozen rainbows arcing over a marble floor veined with black granite, each beam of light a prism shifting through the diamond facets of chandeliers worked into trees, birds, sunbeams, constellations, storms, infernos, typhoons, and a dozen other symbols of Silver strength. I would spend the entire meal staring at the ceiling if not for own my precarious position. At least I'm not next to Maven this time. The princes have to suffer him tonight. But Jon is on my left and Evangeline on my right. I keep my elbows tucked sharply to my sides, not wanting to accidentally touch either of them. Evangeline might stab me, and Jon might share another nauseating premonition.

Luckily, the food is good. I force myself to eat, and I keep away from the liquor. Red servants circulate, and no glass is ever empty. After ten minutes of trying to catch someone's eye, I abandon the pursuit. The servants are smart, and not willing to risk their lives for a glance at me.

I fix my eyes ahead, counting the tables, counting the High Houses. All are here, plus House Calore, represented by Maven alone. He has no cousins or other family that I know of, though I assume they must exist. Like the servants, they're probably smart enough to avoid his jealous wrath and tremulous grip on the throne.

House Iral seems smaller, dulled despite their vibrant blue-and-red outfits. There are nowhere near as many of them, and I wonder how many Irals were sent to Corros Prison. Or maybe they fled court. Sonya is still here, though, her posture elegant and practiced but strangely tense. She's traded her officer's uniform for a sparkling gown and sits beside an older man, resplendent in a collar of rubies and sapphires. Probably the new lord of her house since his predecessor, the Panther, was murdered by a man sitting only a few feet away. I wonder if Sonya told them what I said about her grandmother and Ptolemus. I wonder if they care.

I jolt when Sonya looks up sharply, catching my eye.

Next to me, Jon sighs long and low. He picks up his glass of scarlet wine with one hand and shunts his dinner knife away with the other.

"Mare, could you do me a small favor?" he says calmly.

Even his voice disgusts me. Sneering, I turn to look at him with all the venom I can muster. "Excuse me?"

Something cracks, and pain sears along my cheekbone, cutting skin, burning flesh. I jerk from the sensation, falling sideways, shying away like a spooked animal. My shoulder collides with Jon, and he pitches forward, spilling wine and water over the fine tablecloth. Blood too. There's a lot of blood. I feel it, warm and wet, but I don't look down to see the color. My eyes are on Evangeline, standing from the table, one arm outstretched.

A bullet shudders on the air in front of her, held in place. I assume it matches the one that cut my cheek—and could have done much worse.

Her fist clenches and the bullet rockets backward to where it came from, chased on by splinters of cold steel as they explode from her dress. I watch in horror as blue-and-red figures weave through the metallic storm, dodging, dipping, darting in and out of every blow. They even catch pieces of her metal projecticles and hurl them back, beginning the cycle again in a violent, glittering dance.

Evangeline is not the only one to attack. Sentinels pitch forward, surging over the high table, forming a wall before us. Their movements are perfect, made through years of relentless training. But their ranks have gaps. And some throw their masks away, discarding their flame-like robes. They turn on one another.

The High Houses do the same.

I've never felt so exposed, so helpless, and that's saying quite a bit. In front of me, gods duel. My eyes widen, trying to see it all. Trying to make sense of this. I've never imagined anything like it. An arena battle in the middle of a ballroom. Jewels instead of armor.

Iral and Haven and Laris in their shocking yellow seem to form one side of whatever this is. They back one another, aid one another. Laris windweavers toss Iral silks from one side of the room to the other with sharp gusts, wielding them like living arrows while the Irals fire pistols and throw knives with deadly precision. The Havens have disappeared entirely, but a few Sentinels in front of us drop, felled by invisible attacks.

And the rest, the rest don't know what to do. Some—Samos, Merandus, most of the guards and Sentinels—rally to the high table, rushing to defend Maven, who I can't see. But most fall back, surprised, betrayed, not willing to wade into such a mess and risk their own necks. They defend and do nothing else. They watch to see the direction of the tide.

My heart leaps in my chest. This is my chance. In the chaos, no one will notice me. The manacles have not taken away my thief's instincts or talents.

I push off the floor, finding my feet, not bothering to wonder about Maven or anyone. I focus only on what's in front of me. The closest door. I don't know where it goes, but it will get me away from here, and that's enough. As I move, I grab a knife off the table and set it to work, trying to pick the locks of my manacles.

Someone flees ahead of me, leaving a trail of scarlet blood. He limps but moves fast, ducking through a door. Jon, I realize. Making his escape. He sees the future. Surely he can see the best way out of here.

I wonder if I'll be able to keep up.

I get my answer after a grand total of three steps, when a Sentinel seizes me from behind. He pins my arms to my sides, holding tight. I groan like an annoyed child, exasperated beyond frustration, as my hand drops the knife.

"No, no, no," Samson says as he steps into my path. The Sentinel won't even let me flinch. "We can't have this."

Now I can see what this is. Not a rescue. Not for me. A coup, an assassination attempt. They've come for Maven.

Iral, Haven, and Laris cannot win this battle. They're outnumbered, but they know that. They prepared for it. The Irals are schemers and spies. Their plan is well executed. Already they're making an escape through the shattered windows. I watch, dumbfounded, as they throw themselves out into the sky, catching gales of wind that fling them out and away. Not all of them make it. Nornus swifts catch a few, as does Prince Daraeus, despite a long knife protruding from his shoulder. I assume the Havens are long gone too, though one or two flicker back into my vision, each one bleeding, dying, assaulted by a Merandus whisper's onslaught. Daraeus himself puts out one blurring arm and catches someone by the neck. When he squeezes, a Haven blinks into existence.

The Sentinels who turned, all Laris and Iral, don't make it either. They kneel, angry but unafraid, burning with determination. Without their masks, they don't look so terrifying.

A gurgling sound draws our attention. The Sentinel turns, allowing me to see the center of what was once the feasting table. A crowd clusters where Maven's seat was, some on guard, some kneeling. Through their legs, I see him.

Silver blood bubbles from his neck, gushing through the fingers of the nearest Sentinel, who is trying to keep pressure on a bullet wound. Maven's eyes roll and his mouth moves. He can't speak. He can't even scream. A wet, gasping sort of noise is all he can make.

I'm glad the Sentinel holds me still. Or else I might run to him. Something in me wants to run to him. Whether to finish the job or comfort him as he dies, I don't know. I desire both in equal measure. I want to look into his eyes and see him leave me forever.

But I just can't move, and he just won't die.

The Skonos skin healer, my skin healer, skids to his side, sliding on her knees. I think her name is Wren. An apt name. She is small and darting as her namesake. She snaps her fingers. "Take it out; I have him!" she shouts. "Out, now!"

Ptolemus Samos crouches, abandoning his guarding vigil. He twitches his fingers and a bullet pulls free of Maven's neck, bringing with it a fresh fountain of silver. Maven tries to scream, gargling his own blood.

Brow furrowed, the skin healer works, holding both hands over his wound. She bends as if to put her weight on him. From this angle, I can't see the skin beneath, but the blood stops gushing. The wound that should've killed him heals. Muscle and vein and flesh knit back together, good as new. No scar but the memory.

After a long, gasping moment, Maven hurtles to his feet, and fire explodes from both hands, sending his entourage reeling backward. The table before him flips, blasted back by the strength and rage of his flame. It lands in a resounding heap, spitting puddles of blue-burning alcohol. The rest ignites, fed by Maven's anger. And, I think, terror.

Only Volo has the spine to approach him in such a state.

"Your Majesty, should we evacuate you to the—"

With wicked eyes, Maven turns. Above him, the lightbulbs in the chandeliers burst, spitting flame instead of sparks. "I have no reason to run."

All this in a few moments. The ballroom is in shambles, full of shattered glass, upended tables, and a few very mangled bodies.

Prince Alexandret is among them, slumped dead in his seat of honor with a bullet hole between his eyes.

I don't mourn his loss. His ability was pain.

Naturally, they interrogate me first. I should be used to it by now.

Exhausted, emotionally spent, I slump to the cold stone floor when Samson lets me go. My breathing comes hard, like I've just run a race. I will my heartbeat to normalize, to stop panting, to hold on to some shred of dignity and sense. I cringe as the Arvens lock my manacles back into place; then they pass the key away. The manacles are a relief and a burden both. A shield and a cage.

We've retreated to the grand council chambers this time, the circular room where I saw Walsh die to protect the Scarlet Guard. More room here, more space to try the dozen captured assassins. The Sentinels have learned their lesson, and they keep firm grips on the prisoners, not allowing any movement. Maven leers down from his council seat, flanked on either side by Volo and Daraeus. The latter fumes, torn between livid rage and sorrow. His fellow prince is dead, killed in what I now know was an assassination attempt on Maven. An attempt that, sadly, failed.

"She knew nothing of this. Neither the house rebellion nor Jon's betrayal," Samson tells the room. The terrible chamber seems small, with most of the seats empty and the doors firmly locked. Only Maven's closest advisers remain, looking on, gears turning in their heads.

In his seat, Maven sneers. Almost being murdered doesn't seem to rattle him. "No, this was not the Scarlet Guard's doing. They don't work like this."

"You don't know that," Daraeus snaps, forgetting all his manners and smiles. "You don't know anything about them, no matter what you might say. If the Scarlet Guard has allied with—"

"Corrupted," Evangeline snaps from her place behind Maven's left shoulder. She doesn't have a council seat or a title of her own and has to stand, despite the many empty chairs. "Gods do not ally with insects, but they can be infected by them."

"Pretty words from a pretty girl," Daraeus says, dismissing her outright. She fumes. "What of the rest?"

At Maven's gesture, the next interrogation begins in earnest. A Haven shadow, grasped tightly by Trio himself to keep the woman from fleeing. Without her ability, she seems dim, an echo of her beautiful house. Her red hair is darker, duller, without its usual scarlet gleam. When Samson puts a hand to her temple, she shrieks.

"Her thoughts are of her sister," Samson says without any feeling. Except maybe boredom. "Elane."

I saw her only hours ago, gliding around Evangeline's salon. She gave no indication that she knew of an impending assassination. But no good schemer would.

Maven knows it too. He glares at Evangeline, seething. "I'm told Lady Elane escaped with the majority of her house, fleeing the capital," he says. "Do you have any idea where they might have gone, my dearest?"

She keeps her eyes forward, walking a quickly thinning line. Even with her father and brother so close, I don't think anyone could save her from Maven's wrath if he felt inclined to unleash it. "No, why would I?" she says airily, examining her clawlike nails.

"Because she was your brother's betrothed and your whore," the king replies, matter-of-fact.

If she's ashamed or even apologetic, Evangeline does not show it. "Oh, that." She even scoffs, taking the accusation in stride. "How could she learn much of anything from me? You conspire so well to keep me from councils and politics. If anything, she did you a favor in keeping me pleasantly occupied."

Their bickering reminds me of another king and another queen: Maven's parents, fighting after the Scarlet Guard attacked a party at the Hall of the Sun. Each ripping at the other, leaving deep wounds to be exploited later.

"Then submit to interrogation, Evangeline, and we'll see," he fires back, pointing with one jeweled hand.

"No daughter of mine will ever do such a thing," Volo rumbles, though it hardly seems a threat. Merely a fact. "She had no part in this, and she defended you with her own life. Without Evangeline's and my son's quick action—well, even to *say* it is treason." The old patriarch pulls a frown, wrinkling his white skin, as if the thought is so disgusting. As if he wouldn't celebrate if Maven died. "Long live the king."

In the center of the floor, the Haven woman snarls, trying to shove off Trio. He holds firm, keeping her on her knees. "Yes, long live the king!" she says, glaring at us. "Tiberias the Seventh! Long live the king!"

Cal.

Maven stands, slamming his fists against the arms of his seat. I expect the room to burn, but no fire springs to life. It can't. Not while he sits on Silent Stone. His eyes are the only thing aflame. And then, slowly, with a manic grin, he begins to laugh.

"All this . . . for him?" he says, smirking. "My brother murdered the king, our father, helped murder my mother, and now he tries to murder me. Samson, if you would continue"—he inclines his head in his cousin's direction—"I have no mercy or remorse for traitors. Especially stupid ones."

The rest turn to watch the interrogation continue, to listen to the Haven woman as she spouts secrets of her faction, their goals, their plans. To replace Maven with his brother. To make Cal king as he was born to be. To return things to the way they were.

Through it all, I stare at the boy on the throne. He maintains his mask. Jaw clenched, lips pressed into a thin, unforgiving line. Still fingers, straight back. But his gaze wavers. Something in his eyes has gone far away. And at his collar, the slightest gray flush rises, painting his neck and the tips of his ears.

He's terrified.

For a second, it makes me happy. Then I remember—monsters are most dangerous when they're afraid.

ELEVEN
Cameron

Even though it would have turned me into an icicle, I wanted to stay behind in Trial. Not out of fear, but to prove a point. I'm not some weapon to be used, not like Barrow allowed herself to be. No one gets to tell me where to go or what to do. I'm done with that. I've lived my entire life that way. And every instinct in me tells me to stay away from the Guard's operation in Corvium, a fortress city that swallows every soldier and spits out their bones.

Except that my brother, Morrey, is only a few miles away now, still firmly stuck in a trench. Even with my ability, I'll need help to get to him. And if I want anything from this stupid Guard, I'm going to have to start giving them something in return. Farley made that clear enough.

I like her, more now after she apologized for the "utilizing" comment. She says what she means. She doesn't mope, though she has every right. Not like Cal, who broods around every corner, refusing to help and then relenting when he feels like it. The fallen prince is exhausting. I don't know how Mare could stand him or his inability to choose a damned side—especially when there's only one side he can possibly pick. Even now he blusters, wavering between wanting to protect the Silvers of Corvium and wanting to tear the city apart.

"You need to control the walls," he mutters, standing before Farley and the Colonel. We're operating from our headquarters in Rocasta, a less-defended supply city a few miles away from our objective. "If you control the walls, you can turn the city inside out—or take the walls down entirely. Render Corvium useless. To everyone."

I sit idly by in the sparse room, listening to the back-and-forth from my place next to Ada. Farley's idea. We're two of the more visible newbloods, well known to both kinds of Reds. Including us in these meeting sends a strong message to the rest of the unit. Ada watches with wide eyes, memorizing every word and gesture. Usually Nanny would sit with us, but Nanny is gone. She was a small woman, but she leaves a very large hole. And I know whose fault that is.

My eyes burn into Cal's back. I feel the itch of my ability, and fight the urge to bring him to his knees. He'll kill us for Mare, and he won't kill his own for the rest of the world. It was Nanny's choice to infiltrate Archeon on her own, but everyone knows it wasn't her idea.

Farley is just as angry as I am. She can barely look at Cal, even when speaking to him. "The question now is how to effectively dispatch our own. We can't focus everyone on the walls, important as they are."

"By my count, ten thousand Red soldiers occupy Corvium at any given time." I almost laugh at Ada's humbleness. *By my count*. Her count is perfect, and everyone knows it. "Military protocol dictates one officer to every ten, giving us at least one thousand Silvers inside the city, not accounting for command units and administration. Neutralizing them should be our objective."

Cal crosses his arms, unconvinced even by Ada's perfect, inarguable intelligence. "I'm not so sure. Our goal is to destroy Corvium, to strike Maven's army at its heart. That can be done without"—he stumbles—"without a massacre on both sides."

As if he cares what happens to our side. As if he cares if any one of us dies.

"How do you plan to destroy a city with a thousand Silvers looking on?" I wonder aloud, knowing I won't get much of an answer. "Will the prince ask them to sit quietly and watch?"

"Of course we fight those who resist," the Colonel breaks in. He stares at Cal, daring him to argue. "And they will resist. We know this."

"Do we?" Cal's tone is quietly smug. "Members of Maven's own court tried to kill him last week. If there's division in the High Houses, then there's division in the armed forces. Attacking them outright will only serve as a unifier, in Corvium at least."

My scoff echoes around the room. "So, what, we wait? Let Maven lick his wounds and regroup? Give him time to catch his breath?"

"Give him time to hang himself," Cal snaps back. He matches my scowl. "Give him time to make even more mistakes. Now he's on thin ice with Piedmont, his only ally, and three High Houses are in open rebellion. One of them all but controls the Air Fleet, another a vast intelligence network. Not to mention he still has us and the Lakelanders to worry about. He's scared; he's scrambling. I wouldn't want to be on his throne right now."

"Is that true?" Farley asks, her voice casual. But the words move through the room like knives. They sting him. Anyone can see that. His royal teachings are enough to keep his face still, but his eyes betray him. They flash in the fluorescent light. "Don't lie to us and say you're unconcerned with the other news out of Archeon. The reason Laris and Iral and Haven tried to kill your brother."

He stares. "They attempted a coup because Maven is a tyrant who abuses his power and murders his own."

I slam my fist against the arm of my chair. He's not going to dance his way around this one. "They revolted because they want to make you king!" I shout. To my surprise, he flinches. Maybe he's expecting more than just words. But I keep my ability in check, hard as it may be. "'Long live Tiberias the Seventh.' That's what the assassins said to Maven. Our operatives in Whitefire were clear."

He expels a long, frustrated sigh. He seems aged by this conversation. Brow furrowed, jaw tight. Muscles stand out at his neck and his hands curl into fists. He's a machine about to break—or explode.

"It's not unexpected," he mutters, as if it makes anything better. "There was bound to be a succession crisis eventually. But there's no feasible way anyone can put me back on the throne."

Farley tips her head. "And if they could?" Silently, I cheer her on. She won't let him off as easily as Mare used to. "If they offered the crown, your so-called birthright, in exchange for an end to all this—would you take it?"

The fallen prince of House Calore straightens to look her dead in the eye.

"No."

He's not as good a liar as Mare is.

"As much as I hate to admit it, he has a point about waiting."

I almost cough up the tea Farley poured me. Quickly I set the chipped cup back down on her ramshackle table. "You're not seriously saying that. How can you trust him?"

Farley paces back and forth, crossing her tiny room in only a few long steps. One hand massages her back as she moves, working out another of her aches. Her hair is longer every day, and she keeps it braided back from her face at odd lengths. I would offer her my seat, but she doesn't like to sit much these days. She has to keep moving, for her own comfort and her own nervous energy.

"Of course I don't trust him," she replies, kicking weakly at one of the paint-peeling walls. Her frustration runs as high as her emotions. "But I can trust things about him. I can trust him to act a certain way where certain people are concerned."

"You mean Mare." *Obviously.*

"Mare and his brother. His affection for one plays nicely off his hatred for the other. It might be our only way to keep him around."

"I say let him go, let him rile up a few more Silvers and be another thorn in Maven's side. We don't need him here."

She almost laughs, a bitter sound nowadays. "Yes, I'll just tell Command that we kicked out our most well known and legitimate operative. That will go over very well."

"He's not even really with us—"

"Well, Mare's not really with Maven, but people don't seem to understand that either, do they?" Even though she's right, I have to scowl. "As long as we have Cal, people take notice. No matter how badly we botched that first attempt at Archeon, we still ended up with a Silver prince on our side."

"A bleeding useless prince."

"Annoying, frustrating, a veritable pain in the ass—but not useless."

"Oh yeah? What's he done for us lately besides get Nanny killed?"

"Nanny wasn't forced to go to Archeon, Cameron. She made a choice and she died. That's how it works sometimes."

Nurturing as she sounds, Farley isn't much older than me.

Twenty-two, maybe, at most. I think her maternal instincts are kicking in early.

"Besides the fact that he wins us points with less-hostile Silvers, Montfort has an interest in him."

Montfort. The mysterious Free Republic. The twins, Rash and Tahir, paint the place as a haven of liberty and equality, where Reds, Silvers, and Ardents—what they call newbloods—live in peace together. An impossible place to believe in. But even so, I have to believe in their money, their supplies, their support. Most of our resources come from them in some way.

"What do they want?" I swirl the tea in my cup, letting the heat wash over my face. It's not as cold here as in Irabelle, but winter still creeps through the Rocasta safe house. "A poster boy?"

"Something like that. There's been lots of chatter with Command. I don't have clearance for most of it. They wanted Mare but—"

"She's a bit preoccupied."

Mention of Mare Barrow doesn't affect Farley as much as the memory of Shade, but a flicker of pain washes over her face anyway. She tries to hide it, of course. Farley does her best to appear impenetrable, and usually she is.

"So there's really no chance of rescuing her," I whisper. When she shakes her head, I feel a surprising pang of sadness in my own chest. Infuriating as Mare might be, I still want her back. We need her. And over the long months, I've realized *I* need her too. She knows what it is to be different and in search of someone like you, to fear and be feared in the same measure. Even if she was a condescending twit most of the time.

Farley stops pacing to pour herself another cup of tea. It steams, filling the room with a hot, herbal scent. She takes it in hand but doesn't drink, crossing instead to the foggy window set high in her wall. It bleeds daylight. "I don't see how we can with what we have. Infiltration of Corvium is easy compared to Archeon. It would take a full-scale assault, the kind we can't muster. Especially now, after Nanny and an assassination attempt. Security at Maven's court will be at its highest—worse than a prison. Unless . . ."

"Unless?"

"Cal tells us to wait. To let the Silvers in Corvium turn on each other. To let Maven make his mistakes before we do anything else."

"And it will help Mare too."

Farley nods. "The weak, divided court of a paranoid king will be easier for her to escape." She sighs, staring at her untouched tea. "She's the only one who can save herself now."

The conversation is easy to twist. As much as I want Mare back, I want someone else more. "How many miles are we from the Choke?"

"This again?"

"This always." I push back from the table to get up. I feel like I should be standing. I'm just as tall as Farley, but she always seems like she's looking down at me. I'm young, untrained. I don't know much about the world outside my slum. But that doesn't mean I'm going to sit here and follow orders. "I'm not asking for your help or the Guard's. I just need a map and maybe a gun. I'll do the bleeding rest myself."

She doesn't blink. "Cameron, your brother is embedded in a legion. It's not like pulling out a tooth."

My fist clenches at my side. "You think I came all the way here to sit around and watch Cal spin his wheels?" It's an old argument by now. She easily shuts me down.

"Well, I certainly don't think you came all the way here to get killed," she replies calmly. Her broad shoulders rise just a little, in challenge. "Which is precisely what will happen, no matter how strong or deadly your ability is. And even if you take a dozen Silvers with you, I'm not going to let you die for nothing. Is that clear?"

"My brother is not nothing," I grumble. She's right, but I don't want to admit it. Instead, I avoid her eyes and turn to the wall. My fingers pick at the peeling paint, ripping away pieces in annoyance. A childish thing, but it makes me feel a bit better. "You're not my captain. You don't get to tell me what to do with my life."

"That's true. I'm just a friend who feels inclined to point something out." I hear her shift, her footsteps heavy on the creaking floor. But her touch is light, a brush of her hand on my shoulder. She's robotic in the movement, not really knowing how to comfort another person. Bleakly, I wonder how she and warm, smiling Shade Barrow ever shared a conversation, let alone a bed. "I remember what you told Mare. When we first found you. On the jet, you said that her search for newbloods, to save them, was wrong. A continuation of the blood divide. Favoring one kind of Red over another. And you were right."

"This is not the same. I just want to save my brother."

"How do you think the rest of us got here?" she scoffs. "To save a friend, a sibling, a parent. To save ourselves. We all came here for selfish reasons, Cameron. But we can't be distracted by them. We have to think of the cause. The greater good. And you can do so much more here, with us. We can't lose you . . ."

Too. We can't lose you too. The last word hangs in the air, unspoken. I hear it anyway.

"You're wrong. I didn't come here by choice. I was taken. Mare Barrow forced me to follow, and you all went along with it."

"Cameron, that's a card you have played too many times. You chose to stay a long time ago. You chose to help."

"And what would you choose now, Farley?" I glare at her. She may be my friend, but that doesn't mean I have to back down.

"Excuse me?"

"Would you choose the greater good? Or would you choose Shade?"

When she doesn't respond, her eyes sliding out of focus, I have my answer. I realize I don't want to see her cry and turn my back, making for the door.

"I have to train," I say to no one. I doubt she's still listening.

Training is harder in the Rocasta safe house. We don't have anywhere near enough space, not to mention most of the operatives I know were left in Irabelle. Kilorn, for example. Eager as he is, he's nowhere near ready for all-out battle, and he doesn't have an ability to lean on. He was left behind. But my trainer was not. After all, she's Silver, and the Colonel wasn't about to let her out of his sight.

Sara Skonos waits in the basement of our reinforced warehouse, in a room dedicated to newblood exercises. It's dinnertime, so the other newbloods in this particular sanctuary are upstairs eating with the rest. We have the space to ourselves, not that we need much space at all.

She sits cross-legged, palms flat on a concrete floor that matches the concrete walls. Her notepad is there too, ready to be used if need be. Her eyes track my entrance, the only greeting I'll get. As of yet, we have not found another skin healer to join us, and she remains mute. Even though I'm used to it, the sight of her sunken cheeks and missing tongue makes me cringe. As usual, she pretends not to notice and gestures to the space in front of her.

I sit as she instructs, and fight the familiar urge to run or attack.

She's Silver. She's everything I've been raised to fear, hate, and obey. But I can't find it in myself to despise Sara Skonos the way I do Julian or Cal. It's not that I pity her. I think . . . I understand her. I understand the frustration of knowing what is right and being ignored or punished because of it. I can't count how many times I received half rations for looking at a Silver overseer incorrectly. For talking out of turn. She did the same, except her words were against a reigning queen. And so her words were taken away forever.

Even though she can't speak, Sara has a way of communicating what she wants. She taps me on the knee, forcing me to meet her cloudy gray eyes. Then she dips her face and puts a hand over her heart.

I follow the motions, knowing what she wants. I match her breathing: steady, deep breaths in even succession. A calming mechanism that helps drown out all the thoughts swirling around my head. It clears my mind, allowing me to feel what I usually ignore. My ability hums beneath my skin, constant as always, but now I let myself notice it. Not to use it, but to acknowledge its existence. My silence is still new to me, and I have to get to know it like any other skill.

After long minutes of breathing, she taps me again, making me look up. This time she points at herself.

"Sara, I'm really not in the right mood," I start to tell her, but she draws one hand through the air in a chopping motion. *Shut up,* plain as day.

"I mean it. I could hurt you."

She scoffs deep in her throat, one of the only true vocalizations she can make. It almost sounds like laughter. Then she taps her lips, smirking darkly. She's been hurt far worse.

"Fine, I warned you," I sigh. I wiggle a little, settling deeper into my position. Then I furrow my brow, letting the ability swim around me, deepening, expanding. Until it touches her. And silence descends.

Her eyes widen when it hits. A twinge at first. At least I hope it's just a twinge. I'm only practicing, and I don't intend to pummel her into submission. I think of Mare, able to call up storms, while Cal can make infernos, but both find it difficult to have a simple conversation without exploding. Control takes more practice than brute force.

My ability deepens, and she holds up one finger to denote the level of discomfort. I try to keep the silence in place, constant but steady. It's like holding back a tide. I don't know what it feels like to be silenced. The Silent Stone didn't work on me in Corros Prison, but it stifled, drained—and slowly killed—all the people around me. I can do the same. After about a minute, she puts up a second finger.

"Sara . . . ?"

With her other hand she gestures for me to continue.

I remember our session yesterday. She was on the floor at five, though I knew I could push harder. But incapacitating our only skin healer is neither smart nor something I want to do.

A flush paints her cheeks, but the door to the basement swings open before she can hold up another finger.

My concentration and my silence break, drawing a relieved gasp from her. Both of us whirl to face our disrupter. While she breaks into a rare smile, I scowl.

"Jacos," I mutter in his direction. "We're training, in case you haven't noticed."

One side of his mouth twitches, begging to pull into a sneer of his own, but Julian refrains. Like the rest of us, he looks better here in Rocasta. Supplies are easier to come by. Our clothes are higher quality, quilted and lined against the cold. The food is heartier, the rooms warmer. Julian's color has returned, and his gray-flecked hair looks glossier. He's Silver. He was born to thrive.

"Oh, how foolish of me. I thought you were down here sitting on cold concrete for the fun of it," he replies. Clearly no love lost between us. Sara glares at him, a weak reproach, but it softens him anyway. "My apologies, Cameron," he adds quickly. "I just wanted to tell Sara something."

Sara quirks an eyebrow, a question. When I get up to go, she stops me and, with a dip of her head, asks Julian to continue. He always obeys where she is concerned.

"There's been an exodus from court. Maven expelled dozens of nobles, mostly his father's old advisers and those who might still harbor loyalties to Cal. It's . . . I didn't believe the intelligence report at first. I've never seen anything like it before."

Julian and Sara hold each other's gaze, both pondering what this means. I don't care at all about a few Silver lords and ladies, old friends of Julian and Sara's. "And Mare?" I wonder aloud.

"She's still there, still a prisoner. And any further fractures we may have expected from the rebelling houses . . ." He sighs, shaking his head. "Maven is already at war, and now he prepares for a storm."

I shift on the floor, moving my weight into a more comfortable position. He's right. Cold concrete isn't pleasant. Good thing I'm used to it. "We already knew rescuing her was impossible. What else does this do for us?"

"Well, it's good and it's bad. More enemies for Maven give us more opportunity to work beyond his reach. But he's closing ranks, retreating further into his enclave of protection. We'll never get to him personally."

Next to me, Sara hums low in her throat. She can't say what we're all thinking, so I do.

"Or to Mare."

Julian nods with sobering eyes.

"How is your training coming along?"

He changes topics with whiplash speed, and I stutter out a reply.

"As—as good as it can. We don't have many teachers here."

"Because you refuse to train with my nephew."

"The others can," I say, not bothering to keep the bite from my voice. "But I can't promise I won't kill him, so it's better I don't tempt myself."

Sara tsks, but Julian brushes her off with a wave of his hand. "It's fine, really. You may think I don't understand, that I can't understand your point of view, and you're right. But I'm certainly doing my best to try, Cameron." He takes a daring step toward us, still cross-legged on the floor. I don't like it one bit and scramble to my feet, letting my defensive instincts take over. If I'm going to be this close to Julian Jacos, I want to be ready. "There's no need to be afraid of me, I promise you."

"Silver promises mean nothing." I don't have to snap. The words are harsh enough.

To my surprise, Julian smiles. But the expression is hollow, empty. "Oh, don't I know that," he mutters, more to himself and Sara. "Hold on to your anger. Sara might not agree, but it will help you more than anything else, if you can learn to harness it."

As much as I don't want advice from such a man, I can't help but tuck it away. He trained Mare. I'd be stupid to deny he can help my ability grow. And anger is something I have in spades.

"Any other news?" I ask. "Farley and the Colonel seem to be stalling, or your nephew is stalling them."

"Yes, it seems he is."

"Odd. Thought he was always up for a fight."

Julian offers that strange smile again. "Cal was raised to war the same way you were raised to machines. But you don't want to go back to the factory, do you?"

An answer, any answer, sticks in my throat. *I was a slave; I was forced; it was all I knew.*

"Don't get smart with me, Julian" grinds out instead, searing between my clenched teeth.

He only shrugs. "I'm trying to understand your perspective. Do a bit to understand his."

On another day, I might storm from the room, angry, defensive. Find solace in a broken fuse, a stripped wire. I sit back down instead, taking my place next to Sara. Julian Jacos will not send me scurrying away like a scolded child. I've dealt with overseers far worse than him.

"I watched babies die without seeing the sun. Without breathing fresh air. Slaves to your kind. Have you? When you have, then you can lecture me on perspective, Lord Jacos." I turn from him. "Let me know when the prince finally picks a side. And if he picks the right one."

Then I nod at Sara. "Ready to go again?"

TWELVE
Mare

Months ago, when the Silvers fled the Hall of the Sun, frightened by a Scarlet Guard attack on their precious ball, it was a united act. We left together, as one, heading downriver in succession to regroup in the capital. This is not the same.

Maven's dismissals come in packs. I'm not privy to them, but I notice as the numbers dwindle. A few older advisers missing. The royal treasurer, some generals, members of various councils. *Relieved of their posts,* the rumors say. But I know better. They were close to Cal, close to his father. Maven is smart not to trust them, and ruthless in their removal. He doesn't kill them or make them disappear. He's not stupid enough to trigger another house war. But it's a decisive move, to say the least. Sweeping away obstacles like pieces from a chess board. The results are feasts that look like mouths of missing teeth. Gaps appear, more with every passing day. Most of those asked to leave are older, men and women with ancient allegiances, who remember more and trust their new king less.

Some start to call it the Court of Children.

Many lords and ladies are gone, sent away by the king, but their sons and daughters are left behind. A request. A warning. A threat.

Hostages.

Not even House Merandus escapes his growing paranoia. Only House Samos remains in their entirety, not one of them falling prey to his tempestuous dismissals.

Those still here are devout in their loyalty. Or at least they make it look like it.

That's probably why he summons me more now. Why I see so much of him. I'm the only one with loyalties he can trust. The only one he really knows.

He reads reports over our breakfast, eyes skimming back and forth with blistering speed. It's useless to try to see what they are. He's careful to keep them to his side of the table, turned over when finished, and well out of my reach. Instead of reading the reports, I have to read him. He doesn't bother to surround himself with Silent Stone, not here in his private dining room. Even the Sentinels wait outside, posted at every door and on the other side of the tall windows. I see them, but they can't hear us, as is Maven's design. His uniform jacket is unbuttoned, his hair unkempt, and he doesn't put on his crown this early in the morning. I think this is his little sanctuary, a place where he can trick himself into feeling safe.

He almost looks like the boy I imagined. A second prince, content with his place, unburdened by a crown that was never his.

Over the rim of my water glass, I watch every tick and flash across his face. Narrowed eyes, a tightening jaw. Bad news. The dark circles have returned, and while he eats enough for two people, tearing through the plates in front of us, he seems thinned by the days. I wonder if he has nightmares of the assassination attempt. Nightmares of his mother, dead by my hand. His father, dead by his action. His brother, in exile but a constant threat. Funny, Maven called himself Cal's shadow, but Cal is the shadow now, haunting every corner of Maven's fragile kingdom.

There are reports of the exiled prince everywhere, so prevalent that even I hear about them. They place him in Harbor Bay, Delphie, Rocasta; there's even shaky intelligence hinting that he escaped across the border into the Lakelands. I honestly don't know which, if any, of these rumors are true. He could be in Montfort for all I know. Gone to the safety of a faraway land.

Even though this is Maven's palace, Maven's world, I see Cal in it. The immaculate uniforms, drilling soldiers, flaming candles, gilded walls of portraits and house colors. An empty salon reminds me of dance lessons. If I glance at Maven from the corner of my eye, I can pretend. They're half brothers after all. They share similar features. The dark hair, the elegant lines of a royal face. But Maven is paler, sharper, a skeleton in comparison, body and soul. He is hollowed out.

"You stare so much I wonder if you can read reflections in my eyes," Maven suddenly muses aloud. He flips the page in front of him, hiding what it holds, as he looks up.

His attempt to startle me fails. Instead, I continue spreading an embarrassing amount of butter onto my toast. "If only I could see something in them," I reply, meaning all things. "You're an empty boy."

He doesn't flinch. "And you're useless."

I roll my eyes and idly tap my manacles against the breakfast table. Metal and stone rap against wood like knocking on a door. "Our talks are so fun."

"If you prefer your room . . . ," he warns. Another empty threat he makes every day. We both know this is better than the alternative. At least now I can pretend I'm doing something of use, and he can pretend he isn't entirely alone in this cage he built for himself. For both of us.

It's hard to sleep here, even with the manacles, which means I have a lot of time to think.

And plan.

Julian's books are not only a comfort, but a tool. He's still teaching me, even though we're who knows how many miles apart. In his well-preserved texts, there are new lessons to be learned and utilized. The first—and most important—is divide and conquer. Maven's already done it to me. Now I must return the favor.

"Are you even trying to hunt for Jon?"

Maven is actually startled at my question, the first mention of the newblood who used the assassination attempt to escape. As far as I know, he hasn't been captured. Part of me is bitter. Jon escaped where I couldn't. But at the same time, I'm glad. Jon is a weapon I want far away from Maven Calore.

After a split-second recovery, Maven returns to eating. He shoves a piece of bacon in his mouth, throwing etiquette to the wind. "You and I both know that's not a man who is easily found."

"But you are looking."

"He had knowledge of an attack on his king and did nothing," Maven states, matter-of-fact. "That's tantamount to murder itself. For all we know, he conspired with Houses Iral, Haven, and Laris too."

"I doubt it. If he'd helped them, they would have succeeded. Pity."

He dutifully ignores the jab, continuing to read and eat.

I tip my head, letting my dark hair spill across one shoulder. The gray ends are spreading, leaching upward despite my healer's best efforts. Even House Skonos cannot heal what is already dead.

"Jon saved my life."

Blue eyes meet mine, holding firm.

"Seconds before the attack, he got my attention. He made me turn my head. Or else . . ." I run a finger along my cheekbone. Where the bullet only grazed my cheek, instead of leaving my skull a ruin. The wound healed, but not forgotten. "I must have a part to play in whatever future he sees."

Maven focuses on my face. Not my eyes, but the place where a bullet would have obliterated my skull. "For some reason, you're a difficult person to let die."

For him, for the pageantry, I force a small, bitter laugh.

"What's so funny?"

"How many times have you tried to kill me?"

"Just the once."

"And the sounder was what?" My fingers tremble at the memory. The pain of the device is still fresh in my mind. "Just part of a game?"

Another report flutters in the sunlight, landing facedown. He licks his fingers before raising the next. All business. All for show. "The sounder wasn't designed to kill you, Mare. Just incapacitate you, if need be." A strange look crosses his face. Almost smug, but not exactly. "I didn't even make that thing."

"Clearly. You're not one for ideas. Elara, then?"

"Actually it was Cal."

Oh. Before I can stop myself, I look down, away from him, needing a moment of my own. The sting of betrayal pricks at my insides, if only for a second. It's no use being angry now.

"I can't believe he didn't tell you." Maven presses on. "He's usually very proud of himself. A brilliant thing too. But I don't care for it. I had the device destroyed." His eyes are on my face. Hungry for a reaction.

I keep my expression from changing, despite the sudden skip in my heartbeat. The sounder is gone. Another small gift, another message from the ghost.

"It can easily be rebuilt, though, if you decide to stop cooperating. Cal was kind enough to leave the device plans behind when he ran off with your band of Red rats."

"Escaped," I mumble. *Move on. Don't let him throw you off.* Feigning disinterest, I push the rest of my food around my plate. I do my best to look hurt, as Maven wants me to be, but not let myself feel it. I have to stick to the plan. Twist the conversation as I want to twist it. "You forced him away. All so you could take his place, and be exactly like him."

Like me, Maven forces a laugh to hide how annoyed he is. "You have no idea what he would've been like, with the crown on his head."

I cross my arms, settling back in my chair. This is playing out exactly as I want it to. "I know he would have married Evangeline Samos, continued fighting a useless war, and kept ignoring a country full of angry, oppressed people. Does that sound at all familiar?"

He may be a snake in human form, but even Maven doesn't have a retort for that. He slaps down the report in front of him. Too quickly. It faces up, just for a second, before he turns it over. I glimpse only a few words. *Corvium. Casualties.* Maven sees me see them, and he hisses out a sigh of annoyance.

"As if that will help you," he says quietly. "You're not going anywhere, so why bother?"

"I suppose that's true. My life probably won't last much longer."

He tips his head. Concern furrows his brow, as I hope it will. As I need it to. "What makes you say that?"

I glare up at the ceiling, studying the elaborate molding and the chandelier above us. It flickers with tiny electric bulbs. If only I could feel them.

"You know Evangeline won't let me live. Once she's queen . . . I'm done for." My voice trembles, and I push all my fear into the words. I hope it works. He has to believe me. "It's what she's wanted since the day I fell into her life."

He blinks at me. "You don't think I'll protect you from her?"

"I don't think you can." My fingers pick at my gown. Not as beautiful as the ones made for court, but just as overwrought. "You and I both know how easy it is for a queen to be killed."

The air ripples with heat as he continues to stare, daring me to meet his gaze. My natural instinct is to glare back, but I lean away, refusing to look at him. It will only incense him further. Maven loves an audience. The moment stretches, and I feel bare before him, prey in the path of a predator. That's all I am here. Caged, restrained, leashed. All I have left is my voice, and the pieces of Maven I hope I know.

"She won't touch you."

"And what about the Lakelanders?" I snap my head back up. Tears of anger spring to my eyes, born of frustration, not fear. "When they rip apart your already-splintering kingdom? What happens when they win this endless war and burn your world to embers?" I scoff to myself, heaving a shuddering breath. The tears fall freely now. They must. I have to sell this with every inch of myself. "I guess then we'll end up in the Bowl of Bones together, executed side by side."

By the way he pales, the little color he has draining from his face, I know he's thought the same thing. It plagues him endlessly, a bleeding wound. So I twist the knife.

"You're on the edge of civil war. Even I know that. What's the point in pretending there's a scenario where I make it out of this alive? Either Evangeline kills me or the war does."

"I told you already, I won't let that happen."

The snarl I throw his way doesn't need to be faked. "In what life can I trust anything out of your mouth ever again?"

When he stands, the cold fear pooling in my stomach isn't fake either. As he rounds the table, crossing to me in lean, elegant strides, I lock every muscle, tensing up so I don't shake. But I quiver anyway. I brace myself for a blow as he takes my face in disturbingly soft hands, both thumbs tight under my jaw, inches away from digging into my jugular.

His kiss burns worse than his brand.

The sensation of his lips on mine is the worst kind of violation. But for him, for what I need, I keep my hands fisted in my lap. My nails dig into my flesh instead of his. He needs to believe as his brother believed. He needs to choose me, the way I tried to make Cal choose me before. Still, I can't find it in me to open my mouth, and my jaw remains locked shut.

He breaks the kiss first, and I hope he can't feel my skin crawl beneath his fingers. Instead, his eyes search mine, looking for the lie I keep well hidden.

"I lost every other person I ever loved."

"And whose fault is that?"

Somehow, he trembles worse than I do. He steps back, letting me go, and his fingers scratch at one another. I'm shocked because I recognize the action. I do it too. When the pain in my head is so horrible I need another kind to draw me away. He stops when he notices me staring, clasping both hands to his sides as tightly as he can.

"She broke a lot of my habits," he admits. "Never broke that one. Some things always come back."

"She." Elara. I see her handiwork right in front of me. The boy she shaped into a king through a torture she called love.

He sits back down, slowly. I keep staring, knowing it unsettles him. I put him off balance, and still I don't understand exactly why.

Every other person I ever loved.

I don't know why I'm included in that statement. But I know it's the reason I'm still breathing. Careful, I edge the conversation back to Cal.

"Your brother is alive."

"Unfortunately so."

"And you don't love him?"

He doesn't bother to look up, but his eyes waver on the next report, fixed on a single spot. Not because he's surprised, or even sad. He looks more confused than anything, a little boy trying to solve a puzzle with too many missing pieces. "No," he says finally, lying.

"I don't believe you," I tell him. I even shake my head.

Because I remember them as they were. Brothers, friends, raised together against the rest of the world. Even Maven can't shut himself off from something like that. Even Elara can't break that kind of bond. No matter how many times Maven tried to kill Cal, he can't deny what they were once.

"Believe what you want, Mare," he replies. As before, he puts on an air of disinterest, violently trying to convince me this means nothing to him. "I know for a fact that I don't love my brother."

"Don't lie. I have siblings too. It's a complicated thing, especially between me and my sister. She's always been more talented, better at everything, kinder, smarter. Everyone prefers her to me." I mumble my old fears, spinning them into a web for Maven. "Take it from a person who knows. Losing one of them—losing a brother . . ." My breath hitches, and my mind flies. *Keep going. Use the pain.* "It hurts like nothing else."

"Shade. Right?"

"Keep his name out of your mouth," I snap, forgetting for a moment what I'm trying to do. The wound is too fresh, too raw. He takes it in stride.

"My mother said you used to dream about him," he says. I flinch at the memory, and the thought of her inside my brain. I can still feel her, clawing at the walls of my skull. "But I suppose those weren't dreams at all. It was really him."

"Did she do that with everyone?" I reply. "Was nothing safe from her? Even your dreams?"

He doesn't respond. I push harder.

"Did you ever dream of me?"

Again I cut him without realizing it. He drops his gaze, looking down to the empty plate in front of him. He raises a hand to grab at his water glass, but thinks better of it. His fingers tremble for a second before he shoves them away, out of sight.

"I wouldn't know," he finally says. "I don't dream."

I scoff. "That's impossible. Even for a person like you."

Something dark, something sad, twitches across his face. His jaw tightens and his throat bobs, trying to swallow words he shouldn't speak. They burst from him anyway. His hands reappear, tapping weakly on the table.

"I used to have nightmares. She took that part away when I was a boy. Like Samson said, my mother was a surgeon with minds. She cut out whatever didn't suit."

In recent weeks, a ferocious, fiery anger has replaced the cold hollowness I used to feel. But as Maven speaks, the ice returns. It bleeds through me, a poison, an infection. I don't want to hear what he has to say. His excuses and explanations are nothing to me. He is a monster still, a monster always. And yet I can't stop myself from listening. Because I could be a monster too. If given the wrong chance. If someone broke me, like he is broken.

"My brother. My father. I know I loved them once. I remember it." His hands clench around a butter knife, and he glares at the dull edge. I wonder if he wants to use it on himself or his dead mother. "But I don't feel it. That love isn't there anymore. For any of them. For most things."

"Then why keep me here? If you don't feel anything. Why not just kill me and be done with this?"

"She has a hard time erasing . . . certain kinds of feeling," he admits, meeting my eye. "She tried to do it with Father, to make him forget his love for Coriane. It only made things worse. Besides," he mumbles, "she always said it was better to be heartbroken. The pain makes you stronger. Love makes you weak. And she's right. I learned that before I even knew you."

Another name lingers in the air, unspoken.

"Thomas."

A boy at the war front. Another Red lost to a useless war. *My first real friend,* Maven told me once. I realize now the spaces between those words. The things unsaid. He loved that boy as he claims to love me.

"Thomas," Maven echoes. His grip on the knife tightens. "I felt . . ." Then his brow furrows, deep creases forming between his eyes. He puts his other hand to his temple, massaging an ache I can't understand. "She wasn't there. She never met him. She didn't know. He wasn't even a soldier. It was an accident."

"You said you tried to save him. That your guards stopped you."

"An explosion at headquarters. The reports said it was Lakelander infiltration." Somewhere, a clock ticks as the minutes slide by. His silence stretches as he decides what to say, how far to let the mask slip. But it's already gone. He's bare as he can only be with me. "We were alone. I lost control."

I see it in my mind's eye, filling in what he can't will himself to tell me. An ammunitions depot maybe. Or even a gas line. Both need only flame to kill.

"I didn't burn. He did."

"Maven—"

"Even my mother could not cut that memory away. Even she couldn't make me forget, no matter how I begged her to. I wanted her to take that pain from me, and she tried so many times. Instead, it always got worse."

I know how he's going to answer my question, but I ask all the same.

"Please let me go?"

"I won't."

"Then you're going to let me die too. Like him."

The room crackles with heat, sending sweat down my spine. He stands so quickly, he knocks back his chair, letting it crash to the floor. One fist collides with the tabletop before raking sideways, throwing plates, glasses, and reports to the floor. The papers float for a moment, suspended in air before drifting down to the shattered pile of crystal and porcelain.

"I won't," he growls under his breath, so low I almost don't hear him as he stalks from the room.

The Arvens enter and seize me beneath my arms, pulling me away from the table of papers, all of them slipping from reach.

I'm surprised to learn that Maven's usually meticulous schedule of hearings and court gatherings is suspended for the rest of the day. I guess our conversation had a stronger effect than I expected. His absence confines me to my room, to Julian's books. I force myself to read, if only to block out any memories of the morning. Maven is a talented liar, and I don't trust a single word he speaks. Even if he was telling the truth. Even if he is a product of his mother's meddling, a thorned flower forced to grow a certain way. That doesn't change things. I can't forget everything he's done to me and so many others. When I first met him, I was seduced by his pain. He was the boy in shadow, a forgotten son. I saw myself in him. Second always to Gisa, the bright star in my parents' world. I know now that was by design. He caught me back then, ensnaring me in a prince's trap. Now I'm in a king's cage. But so is he. My chains are Silent Stone. His is the crown.

The country of Norta was forged from smaller kingdoms and lordships, ranging in size from the Samos kingdom of the Rift to the city-state Delphie. Caesar Calore, a Silver lord of Archeon and a talented tactician, united fractured Norta against the looming threat of joint invasion by Piedmont and the Lakelands. Once he crowned himself king, he married his daughter Juliana to Garion Savanna, the ruling high prince of Piedmont. This act cemented a lasting alliance between House Calore and the princes of Piedmont. Many children of Calore and Piedmont royalty upheld the marriage alliance for the following centuries. King Caesar brought an age of prosperity to Norta, and as such, Nortan calendars consider the beginning of his reign the demarcation of the "New Era," or NE.

It takes me three tries to get through the paragraph. Julian's histories are much denser than what I had to learn in school. My thoughts keep drifting. Black hair, blue eyes. Tears Maven refuses to show, even to me. Is it another performance? What do I do if it is? What do I do if it isn't? My heart breaks for him; my heart hardens against him. I push on to avoid such thoughts.

In contrast, relations between newly founded Norta and the extensive Lakelands deteriorated. Following a series of border wars with Prairie in the second century NE, the Lakelands lost vital agricultural territory in the Minnowan region as well as control of the Great River (also known as the Miss). Taxation following the war, as well as the threat of famine and Red rebellion, forced expansion along the Nortan border. Skirmishes sparked on either side. To prevent further bloodshed, King Tiberias the Third of Norta and King Onekad Cygnet of the Lakelands met in a historic summit at the crossing of Maiden Falls. Negotiations fell apart quickly, and in 200 NE, both kingdoms declared war, each blaming the other for the breakdown in their diplomatic relations.

I can't help but laugh. Nothing ever changes.

Known as the Lakelander War in Norta, and the Aggression in the Lakelands, the conflict is still ongoing at the time of writing. Total Silver death tolls number approximately five hundred thousand, most in the first decade of war. Accurate records for Red soldiers are not kept, but

estimates put the total death toll in excess of fifty million, with casualties
more than twice that number. Both Lakelander and Nortan casualties
are equal in proportion to their native Red populations.

It takes longer than I care to admit, but I scratch out the math in my head. Almost one hundred times more. If this book belonged to anyone other than Julian, I would throw it away in rage.

A century of war and wasteful bloodshed.

How can anyone change something like that?

For once I find myself counting on Maven's ability to twist and scheme. Perhaps he can see a way—forge a path—that no one before him has imagined.

THIRTEEN
Mare

A week passes until I leave my room again. Even though they're a gift from Maven, a reminder of his strange obsession with me, I'm glad for Julian's books. They're my only company. A piece of a friend in this place. I keep them close, alongside Gisa's silk scrap.

Pages pass with the days. I work back through the histories, traveling through words that become less and less believable. Three hundred years of Calore kings, centuries of Silver warlords—this is a world I recognize. But the farther I go, the murkier things become.

Written records of the so-called Reformation Period are scarce, though most scholars agree that the period began sometime around 1500 Old Era (or OE) by the modern Nortan calendar. Most records dating before the Reformation, immediately following, during, or prior to the Calamities that befell the continent, were almost entirely destroyed, were lost, or are impossible to read at present. Those recovered are closely studied and guarded within the Royal Archives in Delphie, as well as similar facilities in neighboring kingdoms. The Calamities themselves have been studied at length, using field investigation paired with pre-Silverian myth to postulate events. At the time of writing, many believe that a combination of ultimate human war, geologic shift, climate change, and other natural catastrophes resulted in the near extinction of the human race.

The earliest discovered, translatable records date from approximately 950 OE, but the exact year cannot be verified. One document, The Trial of Barr Rambler, *is an incomplete account of the attempted court trial of an accused thief in reconstructed Delphie. Barr was accused of stealing his neighbor's wagon. During the course of the trial, Barr reportedly broke his chains of binding "as if made of twigs" and escaped despite a full guard. It is believed to be the first record of a Silver displaying his ability. To this day, House Rhambos claims to trace its strongarm bloodline from him. However, this claim is refuted by another court record,* The Trial of Hillman, Tryent, Davids, *wherein three men of Delphie were tried for the subsequent murder of Barr Rambler, who was reported to have no children. The three men were acquitted and later praised by the citizens of Delphie for their work in destroying "the Rambler abomination"* (Delphie Records and Writings, Vol. 1).

The treatment of Barr Rambler was not an isolated incident. Many early writings and documents detail fear and persecution of a rising population of abilitied humans with silver-colored blood. Most banded together for protection, forming communities outside Red-dominated cities. The Reformation Period ended with the rise of Silver societies, some living in conjunction with Red cities, though most eventually overtook their red-blooded counterparts.

Silvers persecuted by Reds. I want to laugh at the thought. How stupid. How impossible. I've lived every day of my life knowing they are gods and we are insects. I cannot even begin to fathom a world where the reverse was true.

These are Julian's books. He saw enough merit here to study them. Still, I feel too unsettled to continue, and I keep my reading to later years. The New Era, the Calore kings. Names and places I know in a civilization I understand.

One day my delivered clothes are plainer than ever. Comfortable, made for utility rather than style. My first indication of something amiss. I almost look like a Security officer, with stretchy pants, a black jacket sparsely embellished with pinprick whorls of ruby beading, and shockingly sensible boots. Polished but worn leather, no heel, just the right amount of pinch, and enough room for my ankle manacles. The ones at the wrist are hidden as usual, covered by gloves. Fur-lined. For the cold. My heart leaps. I've never been so excited about gloves.

"Am I going outside?" I ask Kitten breathlessly, forgetting how good she is at ignoring me. She doesn't disappoint, staring straight ahead as she leads me from my luxurious cell. Clover is always easier to read. The twitch of her lips and narrowed green eyes are affirmation enough. Not to mention that they, too, are both wearing thick coats as well as gloves, albeit the rubber ones to protect their hands from electricity I no longer possess.

Outside. I haven't tasted much more than a breeze from an open window since that day on the steps of the palace. I thought Maven was going to take my head off, so obviously my mind was elsewhere. Now I wish I could remember the cold air of November, the sharp wind bringing winter with it. In my haste, I almost outpace the Arvens. They're quick to yank me in line and make me match their steps. It's a maddening descent, down stairs and corridors I know by heart.

Familiar pressure ripples against me, and I glance over my shoulder.

Egg and Trio join our ranks, bringing up the rear of my Arven guard. They move in unison with Kitten and Clover, steps matching, as we make our way to the entrance hall and Caesar's Square.

Quick as my excitement came, it bleeds away.

Fear gnaws at my insides. I tried to manipulate Maven into making costly mistakes, to make him doubt, to burn the last bridges he has left. But maybe I failed. Maybe he's going to burn me instead.

I focus on the click of my boots on marble. Something solid to anchor my fear. My fists curl in my gloves, begging for a spark to tide me over. It never comes.

The palace seems strangely empty, even more so than usual. Doors are shut fast, while servants flutter through the rooms that aren't closed yet, quick and quiet as mice. They flutter white sheets over furniture and artwork, covering them up in strange shrouds. Few guards, fewer nobles. The ones I pass are young and wide-eyed. I know their houses, their colors, and I can see naked fear on their faces. All are dressed like me, for the cold, for function. For movement.

"Where is everyone going?" I ask no one, because no one is going to answer.

Clover harshly yanks on my ponytail, forcing me to look straight ahead. It doesn't hurt, but the action is jarring. She never handles me this way, not unless I give her a good reason.

I spin through the possibilities. Is this an evacuation? Has the Scarlet Guard attempted another assault on Archeon? Or have the rebelling houses returned to finish what they started? No, it can't be either. This is too calm. We're not running from anything.

As we cross the hall, I take a deep breath, looking around. Marble beneath me, chandeliers above me, tall glimmering mirrors and gilded paintings of Calore ancestors marching up the walls on either side. Red and black banners, silver and gold and crystal. I feel like it's all going to crash down and crush me. Fear creeps down my spine when the doors ahead swing open, metal and glass easing on giant hinges. The first breath of cold wind hits me head-on, making my eyes water.

The winter sun shines bright on the gleaming square, blinding me for a second. I blink rapidly, trying to make my eyes adjust. I can't afford to miss a second of this. The outside world comes into focus steadily. Snow lies deep on the rooftops of the palace and the surrounding structures of Caesar's Square.

Soldiers line either side of the steps leading down from the palace, immaculate in their neat rows. The Arvens lead me through the double row of soldiers, past their guns and uniforms and unblinking eyes. I turn to look over my shoulder as I walk, stealing a glance at the opulent pale hulk of Whitefire Palace. Silhouettes prowl the roof. Officers in black uniforms, soldiers in clouded gray. Even from here, their rifles are clearly visible, silhouetted against a cold blue sky. And those are just the guards I can see. There must be more patrolling the walls, manning the gates, concealed and ready to defend this wretched place. Hundreds, probably, kept for their loyalty and lethal ability. We cross the square alone, for no one, for nothing. What is this?

I note the buildings we pass. The Royal Court, a circular building with smooth marble walls, spiraled columns, and a crystal dome, has gone unused since Maven's coronation. It is a symbol of power, a massive hall large enough to seat the assembled High Houses and their retainers, as well as important members of the Silver citizenry. I've never been inside. I hope I never am. The judiciary courts, where Silver law is made and enacted with brutal efficiency, branch out from the domed structure. Next to their arches and crystal trappings, the

Treasury Hall looks dull. Slab walls—more marble, and I have to won-der how many quarries this place sucked dry—no windows, sitting like a block of stone among sculptures. The wealth of Norta is some-where in there, more defended than the king, locked in vaults drilled deep into the bedrock below us.

"This way," Clover growls, pulling me toward the Treasury.

"Why?" I ask. Again, no one answers.

My heartbeat quickens, hammering against my rib cage, and I struggle to keep my breathing even. Each cold gasp feels like the tick of a clock, steadily counting down the moments before I'm swallowed up.

The doors are thick, thicker than the ones I remember from Corros Prison. They open wide as a yawning mouth, flanked by guards in liveried purple. The Treasury has no grand entrance hall, in sharp con-trast to every other Silver structure I've ever seen. It's just a long white corridor, curving and sloping downward in a steady spiral. Guards stand at attention every ten yards or so, flush against pure white stone. Where the vaults might be, or where I'm going, I can't say.

After exactly six hundred steps, we stop in front of a guard.

Without a word he steps forward and to the side, putting his fingers to the wall behind him. He pushes and the marble glides backward a foot, revealing the silhouette of a door. It slides easily at his touch, wid-ening to create a three-foot gap in the stone. The soldier doesn't strain at all. *Strongarm,* I note.

The stone is thick and heavy. My fear triples, and I swallow hard, feeling my hands start to sweat in my gloves. Maven is finally putting me in a real cell.

Kitten and Clover shove me, trying to take me off guard, but I plant my feet, locking every joint against them. "No!" I shout, driving a shoulder back into one of them. Kitten grunts but doesn't stop, continuing to push while Clover takes me around the middle, lifting me clean off the floor.

"You can't put me down here!" I don't know what card to play, what mask to put on. Do I cry? Do I beg? Do I act like the rebel queen they think I am? Which one will save me? Fear overrules my senses. I gasp like a girl drowning. "Please, I can't—I can't—"

I kick at open air, trying to topple Clover, but she's stronger than I expect. Egg takes my legs, cleanly ignoring my heel as it cracks into his jaw. They carry me like a piece of furniture, without thought or attention.

Twisting, I manage to catch sight of the Treasury guard as the door slides back into place. He hums to himself, nonchalant. Another day on the job for him. I force myself to look forward, at whatever fate awaits me in these white depths.

This vault is empty; its walkway corkscrews like the corridor, albeit in tighter circles. Nothing marks the walls. No distinguishing features, no seams, not even guards. Just lights overhead and stone all around.

"Please." My voice echoes in the silence, alone with the sound of my racing heartbeat.

I stare up at the ceiling, willing this all to be a dream.

When they drop me, I gasp, the wind knocked from my lungs. Still, I roll to my feet as quickly as I can. As I stand, fists clenched, teeth bared, I'm ready to fight and willing to lose. I won't be abandoned here without taking someone's teeth.

The Arvens stand back, side by side, unamused. Uninterested. Their focus is beyond me, behind me.

I whirl to find myself staring, not at another blank wall, but at a winding platform. Newly built, joining with other corridors or vaults or secret passages. It overlooks tracks.

Before my brain can attempt to connect the dots, before even the briefest whisper of excitement can ripple in my mind, Maven speaks, and smashes my hope to pieces.

"Don't get ahead of yourself." His voice echoes from my left, farther down the platform. He stands there, waiting, a guard of Sentinels around him, along with Evangeline and Ptolemus. All of them wear coats like mine, with ample fur to keep them warm. Both Samos children are resplendent in black sable.

Maven steps toward me, grinning with the confidence of a wolf. "The Scarlet Guard aren't the only ones capable of building trains."

The Undertrain rattled and sparked and rusted all over, a tin heap threatening to split apart at its welds. Still, I prefer it to this glamorous slug.

"Your friends gave me the idea, of course," Maven says from his plush seat across from me. He lazes, proud of himself. I see none of his psychic wounds today. They're carefully hidden, either pushed aside or forgotten for the moment.

I fight the urge to curl up in my own seat, and I keep both feet firmly planted on the floor. If something goes wrong, I have to be ready to run. As in the palace, I note every inch of Maven's train, looking for any kind of advantage. I find none. No windows, and Sentinels and Arven guards are planted at either end of the long compartment. It's furnished like a salon, with paintings, upholstered chairs and couches, even crystal lights tinkling with the motion of the train. But as with everything Silver, I see the cracks. The paint has barely dried. I can smell it. The train is brand-new, untested. At the other end of the compartment, Evangeline's eyes dart back and forth, betraying her attempt to seem calm. The train rattles her. I bet she can feel every piece of it moving at high speed. It's a hard sensation to get used to. I never could, always sensing the pulse of machines like the Undertrain or the Blackrun jet. I used to feel the electric blood—I guess she can feel the metal veins.

Her brother sits beside her, glowering at me. He shifts once or twice, nudging her shoulder. Her pained expression relents every time, calmed by his presence. I guess if the new train explodes, they're strong enough to survive the shrapnel.

"They managed to escape so quickly from the Bowl of Bones, riding the ancient rails all the way to Naercey before even I could get there. I figured it wouldn't be so bad to have a little escape route of my own," Maven continues, drumming his fingers on his knee. "You never know what new concoction my brother may dream up in his attempt to overthrow me. Best to be prepared."

"And what are you escaping from right now?" I mumble, trying to keep my voice low.

He only shrugs and laughs. "Don't act so glum, Mare. I'm doing us both a favor." Grinning, he sinks back in his seat. He kicks his feet up, putting them onto the seat beside me. I wrinkle my nose at the action, angling away. "One can only tolerate the prison of Whitefire Palace for so long."

Prison. I bite back a retort, forcing myself to humor him. *You have no idea what a prison is, Maven.*

Without windows or any kind of bearing, I have no way to know where we may be headed or how far this infernal machine can travel. It certainly feels as fast as the Undertrain, if not faster. I doubt we're heading south, to Naercey, a ruined city now abandoned even by the Scarlet Guard. Maven made such a show of destroying the tunnels after the infiltration of Archeon.

He lets me think, watching as I puzzle out the picture around us. He knows I don't have enough pieces to make it whole. Still, he lets me try, and doesn't offer any more explanation.

The minutes tick by, and I turn my focus to Ptolemus. My hate for him has only grown over the last few months. He killed my brother. He took Shade from this world. He would do the same to everyone I love if given the chance. For once, he's without his scaled armor. It makes him seem smaller, weaker, more vulnerable. I fantasize about cutting his throat and staining Maven's freshly painted walls with Silver blood.

"Something interest you?" Ptolemus snarls, meeting my gaze.

"Let her stare," Evangeline says. She leans back in her seat and tips her head, never breaking eye contact. "She can't do much more than that."

"We'll see," I growl back. In my lap, my fingers twitch.

Maven clucks his tongue, chiding. "Ladies."

Before Evangeline can retort, her focus shifts and she looks away, at the walls, at the floor, at the ceiling. Ptolemus matches her action. They sense something I can't. And then the train around us starts to slow, its gears and mechanisms screeching against iron tracks.

"Nearly there, then," Maven says, easing to his feet. He offers me a hand.

For a moment, I entertain the idea of biting his fingers off. Instead, I put my hand in his, ignoring the crawling sensation under my skin. When I stand, his thumb grazes the raised edge of my manacle beneath my glove. A firm reminder of his hold over me. I can't stand it and pull away, folding my arms over my chest to create a barrier between us. Something darkens in his bright eyes, and he puts up a shield of his own.

Maven's train stops so smoothly I barely feel it. The Arvens do, though, and snap to my side, surrounding me with exhausting familiarity. At least I'm not chained up or leashed.

Sentinels flank Maven as the Arvens flank me, their flaming robes and black masks foreboding as always. They let Maven set the pace, and he crosses the length of the compartment. Evangeline and Ptolemus follow, forcing me and my guards to take up the back of the strange procession. We follow them through the door, into a vestibule connecting one compartment to the next. Another door, another long stretch of opulent furnishings, this time in a dining room. Still no windows. Still no hint as to where we might be.

At the next vestibule, a door opens, not ahead, but to the right. The Sentinels duck through first, disappearing, then Maven goes, then the rest. We exit onto another platform, illuminated by harsh lights overhead. It's shockingly clean—another new construction, no doubt—but the air feels damp. Despite the meticulous order of the empty platform, something drips somewhere, echoing around us. I look left and right along the tracks. They fade into blackness on either side. This isn't the end of the line. I shudder to think how much progress Maven has made in only a few months' time.

Up we go, ascending a set of stairs. I resign myself to a long climb, remembering how deep the vault entrance was. So I'm surprised when the stairs level off quickly at another door. This one is reinforced steel, a foreboding omen of what might be beyond. A Sentinel grasps the bar lock and turns it with a grunt. The groan of a massive mechanism answers. Evangeline and Ptolemus don't lift a finger to help. Like me, they watch with thinly veiled fascination. I don't think they know much more than I do. Strange, for a house so closely tied to the king.

Daylight streams through as the steel swings back, revealing gray and blue beyond. Dead trees, their branches splayed like veins, reach into a clear winter sky. As we step out from the train bunker, I take a deep breath. Pine, the sharp cleanness of cold air. We're standing in a clearing surrounded by evergreens and naked oaks. The earth beneath me is frozen, hard-packed dirt beneath a few inches of snow. It chills my toes already.

I dig in my heels, earning one more second of open forest. The Arvens push me along, making me skid. I don't fight so much as methodically slow them down, all the while whipping my head back and forth. I try to get my bearings. Judging by the sun, now beginning its western descent, north is directly ahead of me.

Four military transports, polished to unnatural shine, idle in the path before us. Their engines hum, waiting, the heat of them sending plumes of steam into the air. It's easy to figure which belongs to Maven. The Burning Crown, red, black, and royal silver, is stamped on the sides of the grandest one. It stands almost two feet off the ground, with massive wheels and what must be a reinforced body. Bulletproof, fireproof, deathproof. Everything to protect the boy king.

He climbs inside without hesitation, his cape trailing behind. To my relief, the Arvens don't make me follow, and I'm bodily shoved into another transport. Mine is unmarked. As I duck in, straining for one last glimpse of the open sky, I notice Evangeline and Ptolemus approach their own transport. Black and silver, its metal body covered in spikes. Evangeline probably decorated it herself.

We lurch forward as Egg shuts the door behind him, locking me into the transport with four Arven guards. There is a soldier behind the wheel and a Sentinel in the seat next to him. I resign myself to another journey, crammed in with the Arvens.

At least the transport has windows. I watch, not wanting to blink, as we speed through an achingly familiar forest. When we reach the river, and the widely paved road running next to it, a longing burns through my chest.

That is the Capital River. My river. We're driving north, on the Royal Road. They could throw me from the transport right now, leave me in the dust with nothing, and I could find my way home. Tears spring to my eyes at the thought. What I would do, to myself or anyone else, for the chance to go back home?

But no one is there. No one I care about. They're gone, protected, far away. Home is no longer the place we're from. Home is safe with them. I hope.

I jump as other transports join our convoy. Military-grade, their bodies marked by the black sword of the army. I count almost a dozen in sight, and more stretching into the distance behind us. Many have Silver soldiers visible, either leaning off the side or perched on top in special seats and harnesses. All of them are on alert, ready to act. The Arvens don't look surprised by the new additions. They knew they were coming.

The Royal Road winds through towns on the riverbank. Red towns. We're too far south for us to pass through the Stilts yet, but that doesn't dampen my excitement. Brick mills come into view first, jutting out into the shallows of the river. We speed right for them, entering the outskirts of a thriving mill town. As much as I want to see more, I hope we don't stop. I hope Maven passes right through this place without disruption.

I mostly get my wish. The convoy slows but never stops, rolling through the heart of the town in all its glittering menace. Crowds line the street, waving us on. They cheer for the king, shouting his name, straining to see and be seen. Red merchants to millworkers, the old and young, hundreds of them pressing forward to get a better look. I expect to see Security officers pushing them on, forcing such a raucous welcome. I lean back against my seat, willing myself not to be seen. They're already forced to watch me sit by Maven's side. I don't want to add more fuel to that manipulative fire. To my relief, no one puts me on display. I merely sit and stare at my hands in my lap, hoping for the town to pass by as quickly as possible. In the palace, seeing what I see of Maven, knowing what I do about him, it's easy to forget he has most of the country in his pocket. His grand efforts to turn the tide of opinion against the Scarlet Guard and his enemies seem to be working. These people believe what he says, or perhaps have no opportunity to fight. I don't know which one is worse.

When the town recedes behind us, the cheers still echo in my head. All this for Maven, for the next step in whatever plan he has put in motion.

We must be beyond New Town; that much is clear. There's no pollution in sight. There aren't any estates either. I remember passing River Row on my first journey south, back when I was pretending to be Mareena. We sailed downriver from the Hall of the Sun all the way to Archeon, passing villages, towns, and the luxurious stretch of bank where many High Houses kept their family mansions. I try to remember the maps Julian used to show me. Instead, I only give myself a headache.

The sun dips lower as the convoy turns off after the third cheering town, moving in practiced formation onto a connecting roadway. Heading west. I try to swallow the dip of sadness rising inside. North pulls at me, beckoning even though I cannot follow. The places I know stretch farther and farther away.

I try to keep the compass in my head. West is the Iron Road. The way to the Westlakes, the Lakelands, the Choke. West is war and ruin.

Egg and Trio don't let me move much, so I have to crane my neck to see. I bite my lip as we pass through a set of gates, trying to spot a sign or a symbol. There isn't anything, just bars of wrought iron beneath shockingly green vines of flowering ivy. Well out of season.

The estate is palatial, at the far end of a road lined by immaculate hedges. We spit out into a wide square of stone, with the estate house occupying one side. Our convoy circles in front of it, stopping with the transports splayed out in an arced row. No crowds here, but guards are already waiting outside. The Arvens move quickly and I'm ushered from the transport.

I glare up at charming red brick and white trim, rows of polished windows hung with blooming flower boxes, fluted columns, florid balconies, and the largest tree I've ever seen bursting from the middle of the mansion. Its branches arc over the pointed roof, growing in conjunction with the structure. Not a twig or leaf out place, perfectly sculpted like a piece of living art. Magnolia, I think, judging by the white flowers and the perfumed smell. For a moment, I forget it's winter.

"Welcome, Your Majesty."

The voice isn't one I recognize.

Another girl, my age but tall, lean, pale as the snow that should be here, steps down from one of the many transports that joined ours. Her attention is on Maven, now clambering out of his own transport, and she glides by me to curtsy in front of him. I know her at a glance.

Heron Welle. She competed in Queenstrial long ago, drawing mighty trees out of earth while her house cheered her on. Like so many, she hoped to become a royal bride, chosen to marry Cal. Now she stands at Maven's command, eyes downcast, waiting for his order. She pulls her green-and-gold coat tighter around herself, a defense against the cold and Maven's stare.

Hers is one of the few houses I knew before I was forced into the Silver world. Her father governs the region I was born in. I used to watch his ship pass by on the river, and wave at its green flags with other stupid children.

Maven takes his time, needlessly donning his gloves for the short walk between his transport and the mansion. As he moves, the simple crown nestled in his black curls captures the waning sunlight, winking red and gold.

"Charming place, Heron," he says, making idle small talk. It sounds sinister coming from him. A threat.

"Thank you, Your Majesty. All is well in order for your arrival."

As I'm maneuvered closer, Heron spares a single glance for me. Her only acknowledgment of my existence. She has birdlike features, but on her angular figure they look elegant, refined, and sharply beautiful. I expect her eyes to be green, like everything else about her family and ability. Instead, they are a vibrant deep blue, set off by porcelain skin and auburn hair.

The rest of the transports empty their passengers. More colors, more houses, more guards and soldiers. I spot Samson among them, looking foolish in leather and fur dyed blue. The color and the cold make him paler than ever, a blond icicle of bloodlust. The others give him a wide berth as he prowls to Maven's side. I count a few dozen courtiers at a glance. Enough to make me wonder if even Governor Welle's mansion can hold us all.

Maven acknowledges Samson with a nod of his head before he sets off at a brisk pace, trotting toward the ornate stairs leading up from the square. Heron follows at his heels, as do the Sentinels in their usual flock. Everyone else follows, pulled along by an invisible tether.

A man who can only be the governor rushes from oak-and-gold doors, bowing as he walks. He seems bland in comparison to his home, unremarkable with his weak chin, dirty-blond hair, and a body neither fat nor thin. His clothes make up for it, and then some. He wears boots, butter-soft leather pants, and a jacket worked in ornate brocade, set with flashing emeralds at the collar and hems. They are nothing compared to the ancient medallion around his neck. It bounces against his chest as he walks, a jeweled emblem of the tree guarding his home.

"Your Majesty, I can't tell you how pleased we are to host you," he blusters, bowing one last time. Maven purses his lips into a thin smile, amused by the display. "It's such an honor to be the first destination on your coronation tour."

Disgust curls in my stomach. I'm seized by the image of me parading through the country, a few steps behind Maven, always at his beck and call. On-screen, in front of cameras, it feels degrading, but in person? Before crowds of people like the ones in the town? I may not survive it. Somehow I think I would prefer the prison of Whitefire.

Maven clasps hands with the governor, his smile spreading into something that could pass for genuine. He's good at the act, I'll give him that. "Of course, Cyrus, I could think of no better place to start. Heron speaks so highly of you," he adds, waving her to his side.

She steps quickly, eyes flashing to her father. A look of relief passes between them. Like everything Maven does, her presence is a careful manipulation and a message.

"Shall we?" Maven gestures to the mansion. He sets off, making the rest of us keep up. The governor hurries to flank Maven, still trying to at least look like he has some manner of control here.

Inside, droves of Red servants line the walls in their best uniforms, their shoes polished and eyes on the floor. None look at me, and I keep to myself, musing instead on the governor's mansion. I expected greenwarden artistry and I am not disappointed. Flowers of every kind dominate the foyer, blooming from crystal vases, painted on the walls, molded on the ceiling, worked in glass in the chandeliers or in stone mosaic on the floor. The smell should be overwhelming. Instead, it's intoxicating, calming with every breath. I inhale deeply, allowing myself this one small pleasure.

More of House Welle wait to greet the king, falling over themselves to bow or curtsy or compliment Maven on everything from his laws to his shoes. As he suffers them all, Evangeline joins us, having already discarded her furs with some poor servant.

I tense as she pauses next to me. All the greenery reflects in her clothing, giving her a sickly hue. With a jolt, I realize her father isn't here. He usually hovers between her and Maven at events like this, quick to step in when her temper threatens to boil over. But he isn't here now.

Evangeline says nothing, content to stare at Maven's back. I watch her watch him. Her fist clenches when the governor leans to whisper in Maven's ear. Then he beckons to one of the Silvers waiting, a tall, thin woman with jet-black hair, swooping cheekbones, and cool, ocher skin. If she's part of House Welle, she doesn't look it. Not a scrap of green on her. Instead, her clothes are gray-blue. The woman bows her head stiffly, careful to keep her eyes on Maven's face. His demeanor changes, his smile widening for an instant. He mutters something back, his head bobbing in excitement. I catch a single word.

"Now," he says. The governor and the woman oblige.

They walk away together, Sentinels in tow. I glance at the Arvens, wondering if we're meant to go too, but they don't move.

Evangeline doesn't either. And for whatever reason, her shoulders droop and her body relaxes. Some weight has fallen away.

"Stop staring at me," she snaps, knocking me from my observations.

I drop my head, letting her win this small, insignificant exchange. And I continue to wonder. *What does she know? What does she see that I don't?*

As the Arvens lead me away to whatever my cell for the evening may be, my heart sinks in my chest. I left Julian's books in Whitefire. Nothing will comfort me tonight.

FOURTEEN
Mare

Before my capture, I spent months crisscrossing the country, evading Maven's hunters and recruiting newbloods. I slept on a dirt floor, ate what we could steal, spent all my waking hours either feeling too much or too little, trying my best to stay ahead of all our demons. I didn't handle the pressure well. I shut down and shut out my friends, my family, everyone close to me. Anyone who wanted to help or understand. Of course I regret it. Of course I wish I could go back to the Notch, to Cal and Kilorn and Farley and Shade. I would do things differently. I would be different.

Sadly, no Silver or newblood can change the past. My mistakes cannot be undone, forgotten, or ignored. But I can make amends. I can do something now.

I've seen Norta, but as an outlaw. From the shadows. The view from Maven's side, as part of his extensive entourage, is like the difference between night and day. I shiver beneath my coat, hands clasped together for warmth. Between the crushing power of the Arvens and my manacles, I'm more susceptible to the temperature. Despite my hatred for him, I find myself inching closer to Maven, if only to take advantage of his constant heat. On his other side, Evangeline does the opposite, keeping her distance. She focuses more on Governor Welle than the king, and mutters to him occasionally, her voice low enough not to disturb Maven's speech.

"I'm humbled by your welcome, as well as your support for a young and untested king."

Maven's voice echoes, magnified by microphones and speakers. He doesn't read from any paper and somehow seems to make eye contact with every person crowding the city square below the balcony. Like everything about the king, even the location is a manipulation. We stand above hundreds, looking down, elevated beyond the reach of mere humans. The assembled people of Arborus, Governor Welle's own capital within his domain, stare up, faces raised in a way that makes my skin itch. The Reds jostle for a better look. They're easy to pick out, standing in bunches, covered in mismatched layers, their faces flushed red with cold, while the Silver citizenry sit in furs. Black-uniformed Security officers dot the crowd, vigilant as the Sentinels posted on the balcony and neighboring rooftops.

"It is my hope that this coronation tour allows me not only a deeper understanding of my kingdom, but a deeper understanding of you. Your struggles. Your hopes. Your fears. Because I am certainly afraid." A murmur goes through the crowd below, as well as the assembled party on the balcony. Even Evangeline glances sidelong at Maven, eyes narrowed over the flawless white collar of her fur wrap. "We are a kingdom on the brink, threatening to shatter under the weight of war and terrorism. It is my solemn duty to prevent this from happening, and save us from the horrors of whatever anarchy the Scarlet Guard wishes to instill. So many are dead, in Archeon, in Corvium, in Summerton.

My own mother and father among them. My own brother corrupted by the insurrectionist forces. But even so, I am not alone. I have you. I have Norta." He sighs slowly, a muscle ticking in his cheek. "And we will stand together against the enemies seeking to destroy our way of life, Red and Silver. I pledge my life to eradicating the Scarlet Guard, in any way possible."

The cheers below sound like metal on metal to me, screeching, a horrific noise. I keep my face still, expression carefully neutral. It serves me as well as any shield.

Every day his speech becomes firmer, his words carefully chosen and wielded like knives. Not once does he say the word *rebel* or *revolution*. The Scarlet Guard are always terrorists. Always murderers. Always enemies to our way of life, whatever that may be. And unlike his parents, he is masterfully careful to not insult Reds. The tour moves through Silver estates and Red cities alike. Somehow he seems at home in both, never flinching from the worst his kingdom has to offer. We even visit one of the factory slums, the kind of place I will never forget. I try not to cringe as we pass through the teetering dormitory buildings or when we step out into the polluted air. Maven alone seems unfazed, smiling for the workers and their tattooed necks. He doesn't cover his mouth like Evangeline or retch at the smell like so many others, myself included. He's better at this than I ever expected. He knows, as his parents could not or refused to understand, that seducing Reds to his Silver cause is perhaps his best chance of victory.

In another Red city, on the steps of a Silver mansion, he lays the next brick in a deadly road. One thousand poor farmers look on, not daring to believe, not daring to hope. Even I don't know what he's doing.

"My father's Measures were enacted after a deadly attack that left many government officials dead. It was his attempt to punish the Scarlet Guard for their evil, and, to my shame, it only punished you instead." Before the eyes of so many, he dips his face. It is a stirring sight. A Silver king bowing in front of the Red masses. I have to remind myself that this is Maven. This is a trick. "As of today, I decree the Measures lifted and abolished. They were the mistakes of a well-meaning king, but mistakes all the same."

He glances at me, just for a moment, but the moment is enough for me to know that he cares about my reaction.

The Measures. Conscription age lowered to fifteen. Restrictive curfew. Lethal punishment for any crime. All to turn the Red population of Norta against the Scarlet Guard. All gone in an instant, in one beat of a king's black heart. I should feel happy. I should feel proud. He's doing this because of me. Some part of him thinks this will please me. Some part thinks it will keep me safe. But watching the Reds, my own people, cheer for their oppressor only fills me with dread. I look down to find that my hands are shaking.

What is he doing? What is he planning?

To find out, I must fly as close to the flame as I dare.

He ends his appearances by walking through the crowd, shaking hands with as many Reds as he does Silvers. He cuts through them with ease, Sentinels flanking him in diamond formation. Samson Merandus always has his back, and I wonder how many feel the brush of his mind against their own. He's a better deterrent to a would-be assassin than anything else. Evangeline and I trail behind, both of us with guards. As always, I refuse to smile, to look, to touch anyone. It's safer for them this way.

The transports wait for us, their engines worked to an idle purr.

Above, the overcast sky darkens and I smell snow. While our guards close ranks, tightening formation to allow the king to enter his transport, I quicken my pace as best I can. My heart races and my breath puffs white on the cold air.

"Maven," I say aloud.

Despite the cheering crowd behind us, he hears me and pauses on the step of his transport. He turns with fluid grace, long cape whirling out to show bloodred lining. Unlike the rest of us, he doesn't need to wear fur to keep warm.

I draw my coat tighter, if only to give my nervous hands something more to do. "Did you really mean that?"

At his own transport, Samson stares, eyes boring into mine. He can't read my mind, not while I wear the manacles, but that doesn't make him useless. I rely on my real confusion to create the mask I want to wear.

I have no illusions where Maven is concerned. I know his twisted heart, and that it feels something for me. Something he wants to get rid of, but can never part with. When he waves me to his transport, beckoning for me to join him, I expect to hear Evangeline scoff or protest. She does neither, sweeping away to her own transport. In the cold, she doesn't glitter so brightly. She seems almost human.

The Arvens do not follow, though they try. Maven stops them with a look.

His transport is different from any other I've been in. The driver and front guard are separated from the passengers by a glass window, sealing us in together. The walls and windows are thick, bulletproof. The Sentinels don't slide in either, instead climbing directly onto the transport skeleton, taking up defensive positions at every corner. It's unsettling, to know there's a Sentinel with a gun sitting directly above me. But not as unsettling as the king sitting across from me, staring, waiting.

He eyes my hands, watching me rub my frozen fingers together.

"Are you cold?" he murmurs.

Quickly I tuck my hands under my legs to warm them up. The transport accelerates forward. "Are you really going to do it? End the Measures?"

"You think I would lie?"

I can't help but laugh darkly. In the back of my mind, I wish for a knife. I wonder if he could incinerate me before I slit his throat. "You? Never."

He smirks and shrugs, shifting to get more comfortable on the plush seats. "I meant what I said. The Measures were a mistake. Enacting them did more harm than good."

"To Reds? Or to you?"

"To both, of course. Although I would thank my father if I could. I expect righting his wrongs will win me support among your people." The cold detachment in his voice is discomforting, to say the least. I know now it comes from memories of his father. Poisoned things, drained of any love or happiness. "I'm afraid your Scarlet Guard won't have many sympathizers left by the time this is done. I'm going to end them without another useless war."

"You think giving people crumbs is going to placate them?" I growl, gesturing to the windows with my chin. Farms, barren for the winter, stretch out to the hills. "Oh, lovely, the king has given me back two years of my child's life. Doesn't matter that they're still going to be taken away eventually."

His smirk only widens. "You think that?"

"I do. That's how this kingdom is. That's how it's always been."

"We'll see." Leaning farther, he puts a foot up on the seat next to me. He even removes his crown, spins it between his hands. Bronze and iron flames glint in the low light, reflecting my face and his. Slowly, I edge away, crowding myself into the corner.

"I suppose I taught you a hard lesson," he says. "You missed so much last time, and now you trust nothing. You're always watching, looking for information you're never going to use. Have you figured out where we're going yet? Or why?"

I take a breath. I feel like I'm back in Julian's classroom, being tested on a map. The stakes feel much higher here. "We're on the Iron Road now, heading northwest. To Corvium."

He has the gall to wink. "Close."

"We're not . . ." I blink quickly, trying to think. My brain buzzes through all the pieces I've jealously collected over the days. Shards of news, bits of gossip. "Rocasta? Are you going after Cal?"

Maven settles back farther, amused. "So small-minded. Why would I waste time chasing rumors of my exiled brother? I have a war to end and a rebellion to prevent."

"A war to . . . end?"

"You said yourself, the Lakelands will overthrow us if given the chance. I'm not going to let that happen. Especially with Piedmont focused elsewhere, on their own multitude of troubles. I have to handle these matters myself." Despite the warmth of the transport, due in large part to the fire king sitting in front of me, I feel a finger of ice trail down my spine.

I used to dream of the Choke. The place where my father lost his leg, where my brothers almost lost their lives. Where so many Reds die. A waste of ash and blood.

"You're not a warrior, Maven. You're not a general or a soldier. How can you possibly hope to defeat them when—"

"When others couldn't? When Father couldn't? When Cal couldn't?" he snaps. Each word sounds like the crack of bone. "You're right, I'm not like them. War is not what I was made for."

Made. He says it with such ease. Maven Calore is not his own self. He told me as much. He is a construct, a creation of his mother's additions and subtractions. A mechanical, a machine, soulless and lost. What a horror, to know that someone like this holds our fates in the palm of his quivering hand.

"It will be no loss, not truly," he drones on to distract us both. "Our military economy will simply turn its attention to the Scarlet Guard. And then whoever we decide to fear next. Whatever avenue is best for population control—"

If not for the manacles, my rage would certainly turn the transport into a heap of electrified scrap. Instead, I jump forward, lunging, hands stretched out to grab him by the collar. My fingers worm beneath the lapels of his jacket and I seize fabric in both fists. Without thinking, I shove, pushing, smashing him back into his seat. He flinches, a hand's breadth from my face, breathing hard. He's just as surprised as I am. No easy thing. I immediately go numb with shock, unable to move, paralyzed by fear.

He stares up at me, eye to eye, lashes dark and long. I'm so close to him I can see his pupils dilate. I wish I could disappear. I wish I were on the other side of the world. Slowly, steadily, his hands find mine. They tighten on my wrists, feeling manacle and bone. Then he pries my fists from his chest. I let him move me, too terrified for anything else. My skin crawls at his touch, even beneath gloves. I attacked him. Maven. The king. One word, one tap on the window, and a Sentinel will rip out my spine. Or he could kill me himself. Burn me alive.

"Sit back down," he whispers, every word sharp. Giving me one single chance.

Like a scrambling cat, I do as he says, retreating to my corner.

He recovers faster than I do and shakes his head with the ghost of a smile. Quickly he smooths his jacket and brushes back a lock of rumpled hair.

"You're a smart girl, Mare. Don't tell me you never connected those particular dots."

My breath comes hard, as if there's a stone sitting on my chest. I feel heat rise in my cheeks, both out of anger and shame. "They want our coast. Our electricity. We want their farmlands, resources . . ." I stumble over the words I was taught in a ramshackle schoolhouse. The look on Maven's face only becomes more amused. "In Julian's books . . . the kings disagreed. Two men arguing over a chessboard like spoiled children. They're the reason for all this. For a hundred years of war."

"I thought Julian taught you to read between the lines. To see the words left unsaid." He shakes his head, despairing of me. "I suppose even he could not undo your years of poor education. Another well-used tactic, I might add."

That I knew. That I've always known, and lamented. Reds are kept stupid, kept ignorant. It makes us weaker than we already are. My own parents can't even read.

I blink away hot tears of frustration. *You knew all this,* I tell myself, trying to calm down. *The war is a ruse, a cover to keep Reds under control. One conflict may end, but another will always begin.*

It twists my insides to realize how rigged the game has been, for everyone, for so very long.

"Stupid people are easier to control. Why do you think my mother kept my father around for so long? He was a drunk, a heartbroken imbecile, blind to so much, content to keep things as they were. Easy to control, easy to use. A person to manipulate—and blame."

Furious, I swipe at my face, trying to hide any evidence of my emotions. Maven watches anyway, his expression softening a little. As if that helps anything. "So what are two Silver kingdoms going to do once they stop throwing Reds at each other?" I hiss. "Start marching us off cliffs at random? Pull names out of a lottery?"

He rests a hand on his chin. "I can't believe Cal never told you any of this. Although he wasn't really jumping at the opportunity to change things, not even for you. Probably didn't think you could handle it— or, well, perhaps he didn't think you would understand it—"

My fist slams against the bulletproof glass of the window. It smarts instantly, and I bury myself in the pain, using it to keep any thoughts of Cal at bay. I can't let myself fall into that drowning spiral, even if it's true. Even though Cal was once willing to uphold these horrors. "Don't," I snap at him. "Don't."

"I'm not a fool, little lightning girl." His snarl matches my own. "If you're going to play in my head, I'm going to play in yours. It's what we're good at."

I was cold before, but now the heat of his anger threatens to consume me. Feeling sick, I press my cheek against the cool glass of the window and shut my eyes. "Don't compare me to you. We're not the same."

"People like us," he scoffs. "We lie to everyone. Especially ourselves."

I want to punch the window again. Instead, I tuck my fists tight under my arms, trying to make myself smaller. Maybe I'll just shrink away and disappear. With every breath, I regret getting into his transport more and more.

"You'll never get the Lakelands to agree," I say.

I hear him laugh deep in his throat. "Funny. They already have."

My eyes fly open in shock.

He nods, looking pleased with himself. "Governor Welle facilitated a meeting with one of their top ministers. He has contacts in the north and is easily . . . persuaded."

"Probably because you hold his daughter hostage."

"Probably," he agrees.

So that's what this tour is. A solidifying of power, the creation of a new alliance. A twisting of arms and bending of wills by whatever means necessary. I knew it was for something other than spectacle, but this—this I could not fathom. I think of Farley, the Colonel, their Lakelander soldiers pledged to the Scarlet Guard. What will a truce do to them?

"Don't look so glum. I'm ending a war millions died for, and bringing peace to a country that no longer knows the meaning of the word. You should be proud of me. You should be thanking me. Don't—" He puts his hands up in defense as I spit at him.

"You really need to figure out another way to express your anger," he grumbles, wiping at his uniform.

"Take off my manacles and I'll show you one."

He barks out a laugh. "Yes, of course, Miss Barrow."

Outside, the sky darkens and the world fades to gray. I put a palm to the glass, willing myself to fall through. Nothing happens. I'm still here.

"I must say, I am surprised," he adds. "We have far more in common with the Lakelands than you think."

My jaw tightens and I speak through gritted teeth. "You both use Reds as slaves and cannon fodder."

He sits up so quickly I flinch. "We both want to end the Scarlet Guard."

It's almost comical. Every step I take explodes in my face. I tried to save Kilorn from conscription and maimed my sister instead. I became a maid to help my family and within hours became a prisoner. I believed Maven's words and Maven's false heart. I trusted Cal to choose me. I raided a prison to free people and ended up clutching Shade's corpse. I sacrificed myself to save the people I love. I gave Maven a weapon. And now, try as I might to thwart his reign from the inside, I think I've done something much worse. What will a united Lakelands and Norta look like?

Despite what Maven said, we head to Rocasta anyway, barreling on after more coronation stops throughout the Westlakes region. We won't stay. Either there isn't a stately home suitable enough for Maven's court, or he simply doesn't want to be there. I can see why. Rocasta is a military city. Not a fortress like Corvium, but built to support the army all the same. An ugly thing, formed for function. The city sits several miles off the banks of Lake Tarion, and the Iron Road runs through its heart. It bisects Rocasta like a blade, separating the wealthier Silver sector of the city from the Red. With no walls to speak of, the city creeps up on me. The shadows of houses and buildings appear out of the white blindness of a blizzard. Silver storms work to keep our road clear, battling the weather to keep the king on schedule. They stand on top of our transports, directing the snow and ice around us with even motions. Without them, the weather would be much worse, a hammer of brutal winter.

Still, snow blasts against the windows of my transport, obscuring the world outside. There are no more windweavers from the talented House Laris. They're either dead or gone, having fled with the other rebelling houses, and the Silvers remaining can only do so much.

From what little I can see, Rocasta carries on despite the storm. Red workers move to and fro, clutching at lanterns, their lights bobbing through the haze like fish in murky water. They're used to this kind of weather so close to the lakes.

I settle down into my long coat, glad for the warmth, even if the coat is a bloodred monstrosity. I glance at the Arvens, still clad in their usual white.

"Are you scared?" I chatter to the empty air. I don't wait for their nonexistent response, all of them quietly focused on ignoring my voice. "We could lose you in a storm like this." I sigh to myself, crossing my arms. "Wishful thinking."

Maven's transport rolls ahead of mine, spotted with Sentinel guards. Like my coat, they stand out sharply in the snowstorm, their flaming robes a beacon to the rest of us. I'm surprised they don't take off their masks despite the low visibility. They must revel in looking inhuman and frightening—monsters to defend another monster.

Our convoy turns off the Iron Road somewhere near the center of the city, speeding down a wide avenue crisscrossed with twinkling lights. Opulent town houses and walled city manors rise up from the street, their windows warm and inviting. Up ahead, a clock tower fades in and out of visibility, occasionally obscured by drifting gusts of snow. It tolls three o'clock as we approach, gonging peals of sound that seem to reverberate inside my rib cage.

Dark shadows plunge along the street, deepening with every passing second as the storm gets stronger. We're in the Silver sector, evidenced by the lack of trash and bedraggled Reds roaming the alleys. Enemy territory. As if I'm not already as deeply behind enemy lines as possible.

At court, there were rumors about Rocasta, and Cal in particular. A few soldiers had received a tip that he was in the city, or some old man had thought he'd seen him and wanted rations in exchange for the information. But the same could be said of so many places. He'd be stupid to come here, to a city still firmly under Maven's control. Especially with Corvium so close by. If he's smart, he is far away, well hidden, helping the Scarlet Guard as best he can. Strange to think that House Laris, House Iral, and House Haven rebelled in his honor, for an exiled prince who will never claim the throne. What a waste.

The administrative building beneath the clock tower is ornate compared to the rest of Rocasta, more akin to the columns and crystal of Whitefire Palace. Our convoy glides to a halt before it, spitting us out into the snow.

I hustle up the steps as quickly as I can, drawing up the infuriating red collar against the cold. Inside, I expect warmth and a waiting audience to hang on Maven's every calculated word. Instead, we find chaos.

This was once a grand meeting hall: the walls are lined with plush benches and seating, now pushed aside. Most have been stacked on top of one another, cleared to make room on the main floor. I'm seized by the scent of blood. A strange thing for a hall full of Silvers.

But then I see: it is not so much a hall as a hospital.

All the wounded are officers, laid out on cots in neat rows. I count three dozen at a glance. Their liveried uniforms and neat medals mark them as military of varying ranks, with insignia from any number of High Houses. Skin healers attend as fast as they can, but only two are on duty, marked by the red-and-silver crosses on their shoulders. They sprint back and forth, seeing to injuries in order of seriousness. One jumps up from a moaning man to kneel over a woman coughing up silver blood, her chin metal-bright with the liquid.

"Sentinel Skonos," Maven says gravely. "Help who you can."

One of his masked guards reacts with a stilted bow, breaking rank with the rest of the king's defenders.

More of us file in, crowding an already-crowded room. A few members of court abandon propriety to search the soldiers, looking for family. Others are simply horrified. Their kind aren't meant to bleed. Not like this.

Ahead of me, Maven looks back and forth, hands on his hips. If I didn't know him better, I would think him affected, angry or sad. But this is about to be another performance. Even though these are Silver officers, I feel a pang of pity for them.

The hospital hall is proof my Arvens are not made of stone. To my surprise, Kitten is the one to break first, her eyes watering with tears as she looks around. She fixes her gaze on the far end of the hall. White shrouds cover bodies. Corpses. A dozen dead.

At my feet, a young man hisses out a breath. He keeps a hand pressed to his chest, putting pressure on what must be an internal wound. I lock eyes with him, noting his uniform and his face. Older than me, classically handsome beneath streaks of silver blood. Black-and-gold house colors. House Provos, a telky. It doesn't take him long to recognize me. His brows raise a little in realization, and he struggles for another breath. Beneath my gaze, he shakes. He's afraid of me.

"What happened?" I ask him. In the din of the hall, my voice is barely more than a whisper.

I don't know why he responds. Maybe he thinks I'll kill him if he doesn't. Maybe he wants someone to know what's really going on.

"Corvium," he murmurs back. The Provos officer wheezes, fighting to push out the words. "Scarlet Guard. It's a massacre."

Fear shivers in my voice. "For who?"

He hesitates, and I wait.

Finally he draws a ragged breath.

"Both."

FIFTEEN
Cameron

I didn't know what could possibly spur the exiled prince to action—until King Maven began his bleeding coronation tour. Clearly a ruse, definitely another plot. And it was headed straight for us. Everyone suspected an attack. And we had to strike first.

Cal was right about one thing. Taking the walls of Corvium was our best plan of action.

So he did it two days ago.

Working in conjunction with the Colonel and rebels already inside the fortress city, Cal led a strike force of Scarlet Guard and newblood soldiers. The blizzard was their cover, and the shock of an assault served them well. Cal knew better than to ask me to join. I waited back in Rocasta with Farley. Both of us paced by the radio, eager for news. I fell asleep, but she shook me awake before dawn, grinning. We held the walls. Corvium never saw it coming. The city boiled in chaos.

And we could no longer stay behind. Not even me. Admittedly, I wanted to go. Not to fight, but to see what victory actually looked like. And of course to get one step closer to the Choke, my brother, and some semblance of purpose.

So here I am, shrouded in the tree line with the rest of Farley's unit, looking out at black walls and blacker smoke. Corvium burns from within. I can't see much, but I know the reports. Thousands of Red soldiers, some spurred on by the Guard, turned on their officers as soon as Cal and the Colonel attacked. The city was already a powder keg. Fitting that a fire prince lit the fuse and let it explode. Even now, a day later, the fighting continues as we take the city, street by street. The occasional burst of gunfire breaks the relative silence, making me flinch.

I look away, trying to see farther than human reach. The sky here is dark already, the sun obscured by a cloudy gray sky. To the northwest, in the Choke, the clouds are black, heavy with ash and death. Morrey is out there, somewhere. Even though Maven released the underage conscripts, his unit hasn't moved, according to our last intelligence reports. They're the farthest away, deep in a trench. And the Scarlet Guard happens to be currently occupying the place his unit would return to. I try to block out the image of my twin huddled against the cold, his uniform too big, his eyes dark and sunken. But the thought is burned into my brain. I turn away, back to Corvium, to the task at hand. I need to keep my focus here. The sooner we take the city, the sooner we can get the conscripts moving. *And then what?* I ask myself. *Send him home? To another hellhole?*

I have no answers for the voice in my head. I can barely stomach the idea of sending Morrey back to the factories of New Town, even if it means sending him back to our parents. They're my next goal, after I get my brother back. One impossible dream after another.

"Two Silvers just threw a Red soldier from a tower." Ada squints into a pair of binoculars. Next to her, Farley remains still, arms calmly folded across her chest.

Ada continues to scan the walls, reading signals. In the gray light, her golden skin takes on a sallow hue. I hope she isn't getting sick.

"They're solidifying their position, retreating and regrouping into the central sector, behind the second ring wall. I calculate fifty at least," she murmurs.

Fifty. I try to swallow my fear. I tell myself there's no reason to be afraid. There's an army between us and them. And no one is stupid enough to try to force me anywhere I don't want to go. Not now, not with months of training behind me.

"Casualties?"

"A hundred of the Silver garrison dead. Most of the injured escaped with the rest into the wilderness. Probably to Rocasta. And there were less than a thousand in the city. Many had defected to the rebelling houses before Cal's assault."

"What about Cal's newest report?" Farley asks Ada. "The Silvers deserting?"

"I included that in my calculations." She almost sounds annoyed. Almost. Ada has a calmer disposition than any of us. "Seventy-eight are in holding now, under Cal's protection."

I put my hands on my hips, setting my weight. "There's a difference between defection and surrender. They don't want to join us; they just don't want to end up dead. They know Cal will show mercy."

"Would you rather he kill them all? Set everyone against us?" Farley snaps back, turning to me. After a second, she waves a hand dismissively. "There's over five hundred of them still out there, ready to come back and slaughter us all."

Ada ignores our jabbering and keeps her vigil. Up until she joined the Scarlet Guard, she was a housemaid to a Silver governor. She's used to much worse than us. "I see Julian and Sara above the Prayer Gate," she says.

I feel a squeeze of comfort. When Cal radioed in, he didn't mention any casualties on his team, but nothing is ever certain. I'm glad Sara is all right. I squint toward the forbidding Prayer Gate, looking for the black-and-gold entry on the east end of the Corvium walls. On top of the parapets, a red flag waves back and forth, barely a glimmer of color against the overcast sky. Ada translates. "They're signaling for us. Safe passage."

She glances at Farley, waiting for her order. With the Colonel in the city, she's the ranking officer here, and her word is good as law. Though she gives no indication of it, I realize she must be weighing her options. We have to cross open ground to get to the gates. It could easily be a trap.

"Do you see the Colonel?"

Good. She doesn't trust a Silver. Not with our lives.

"No," Ada breathes. She scans the walls again, her bright eyes taking in every block of stone. I watch her motions as Farley waits, still and stern. "Cal is with them."

"Fine," Farley says suddenly, her eyes lividly blue and resolute. "Let's move out."

I follow her begrudgingly. As much as I may hate to admit it, Cal isn't the type to double-cross us. Not fatally, at least. He's not his brother. I meet Ada's eyes over Farley's shoulder. The other newblood inclines her head a little as we walk.

I shove clenched fists into my pockets. If I look like a sullen teenager, I don't care. That's what I am: a scared, sullen teenager who can kill with a look. Fear eats me up. Fear of the city—and fear of myself.

I haven't used my ability outside training in months, not since the magnetron bastards pulled our jet out of the sky. But I remember what it feels like, to use silence as a weapon. In Corros Prison, I killed people with it. Horrible people. Silvers keeping others like me trapped to slowly die. And the memory still makes me sick. I felt their hearts stop. I felt their deaths like they were happening to me. Such power—it frightens me. It makes me wonder what I could become. I think of Mare, the way she ricocheted between violent rage and numb detachment. Is that the price of abilities like ours? Do we have to choose—become empty, or become monsters?

We set out in silence, all of us hyperaware of our precarious position. We stand out sharply in the fresh snow, picking along in one another's footprints. The newbloods in Farley's unit are particularly on edge. One of Mare's own, Lory, leads us with the awareness of a bloodhound, her head whipping back and forth. Her senses are incredibly heightened, so if there's any imminent attack, she'll see it, hear it, or smell it coming. After the raid on Corros Prison, after Mare was taken, she started dyeing her hair bloodred. It looks like a wound against the snow and iron sky. I level my gaze on her shoulder blades, ready to run if she so much as hesitates.

Even pregnant, Farley manages to look commanding. She pulls the rifle from her back, holds it in both hands. But she isn't as alert as the others. Again her eyes slide in and out of focus. I feel a familiar pang of sadness for her.

"Did you come here with Shade?" I ask her quietly.

She snaps her head in my direction. "Why do you say that?"

"For a spy, you're pretty easy to read sometimes."

Her fingers drum along the barrel of her gun. "Like I said, Shade is still our main source of information on Corvium. I ran his operation here. That's all."

"Sure, Farley."

We continue on in silence. Our breath mists on the air and the cold sets in, taking my toes first. In New Town we had winter, but never like this. Something to do with the pollution. And the heat from the factories kept us sweating at work, even in the depths of winter.

Farley is a Lakelander by birth, better suited to the weather. She doesn't seem to notice the snow or the prickling cold. Her mind is still obviously somewhere else. With someone else.

"I guess it's a good thing I didn't go after my brother," I mutter to the silence. Both for myself and for her. Something else to think about. "I'm glad he isn't here."

She glances at me sidelong. Her eyes narrow with suspicion. "Is Cameron Cole admitting she was wrong about something?"

"I can do that much. I'm not Mare."

Another person might think that rude to say. Farley grins instead. "Shade was stubborn too. Family trait."

I expect his name to act as an anchor, dragging her down. Instead, it keeps her moving, one foot in front of the other. One word after the next. "I met him a few miles from here. I was supposed to be recruiting Whistle operatives from the Nortan black market. Use organizations already in place to better facilitate the Scarlet Guard. The Whistle in the Stilts gave me a lead on some soldiers up here who might be willing to coordinate."

"Shade was one of them."

She nods, thoughtful. "He was assigned to Corvium with the support troops. An officer's aide. A good position for him, even better for us. He fed the Scarlet Guard miles of information, all funneled through me. Until it became clear he couldn't stay any longer. He was being transferred to another legion. Someone knew he had an ability, and they were going to execute him for it."

I've never heard this story. I doubt few have. Farley is not exactly forthcoming with her personal history. Why she's telling me now, I can't say. But I can see she needs to. I let her talk, giving her what she wants.

"And then when his sister . . . I've never seen him so terrified. We watched Queenstrial together. Watched her fall, watched her lightning. He thought the Silvers were going to kill her. You know the rest of that, I assume." She bites a lip, looking down the length of her rifle. "It was his idea. We already had to get him out of the army to protect him. So he faked his execution report. Helped with the paperwork himself. Then he was gone. Silvers don't care enough to follow through on dead Reds. Of course, his family minded. That part stuck him for a while."

"But he still did it." I try to be understanding, but I can't imagine putting my own family through something like that, not for anything.

"He had to. And—and it served as a good motivation. Mare joined up after she found out. One Barrow for another."

"So that part of her speech wasn't a lie." I think about what Mare was forced to say, glaring down a camera like it was a firing squad. *They asked if I wanted vengeance for his death.* "No wonder she has personality issues. No one tells the girl the truth about anything."

"It'll be a long road back for her," Farley murmurs.

"For everyone."

"And now she's on that infernal tour with the king," Farley rattles on. She spools up like a machine, her voice gaining momentum and strength with every passing second. Shade's ghost disappears. "It will make things easier. Still horribly difficult, of course, but the knot is loosened."

"Is there a plan in place? She's getting closer by the day. Arborus, the Iron Road—"

"She was in Rocasta yesterday."

The silence around us shifts. If the rest of our unit weren't listening before, they certainly are now. I look back to lock my gaze on Ada. Her liquid-amber eyes widen, and I can almost see the cogs turning in her flawless mind.

Farley presses on. "The king visited the wounded soldiers evacuated from the first wave of attack. I didn't know until we were halfway here. If I had, maybe . . ." she breathes. "Well, it's too late for that now."

"The king practically travels with an army," I tell her. "She's guarded night and day. There was nothing you could have done, not with just us."

Still her cheeks flush, and not from the cold. Her fingers keep tapping idly on the stock of her gun. "Probably not," she replies. "Probably not." Softer, to convince herself.

Corvium casts a shadow over us, and the temperature drops in the gloomy shade. I pull up the neck of my collar farther, trying to burrow into its warmth. The black-walled monstrosity seems to howl at us.

"There. The Prayer Gate." Farley points to an open mouth of iron fangs and golden teeth. Blocks of Silent Stone line the arch, but I can't feel them. They don't affect me. To my relief, Red soldiers man the gate, marked by rust-colored uniforms and worn boots. We move forward, off the snowy road and into the jaws of Corvium. Farley looks up at the Prayer Gate as we pass through, her eyes wide, blue, and trembling. Under her breath, I hear her whisper something to herself.

"As you enter, you pray to leave. As you leave, you pray never to return."

Even though no one is listening, I pray too.

Cal bends over a desk, knuckles pressed against the flat of the wood. His armor piles in a heap in the corner, plates of black leather discarded to show the muscled hulk of the young man beneath. Sweat plasters black hair to his forehead and paints glistening lines of exertion down his neck. Not from heat, though his ability warms the room better than any fire. No, this is fear. Shame. I wonder how many Silvers he was forced to kill. *Not enough,* part of me whispers. Still, the sight of him, the horrors of the siege plainly written on his face, gives even me enough reason to pause. I know this is not easy. It can't be.

He stares at nothing, bronze eyes boring holes. He doesn't move when I enter the room, trailing behind Farley. She goes to the Colonel, sitting across from him, one hand on his temple, the other smoothing a map or schematic of some kind. Probably Corvium, judging by the octagonal shape and expanding rings that must be walls.

I feel Ada at my back, hesitant to join us. I have to give her a nudge. She's better at this than anyone, her exquisite brain a gift to the Scarlet Guard. But a maid's training is hard to break.

"Go on," I murmur, putting a hand on her wrist. Her skin isn't as dark as mine, but in the shadows we all start to blend together.

She gives me a tiny nod and an even tinier smile. "Which ring are they in? Central?"

"Core tower," the Colonel replies. He raps the corresponding place on the map. "Well fortified, even at the subterranean levels. Learned that the hard way."

Ada sighs. "Yes, the core is built for something like this. A final stand, well armed and provisioned. Sealed twice over. And stuffed to the brim with fifty trained Silvers. With the bottleneck, there might as well be five times that number in there."

"Like spiders in a hole," I mutter.

The Colonel scoffs. "Maybe they'll start to eat each other."

Cal's wince does not go unnoticed. "Not while a common enemy hammers at the door. Nothing unites Silvers so much as someone to hate." He doesn't look up from the desk, keeping his eyes fixed on the wood. The meaning is clear. "Especially now that everyone knows the king is near." His face darkens, a storm cloud. "They can wait."

With a low growl, Farley finishes the thought for him. "And we can't."

"If ordered, the legions of the Choke can hard march back here in a day's time. Less if . . . motivated." Ada wavers over the last word. She doesn't need to elaborate. I can already see my brother, technically freed by Maven's new laws, being driven on by Silver officers, forced to run through the snow. Only to throw himself against his own.

"Surely the Reds would join us," I say, thinking aloud, if only to combat the images in my head. "Let Maven send his armies. It will only bolster ours. The soldiers will turn like the ones here did."

"She might have a point—" the Colonel begins, agreeing with me for once. A strange sensation. But Farley cuts him off.

"Might. The garrison in Corvium has been stirred up for months, inciting its own havoc, pushed and prodded and boiled to this explosion. I can't say the same for the legions. Or the amount of Silvers he'll convince into service."

Ada agrees with her, nodding along. "King Maven has been careful with the Corvium narrative. He paints everything here as terrorism, not rebellion. Anarchy. The work of a bloodthirsty, genocidal Scarlet

Guard. The Reds of the legions, the Reds of the kingdom, have no idea what's happening here."

Seething, Farley puts a protective hand on her belly. "I've lost enough on ifs and maybes."

"We all have," Cal says, his voice distant. Finally he pulls away from the desk and turns his back on us all. He crosses to the window in a few long strides, looking out over a city still burning.

Smoke drifts on the icy wind, spitting black into the sky. It reminds me of the factories. I shudder to remember them. The tattoo on my neck itches, but I don't scratch with my crooked fingers. Broken too many times to count. Sara asked to fix them once. I didn't let her. Like the tattoo, like the smoke, they remind me of what I came from, and what no one else should endure.

"I don't suppose you have any ideas for this?" Farley asks, taking the map from her father's hands. She glances sidelong at the exiled prince.

Cal shrugs, his broad shoulders rolling in silhouette. "Too many. All bad. Unless—".

"I'm not going to let them walk out of here," the Colonel snaps. He sounds annoyed. I suppose they argued this through already. "Maven is too close. They'll run to his side and come back with a vengeance, with more warriors."

The gleaming bracelet at Cal's wrist flickers, birthing sparks that travel along his arm in a quick burst of red flame. "Maven is coming anyway! You heard the reports. He's already in Rocasta and moving west. He's marching here in a parade, waving and smiling to hide that he's coming to take back Corvium. And he'll do it if you fight him in a broken city with our backs against a cage of wolves!" He spins around to face the Colonel, shoulders still smoldering with embers. Usually he can control himself enough to save his clothes. Not so now. Smoke clings to him, revealing charred holes in his undershirt. "A battle on two fronts is suicide."

"And what about hostages? You mean to tell me there's no one of value in that tower?" the Colonel barks back.

"Not to Maven. He already has the only person he would ever trade anything for."

"So we can't starve them, can't release them, can't bargain." Farley ticks off words on her hand.

"And you can't kill them all." I tap a finger against my lip. Cal looks at me, surprised. I simply shrug. "If there was a way, if it was acceptable, the Colonel would have done it already."

"Ada?" Farley prods softly. "Can you see anything we can't?"

Her eyes fly back and forth, scanning the schematic as well as her memories. Figures, strategies, everything at her mammoth disposal. Her silence is not at all comforting.

"What we need is that bleeding seer," I mumble. I never met Jon, the one who made it possible for Mare to find and capture me. But I've seen him enough on Maven's broadcasts. "Make him do the work for us."

"If he wanted to help, he'd be here. But that damned ghost is in the wind," Cal curses. "Didn't even have the decency to take Mare with him when he escaped."

"No use dwelling on what we can't change." Farley scuffs her boot against the cold floor. "So is brute force the only thing left to us? Take the tower down stone by stone? Pay for every inch with a gallon of blood?"

Before Cal can explode again, the door wrenches open. Julian and Sara all but tumble inside, both of them wide-eyed and silver-flushed. The Colonel jumps to his feet, in surprise and defense. None of us are fools where Silvers are concerned. Our fear of them is bone-deep, bred into our blood.

"What is it?" he asks, his red eye a scarlet gleam. "Done with the interrogation so soon?"

Julian bristles at the word *interrogation*, sneering. "My questions are a mercy compared to what you would do."

"Pah," Farley scoffs. She eyes Cal and he shifts, embarrassed under her gaze. "Don't tell me about Silver mercy."

I care little for Julian and trust him less, but the look on Sara's face is startling. She stares at me, her gray face full of pity and fear. "What is it?" I ask her, though I know only Julian can answer. Even in Corvium, she hasn't yet found another skin healer willing to return her tongue. All of them must be in the core tower, or dead.

"General Macanthos oversees training command," Julian says. Like Sara, he glances at me with hesitation. My pulse pounds in my ears. Whatever he's about to say, I won't like. "Before the siege, part of a legion was recalled for further instruction. They were unfit to man the trenches. Even for Reds."

My rushing blood starts to howl in my ears, a gale that almost drowns Julian out. I feel Ada step to my side, her shoulder brushing mine. She knows where this is going. I do too.

"We retrieved the rolls. A few hundred children of the Dagger Legion, called back to Corvium. Unreleased, even after Maven's decree. We accounted for most, but some . . ." Julian forces himself on, though he stumbles over the words. "They're hostages. In the core, with the remaining Silver officers."

I put a hand to the cool office wall, letting it steady me. My silence begs, pushing beneath my skin, wanting to expand and drag down everything in the room. I have to say the words myself, because apparently Julian won't. "My brother is in there."

The Silver bastard hesitates, drawing it out. Finally, he speaks. "We think so."

The roar of my thrumming heart overpowers their voices. I hear nothing as I run from the room, evading their hands, sprinting down through the administrative headquarters. If anyone follows, I don't know. I don't care.

The only thing on my mind is Morrey. Morrey and the fifty soon-to-be corpses standing between us.

I am not Mare Barrow. I will not give my brother to this.

My silence curls around me, heavy as smoke, soft as feathers, dripping from every pore like sweat. It isn't a physical thing. It won't tear the core down for me. My ability is for flesh and flesh alone. I've been practicing. It scares me, but I need it. Like a hurricane, the silence churns around me, surrounding the eye of a growing storm.

I don't know where I'm going, but Corvium is easy to navigate. And the core is self-explanatory. The city is orderly, well planned, a giant gear. I understand that. My feet slam against the pavement, propelling me through the outer ward. On my left, the high walls of Corvium scrape at the sky. To the right, barracks, offices, training facilities pile against the second ring of granite walls. I have to find the next gate, start working inward. My crimson scarf is camouflage enough. I look like Scarlet Guard. I could be Scarlet Guard. The Red soldiers let me run, too distracted or too excited or too busy to care about another wayward rebel tearing through their midst. They've overthrown their masters. I'm as good as invisible to them.

But not to His Bleeding Royal Highness, Tiberias Calore.

He grabs my arm, forcing me to spin. If not for my silence pulsing around us, I know he would be on fire. The prince is smart, using our momentum to toss me back—and keep himself out of my deadly hands.

"Cameron!" he shouts, one hand outstretched. His fingers flicker, the flames on them gasping for air. When he takes another step back, planting himself firmly in my path, they blaze stronger, licking up to his elbow. His armor is back on. Interlocking plates of leather and steel thicken his silhouette. "Cameron, you'll die if you go in the tower alone. They'll rip you apart."

"What do you care?" I snarl back. My bones lock, joints tightening, and I push a bit more. The silence reaches him. His fire gutters and his throat bobs. He feels it. I'm hurting him. *Hold it. Remember your constant. Not too much, not too little.* I push a bit more and he takes another step back, another step in the direction I must go. The second gate taunts me from over his shoulder. "I'm here for one reason." I don't want to fight him. I just want him to stand aside. "I'm not letting your people kill him."

"I know!" he growls back, his voice guttural. I wonder if all of his fire kind have eyes like his. Eyes that burn and smolder. "I know you're going in there. So would I if—so would I."

"Then let me go."

He sets his jaw, a picture of determination. A mountain. Even now, in burned clothes, bruised, his body a wreck and his mind a ruin, he looks like a king. Cal is exactly the kind of person who will never kneel. It's not in him. He was not made that way.

But I've been broken too many times to break again.

"Cal, let me go. Let me get him." It sounds like begging.

This time he steps forward. And the flames on his fingers turn blue, so hot they singe the air. Still they waver before my ability, fighting to breathe, fighting to burn. I could snuff them out if I wanted to. I could seize all that he is and tear him apart, kill him, feel every centimeter of him die. Part of me wants to. A foolish part, ruled by anger and rage and blind vengeance. I let it fuel my ability, let it make me strong, but I don't let it control me. Just as Sara taught. It's a thin line to walk.

His eyes narrow, as if he knows what I'm thinking. So I'm surprised when he says the words. I almost don't hear them over the sound of my hammering heart.

"Let me help."

Before the Scarlet Guard, I used to think allies operated on exactly the same page. Machines in tandem, working toward the same goal. How naive of me. Cal and I are seemingly on the same side, but we absolutely do not want the same thing.

He's open with his plan. Detailing it fully. Enough for me to realize how he intends to use my rage, use my brother, to fulfill his own ends. *Distract the guards, get into the core tower, use your silence as a shield, and make the Silvers hand over their hostages in exchange for freedom. Julian will open the gates; I'll escort them myself. No bloodshed. No more siege. Corvium will be entirely ours.*

A good plan. Except the Silver garrison will go free, released to rejoin Maven's army.

I grew up in a slum, but I'm not stupid. And I'm certainly not some moon-eyed girl about to swoon over Cal's angled jaw and crooked smile either. His charm has its limits. He's used to bewitching Barrow, not me.

If only the prince had a bit more edge. Cal is too softhearted for his own good. He won't leave the Silver soldiers to the Colonel's nonexistent mercy, even if the only alternative is letting them go just to fight us again.

"How long do you need?" I ask. Lying to his face isn't difficult. Not when I know he's trying to trick me too.

He grins. He thinks he's won me over. *Perfect.* "A few hours to get my ducks in a row. Julian, Sara—"

"Fine. I'll be at the outer barracks when you're ready." I turn away, forcing an oh-so-thoughtful stare into the distance. The wind picks up, stirring my braids. It feels warmer, not because of Cal, but from the sun. Spring will be here eventually. "Need to clear my head."

The prince nods in understanding. He claps a fiery hand on my shoulder, giving it a squeeze. In reply, I force a smile that feels more like a grimace. As soon as I turn my back, I let it drop. He stays behind, his eyes burning holes into my back until the gentle curve of the ring wall obstructs me from view. Despite the rising temperature, a shiver trembles down my spine. I can't let Cal do this. But I'm not going to let Morrey spend one more second in that tower.

Up ahead, Farley marches in my direction, moving as fast as her body will allow. Her face darkens when she spots me, her brow furrowing so intensely her entire face turns beet red. It makes the pearly white scar at the side of her mouth stand out worse than usual. All in all, an intimidating sight.

"Cole," she snaps, her voice as stern as her father's. "I was afraid you were about to go and do something really stupid."

"Not me," I reply, dropping to a mutter. She cocks her head, and I motion for her to follow.

Once we're safely inside a storeroom, I tell her everything as fast as I can. She huffs through it all, as if Cal's plan is just an annoyance and not completely dangerous to us all.

"He's putting the entire city at risk," I finish, exasperated. "And if he goes through with it—"

"I know. But I told you before: Montfort and Command want Cal with us, at almost any cost. He's all but bulletproof. Anyone else would be shot for insurrection." Farley scratches both hands along her scalp, pulling at stray bits of her blond hair. "I don't want to do that, but a soldier who has no incentive to take orders and harbors his own agenda is not someone I want watching my back."

"Command." I hate the word, and whoever the hell it stands for. "Beginning to think they may not have our best interests at heart."

Farley doesn't disagree. "It's hard, putting all our faith in them. But they see what we don't, what we can't. And now . . ." She heaves a breath. Her eyes lock on the floor with laser focus. "I hear Montfort is about to get a lot more involved."

"What does that mean?"

"I'm not entirely sure."

I scoff. "Don't have the full picture? I'm shocked."

The glare she aims at me could cut through bone. "The system isn't perfect, but it protects us. If you're going to be sullen, I'm not going to help."

"Oh, now you have ideas?"

She grins darkly.

"A few."

Harrick hasn't lost his tendency to twitch.

He bobs his head up and down as Farley hisses our plan, lips moving quickly. She won't be going into the tower with us, but she's going to make sure we can actually get in.

Harrick seems wary. He isn't a warrior. He didn't come to Corros and he didn't participate in the Corvium raid either, even though his illusions would have helped immensely. He arrived with the rest of us, trailing behind the pregnant captain. Something happened to him back when we still had Mare, on a newblood recruitment gone wrong. Since then, he's stayed out of the fray, on the defense instead of in the thick of battle. I envy him. He doesn't know what it feels like to kill someone.

"How many hostages?" he asks, voice quivering like his fingers. A red flush blooms in his cheeks, spreading beneath winter-paled skin.

"At least twenty," I answer as quickly as I can. "We think my brother is one of them."

"With at least fifty Silvers on guard," Farley adds. She doesn't gloss over the danger. She won't trick him into doing this.

"Oh," he mumbles. "Oh dear."

Farley nods. "It's up to you, of course. We can find other ways."

"But none with less chance of bloodshed."

"That's right. Your illusions—" I press on, but he holds up a trembling hand. I wonder if his ability shakes like he does.

His mouth opens, but no words come out. I wait on tenterhooks, imploring him with every nerve in my body. He has to see how important this is. He has to.

"Fine."

I have to restrain myself from celebrating. This is a good step, but not victory, and I can't lose sight of that until Morrey is safe. "Thank you." I clasp his hands, letting them shake in mine. "Thank you so much."

He blinks rapidly, brown eyes meeting mine. "Don't thank me until it's over."

"Isn't that the truth?" Farley mutters. She tries not to look grim, for our sakes. Her plan is hasty, but Cal is forcing our hand. "All right, follow me," she says. "This is going to be quick, quiet, and with a little luck clean."

We follow in her wake as she dodges soldiers of the Scarlet Guard as well as the Reds defecting to our side. Many touch their brows in deference to her. She's a well-known figure in the organization, and we're banking on the level of respect she commands. I pull at my braids as we go, tightening them as best I can. The tug is a good pain. It keeps me sharp. And it gives my hands something to do. Or else I might twitch as badly as Harrick.

With Farley leading the way, no one stops us at the ring gates, and we march to the center of Corvium, where the core tower looms. Black granite thrusts into the sky, dotted with windows and balconies. All are neatly shut, while soldiers ring the base in the dozens, keeping watch over the two fortified entrances to the tower. Colonel's orders, I bet. He wasted no time doubling the guard after he realized I want in—and Cal wants the Silvers out. The captain doesn't lead us up to the tower, but past it, into one of the structures built up against the central ring wall. Like the rest of the city, it is gold, iron, and black stone, shadowed even in broad daylight.

My heartbeat thuds, faster with every step forward into the gloom of one of the many prisons dotting Corvium. As planned, Farley leads us down a staircase, and we descend to the cell level. My skin crawls at the sight of bars, the stone walls waxy in the dim light of too few bulbs. At least the cells are empty. Cal's defecting Silvers are over the Prayer Gate, confined to the room directly above arches of Silent Stone, where their abilities are nonexistent.

"I'll distract the lower-level guards while Harrick slips you both past," she says quietly, trying not to let her voice echo. Farley smoothly passes me two keys. "Iron first." She indicates the rough, black metal key as big as my fist, then the glinting, dainty one with sharp teeth. "Silver second."

I tuck them into separate pockets, easily within reach. "Got it."

"I can't muffle sound as well as sight yet, so we have to be as quiet as possible," Harrick murmurs. He nudges the inside of my arm and matches his steps to mine. "Stay close. Let me keep the illusion as small as I can for as long as possible."

I nod, understanding. Harrick needs to save his strength for the hostages.

The cells wind deeper and deeper into the ground beneath Corvium. It gets damper and colder by the minute, until my breath fogs. When light blazes around a corner, I feel no comfort. This is as far as Farley goes.

She gestures silently, waving us both back. I tuck closer to Harrick. This is it. Excitement and fear rage through me. *I'm coming, Morrey.*

My brother is close, surrounded by people who would kill him. I don't have time to care if they kill me.

Something wobbles before my vision, dropping like a curtain. The illusion. Harrick braces me against his chest and we walk together, our footsteps matching. We can see everything well enough, but when Farley looks back to check, her eyes search wildly, sweeping back and forth. She can't see us. And neither can the Guardsmen around the corner.

"Everything okay down here?" she crows, stomping on the stone much louder than necessary. Harrick and I follow at a safe distance and turn the passage to see six well-armed soldiers with red scarves and tactical gear. They stand across the narrow hall, shoulder to shoulder, firmly set.

They jump to attention in Farley's presence. One, a meaty man with a neck bigger than my thigh, addresses her on behalf of the rest. "Yes, Captain. No sign of movement. If the Silvers intend to make an escape attempt, it won't be through the tunnels. Even they aren't that foolish."

Farley clenches her jaw. "Good. Keep your eyes—oh!"

Wincing, she doubles over, bracing a hand on one of the midnight-black walls. The other clutches her belly. Her face furrows in pain.

The Guardsmen are quick to aid her, three jumping to her side in an instant. They leave a gap in their ranks much bigger than they need. Harrick and I move quickly, sliding along the opposite wall to reach the sealed door dead-ending the passage. Farley watches the door as she kneels, still faking a cramp or something worse. The illusion around me ripples a bit more, indicating Harrick's concentration. He's not just hiding us now, but a door yawning open behind a half-dozen soldiers assigned to protect it.

Farley yelps as I shove the iron key into the lock, twisting the mechanism. She keeps it up, her hisses of discomfort and cries of pain alternating in steady rhythm to distract from any squeaky hinges. Luckily, the door is well oiled. When it swings open, no one can see, and no one hears.

I shut it slowly, preventing the slam of iron on granite. The light disappears inch by inch, until we are left in almost pitch-black darkness. Not even Farley or her soldiers' fussing follows, sufficiently muffled by the closed door.

"Let's go," I tell him, linking my arm to his tightly.

One, two, three, four . . . I count my steps in the darkness, one hand trailing on the freezing cold wall.

Adrenaline kicks in when we reach the second door, now directly below the core tower. I didn't have enough time to memorize its structure, but I know the basics. Enough to get to the hostages and walk them right out into the safety of the central ward. Without hostages, the Silvers will have nothing to bargain with. They'll have to submit.

Feeling along the door, I poke around for the keyhole. It's small, and it takes a good amount of scraping to get the key in the lock properly. "Here we go," I murmur. A warning to Harrick, and to myself.

As I ease open the way into the tower, I realize this could be the last thing I ever do. Even with my ability and Harrick's, we're no match for fifty Silvers. We die if this goes wrong. And the hostages, already subjected to so many horrors, will probably die too.

I won't let that happen. I can't.

The adjoining chamber is just as dark as the tunnel, but warmer. The tower is tightly sealed against the elements, just like Farley said. Harrick crowds in behind me and we shut the door together. His hand brushes mine. It isn't twitching now. Good.

There should be some stairs . . . yes. I nudge my toes against a bottom step. Keeping my grip on Harrick's wrist, I lead us up, toward dim but steadily growing light. Two flights up, just like the two flights down we took in the prison cells.

Murmurs reverberate off the walls, deep enough to hear but too muffled to decipher. Harried voices, whispered arguments. I blink rapidly as the darkness lifts and we reach the ground floor of the tower, our heads poking up from the steps. Warm light pools around us, illuminating the circular stairwell twisting up the tall, central chamber. The spine of the tower. Doors branch off at several landings, each one bolted shut. My heart beats a thunderous rhythm, so loud I think the Silvers might hear it.

Two of them patrol the stairwell, tense and ready for an assault. But we're not soldiers and we aren't Scarlet Guard. Their figures ripple slightly, like the surface of disturbed water. Harrick's illusions are back, shielding us both from unfriendly eyes.

We move as one, following the voices. I can barely stand to breathe as we ascend the steps, making for the central chamber about three stories up. In Farley's schematics, it spread the width of the tower, occupying an entire floor. That's where the hostages will be, and the bulk of the Silvers holding out for Maven's rescue or Cal's mercy.

The Silver patrolmen are heavily muscled. Strongarms. Both have stone-gray faces and arms the size of tree trunks. They can't snap me in two, not if I use my silence. But my ability has no effect on guns, and both have many. Double pistols, along with rifles slung across their shoulders. The tower is well stocked for a siege, and I guess that means they have more than enough ammunition to hold out.

One strongarm descends the stairs as we approach, his footsteps lumbering. I thank whatever idiot Silver put him on watch. His ability is brute force, nothing sensory. But he would certainly feel us if we bumped into him.

We slip by him slowly, our backs edged against the exterior tower wall. He passes without so much as a whiff of uncertainty, his focus elsewhere.

The other strongarm is more difficult to pass. He leans against a door, long legs angled out in front of him. They almost block the steps entirely, forcing Harrick and me to the far side of the stairs. I'm grateful for my height. It allows me to step over him without incident. Harrick is not so graceful. His twitching returns tenfold as he straddles the steps, trying not to make a sound.

Gritting my teeth, I let silence pool beneath my skin. I wonder if I can kill both these men before they raise the alarm. I already feel sick at the thought.

But then Harrick lurches forward, his foot catching the next step. It doesn't make much noise, but enough to stir the Silver. He looks back and forth, and I freeze, gripping Harrick's outstretched wrist. Terror claws at my throat, begging to scream out.

When he turns his back, looking down at his comrade, I nudge Harrick.

"Lykos, you hear something?" the strongarm calls down.

"Not a thing," the other responds.

Each word covers our darting steps, allowing us to reach the top of the stairs and the door cracked ajar. I breathe the quietest sigh of relief imaginable. My hands are shaking too.

Inside the room, voices bicker. "We have to surrender," someone says.

Barks of opposition sound in response, drowning out our entry. We slip in like mice and find ourselves in a room crawling with hungry cats. Silver officers congregate along the walls, most of them wounded. The smell of blood is overpowering. Moans of pain permeate the many arguments arcing across the chamber. Officers shout each other down, their faces pale with fear, grief, and agony. Several of the wounded seem to be dying. I gag at the sight and stench of men and women in all states of injury. No healers here, I realize. These Silver wounds won't disappear with the wave of a hand.

Even so, I'm not made of ice or stone. The ones with the worst injuries are lined up along the curved exterior wall, just a few yards from my feet. The closest one is a woman, her face scraped with cuts. Silver blood pools beneath her hands as she tries in vain to keep her guts inside her body. Her mouth flaps open and closed, a dying fish gasping for air. Her pain is too deep for ramblings or screams. I swallow hard. A strange thought comes to me: *I could put her out of her misery if I wanted.* I could extend a hand of silence and help her slip away in peace.

Just the idea is enough to make me gag, and I have to turn away.

"Surrender is not an option. The Scarlet Guard will kill us, or worse . . . ?"

"Worse?" sputters one of the officers lying on the floor, his body bruised and bandaged. "Look around, Chyron!"

I glance around, daring to hope. If they keep shouting at one another, this will be so much easier. On the far side of the room, I spot them. Huddled together, their flesh pink and brown, their blood Red, are no less than twenty fifteen-year-olds. Only fear keeps me rooted in place, separated from everything I want by a stretch of deadly, angry killing machines.

Morrey. Seconds away. Inches away.

We cross the chamber as carefully as we climbed the steps, and twice as slowly. The Silvers with lesser wounds rove about, either tending to the more seriously injured or walking off their nerves. I've never seen Silvers like this. Off guard, up close. So human. An older female officer with a riot of badges holds the hand of a young man, maybe eighteen. His face is bone white, drained of blood, and he blinks calmly at the ceiling, waiting to die. The body next to him is already there. I hold back a gasp, forcing myself to breathe evenly and quietly. Even with so many distractions, I'm not taking a chance.

"Tell my mother I love her," one of the dying murmurs.

Another almost corpse calls for a man who isn't here, yelping out his name.

Death looms like a cloud. It shadows me too. I could die here, same as the rest. *If Harrick tires, if I step somewhere I shouldn't.* I try to ignore everything but my own two feet and the goal in front of me. But the farther I go into the chamber, the harder that is. The floor swims before my eyes, and not from Harrick's illusion. Am I . . . am I crying? For them?

Angry, I wipe the tears away before they can fall and leave tracks. As much as I know I hate these people, I can't find it in me to hate right now. All the rage I felt an hour ago is gone, replaced by strange pity.

The hostages are now close enough for me to touch, and one silhouette is as familiar as my own face. Curly black hair, midnight skin, gangly limbs, big hands with crooked fingers. The widest, brightest smile I've ever seen, though that is far, far away right now. If I could, I would tackle Morrey and never let him go. Instead, I creep up behind and slowly, surely crouch until I'm right next to his ear. I hope beyond hope he doesn't startle.

"Morrey, it's Cameron."

His body jolts, but he doesn't make a sound.

"I'm with a newblood; he can make us invisible. I'm going to get you out of here, but you have to do exactly as I say."

He turns his head, just so, his eyes wide and afraid. He has our mother's eyes, kohl black with heavy lashes. I resist the urge to hug him. Slowly, he shakes his head back and forth.

"Yes. I can do it," I breathe. "Tell the others what I just told you. Be discreet. Don't let the Silvers see. Do it, Morrey."

After another long moment he clenches his teeth and concedes.

It doesn't take long for knowledge of our presence to sweep through them. No one questions it. They don't have the luxury of doing that, not here, in the belly of the beast.

"What you're about to see isn't real."

I gesture to Harrick, who nods. He's ready. Slowly, we move to our knees, crouching down to blend in with them. When his illusion on us lifts, the Silvers won't notice us at first. Distracted. Hopefully.

My message travels quickly. The hostages tense. Even though they're the same age as me, they seem older, worn by the months training to fight and then spent in a trench. Even Morrey, though he looks better fed than he ever was at home. Still invisible to his eye, I reach out and tentatively take his hand. His fingers close on mine, holding tight. And the illusion rendering us invisible drops. Two more bodies join the circle of hostages. The others blink at us, struggling to mask their surprise.

"Here we go," Harrick murmurs.

Behind us, the Silvers continue bickering over the dead and dying. They don't spare a thought for the hostages.

Harrick narrows his eyes, focusing on the curving tower wall to our right. He breathes heavily, air whistling through his nose and out his mouth. Gathering his strength. I brace myself for the blow, even though I know it doesn't exist.

Suddenly the wall explodes inward in a bloom of fire and stone, exposing the tower to the sky. The Silvers shudder, scampering back from what they think is an attack. Airjets scream past, swooping through the false clouds. I blink, not believing my eyes. I shouldn't believe my eyes. This isn't real. But it looks amazingly, impossibly real.

Not that I have time to gape.

Harrick and I jump to our feet, herding the others with us. We bolt through the fire, flames licking close enough to burn us through. I flinch even though I know it isn't there. The fire is distraction enough, startling the Silvers so that we can stampede through the door and onto the stairs.

I push on, leading the pack, while Harrick keeps the rear. He waves his arms like a dancer, weaving illusions out of thin air. Fire, smoke, another round of missiles. All of it keeps the Silvers from pursuing us, cowering from his spooling images. Silence blooms from me, a sphere of deadly power to fell the two Silver lookouts. Morrey clips my heels, almost making me trip, but he catches my arm, keeping me from going over the rail.

"Stop!" The first strongarm charges at me, head lowered like a bull. I pulse silence into his body, ramming my ability down his throat. He stumbles, feeling the full weight of my power. I feel it too, death rolling through his flesh. I have to kill him. And quickly. The force of my need crushes blood from his mouth and eyes as pieces of his body die off, organs one after the other. I smother the life from him faster than I've ever killed anyone before.

The other strongarm dies even faster. When I hit him with another exhausting pummel of silence, he trips sideways and falls headfirst. His skull cracks open on the stone floor, spilling blood and brain matter. A sob chokes in my chest, and I have no time to question my sudden disgust with myself. *For Morrey. For Morrey.*

My brother looks as agonized as I feel, his eyes glued to the dead strongarm bleeding all over the floor. I tell myself he's just shocked, and not terrified of me.

"Go!" I bellow, voice choked with shame. Thankfully he does as I say, sprinting to the lower level with the rest.

Even though the ground entrance is blocked up, the hostages make quick work of it, tearing down the Silver fortifications until the double doors are laid bare, a single lock standing between all of us and freedom.

I vault over the strongarm's crushed skull, tossing the small silver key. Morrey catches it. His conscription and my imprisonment have not stamped out our bond as twins. Sunlight streams through as he hauls the doors open and lunges into the fresh air, the other hostages sprinting with him.

Harrick comes flying down the stairs, false fire spewing in his wake. He waves me on, telling me to go, but I stay rooted. I'm not leaving without the illusionary.

We stumble out together, clutching each other tightly to face down a square full of perplexed guards armed to the teeth. They allow us through at Farley's orders. She shouts nearby, directing them to focus on the tower entrance, in case the Silvers attempt to make a stand.

I don't hear her words. I just keep walking until I have my brother in my arms. His heart beats rapidly in his chest. I revel in the sound. He's here. He's alive.

Not like the strongarms.

I still feel it, what I did to them.

What I did to every single person I ever killed.

The memories make me dizzy with shame. All for Morrey, all to survive. But no more.

I don't have to be a murderer alongside everything else.

He clutches at me, eyes rolling in terror. "The Scarlet Guard," he hisses, holding me close. "Cam, we have to run."

"You're safe; you're with us now. They can't hurt you, Morrey!"

But instead of calming down, his fear triples. Morrey's grip on me tightens as his head whips back and forth, taking stock of Farley's soldiers. "Do they know what you are? Cam, do they know?"

Shame bleeds into confusion. I push back from him a little, to get a better look at his face. He breathes heavily. "What I *am*?"

"They'll kill you for it. The Scarlet Guard will kill you for what you are."

Each word hits me like a hammer. And then I realize my brother isn't the only one still afraid. The rest of his unit, the other teenagers, cluster together for safety, every one of them keeping clear of the Guard soldiers. Farley meets my eye from a few feet away, just as puzzled as I am.

Then I see her from my brother's point of view. See them all for what he's been told to see.

Terrorists. Murderers. The reason they were conscripted in the first place.

I try to pull Morrey into a hug, try to whisper an explanation.

He just goes cold in my arms. "You're one of them," he spits, looking at me with so much anger and accusation my knees buckle. "You're Scarlet Guard."

My soul fills with dread.

Maven took Mare's brother.

Did he take mine too?

SIXTEEN
Mare

I can't see Corvium through the low cloud cover. I stare anyway, my eyes glued on the eastern horizon stretching out behind us. The Scarlet Guard took the city. They control it now. We had to skirt around, giving the hostile city a wide berth. Maven is doing his best to keep it quiet; even he can't hide such massive defeat. I wonder how the news will land across the kingdom. Will Reds celebrate? Will Silvers retaliate? I remember the riots that followed other attacks by the Scarlet Guard. Of course there will be repercussions. Corvium is an act of war. Finally, the Scarlet Guard has planted a flag that cannot simply be torn down.

My friends are so close I feel as if I could run to them. Tear the manacles off, kill the Arven guards, jump from the transport and disappear into the gray gloom, sprinting through the bare winter forest. In the daydream, they wait for me outside the walls of a broken fortress. The Colonel, his eye crimson, his weathered face and the gun on his hip a comfort like nothing else. Farley with him, bold and tall and resolute as I remember. Cameron, her silence a shield rather than a prison. Kilorn, familiar as my own two hands. Cal, angry and broken as I am, the embers of his rage ready to burn all thoughts of Maven from my mind. I imagine leaping into their arms, begging them to take me away, take me anywhere. Take me to my family, take me home. Make me forget.

No, not forget. It would be a sin to forget my imprisonment. A waste. I know Maven as no one else does. I know the holes in his brain, the pieces he can never make fit. And I've seen his court splinter first-hand. If I can escape, if I can be rescued, I can do some good still. I can make my fool's bargain worth the terrible cost—and I can start to right so many wrongs.

Even though the transport windows are tightly sealed, I smell smoke. Ash. Gunpowder. The metallic, sour bite of a century of blood. The Choke nears, closer with every passing second as Maven's convoy speeds west. I hope my nightmares of this place were worse than the reality.

Kitten and Clover are still at my sides, their hands gloved and flat upon their knees. Ready to grab me, ready to hold me down. The other guards, Trio and Egg, perch above, on the transport skeleton, harnessed to the moving vehicle. A precaution, now that we're so close to the war zone. Not to mention a few miles from a city occupied by revolution. All four remain vigilant as ever. Both to keep me imprisoned—and to keep me safe.

Outside, the forest lining the last miles of the Iron Road thins into nothing. Naked branches fall away to reveal hard earth barely worthy of snow. The Choke is an ugly place. Gray dirt, gray skies, blending so perfectly I don't know where the land ends and sky begins. I almost expect to hear explosions in the distance. Dad said you could always hear the bombs, even from miles away. I suppose that isn't the case any-more, not if Maven's gambit succeeds. I'm ending a war that millions died for. Just to keep killing under another name.

The convoy presses on toward the forward camps, a collection of buildings that remind me of the Scarlet Guard base on Tuck. They fade into the distance in either direction. Barracks, mostly. Coffins for the living. My brothers lived in those once. My father too. It might be my turn to keep up the tradition.

As in the cities along the coronation tour, people turn out to watch King Maven and his retinue. Soldiers in red, in black, in clouded gray. They line the main avenue bisecting the Choke camp with military precision, each one dipping their heads in respect. I don't bother trying to count how many hundreds there are. It's too depressing. Instead, I clasp my hands together, tight enough to give me another pain to dwell on. The injured Silver officer in Rocasta said Corvium was a massacre. *Don't,* I tell myself. *Don't go there.* Of course my mind does anyway. It's impossible to avoid the horrors you really don't want to think about. *Massacre.* Both sides. Red and Silver, Scarlet Guard and Maven's army. Cal survived, that much I know from Maven's demeanor. But Farley, Kilorn, Cameron, my brothers, the rest? So many names and faces who probably assaulted the walls of Corvium. What happened to them?

I press my fingers to my eyes, trying to keep the tears back. The effort exhausts me, but I refuse to cry in front of Kitten and Clover.

To my surprise, the convoy does not stop in the center of the Choke camp, even though there's a square that looks perfectly suited to another of Maven's honeyed speeches. A few of the transports, each carrying scions of several High Houses, peel off, but we speed through, pressing on, deeper and deeper. Even though they try to hide it, Kitten and Clover grow more on edge, their eyes darting between the windows and each other. They don't like this. *Good. Let them squirm.*

Bold as I feel, a shadow of dread falls over me too. Is Maven out of his mind? Where is he taking us—all of us? Certainly he would not drive the court into a trench or a minefield or worse. The transports pick up speed, rolling faster and faster over earth packed hard into a roadway. In the distance, artillery cannons and heavy guns stand in hulking wrecks of iron, twisted shadows like black skeletons. Within a mile, we cross the first trench lines, our vehicles snarling over hastily built bridges. More trenches follow. For reserves, support, communication. Weaving like the passages of the Notch, burrowing into frozen mud. I lose count after a dozen. Either the trenches are abandoned or the soldiers are well hidden. I can't see a single scrap of red uniform.

This could be a trap, for all we know. The scheming of an old king meant to ensnare and defeat a young boy. Part of me wants that to be true. If I can't kill Maven, maybe the king of the Lakelands will do it for me. House Cygnet, nymphs. Ruling for hundreds of years. That's as much as I know about the enemy monarch. His kingdom is like ours, divided by blood, ruled by noble Silver houses. And afflicted by the Scarlet Guard, apparently. Like Maven, he must be bent on maintaining power at all costs, through any means. Even collusion with an old enemy.

In the east, the clouds break, and a few beams of sunlight illuminate the harsh land around us. No trees as far as the eye can see. We cross over the frontline trench and I gasp at the sight. Red soldiers crowd together in long lines, six bodies deep, their uniforms colored in varying shades of rust and crimson. They pool like blood in a wound. Hands on ladders, they shiver in the cold. Ready to rush out of their trench and into the deadly kill zone of the Choke should their king command it. I spot Silver officers among them, denoted by their gray-and-black uniforms. Maven is young, but not stupid. If this is a Lakelander trick, he's ready to fight his way out. I assume the king of the Lakelands has another army waiting, in his own trenches on the other side. More Red soldiers to discard.

As the tires of our transport hit the other side, Clover tightens next to me. She keeps her electric-green eyes forward, trying to stay calm. A sheen of sweat gleams on her forehead, betraying her fear.

The true wasteland of the Choke is pocked with craters from two armies' worth of artillery fire. Some of the holes must be decades old. Barbed wire tangles in the frozen mud. Up ahead, on the lead transport, a telky and a magnetron work in tandem. They sweep their arms back and forth, wrenching any debris from the path of the convoy. Bits of coiled iron go spinning off in every direction. And, I assume, bones. Reds have been dying here for generations. The dirt is littered with their dust.

In my nightmares, this place stretches on forever, in every direction. But instead of continuing forward into oblivion, the convoy slows a little more than a half mile beyond the frontline trenches. As our transports circle and weave, arranging themselves in a half-moon arc, I almost erupt with nervous laughter. Of all things, in all places—we're stopping at a pavilion. The contrast is jarring. It's brand-new, with white columns and silky curtains swaying in the poisoned wind. Constructed for one purpose and one purpose alone. A summit, a meeting, like the one so long ago. When two kings decided to begin a century of war.

A Sentinel wrenches open my transport door, beckoning for us to step down. Clover hesitates a half second and Kitten clears her throat, urging her on. I move between them, escorted down onto the obliterated earth. Rocks and dirt make the ground uneven under my feet. I pray nothing splinters beneath me. A skull, a rib, a femur, or a spine. I don't need more proof that I'm walking through an endless graveyard.

Clover is not the only one afraid. Even the Sentinels move slowly, on edge, their masked faces sweeping back and forth. For once, they think of their own safety as well as Maven's. And the rest of the remaining court—Evangeline, Ptolemus, Samson—they idle by their transports. Their eyes dart; their noses wrinkle. They can smell death and danger as well as I can. One wrong move, one hint of a threat, and they'll bolt. Evangeline has discarded her furs for armor. Steel coats her from neck to wrist and toe. She quickly frees her fingers from her leather gloves, baring her skin to the cold air. Better for a fight. I feel the itch to do the same, not that it will help me at all. The manacles are strong as ever.

The only one who seems unaffected is Maven. The dying winter suits him, making his pale skin stand out in a way that is oddly elegant. Even the shadows around his eyes, dark as always, black and bruise-like, make him tragically beautiful. Today he wears as much regalia as he dares. A boy king, but a king all the same, about to look into the eyes of someone who is supposedly his greatest opponent. The crown on his head seems natural now, refitted to sit low across his brow. It spits bronze and iron flames through his glossy black hair. Even in the gray light of the Choke, his medals and badges gleam, silver and ruby and onyx. A cape, patterned with brocade red as flame, completes the ensemble and the image of a fiery king. But the Choke consumes us all. Dirt speckles his polished black boots as he walks forward, fighting the deep instinct to fear this place. Impatient, he casts one look over his shoulder, eyeing the dozens he dragged here. His fire-blue eyes are warning enough. We must go with him. I am not afraid of death, and so I am the first to follow him into what could be a grave.

The king of the Lakelands is already waiting.

He sprawls in a simple chair, a small man against the massive flag hung behind him. It is cobalt, worked with a four-petaled flower in silver and white. His milky-blue metal transports splay out on the other side of the pavilion, arranged in mirror image to our own. I count more than a dozen at a glance, all of them crawling with the Lakelander version of Sentinel guards. More flank the Lakeland king and his entourage. They don't wear masks or robes, but tactical armor in flashing plates of deep sapphire. They stand, silent, stoic, with faces like carved stone. Each one a warrior trained from birth or close to it. I know none of their abilities, nor those of the king's companions. The court of the Lakelands is not something I studied in my lessons with Lady Blonos centuries ago.

As we approach, the king comes into better focus. I stare at him, trying to see the man beneath the crown of white gold, topaz, turquoise, and dark lapis lazuli. For as much as Maven favors red and black, this king favors his blue. After all, he is a nymph, a manipulator of water. It's fitting. I expect his eyes to be blue as well—instead, they are storm gray, matching the hard iron of his long, straight hair. I find myself comparing him to Maven's father, the only other king I've ever known. He stands in stark contrast. Where Tiberias the Sixth was hefty, bearded, his face and body bloated by alcohol, the Lakelander king is slight, clean-shaven, and clear-eyed with dark skin. As with all Silvers, a gray-blue undertone cools his complexion. When he stands, he is graceful, his sweeping movements akin to a dancer's. He wears no armor or dress uniform. Only robes of shimmering silver and cobalt, bright and foreboding as his flag.

"King Maven of House Calore," he says, inclining his head just so as Maven steps onto the pavilion. Black silk slithers over white marble.

"King Orrec of House Cygnet," Maven responds in kind. He is careful to bow lower than his opponent, with a smile fixed firmly upon his lips. "If only my father were here to see this."

"Your mother too," Orrec says. No bite to the words, but Maven straightens up quickly, as if suddenly presented with a threat. "My condolences. You are far too young to experience so much loss." He has an accent, his words finding a strange melody. His eyes twitch over Maven's shoulder, past me, to Samson following us in his Merandus blues. "You were informed of my . . . requests?"

"Of course." Maven juts a chin over his shoulder. He glances at me for a second; then, like Orrec's, his gaze slides to Samson. "Cousin, if you would not mind waiting in your transport."

"Cousin—" Samson says with as much opposition as he dares. Still, he stops in his tracks, feet planted several yards from the pavilion platform. There is no argument to make, not here. King Orrec's guards tighten, hands moving to their array of weapons. Guns, swords, the very air around us. Anything they might call upon to keep a whisper from getting too close to their king and his mind. If only the court of Norta were the same.

Finally, Samson relents. He bows low, arms sweeping out at his sides in sharp, practiced movements. "Yes, Your Majesty."

Only when he turns around, walks back to the vehicles, and disappears from sight do the Lakelander guards relax. And King Orrec smiles tightly, waving Maven forward to face him. Like a child invited to beg.

Instead, Maven turns to the seat set opposite. It isn't Silent Stone, isn't safe, but he settles into it without a blink of hesitation. He leans back and crosses his legs, letting his cape drape over one arm while the other lies free. His hand dangles—with his flamemaker bracelet clearly visible.

The rest of us congregate around him, taking seats to match the court of the Lakelands now facing us. Evangeline and Ptolemus take

Maven's right, as does their father. When he joined our convoy, I don't know. Governor Welle is here too, his green robes sickly against the gray of the Choke. The absence of Houses Iral, Laris, and Haven seems glaring to my eye, their ranks replaced by other advisers. My four Arven guards flank me as I sit, so close I can hear them breathing. I focus instead on the people in front of me, the Lakelanders. The king's closest advisers, confidants, diplomats, and generals. People to be feared almost as much as the king himself. No introductions are made, but I quickly realize who is most important among them. She sits at the king's right-hand side, the place Evangeline currently occupies.

A very young queen, maybe? No, the family resemblance is too strong. She has to be the princess of the Lakelands, with eyes like her father's and her own crown of flawless blue gems. Her straight black hair gleams, beaded with pearl and sapphire. As I stare, she feels my eyes—and she stares right back.

Maven speaks first, breaking my observations. "For the first time in a century, we find ourselves in agreement."

"That we do." Orrec nods. His jeweled brow flashes in the weakening sunlight. "The Scarlet Guard and all its ilk must be eradicated. Quickly, lest their disease spread further than it already has. Lest Reds in other regions be seduced by their false promises. I hear rumors of trouble in Piedmont?"

"Rumors, yes." My black-hearted king concedes nothing more than he wants to. "You know how the princes can be. Always arguing among themselves."

Orrec almost smirks. "Indeed. The Prairie lords are quite the same."

"In regard to the terms—"

"Not so fast, my young friend. I should like to know the state of your house before I walk through the door."

Even from my seat I can feel Maven tighten. "Ask what you wish."

"House Iral? House Laris? House Haven?" Orrec's eyes sweep down our line, missing nothing. His gaze skirts over me, faltering for half a second. "I see none of them here."

"So?"

"So the reports are true. They have rebelled against their rightful king."

"Yes."

"In support of an exile."

"Yes."

"And what of your army of newbloods?"

"It grows with every passing day," Maven says. "Another weapon we all must learn to wield."

"Like her." The king of the Lakelands tips his head in my direction. "The lightning girl is a mighty trophy."

My fists clench on my knees. Of course, he's right. I'm little more than a trophy for Maven to drag around, using my face and my forced words to draw more to his side. I don't flush, though. I've had a long time to get used to my shame.

If Maven looks my way, I don't know. I won't look at him.

"A trophy, yes, and a symbol too," Maven says. "The Scarlet Guard is flesh and blood, not ghosts. Flesh and blood can be controlled, defeated, and destroyed."

The king clucks his tongue, as if in pity. Quickly, he stands, his robes swirling around him like a tossing river. Maven stands too, and meets him in the center of the pavilion. They size each other up, one devouring the other. Neither wants to be the first to break. I feel the very air around me tighten: hot, then cold, then dry, then clammy. The will of two Silver kings rages around us all.

I don't know what Orrec sees in Maven, but suddenly he relents and extends one dark hand. Rings of state wink on all his fingers. "Well, they'll be dealt with soon enough. Your rebel Silvers too. Three houses against the might of two kingdoms is nothing at all."

With a dip of his head, Maven returns the gesture. He grips Orrec's hand in his.

Dimly, I wonder how the hell Mare Barrow of the Stilts ended up here. A few feet from two kings, watching one more piece of our bloody history lock into place. Julian will lose his mind when I tell him. *When.* Because I will see him again. See them all again.

"Now for the terms," Orrec pushes on. And I realize he has not let go of Maven's fingers. So do the Sentinels. They take one menacing step forward in tandem, their robes of flame hiding any number of weapons. On the other side of the platform, the Lakelander guards do the same. Each side daring the other to take the step that will end in bloodshed.

Maven doesn't try to wrench away, or push closer. He merely stands firm, unmoved, unafraid. "The terms are sound," he replies, his voice even. I can't see his face. "The Choke divided evenly, the old borders maintained and opened for travel. You'll have equal use of the Capital River and the Eris Canal—"

"While your brother lives, I need guarantees."

"My brother is a traitor, an exile. He will be dead soon enough."

"That's my point, boy. As soon as he is gone, as soon as we tear the Scarlet Guard limb from limb—will you return to the old ways? The old enemies? Will you find yourself once again drowning in Red bodies and in need of somewhere to throw them?" Orrec's face darkens, flushing gray and purple. His cold, detached manner fades into anger.

"Population control is one matter, but the war, the endless push and pull, it is little more than madness. I will not spill one more drop of Silver blood because you can't command your Red rats."

Maven leans forward, matching Orrec's intensity. "Our treaty will be signed here, broadcast across every city, to every man, woman, and child of my kingdom. Everyone will know this war has ended. Everyone in Norta, at least. I know you don't have the same capabilities in the Lakelands, old man. But I trust you'll do your best to inform as much of your backwater kingdom as possible."

A shudder goes through us all. Fear in the Silvers, but excitement in me. *Destroy each other,* I whisper in my head. *Turn each other inside out.* I have no doubt a nymph king would have little issue drowning Maven where he stands.

Orrec bares his teeth. "You don't know anything about my country."

"I know the Scarlet Guard began in your house, not mine," Maven spits back. With his free hand he gestures, telling his Sentinels to back down. Foolish, posturing boy. I hope it gets him killed. "Don't act like you're doing me a favor. You need this as much as we do."

"Then I want your word, Maven Calore."

"You have it—"

"Your word and your hand. The strongest bond you can make."

Oh.

My eyes fly from Maven, locked in a grip with the king of the Lakelands, to Evangeline. She sits still, as if frozen, her gaze on the marble floor and nowhere else. I expect her to stand up and scream, to turn this place into a wreck of shrapnel. But she doesn't move. Even Ptolemus, her lapdog of a brother, stays firmly in his seat. And their father in his Samos blacks broods as always. No change in him that I can see. No indication that Evangeline is about to lose the position she fought so hard to obtain.

Across the pavilion, the Lakelander princess seems hewn from stone. She doesn't even blink. She knew this was coming.

Once, when Maven's father told him he was to marry me, he choked in surprise. He put on a good show, blustering and arguing. He pretended not to know what that proposal was about, what it meant. Like me, he has worn a thousand masks and played a million different parts. Today he performs as king, and kings are never surprised, never caught off guard. If he is shocked, he doesn't show it. I hear nothing but steel in his voice.

"It would be an honor to call you father," he says.

Finally, Orrec lets go of Maven's hand. "And an honor to call you son."

Both could not be more false.

To my right, someone's chair scrapes against marble. Followed quickly by two more. In a flurry of metal and black, House Samos hurries from the pavilion. Evangeline leads her brother and father, never looking back, her hands open at her sides. Her shoulders drop and her meticulously straight posture seems lessened somehow.

She is relieved.

Maven doesn't watch her go, wholly focused on the task at hand. The task being the Lakelander princess.

"My lady," he says, bowing in her direction.

She merely inclines her head, never breaking her steely gaze.

"In the eyes of my noble court, I would ask for your hand in marriage." I've heard these words before. From the same boy. Spoken in front of a crowd, each word sounding like a lock twisting shut. "I pledge myself to you, Iris Cygnet, princess of the Lakelands. Will you accept?"

Iris is beautiful, more graceful than her father. Not a dancer, though, but a hunter. She stands on long limbs, unfolding herself from her seat in a cascade of soft sapphire velvet and full, feminine curves. I glimpse leather leggings between the slashes of her gown. Well-worn, cracked at the knees. She did not come here unprepared. And like so many here, she doesn't wear gloves, despite the cold. The hand she extends to Maven is amber-skinned, long-fingered, unadorned. Still, her eyes do not waver, even as a mist forms from the air, swirling around her out-stretched hand. It glimmers before my eyes, tiny droplets of moisture condensing to life. They become tiny, crystal beads of water, each one a pinprick of refracting light as they twist and move.

Her first words are in a language I do not know. Lakelander. It is heartbreakingly beautiful, one word flowing into the next like a spoken song, like water. Then, in accented Nortan—

"I put my hand in yours, and pledge my life to yours," she replies, after her own traditions and the customs of her kingdom. "I accept, Your Majesty."

He puts his bare hand out to take hers, the bracelet at his wrist sparking as he moves. A current of fire hits the air, snakelike and curl-ing around their joined fingers. It does not burn her, though it certainly passes close enough to try. Iris never flinches. Never blinks.

And so one war is ended.

SEVENTEEN
Mare

It takes many days to return to Archeon. Not because of the distance. Not because the king of the Lakelands brought no less than one thousand people with him, courtiers and soldiers and even Red servants. But because the entire kingdom of Norta suddenly has something to celebrate. The end of a war, and an upcoming wedding. Maven's now-endless convoy snakes down the Iron Road and then the Royal Road at a crawl. Silvers and Reds alike turn out to cheer, begging for a glimpse of their king. Maven always obliges, stopping to meet crowds with Iris at his side. Despite the deeply bred hatred for the Lakelands we are supposed to have, Nortans bow before her. She is a curiosity and a blessing. A bridge. Even King Orrec receives lukewarm welcomes. Polite clapping, respectful bows. An old enemy turned into an ally for the long road ahead.

That's what Maven says at every turn. "Norta and the Lakelands stand united now, bound together for the long road ahead. Against all dangers threatening our kingdoms." He means the Scarlet Guard. He means Corvium. He means Cal, the rebelling houses, anything and everything that might threaten his tenuous grip on power.

There is no one alive to remember the days before war. My country does not know what peace looks like. No wonder they mistake this for peace. I want to scream at every Red face I pass. I want to carve the words on my body so everyone has to see. *Trap. Lie. Conspiracy.* Not that my words mean anything anymore. I've been someone else's puppet for too long. My voice is not my own. Only my actions are, and those are severely limited by circumstances. I would despair of myself if I could, but my days of wallowing are long behind me. They have to be. Or else I will simply drown, a hollow doll dragged behind a child, empty in every inch.

I will escape. I will escape. I will escape. I don't dare whisper the words aloud. They run through my mind instead, their rhythm in time with my heartbeat.

No one speaks to me during our journey. Not even Maven. He's busy feeling out his new betrothed. I get the sense she knows what kind of person he is, and is prepared for him. As with her father, I hope they kill each other.

The tall spires of Archeon are familiar, but not a comfort. The convoy rolls back into the jaws of a cage I know all too well. Through the city, up the steep roads to the palatial compound of Caesar's Square and Whitefire. The sun is deceptively bright against a clear blue sky. It's almost spring. Strange. Part of me thought winter would last forever, mirroring my imprisonment. I don't know if I can stomach watching the seasons turn from inside my royal cell.

I will escape. I will escape. I will escape.

Egg and Trio all but pass me between each other, pulling me down from the transport and marching me up the steps of Whitefire. The air is warm, wet, smelling fresh and clean. A few more minutes in the sunlight and I might start sweating beneath my scarlet-and-silver jacket. But I'm inside the palace again in a few seconds, walking beneath a king's ransom of chandeliers. They don't bother me so much, not after my first and only escape attempt. In fact, they almost make me smile.

"Happy to be home?"

I'm equally startled by someone speaking to me and by exactly who is speaking to me.

I resist the deep urge to bow, keeping my spine straight as I stop to face her. The Arvens halt as well, close enough to grab me if they have to. I feel a ripple of their ability draining bits of my energy. Her own guards are just as on edge, their attentions on the hall around us. I suppose they still think of Archeon and Norta as enemy territory.

"Princess," I reply. The title tastes sour, but I don't see much use in directly antagonizing yet another one of Maven's betrotheds.

Her traveling outfit is deceptively plain. Just leggings and a dark blue jacket, cinched at the waist to better show her hourglass figure. No jewelry, no crown. Her hair is simple, pulled back into a single black braid. She could pass for a normal Silver. Wealthy, but not royal. Even her face remains neutral. No smile, no sneer. No judgment of the lightning girl in her chains. Compared to the nobles I've known, it makes for a jarring contrast and an inconvenient one. I know nothing about her. For all I know, she could be worse than Evangeline. Or even Elara. I have no idea who this young woman is, or what she thinks of me. It makes me uneasy.

And Iris can tell.

"No, I would think not," she pushes on. "Walk with me?"

She puts out a hand, crooking it in invitation. There is a decent chance my eyes bug out of my head. But I do as she asks. She sets a quick but not impossible pace, forcing both sets of guards to follow us through the entrance hall.

"Despite the name, Whitefire seems a cold place." Iris looks up at the ceiling. The chandeliers reflect in her gray eyes, making them starry. "I would not want to be imprisoned here."

I scoff deep in my throat. The poor fool is about to be Maven's queen. I can think of no worse prison than that.

"Something funny, Mare Barrow?" she purrs.

"Nothing, Your Highness."

Her eyes rove over me. They linger on my wrists, at the long sleeves hiding my manacles. Slowly, she touches one and draws in a breath. Despite the Silent Stone and the instinctive fear it inspires, she doesn't flinch. "My father keeps pets as well. Perhaps it's something kings do."

Months ago, I would have snapped at her. *I'm not a pet.* But she isn't wrong. Instead, I shrug. "I haven't met enough kings to know."

"Three kings for a Red girl born to poor nothings. One must wonder if the gods love or hate you."

I don't know whether to laugh or sneer. "There are no gods."

"Not in Norta. Not for you." Her expression softens. She glances over her shoulder, at the many courtiers and nobles as they mill about. Most don't bother to hide their ogling. If it annoys her, she doesn't show it. "I wonder if they can hear me in a godless place like this. There isn't even a temple. I must ask Maven to build me one."

Many strange people have passed through my life. But all of them have pieces I can understand. Emotions I know, dreams, fears. I blink at Princess Iris and realize that the more she speaks, the more confusing she becomes. She seems intelligent, strong, self-assured, but why would a person like that agree to marry such an obvious monster? Certainly she sees him for what he is. And it can't be blind ambition driving her here. She's a princess already, daughter of a king. What does she want? Or did she even have a choice? Her talk of gods is even more confusing. We have no such beliefs. How can we?

"Are you memorizing my face?" she asks quietly as I try to read her. I get the sense she is doing the same, observing me like I'm a complicated piece of art. "Or simply trying to steal a few more moments outside a locked room? If the latter, I do not blame you. If the former, I have a feeling you'll be seeing a great deal of me, and I of you."

From anyone else, it might sound like a threat. But I don't think Iris cares enough about me for that. At least she doesn't seem the jealous type. That would require her to have any sort of feeling for Maven, something I sorely doubt.

"Take me to the throne room."

My lips twitch, wanting to smile. Usually the people here make requests that are truly iron commands. Iris is the opposite. Her command sounds like a question. "Fine," I mutter, letting my feet guide us. The Arvens don't dare try to pull me away. Iris Cygnet is not Evangeline Samos. Crossing her could be considered an act of war. I can't help smirking over my shoulder at Trio and Egg. Both glower back. Their irritation makes me grin, even through the itch of my scars.

"You are an odd sort of prisoner, Miss Barrow. I did not realize that, while Maven paints you as a lady in his broadcasts, he requires you to be one at all times."

Lady. The title never truly applied to me, and never will. "I'm just a well-dressed and tightly leashed lapdog."

"What a peculiar king to keep you as he does. You're an enemy of the state, a valuable piece of propaganda, and somehow treated as near royalty. But then boys are so strange with their toys. Especially those accustomed to losing things. They hold on more tightly than the rest."

"And what would you do with me?" I answer back. As queen, Iris could hold my life in her hands. She could end it, or make it even worse. "If you were in his position?"

Iris dodges the question artfully. "I won't ever make the mistake of trying to put myself in his head. That is not a place any sane person should be." Then she laughs to herself. "I assume his mother spent a good amount of time there."

For as much as Elara hated me and my existence, I think she would hate Iris more. The young princess is formidable to say the least. "You're lucky you never had to meet her."

"And I thank you for that," Iris replies. "Though I hope you don't keep up the tradition of killing queens. Even lapdogs bite." She blinks at me, gray eyes piercing. "Will you?"

I'm not stupid enough to respond. *No* would be a naked lie. *Yes* could land me yet another royal enemy. She smirks at my silence.

It's not a long walk to the grand chamber where Maven holds court. After so many days before the broadcast cameras, forced to stomach newblood after newblood pledging their loyalty to him, I know it intimately. Usually the dais is crowded with seats, but they've been removed in our absence, leaving only the gray, forbidding throne. Iris glares at it as we approach.

"An interesting tactic," she mutters when we reach it. As with my manacles, she runs a finger down the blocks of Silent Stone. "Necessary too. With so many whispers allowed at court."

"Allowed?"

"They are not welcome in the court of the Lakelands. They cannot pass through the walls of our capital, Detraon, or enter the palace without proper escorts. And no whisper is permitted within twenty feet of the monarch," Iris explains. "In fact, I know of no noble families who can claim such an ability in my country."

"They don't exist?"

"Not where I come from. Not anymore."

The implication hangs in the air like smoke.

She pulls away from the throne, tipping her head back and forth. She doesn't like whatever she sees. Her lips purse into a thin line. "How many times have you felt the touch of a Merandus in your head?"

For a split second, I try to remember. *Stupid.* "Too many times to count," I tell her with a shrug. "First Elara, then Samson. I can't decide who was worse. I know now that the queen could look into my mind without me even knowing. But he . . ." My voice falters. The memory is a painful one, drawing out a drilling pressure at my temples. I try to massage away the ache. "Samson, you feel every second he's in there."

Her face grays. "So many eyes in this place," she says, glancing first at my guards and then at the walls. At the security cameras looking over every inch of the open chamber, watching us. "They are welcome to watch."

Slowly, she removes her jacket and folds it over her arm. The shirt beneath is white, fastened high at her throat, but backless. She turns, under the guise of examining the throne room. Really, she's showing off. Her back is muscular, powerful, carved of long lines. Black tattoos cover her from the base of her scalp, down her neck, across her shoulder blades, all to the base of her spine. *Roots,* I think first. I'm wrong. Not roots, but whorls of water, curling and spilling over her skin in perfect lines. They ripple as she moves, a living thing. Finally she roves back to face me. The smallest smirk plays on her lips.

It disappears in an instant as her gaze shifts past me. I don't have to turn around to know who approaches, who leads the many footsteps echoing off the marble and into my skull.

"I would be happy to give you a tour, Iris," Maven says. "Your father is settling into his apartments, but I'm sure he won't mind if we get to know each other better."

The Arvens and Lakelander guards drop back, giving the king and his Sentinels space. Blue uniforms, white, red-orange. Their silhouettes and colors are so ingrained in me I know them out of the corner of my eye. None so much as the pale young king. I feel him as much as I see him, his cloying warmth threatening to engulf me. He stops a few inches from my side, close enough to take me by the hand if he wants to. I shudder at the thought.

"I would like that very much," Iris replies. She dips her head in an oddly stilted manner. Bowing does not come easily to her. "I was just remarking to Miss Barrow about your"—she searches for the right word, glancing back at the stark throne—"decorations."

Maven offers a tight smile. "A precaution. My father was assassinated, and attempts have been made on me as well."

"Could a chair of Silent Stone have saved your father?" she asks innocently.

A current of heat pulses through the air. Like Iris, I feel the need to shed my jacket too, lest Maven's temper sweat me out of it.

"No, my brother decided that cutting his head off was his best option," he says bluntly. "Not much defense against that."

It happened in this very palace. A few passages and rooms away, up some stairs to a place with no windows and soundproofed walls. When the guards dragged me there, I was in a daze, terrified that Maven and I were about to be executed for treason. Instead, the king ended up in two pieces. His head, his body, a rush of silver splattered in between. Instead, Maven took the crown. My fists clench at the memory.

"How horrible," Iris murmurs. I feel her eyes on me.

"Yes, wasn't it, Mare?"

His sudden hand on my arm burns like his brand. My control threatens to snap, and I glare at him sidelong. "Yes," I force out through clenched teeth. "Horrible."

Maven nods in agreement, clenching his jaw to make the bones of his face tighten. I can't believe he has the gall to look morose. To seem sad. He is neither. He can't be. His mother took away the pieces of him that loved his brother and father. I wish she'd taken the part that loves me. Instead, it festers, poisoning us both with its corruption. Black rot eats at his brain and at any bit of him that might be human. He knows it too. Knows there's something wrong, something he cannot fix with ability or power. He is broken, and there is no healer on this earth who can make him whole.

"Well, before I take you through my home, there's someone else who would like to meet my future bride. Sentinel Nornus, if you would?" Maven gestures over his soldier. At his command, the Sentinel in question blurs into a blaze of red and orange, racing to the entrance and back again in a blistering second. A swift. In his robes, he seems a fireball.

Figures follow in his wake, their house colors familiar.

"Princess Iris, this is the ruling lord of House Samos, and his family," Maven says, waving a hand between his new betrothed and the old one.

Evangeline stands out in sharp contrast to the simply clothed Iris. I wonder how long it took her to create the molten, metal liquid hugging every curve of her body like glistening tar. No more crowns and tiaras for her, but her jewelry more than makes up for it. She wears silver chains at her neck, wrists, and ears, fine as thread and studded with diamonds. Her brother's appearance is different too, absent his usual armor or fur. His rippling silhouette is still threatening enough, but Ptolemus looks more like his father now, in flawless black velvet with a sparkling silver chain. Volo leads his children, with someone I don't recognize at his side. But I can certainly guess who she is.

In that instant, I understand a bit more of Evangeline. Her mother is a frightful sight. Not because she's ugly. On the contrary, the older woman is severely beautiful. She gave Evangeline her angular black eyes and flawless porcelain skin, but not her slick, straight raven hair and dainty figure. This woman looks like I could snap her in two, manacles and all. Probably part of her facade. She wears her own house colors, black and emerald green, alongside Samos silver to denote her allegiances. *Viper.* Lady Blonos's voice sneers in my head. Black and green are the colors of House Viper. Evangeline's mother is an animos. As she gets closer, her shimmering dress comes into better focus. And I realize why Evangeline is so insistent on wearing her ability. It's a family tradition.

Her mother isn't wearing jewelry. She's wearing snakes.

On her wrists, around her neck. Thin, black, and moving slowly, their scales gleaming like spilled oil. Equal parts fear and disgust jolt through me. Suddenly I want to sprint to my room, lock the door, and put as much distance as I can between myself and the wriggling creatures. Instead, they get closer with her every footstep. And I thought Evangeline was bad.

"Lord Volo; his wife, Larentia of House Viper; their son, Ptolemus; and their daughter, Evangeline. Well-regarded and valuable members of my court," Maven explains, gesturing to each in turn. He smiles openly, showing teeth.

"I'm sorry we were not able to properly meet you sooner." Volo steps forward to take Iris's outstretched hand. With his silver beard freshly trimmed, it's easy to see the resemblance between him and his children. Strong bones, elegant lines, long noses, and lips permanently curled into a sneer. His skin looks paler against Iris's as he brushes a kiss to her bare knuckles. "We were called away to attend matters in our own lands."

Iris dips her brow. A picture of grace now. "No apology is required, my lord."

Over their clasped hands, Maven catches my eye. He quirks an eyebrow in amusement. If I could, I would ask him what he promised—or what he threatened House Samos with. Two Calore kings have slipped through their fingers. So much scheming and plotting, for nothing. I know Evangeline didn't love Maven, or even like him, but she was raised to be a queen. Her purpose was stolen twice. She failed herself and, worse, failed her house. At least now she has someone other than me to blame.

Evangeline glances in my direction, her lashes dark and long. They flutter for a moment as her eyes waver, ticking back and forth like the pendulum of an old clock. I take a small step away from Iris to put some distance between us. Now that the Samos daughter has a new rival to hate, I don't want to give her the wrong impression.

"And you were betrothed to the king?" Iris pulls her hand back from Volo and knits her fingers together. Evangeline's eyes move away from me to face the princess. For once, I see her on an even field with an equal opponent. Maybe I'll get lucky and Evangeline will misstep, threaten Iris the way she used to threaten me. I have a feeling Iris won't tolerate a word of it.

"For a time, yes," Evangeline says. "And his brother before him."

The princess is not surprised. I assume the Lakelands are well informed of the Nortan royals. "Well, I'm glad you've returned to court. We will require a good amount of help in organizing our wedding."

I bite my lip so hard I almost draw blood. Better that than laughing out loud as Iris pours salt into so many Samos wounds. Across from me, Maven turns his head to hide a sneer.

One of the snakes hisses, a low, droning sound impossible to mistake. But Larentia quickly curtsies, sweeping out the fabric of her shimmering gown.

"We are at your disposal, Your Highness," she says. Her voice is deep, rich as syrup. As we watch, the thickest snake, around her neck, nuzzles up past her ear and into her hair. *Revolting.* "It would be an honor to aid you however we can." I half expect her to elbow Evangeline into agreeing. Instead, the Viper woman turns her attention on me, so quickly I don't have time to look away. "Is there a reason the prisoner is staring at me?"

"None," I respond, teeth clicking together.

Larentia takes my eye contact as a challenge. Like an animal. She steps forward, closing the distance between us. We're the same height. The snake in her hair continues hissing, coiling and twisting down onto her collarbone. Its jewel-bright eyes meet mine, and its forked black tongue licks the air, darting out between long fangs. Even though I stand my ground, I can't help but swallow hard, my mouth suddenly dry. The snake keeps watching me.

"They say you are different," Larentia mutters. "But your fear smells the same as that of every vile Red rat I've ever had the misfortune to know."

Red rat. Red rat.

I've heard that so many times. Thought it about myself. From her lips, it cracks something in me. The control I've worked so hard to maintain, that I must keep if I want to stay alive, threatens to unravel. I take a dragging breath, willing myself to keep still. Her snakes continue hissing, curling over one another in black tangles of scale and spine. Some are long enough to reach me if she wills it so.

Maven sighs low in his throat. "Guards, I think it's time Miss Barrow was returned to her room."

I spin on my heel before the Arvens can jump to my side, retreating into the so-called safety of their presence. *Something about the snakes,* I tell myself. *I couldn't stand them. No wonder Evangeline is horrific, with a mother like that to raise her.*

As I flee back to my rooms, I'm seized by an unwelcome sensation. Relief. Gratitude. To Maven.

I crush that vile burst of emotion with all the rage I have. Maven is a monster. I feel nothing but hatred toward him. I cannot allow anything else, even pity, to creep in.

I MUST ESCAPE.

Two long months pass.

Maven's wedding will be ten times the production that the Parting Ball, or even Queenstrial, was. Silver nobles flood back into the capital, bringing entourages with them from all corners of Norta. Even the ones the king exiled. Maven feels safe enough in his new alliance to allow even smiling enemies through his door. Though most have city houses of their own, many take up residence in Whitefire, until the palace itself seems ready to burst at the seams. I'm kept to my room mostly. I don't mind. It's better this way. But even from my cell, I can feel the impending storm of a wedding. The tangible union of Norta and the Lakelands.

The courtyard below my window, empty all winter long, flourishes in a suddenly warm and green spring. Nobles walk through the magnolia trees at a lazy pace, some arm in arm. Always whispering, always scheming or gossiping. I wish I could read lips. I might learn something other than which houses seem to congregate together, their colors brighter in the sunlight. Maven would have to be a fool to think they aren't plotting against him or his bride. And he is many things, but not that.

The old routine I used to pass my first month of isolation—wake, eat, sit, scream, repeat—doesn't serve anymore. I have more useful ways to pass the time. There are no pens and paper, and I don't bother to ask. No use leaving scraps. Instead, I stare at Julian's books, idly turning pages. Sometimes I latch on to jotted notes, annotations scrawled in Julian's handwriting. *Interesting*; *curious*; *corroborate with volume IV.* Idle words with little meaning. I brush my fingers along the letters anyway, feeling dry ink and the press of a long-gone pen. Enough of Julian to keep me thinking, reading between lines on the page and words spoken aloud.

He ruminates on one volume in particular, thinner than the histories but densely packed with text. Its spine is badly broken, the pages cluttered with Julian's writing. I can almost feel the warmth of his hands as they smoothed the tattered pages.

On Origins, the cover says in embossed black lettering, followed by the names of a dozen Silver scholars who wrote the many essays and arguments within the small book. Most of it is too complex for my understanding, but I sift through it anyway. If only for Julian.

He marked one passage in particular, dog-earing the page and underlining a few sentences. Something about mutations, changes. The result of ancient weaponry we no longer possess and can no longer create. One of the scholars believes it made Silvers. Others disagree. A few mention gods instead, perhaps the ones that Iris follows.

Julian makes his own position clear in notes at the bottom of the page.

Strange that so many thought themselves gods, or a god's chosen, he wrote. *Blessed by something greater. Elevated to what we are. When all evidence points to the opposite. Our abilities came from corruption, from a scourge that killed most. We were not a god's chosen, but a god's cursed.*

I blink at the words and wonder. *If Silvers are cursed, then what are newbloods? Worse?*

Or is Julian wrong? Are we chosen too? And for what?

Men and women much smarter than me have no answers, and neither do I. Not to mention, I have more pressing things to think about.

I plan while I eat breakfast, chewing slowly as I run through what I know. A royal wedding will be organized chaos. Extra security, more guards than I can count, but still a good enough chance. Servants everywhere, drunk nobles, a foreign princess to distract the people usually focused on me. I'd be stupid not to try something. Cal would be stupid not to try something.

I glare at the pages in hand, at white paper and black ink. Nanny tried to save me and Nanny ended up dead. A waste of life. And I selfishly want them to try again. Because if I stay here much longer, if I have to live the rest of my life a few steps behind Maven, with his haunting eyes and his missing pieces and his hatred for everyone in this world—

Hatred for everyone but—

"Stop," I hiss to myself, fighting the urge to let in the silk monster knocking at the walls of my mind. "Stop it."

Memorization of the layout of Whitefire is a good distraction, the one I usually rely on. Two lefts from my door, through a gallery of statues, left again down a spiraling stair . . . I trace the way to the throne room, the entrance hall, the banquet hall, different studies and council chambers, Evangeline's quarters, Maven's old bedroom. Every step I've taken here I memorize. The better I know the palace, the better chance I have of escaping when the opportunity arises. Certainly Maven will marry Iris in the Royal Court, if not in Caesar's Square itself. Nowhere else can hold so many guests and guards. I can't see the court from my window, and I've never been inside, but I'll cross that bridge when I come to it.

Maven hasn't dragged me to his side since we returned. *Good,* I tell myself. An empty room and days of silence are better than his cloying words. Still, I feel a tug of disappointment every night when I shut my eyes. I'm lonely; I'm afraid; I'm selfish. I feel emptied out by the Silent Stone and the months I've spent here, walking the edge of another razor. It would be so easy to let the broken pieces of me fall apart. It would be so easy to let him put me back together however he wishes. Maybe, in a few years, it won't even feel like a prison.

No.

For the first time in a while, I smash my breakfast plate against the wall, screaming as I do it. The water glass next. It explodes in crystal shards. Broken things make me feel a bit better.

My door bursts open in half a second as the Arvens enter. Egg is the first to my side, holding me back in my chair. His grip is firm, preventing me from getting up. Now they know better than to let me anywhere near the wreckage as they clean.

"Maybe you should start giving me plastic," I scoff to no one. "Seems like a better idea."

Egg wants to hit me. His fingers dig into my shoulders, probably leaving bruises. The Silent Stone makes the hurt bite bone-deep. My stomach twists as I realize I can barely remember what it's like not to be in constant, smothering pain and anguish.

The other guards sweep away the debris, unflinching as glass drags over their gloved hands. Only when they disappear, their throbbing presence melting away, do I once again have the strength to stand. Annoyed, I slam shut the book I wasn't reading. *Genealogy of Nortan Nobility, Volume IX*, the cover says. Useless.

With nothing better to do, I put it back on the shelf. The leatherbound book slides in neatly between its brothers, volumes VIII and X. Maybe I'll pull the other books down and rearrange them. Waste a few seconds of the endless hours.

I end up on the floor instead, trying to stretch a bit farther than I did yesterday. My old agility is a faint memory, restricted by circumstance. I try anyway, inching my fingers toward my toes. The muscles in my legs burn, a better feeling than the ache. I chase the pain. It's one of the only things to remind me I'm still alive in this shell.

The minutes bleed into one another and time stretches with me. Outside, the light shifts as spring clouds chase each other across the sun.

The knock on my door is soft, uncertain. No one has ever bothered to knock before, and my heart leaps. But the rush of adrenaline dies off. A rescuer would not knock.

Evangeline pushes open the door, not waiting for an invitation.

I don't move, rooted to the spot by a sudden rush of fear. I draw my legs up under myself. Ready to spring if I need to.

She looks down her nose at me, her usual superior self in a long, glinting coat and tightly sewn leather leggings. For a moment she stands still, and we trade glances in the silence.

"Are you so dangerous they can't even let you open a window?" She sniffs at the air. "It stinks in here."

My tightened muscles relax a little. "So you're bored," I mutter. "Go rattle someone else's cage."

"Perhaps later. But for now, you're going to be of use."

"I really don't feel like being your dartboard."

She smacks her lips. "Oh, not mine."

With one hand, she seizes me under the armpit and hoists me to my feet. As soon as her arm enters the sphere of my Silent Stone, her sleeve falls away, collapsing to the floor in bits of gleaming metal dust. It quickly reattaches and falls again, moving in an even, strange rhythm as she marches me from my room.

I don't struggle. There's no point in it. Eventually she loosens her bruising grip and lets me walk without the pinch of her hand.

"If you wanted to take the pet for a walk, all you had to do was ask," I growl at her, massaging my newest bruise. "Don't you have a new rival to hate? Or is it easier to pick on a prisoner rather than a princess?"

"Iris is far too calm for my liking," she shoots back. "You still have some bite, at least."

"Good to know I amuse you." The passage twists in front of us. Left, right, right. The blueprint of Whitefire sharpens in my mind's eye. We pass the phoenix tapestries in red and black, edges studded with real gemstones. Then a gallery of statues and paintings dedicated to Caesar Calore, the first king of Norta. Beyond it, down a half flight of marble steps, is what I call the Battle Hall. A stretching passage illuminated by skylights, the walls on either side dominated by two monstrous paintings, inspired by the Lakelander War, stretching from floor to ceiling. But she doesn't lead me past painted scenes of death and glory. We're not going down to the court levels of the palace. The halls become more ornate, but with fewer public displays of opulence as she leads me to the royal residences. An increasing number of gilded paintings of kings, politicians, and warriors watch me go, most of them with the characteristic Calore black hair.

"Has King Maven let you keep your rooms, at least? Even though he took your crown?"

Her lips twist. Into a smirk, not a scowl. "See? You never disappoint. All bite, Mare Barrow."

I've never been to these doors before. But I can guess where they lead. Too grand to be for anyone but a king. White lacquered wood, silver and gold trim, inlaid with mother of pearl and ruby. Evangeline doesn't knock this time and throws the doors open, only to find an opulent antechamber lined by six Sentinels. They bristle at our presence, hands straying to weapons, eyes sharp behind their glittering masks.

She doesn't balk. "Tell the king Mare Barrow is here to see him."

"The king is indisposed," one answers. His voice trembles with power. A banshee. He could scream us both deaf if given the chance. "Be gone, Lady Samos."

Evangeline shows no fear and runs a hand through her long silver braid. "Tell him," she says again. She doesn't have to drop her voice or snarl to be threatening. "He'll want to know."

My heart pounds in my chest. *What is she doing? Why?* The last time she decided to parade me around Whitefire, I ended up at the mercy of Samson Merandus, my mind split open for him to sift through. She has an agenda. She has motives. If only I knew what they were, so I could do the opposite.

One of the Sentinels breaks before she does. He is a broad man, his muscles evident even beneath the folds of his fiery robes. He inclines his face, the black jewels of his mask catching the light. "A moment, my lady." I can't stand Maven's chambers. Just being here feels like stepping into quicksand. Plunging into the ocean, falling off a cliff. *Send us away. Send us away.*

The Sentinel returns quickly. When he waves off his comrades, my stomach drops. "This way, Barrow." He beckons to me.

Evangeline gives me the slightest nudge, putting pressure on the base of my spine. Perfectly executed. I lurch forward.

"Just Barrow," the Sentinel adds. He eyes the Arvens in succession.

They stay in place, letting me go. So does Evangeline. Her eyes darken, blacker than ever. I'm seized by the strange urge to grab her and bring her with me. Facing Maven alone, here, is suddenly terrifying.

The Sentinel, probably a Rhambos strongarm, doesn't have to touch me to herd me in the proper direction. We cross through a sitting room flooded with sunlight, oddly empty and barely decorated. No house colors, no paintings or sculptures, or even books. Cal's old room was cluttered, bursting with different types of armor, his precious manuals, even a game board. Pieces of him strewn everywhere. Maven is not his brother. He has no cause to perform, not here, and the room reflects the hollow boy he truly is inside.

His bed is strangely small. Built for a child, even though the room was clearly arranged to hold something much, much bigger. The walls of his bedroom are white, unadorned. The windows are the only decoration, overlooking a corner of Caesar's Square, the Capital River, and the bridge I once helped destroy. It spans the water, connecting Whitefire to the eastern half of the city. Greenery bursts to life in every direction, peppered with blossoms.

Slowly, the Sentinel clears his throat. I glance at him and shiver when I realize he's going to abandon me too. "That way," he says, pointing at another set of doors.

It would be easier if someone dragged me. If the Sentinel put a gun to my head and made me walk through. Blaming my moving feet on another person would hurt less. Instead, it's only me. Boredom. Morbid curiosity. The constant ache of pain and loneliness. I live in a shrinking world where the only thing I can trust is Maven's obsession. Like the manacles, it is a shield and a slow, smothering death.

The doors swing inward, gliding over white marble tile. Steam spirals on the air. Not from the fire king himself, but hot water. It boils lazily around him, milky with soap and scented oils. Unlike his bed, the bath is large, standing on clawed silver feet. He rests an elbow on either side of the flawless porcelain, fingers trailing lazily through the swirling water.

Maven tracks me as I enter, his eyes electric and lethal. I've never seen him so off guard and so angry. A smarter girl would turn and run. Instead, I shut the door behind me.

There are no seats, so I remain standing. I'm not sure where to look, so I focus on his face. His hair is mussed, soaking wet. Dark curls cling to his skin.

"I'm busy," he whispers.

"You didn't have to let me in." I wish I could call back the words as soon as I speak them.

"Yes I did," he says, meaning all things. Then he blinks, breaking his stare. He leans back, tipping his head against the porcelain so he can stare up at the ceiling. "What do you need?"

A way out, forgiveness, a good night's sleep, my family. The list stretches, endless.

"Evangeline dragged me here. I don't want anything from you."

He makes a noise low in his throat. Almost a laugh. "Evangeline. My Sentinels are cowards."

If Maven were my friend, I would warn him not to underestimate a daughter of House Samos. Instead, I hold my tongue. The steam sticks to my skin, feverish as hot flesh.

"She brought you here to convince me," he says.

"Convince you to do what?"

"Marry Iris, don't marry Iris. She certainly didn't send you in here for a tea party."

"No." Evangeline will keep scheming for a queen's crown up until the second Maven puts it on another girl's head. It's what she was made for. Just like Maven was made for other, more horrible things.

"She thinks what I feel for you can cloud my judgment. Foolish."

I flinch. The brand on my collarbone sears beneath my shirt.

"Heard you started smashing things again," he continues.

"You have bad taste in china."

He grins at the ceiling. A crooked smile. Like his brother's. For a second, Maven's face becomes Cal's, their features shifting. With a jolt, I realize I've been here longer than I even knew Cal. I know Maven's face better than his.

He shifts, making the water ripple as he dangles an arm out of the bath. I wrench my eyes away, look down at the tile. I have three brothers, and a father who can't walk. I spent months sharing a glorified hole with a dozen stinking men and boys. I'm not a stranger to the male form. Doesn't mean I want to see more of Maven than I must. Again I feel myself on the edge of quicksand.

"The wedding is tomorrow," he finally says. His voice echoes off the marble.

"Oh."

"You didn't know?"

"How could I? I'm not exactly kept informed."

Maven shrugs, raising his shoulders. Another shift of the water, showing more of his white skin. "Yes, well, I didn't really think you were going to start breaking things over me, but . . ." He pauses and looks my way. My body prickles. "It felt good to wonder."

If there were no consequences, I would scowl and scream and claw his eyes out. Tell Maven that even though my time with his brother was fleeting, I still remember every heartbeat we shared. The feel of him pressed up against me as we slept, alone together, trading nightmares. His hand at my neck, flesh on flesh, making me look at him as we dropped from the sky. What he smells like. What he tastes like. *I love your brother, Maven. You were right. You are only a shadow, and who looks at shadows when they have flame? Who would ever choose a monster over a god?* I can't hurt Maven with lightning, but I can destroy him with words. Poke at his weak spots, open his wounds. Let him bleed and scab over into something worse than he ever was before.

The words I manage to speak are quite different.

"Do you like Iris?" I ask instead.

He scratches a hand along his scalp and huffs, childlike. "As if that has anything to do with it."

"Well, she is the first new relationship you'll have since your mother died. It'll be interesting to see how that plays without her poison in you." I drum my fingers at my side. The words sink in slowly, and he barely nods. Agreeing. I feel a surge of pity for him. I fight it tooth and nail. "And you were betrothed two months ago. It seems fast, faster than your engagement to Evangeline at least."

"That tends to happen when an entire army hangs in the balance," he says sharply. "Lakelanders are not known for their patience."

I scoff. "And House Samos is so accommodating?"

A corner of his mouth lifts in ghost of that crooked smile. He fiddles with one of his flamemaker bracelets, slowly spinning the silver circle around a fine-boned wrist. "They have their uses."

"I thought Evangeline would have turned you into a pincushion by now."

His smile spreads. "If she kills me, she loses whatever chance she thinks she has, however fleeting. Not that her father would ever allow it. House Samos maintains a position of great power, even if she isn't queen. But what a queen she would have made."

"I can only imagine." The thought shudders through me. Crowns of needles and daggers and razors, her mother in jeweled snakes and her father holding Maven's puppet strings.

"I can't," he admits. "Not really. Even now, I only ever see her as Cal's queen."

"You didn't have to choose her after you framed him—"

"Well, I couldn't exactly choose the person I wanted, could I?" he snaps. Instead of heat, I feel the air around us turn cold. Enough to make goose bumps prickle across my skin as he glares at me, his eyes a livid, burning blue. The steam on the air clears on the current of cooler air, removing the faint barrier between us.

Shivering, I force myself to the closest window, putting my back to him. Outside, the magnolia trees shudder on a light breeze, their blossoms white and cream and rosy in the sunshine. Such simple beauty has no place here without the corruption of blood or ambition or betrayal.

"You threw me into an arena to die," I tell him slowly. As if either of us could forget. "You keep me chained up in your palace, guarded night and day, You let me waste away, sick—"

"You think I enjoy seeing you like this?" he murmurs. "You think I want to keep you a prisoner?" Something hitches in his breath. "It's the only way you'll stay with me." Water sloshes over his hands as he draws them back and forth.

I focus on the sound instead of his voice. Even though I know what he's doing, even though I can feel his grip on me tightening, I can't stop it from pulling me under. It would be too easy to let myself drown. Part of me wants to.

I keep my eyes on the window. For once, I'm glad for the all-too-familiar ache of Silent Stone. It is an undeniable reminder of what he is, and what his love means for me.

"You tried to murder everyone I care about. You killed children." A baby, bloodstained, a note in its little fist. I remember it so vividly it could be a nightmare. I don't try to force the image away. I need to remember it. I need to remember what he is. "Because of you, my brother is dead."

I spin to him, barking out a harsh, vengeful laugh. Anger clears my head.

He sits up sharply, his naked torso almost as white as the bathwater.

"And you killed my mother. You took my brother. You took my father. The second you fell into the world, the wheels were in motion. My mother looked into your head and saw opportunity. She saw a chance she had been looking for forever. If you hadn't—if you had never—" He stumbles, the words coming faster than he can stop them. Then he grits his teeth, clamping down on anything more damning. Another breath of silence. "I don't want to know what would have been."

"I know," I snarl. "I would've ended up in a trench, obliterated or torn apart or barely surviving as the walking dead. I know what

I would have become, because a million others live it. My father, my brothers, too many people."

"Knowing what you know now . . . would you go back? Would you choose that life? Conscription, your muddy town, your family, that river boy?"

So many are dead because of me, because of what I am. If I were just a Red, just Mare Barrow, they would be alive. Shade would be alive. My thoughts hinge on him. I would trade so many things to have him back. I'd trade myself a thousand times. But then there are the newbloods found and saved. Rebellions aided. A war ended. Silvers tearing at one another. Reds uniting. I had a hand in all of it, however small. Mistakes were made. My mistakes. Too many to count. I am worlds away from perfect, or even good. The true question eats at my brain. What Maven is really asking. *Would you give up your ability, would you trade your power, to go back?* I don't need time to figure out an answer.

"No," I whisper. I don't remember moving so close to him, my hand closing on one side of the porcelain bath. "No, I wouldn't."

The confession burns worse than flame, eating at my insides. I hate him for what he makes me feel, what he makes me realize. I wonder if I can move fast enough to incapacitate him. Clench a fist, bust his jaw with the hard manacle. Can skin healers regrow teeth? No real point in trying. I wouldn't live to find out.

He stares up at me. "Those who know what it's like in the dark will do anything to stay in the light."

"Don't act like we're the same."

"The same? No." He shakes his head. "But perhaps . . . we're even."

"Even?" Again I want to tear him apart. Use my nails, my teeth to rip his throat. The insinuation cuts. Almost as much as the fact that he might be right.

"I used to ask Jon if he could see futures that no longer exist. He said the paths were always changing. An easy lie. It let him manipulate me in a way even Samson couldn't. And when he led me to you, well, I didn't argue. How was I supposed to know what a poison you would be?"

"If I'm a poison, then get rid of me. Stop torturing us both!"

"You know I can't do that, no matter how much I may want to." His lashes flicker and his eyes go far away. Somewhere even I can't reach him. "You're like Thomas was. You are the only person I care about, the only person who reminds me I am alive. Not empty. And not alone."

Alive. Not empty. Not alone.

Each confession is an arrow, piercing every nerve ending until my body turns to cold fire. I hate that Maven can say such things. I hate that he feels what I feel, fears what I fear. I hate it; I hate it. And if I could change who am, how I think, I would. But I can't. If Iris's gods are real, they certainly know I've tried.

"Jon would not tell me about the dead futures—the ones no longer possible. I think about them, though," he mumbles. "A Silver king, a Red queen. How would things have changed? How many would still be alive?"

"Not your father. Not Cal. And certainly not me."

"I know it's just a dream, Mare," he snaps. Like a child corrected in the classroom. "Any window we had, however small, is gone."

"Because of you."

"Yes." Softer, an admission of his own. "Yes."

Never breaking eye contact, Maven slips the flamemaker bracelet from his wrist. It's slow, deliberate, methodic. I hear it hit the floor and roll, silver metal ringing against the marble. The other quickly follows.

Still watching, he leans back in the bath and tips his head. Exposing his neck. At my side, my hands twitch. It would be so easy. Wrap my brown fingers around his pale neck. Put all my weight into it. Pin him down. Cal is afraid of water. Is Maven? I could drown him. Kill him. Let the bathwater boil us both. He dares me to do it. Part of him might want me to do it. Or it could be one of the thousand traps I've fallen for. Another trick of Maven Calore.

He blinks and exhales, letting go of something deep inside himself. It breaks the spell and the moment shatters.

"You'll be one of Iris's ladies tomorrow. Enjoy yourself."

One more arrow to the gut.

I wish for another glass to smash against the wall. A lady-in-waiting for the wedding of the century. No chance of slipping away. I'll have to stand before the entire court. Guards everywhere. Eyes everywhere. I want to scream.

Use the anger. Use the rage, I try to tell myself. Instead, it just consumes me and turns to despair.

Maven just gestures lazily with an open hand. "There's the door."

I try not to look back as I go, but I can't help myself. Maven stares at the ceiling, his eyes empty. And I hear Julian in my head, whispering the words he wrote.

Not a god's chosen, but a god's cursed.

EIGHTEEN
Mare

For once, I am not the object of torture. If I had the opportunity, I would thank Iris for allowing me to sit to the side and be ignored. Evangeline takes my place instead. She tries to look serene, unaffected by the scene around us. The rest of the bridal entourage keeps glancing at her, the girl they were supposed to serve. At any moment, I expect her to curl up like one of her mother's snakes and start hissing at every person who dares come within a few feet of her gilded chair. After all, these chambers used to be hers.

The salon is redecorated for its new occupant and rightfully so. Bright blue wall hangings, fresh flowers in clear water, and several gentle fountains make it unmistakable. A princess of the Lakelands reigns here.

In the center of the room, Iris surrounds herself with servants, Red maids infinitely skilled in the art of beauty. She needs little help. Her cliff-high cheekbones and dark eyes are magnificent enough without paint. One maid intricately braids her black hair into a crown, fastening it with sapphire and pearl pins. Another rubs sparkling blush to sculpt an already beautiful bone structure into something ethereal and otherworldly. Her lips are a deep purple, expertly drawn. The dress itself, white fading to bright, shimmering blue at the hem, sets off her dark skin with a glow like the sky moments after a sunset. Even though appearance is the last thing I should be worried about, I feel like a discarded doll next to her. I'm in red again, simple in comparison to my usual jewels and brocade. If I were a bit healthier, I might look beautiful too. Not that I mind. I'm not supposed to shine, I don't want to shine—and next to her, I certainly won't.

Evangeline couldn't contrast Iris more if she tried—and she certainly tried. While Iris eagerly plays the part of a young, blushing bride, Evangeline has willingly accepted the role of the girl scorned and cast aside. Her dress is metal so iridescent it could be made of pearl, with razored white feathers and silver inlay throughout. Her own maids flutter about, putting the finishing touches on her appearance. She stares at Iris through it all, black eyes never wavering. Only when her mother moves to her side does she break focus, and then only to inch away from the emerald-green butterflies decorating Larentia's skirts. Their wings flutter idly, as if in a breeze. A gentle reminder that they are living things, attached to the Viper woman by ability alone. I hope she doesn't intend to sit.

I've seen weddings before, back home in the Stilts. Crude gatherings. A few binding words and a hasty party. Families scrounge to provide enough food for the invited guests, while those who wander through get nothing more than a good show. Kilorn and I used to try to pinch leftovers, if there were any. Fill our pockets with bread rolls and slink off to enjoy the spoils. I don't think I'll be doing that today.

The only thing I'll be holding on to is Iris's long train and my own sanity.

"Pity more of your family could not be here to attend, Your Highness."

An older woman, her hair entirely gray, distances herself from the many Silver ladies awaiting Iris. She crosses her arms over an immaculate black dress uniform. Unlike most officers, her badges are few, but still impressive. I've never seen her before, though there's something familiar about her face. But from this angle, with her features in profile, I can't place it.

Iris inclines her head to the woman. Behind her, two maids fasten a shimmering veil in place. "My mother is ruling queen of the Lakelands. She must always sit the throne. And my older sister, her heir, is loath to leave our kingdom."

"Understandable, in such tumultuous times." The older woman bows back, but not as deeply as one would expect. "My congratulations, Princess Iris."

"My thanks, Your Majesty. I'm glad you were able to join us."

Majesty?

The older woman turns fully, putting her back to Iris as the maids finish their work. Her eyes fall on me, narrowing in the slightest. With one hand she beckons. A giant black gem flashes on her ring finger. On either side, Kitten and Clover bump me forward, pushing me at the woman who somehow commands a title.

"Miss Barrow," she says. The woman is sturdy, with a thick waist, and she has a few good inches on me. I glance at her uniform, looking for house colors to distinguish who she might be.

"Your Majesty?" I reply, using the title. It sounds like a question, and truly, it is.

She offers an amused smile. "I wish I had met you before. When you were masquerading as Mareena Titanos and not reduced to this"—she touches my cheek lightly, making me flinch—"this person wasting away. Maybe then I could understand why my grandson threw his kingdom away for you."

Her eyes are bronze. Red-gold. I would know her eyes anywhere.

Despite the wedding party milling around us, the clouds of silk and perfume, I feel myself slide back into that horrible moment when a king lost his head and a son lost his father. And this woman lost them both.

Out of the depths of memory, my moments wasted reading histories, I remember her name. Anabel, of House Lerolan. Queen Anabel. Mother to Tiberias the Sixth. Cal's grandmother. Now I see her crown, rose gold and black diamonds nestled into her neatly tied hair. A little thing compared to what royals usually prance around in.

She pulls her hand away. All the better. Anabel is an oblivion. I don't want her fingers anywhere near me. They could destroy me with a touch.

"I'm sorry about your son." King Tiberias was not a kind man, not to me, not to Maven, not to more than half his country living and dying as slaves. But he loved Cal's mother. He loved his children. He was not evil. Just weak.

Her gaze never breaks. "Odd, since you helped kill him."

There is no accusation in her voice. No anger. No rage.

She is lying.

The Royal Court is devoid of color. Just white walls and black columns, marble and granite and crystal. It devours a rainbow crowd. Nobles flood through its doors, their gowns and suits and uniforms dyed in every glittering shade. The last of them hurry, scrambling to get inside before the royal bride and her own parade begin their march across Caesar's Square. Hundreds more Silvers crowd across the tiled expanse, too common to merit an invitation to the wedding itself. They wait in droves, on either side of a cleared pathway lined by an even distribution of Nortan and Lakelander guards. Cameras watch too, elevated on platforms. And the kingdom watches with them.

From my vantage point, sandwiched in the Whitefire entrance, I can just see over Iris's shoulder.

She keeps quiet, not a hair out of place. Serene as still water. I don't know how she can stand it. Her royal father has her arm, his cobalt-blue robes electric against the white sleeve of her wedding gown. Today his crown is silver and sapphire, matching hers. They do not speak to each other, focused on the path ahead.

Her train feels like liquid in my hands. Silk so fine it might slip through my fingers. I keep a good grip, if only to avoid drawing more attention than I need to. For once, I'm glad to have Evangeline at my side. She holds the other corner of Iris's train. Judging by the whispers of the other ladies-in-waiting, the sight is a near scandal. They focus on her instead of me. No one bothers to bait the lightning girl without her sparks. Evangeline takes it all in stride, jaw set and shut. She hasn't spoken to me at all. Another small blessing.

Somewhere, a horn blows. And the crowd responds, turning toward the palace in unison, a sea of eyes. I feel each look as we step forward, onto the landing, down the stairs, into the jaws of a Silver spectacle. The last time I saw a crowd here, I was kneeling and collared, bloody and bruised and heartbroken. I am still all those things. My fingers tremble. Guards press in, while Kitten and Clover stick behind me in simple but suitable gowns. The crowd pushes closer, and Evangeline is so near she could knife me between the ribs without blinking. My lungs feel tight; my chest constricts and my throat seems to close. I swallow hard and force out a long breath. *Calm down.* I focus on the dress in my hands, the inches in front of me.

I think I feel a drop of water hit my cheek. I pray it's rain and not nervous tears.

"Pull yourself together, Barrow," a voice hisses. It could be Evangeline's. As with Maven, I feel a sick burst of gratitude for the meager support. I try to push it away. I try to reason with myself. But like a dog starved, I'll take whatever scraps I'm given. Whatever passes for kindness in this lonely cage.

My vision spirals. If not for my feet, my dear, quick, sure feet, I might stumble. Each step comes harder than the last. Panic spikes up my spine. I drown myself in the white of Iris's dress. I even count heartbeats. Anything to keep moving. I don't know why, but this wedding feels like the closing of a thousand doors. Maven has doubled his strength and tightened his grip. I'll never escape him. Not after this.

The stone beneath me changes. Smooth, square tiles become steps. I bump on the first but right myself, holding up the train. Doing the only thing I'm still able to do. Stand to the side, kneel, shrivel away, turn bitter and hungry in the shadows. Is this the rest of my life?

Before I enter the maw of the Royal Court too, I glance up. Past the sculptures of fire and stars and swords and ancient kings, past the crystal reaches of the glittering dome. To the sky. Clouds gather in the distance. A few have already reached the square, moving steadily in the wind. They dissipate slowly, unraveling into wisps of nothing. Rain wants to gather, but something, probably Silver storms, controlling the weather won't let it. Nothing will be allowed to ruin this day.

And then the sky disappears, replaced by a vaulted ceiling. Smooth limestone arches overhead, banded with silver spirals of forged flame. Red-and-black banners of Norta and blue banners of the Lakelands decorate either side of the antechamber, as if anyone could forget the kingdoms whose union we're about to witness. The murmurs of a thousand onlookers sound like humming bees, increasing with every step forward I take. Ahead, the passage widens into the central chamber of the Royal Court, a magnificent circular hall beneath the crystal dome. The sun climbs across the clear panes, illuminating the spectacle below. Every seat is full, ringed out from the middle of the chamber in a halo of flashing color. The crowd waits, breathless. I can't see Maven yet, but I can guess where he will be.

Anyone else would hesitate, even a little. Iris does not. She never breaks pace as we cross into the light. A thousand bodies standing up is almost deafening, and the noise echoes around the chamber. Rustling clothes, shifting movement, whispers. I stay focused on my breathing. My heart races anyway. I want to look up, note the entrances, the branching passages, the pieces of this place I can use. But I can barely walk, let alone plan another ill-fated escape.

It feels like years pass before we reach the center. Maven waits, his cape just as opulent as Iris's train and nearly as long. He cuts an impressive figure in flashing red and white instead of black. The crown is newly made, wrought of silver and rubies worked into flame. It gleams when he moves, turning his head to face his approaching bride and her entourage. His eyes find me first. I know him well enough to recognize regret. It flickers, alive for a moment, dancing like the wick of a lit candle. And, just as easily, it disappears, trailing a memory like smoke. I hate him, especially because I can't fight the now-familiar surge of pity for the shadow of the flame. Monsters are made. So was Maven. Who knows who he was supposed to be?

The ceremony takes the better part of an hour, and I have to stand through all of it alongside Evangeline and the rest of the bridal parade. Maven and Iris trade words back and forth, oaths and pledges urged on by a Nortan judge. A woman in plain indigo robes speaks as well. From the Lakelands, I assume—maybe an envoy of their gods? I hardly listen. All I can think about is an army in red and blue, marching across the world. Clouds continue to roll in, each one darker than the last as they pass the dome overhead. And each one disintegrates. The storm wants to break, but it just can't seem to.

I know the feeling.

"From this day until my last day, I pledge myself to you, Iris of House Cygnet, princess of the Lakelands."

In front of me, Maven holds out his hand. Fire licks at the tips of his fingers, gentle and weak as candle flame. I could blow it out if I tried.

"From this day until my last day, I pledge myself to you, Maven of House Calore, king of Norta."

Iris mirrors his action, putting out her own hand. Her white sleeve, edged in bright blue, falls back gracefully, exposing more of her smooth arm as it leaches moisture from the air. A sphere of clear, trembling water fills her palm. When she joins hands with Maven, one ability destroys the other without even the hiss of steam or smoke. A peaceful union is made, and sealed with a brush of their lips.

He doesn't kiss her the way he kissed me. Any fire he might have is far away.

I wish I were too.

The applause shudders in me, loud as a thunderclap. Most people cheer. I don't blame them. This is the last nail in the coffin of the Lakelander War. Even though Reds died in the thousands, the millions, Silvers died too. I won't begrudge them their celebrations of peace.

Another rumble sounds as many seats around the Royal Court shift, pushing back along stone. I flinch, wondering if we're about to be crushed in a tide of well-wishers. Instead, Sentinels press in. I clutch at Iris's train like a lifeline, letting her swift motions pull me through the heaving crowd and back out into Caesar's Square.

Of course, the crush of noise only increases tenfold. Flags wave, cheers erupt, and sprinkles of paper drift down on us. I dip my head, trying to block it out. Instead, my ears start to ring. The sound doesn't go away, no matter how much I shake my head. One of the Arvens takes my elbow, her fingers digging into flesh as more and more people press in around us. The Sentinels shout something, instructing the crowd to stay back. Maven turns to look over his shoulder, his face flushed gray in excitement or nerves or both. The ringing intensifies, and I have to let go of Iris's train to cover my ears. It does nothing except slow me down, pulling me out of her circle of safety. She carries on, arm in arm with her new husband, with Evangeline trailing them both. The tide separates us.

Maven sees me stop and raises an eyebrow, his lips parting to ask a question. His steps slow.

Then the sky turns black.

Storm clouds bloom, dark and heavy, arcing over us like an inferno's smoke. Lightning streaks across the clouds, bolts tinged white and blue and green. Each one jagged, vicious, destructive. Unnatural.

My heartbeat roars loud enough to drown out the crowd. But not the thunder.

The sound rattles in my chest, so close and so explosive it shakes the air. I taste it on my tongue.

I don't get to see the next thunderbolt before Kitten and Clover throw me to the ground, our dresses be damned. They pin my shoulders, digging into aching muscles with their hands and their ability. Silence floods my body, fast and strong enough to push the air from my lungs. I gasp, struggling to breathe. My fingers scrabble over the tiled ground, feeling for something to grab. If I could breathe, I would laugh. This is not the first time someone has held me down in Caesar's Square.

Another clap of thunder, another flash of blue light. The resulting push of Arven silence almost makes me vomit up my guts.

"Don't kill her, Janny. Don't!" Clover growls. *Janny.* Kitten's real name. "It'll be our heads if she dies."

"It's not me," I try to choke out. "It's not me."

If Kitten and Clover can hear, they don't show it. Their pressure never lessens, a new constant of pain.

Unable to scream, I force my head up, looking for someone to help me. Looking for Maven. He'll stop this. I hate myself for thinking it.

Legs cross my vision, black uniforms, civilian colors, and distant, fleeing red-orange robes. The Sentinels keep moving, tight in their formation. Like at the banquet that ended in a near assassination, they spring into well-practiced action, focused on their one and only purpose: defend the king. They change direction quickly, herding Maven not toward the palace, but to the Treasury. To his train. To his escape.

Escape from what?

The freak storm isn't mine. The lightning isn't mine.

"Follow the king," Kitten—Janny—snarls. She hoists me onto wobbly legs, and I almost fall again. The Arvens don't let me. Neither does the sudden wall of uniformed officers. They surround me in diamond formation, perfect for cutting through the surging crowd. The Arvens lessen their pulsing ability, if only to allow me to walk.

We push on as one while the lightning overhead intensifies. No rain yet. And it's not nearly hot enough or arid enough for dry lightning. Strange. If only I could feel it. Use it. Draw the jagged lines out of the sky and obliterate every single person around me.

The crowd is perplexed. Most look up; a few point. Some try to back away but find themselves hemmed in by one another. I glance between the faces, looking for an explanation. I see only confusion and fear. If the crowd panics, I wonder if even the Security officers can stop them from trampling us.

Up ahead, Maven's Sentinels widen the gap between us. A few have taken to tossing people. A strongarm bodily shoves a man back several yards, while a telky sweeps away three or four with a wave of her hand. The crowd gives them a wide berth after that, clearing the space around the fleeing king and new queen. Through the tumult, I catch his eyes as he looks back to search for me. They are wide and wild now, vividly blue even from so far away. His lips move, shouting something I can't hear over the thunder and the rising panic.

"Hurry!" Clover barks, pushing me onward toward the gap.

Our guards become aggressive, their abilities presenting. A swift lunges back and forth, pressing people back from our path. He blurs between bodies, a whirlwind. And then he stops cold.

The gunshot catches the swift between the eyes. Too close to dodge, too fast to escape. His head snaps back in an arc of blood and brain.

I don't know the woman holding the gun. She has blue hair, jagged blue tattoos—and a bloody crimson scarf wrapped around her wrist. The crowd shudders around her, shocked for an instant, before springing into full-blown chaos.

With one hand still aiming her pistol, the blue-haired woman raises the other.

Lightning rips out of the sky.

It crashes toward the circle of Sentinels. She has deadly aim.

I tense, expecting an explosion. Instead, the blue-tinged lightning hits a sudden arc of shimmering water, running across the liquid but not through. It veins and flashes, almost blinding, but disappears in an instant, leaving only the watery shield. Beneath it, Maven, Evangeline, and even the Sentinels crouch, hands over their heads. Only Iris is left standing.

The water pools around her, curling and twisting like one of Larentia's snakes. It grows with every second, leaching so quickly I taste the air drying on my tongue. Iris wastes no time, tearing off her veil. Dimly, I hope it doesn't rain. I don't want to know what Iris can do with rain.

Lakelander guards fight through the crowd, their dark blue forms trying to break through the fleeing crowd. Security officers meet the same obstacle and get caught up, tangled in the mess. Silvers dart in every direction. Some toward the commotion, others away from danger. I'm torn between wanting to run with them and wanting to run toward the blue-haired woman. My brain buzzes as adrenaline courses through me, fighting tooth and nail against the silence smothering my being. *Lightning. She wields lightning. She's a newblood. Like me.* The thought almost makes me cry with happiness. If she doesn't get out of here fast, she'll end up a corpse.

"Run!" I try to scream. It comes out a whisper.

"Get the king to safety!" Evangeline's voice carries as she jumps to her feet. Her gown quickly shifts into armor, scaling across her skin in pearly plates. "Evacuate!"

A few of the Sentinels comply, pulling Maven into their protective formation. His hand sparks with weak flame. It sputters, matching his fear. The rest of his detail draw guns of their own or explode into their abilities. A banshee Sentinel opens his mouth to scream but drops to a knee, gasping. He tears at his throat. He can't breathe. But why, who? His comrades drag him back as he continues to choke.

Another lightning bolt streaks overhead, this one too bright to look at. When I open my eyes again, the blue-haired woman is gone, lost in the crowd. Somewhere, gunfire peppers the air.

Gasping, I realize not everyone in the crowd is running away. Not all of them are afraid, or even confused by the outburst of violence. They move differently, with purpose, motive, a mission. Black pistols gleam, flashing as they dig into a guard's back or stomach. Knives glint in the growing dark. The screams of fear become screams of pain. Bodies fall, slumping against the tile of the square.

I remember the riots in Summerton. Reds hunted down and tortured. A mob turning on the weakest among them. It was disorganized, chaotic, without any order. This is the opposite. What looks like wild panic is the careful work of a few dozen assassins in a crowd of hundreds. With a grin, I realize they all have something in common. As the hysteria grows, each one dons a red scarf.

The Scarlet Guard is here.

Cal, Kilorn, Farley, Cameron, Bree, Tramy, the Colonel.

They're here.

With everything I have, I butt my head back and crack my skull against Clover's nose. She howls, and silver blood spurts down her face. In an instant her grip on me breaks, leaving only Kitten. I drive an elbow into her gut, hoping to throw her off. She lets go of my shoulder, only to wrap her arm around my neck and squeeze.

I twist, trying to get enough room to bend my neck and bite. No chance. She increases the pressure, threatening to crush my windpipe. My vision spots, and I feel myself being pulled backward. Away from the Treasury, Maven, his Sentinels. Through the lethal crowd. I trip backward as we reach the steps. I kick weakly, trying to catch on to anything. The Security officers dodge my poor efforts. Some drop to their knees, guns raised, covering the retreat. Clover looms over me, the bottom half of her face painted with mirrored blood.

"Double back through Whitefire. We have to keep orders," she hisses at Kitten.

I try to shout for help, but I can't summon air enough to make noise. And it wouldn't be any use. Something louder than thunder screams across the sky. Two somethings. Three. Six. Metal birds with razor wings. Snapdragons? The Blackrun? But these airjets look different from the ones I know. Sleeker, faster. Maven's new fleet, probably. In the distance, an explosion blooms with petals of red fire and black smoke. Are they bombing the square, or bombing the Scarlet Guard?

As the Arvens drag me into the palace, another Silver almost collides with us. I reach out. Maybe this person will help.

Samson Merandus sneers down, wrenching one arm out of my grip. I pull back like his touch burns. Just the sight of him is enough to bring on a splitting headache. He wasn't allowed to attend the wedding, but he's still dressed for it, immaculate in a navy suit with his ash-blond hair slicked to his skull.

"Lose her and I'll turn you all inside out!" he snarls over his shoulder.

The Arvens look more frightened of him than of anyone else. They nod vigorously, as do the three remaining officers. All of them know what a Merandus whisper can do. If I needed any more incentive to escape, knowing that Samson will obliterate their minds is certainly it.

In my last glimpse of the square, black shadows loom out of the clouds, coming closer and closer. More airships. But these are heavy, swollen, not built for speed or even combat. Maybe they're coming in to land. I never see them touch down.

I fight as much as I can, which is to say I mumble and squirm under the weight of silence. It slows my guards down, but only a little. Every inch feels hard won but futile. We keep moving. The halls of Whitefire spiral out around us. With my memorization, I know exactly where we are headed. Toward the east wing, the closest part of the palace to the Treasury. There must be passages to it, another way to Maven's forsaken train. Any hope of escape will disappear the second they get me underground.

Three gunshots ring out, echoing so close I feel them in my chest. Whatever's happening in the square is slowly bleeding into the palace. In the window, red flame bursts into the air. From an explosion or a person, I don't know. I can only hope. *Cal. I'm in here. Cal.* I picture him just outside, an inferno of rage and destruction. Gun in one hand, fire in the other, bringing down all his pain and fury. If he can't save me, I hope he can at least rip apart the monster that used to be his brother.

"The rebels are storming Whitefire!"

I jolt at the sound of Evangeline Samos. Her boots ring hard against the marble floor, each step the blow of an angry hammer. Silver blood stains the left side of her face, and her elaborate hair is a mess, tangled and windblown. She smells like smoke.

Her brother is nowhere to be found, but she isn't alone. Wren, the Skonos skin healer who spent so many days trying to make me look alive, trails her closely. Probably dragged along to make sure Evangeline doesn't have to suffer scratches for more than an instant.

Like Cal and Maven, Evangeline is no stranger to military training or protocol. She stays on her toes, ready to react. "The lower library and old gallery are overrun. We have to take her this way." She points her chin to a branching hall perpendicular to ours. Outside, lightning flashes. It reflects against her armor. "You three"—she snaps her fingers at three of the guards—"defend our backs."

My heart sinks in my chest. Evangeline will personally make sure I get on that train.

"I'm going to kill you one day," I curse at her around Kitten's grip.

She lets the threat glance off, too busy barking orders. The guards obey eagerly, dropping back to cover our retreat. They're happy to have someone take charge in this infernal mess.

"What's happening out there?" Clover growls as we hurry along. Fear corrupts her voice. "You, reset my nose," she adds, grabbing Wren by the arm. The Skonos skin healer works on the fly, popping Clover's broken nose back into place with an audible crack.

Evangeline looks over her shoulder, not at Clover but at the passage behind us. It darkens as the storm outside turns day to night. Fear crosses her face. An unfamiliar thing to see in her. "There were plants in the crowd, disguised as Silver nobles. Newbloods, we think. Strong enough to hold their own until . . ." She checks around a corner before waving us on. "The Scarlet Guard took over Corvium, but I didn't think they had this many people. True soldiers, trained, well armed. Dropped right out of the sky like damn insects."

"How did they get in? We're under full security protocols for the wedding. Over a thousand Silver troops, plus Maven's newblood pets—" Kitten blusters. She cuts herself off as two figures in white pop out of a doorway. The weight of their silence slams into me, making my knees buckle. "Caz, Brecker, with us!"

I think Egg and Trio are better names. They skid across the marble floor, sprinting to join my moving prison. If I had the energy, I would weep. Four Arvens and Evangeline. Any whisper of hope disappears. It won't even help to beg.

"They can't win. It's a lost cause," Clover presses on.

"They're not here to win the capital. They're here for her," Evangeline snaps.

Egg shoves me onward. "Waste of effort for this sack of bones."

We round another corner, to the long, stretching Battle Hall. Compared to the turmoil in the square, it seems serene, its painted scenes of war far away from the chaos. They tower, dwarfing all of us in their old grandeur. If not for the distant sound of screaming airjets and concussive thunder, I could trick myself into believing all that was a dream.

"Indeed," Evangeline says. Her steps falter so slightly the others don't notice. But I do. "What a waste of effort."

She twists with smooth, feline grace, both hands darting out. I see it all as if time itself has slowed. The plates of her armor fly from both wrists, quick and deadly as bullets. Their edges gleam, sharpening to razors. They hiss through air. And flesh.

The sudden drop of silence feels like the lifting of immense weight. Clover's arm falls from my neck, her grip slack. She falls too.

Four heads tumble to the floor, leaking blood. The bodies follow, all in white, hands gloved in plastic. Their eyes are open. They never had a chance. Blood—the smell, the sight—assaults my senses, and I taste bile rising in my throat. The only thing that keeps me from retching is the jagged spike of fear and realization.

Evangeline isn't going to take me to the train. She's going to kill me. She's going to end this.

She looks shockingly calm for having just murdered four of her own. The plates of metal return to her arms, sliding back into place. Wren the skin healer doesn't move, her eyes on the ceiling. She won't watch what's going to happen next.

It will be no use to run. I might as well face it.

"Get in my way and I'll kill you slowly," she whispers, stepping over a corpse to grab me by the neck. Her breath washes over me. Warm, tinged with mint. "Little lightning girl."

"Then get it over with," I force through my teeth.

At this range, I realize her eyes are not black but charcoal gray. Storm-cloud eyes. They narrow as she tries to decide how to kill me. It will have to be by hand. My manacles won't let her abilities touch my skin. But a single knife will do the trick just fine. I hope it's quick, though I doubt she has enough mercy for such a thing.

"Wren, if you please," Evangeline says, putting out her hand.

Instead of a dagger, the skin healer pulls a key from a pocket on Trio's now headless corpse. She presses it into Evangeline's palm.

I go numb.

"You know what this is." How could I not? I have dreamed of that key. "I'm going to make you a bargain."

"Make it," I whisper, my eyes never wavering from the spiky bit of black iron. "I'll give you anything."

Evangeline grabs my jaw, forcing me to look at her. I've never seen her so desperate, not even in the arena. Her eyes waver and her lower lip trembles. "You lost your brother. Don't take mine."

Rage flares in my stomach. Anything but that. Because I've dreamed of Ptolemus too. Slitting his throat, cutting him apart, electrocuting him. He killed Shade. A life for a life. A brother for a brother.

Her fingers dig into my skin, nails threatening to pierce flesh. "You lie and I'll kill you where you stand. Then I'll kill the rest of your family." Somewhere in the twisting halls of the palace, the echoes of battle rise. "Mare Barrow, make your choice. Let Ptolemus live."

"He'll live," I croak out.

"Swear it."

"I swear it."

Tears gather as she moves, quickly sliding off one manacle after the other. Evangeline tosses each one as far as she can. By the time she finishes, I'm a weeping mess.

Without the manacles, the Silent Stone, the world feels empty. Weightless. I'm afraid I might float away. Still, the weakness is almost debilitating, worse than my last escape attempt. Six months of it will not disappear in an instant. I try to reach with my ability, try to feel the lightbulbs above my head. I can barely sense the buzz of them. I doubt I could even shut them off, something I used to take for granted.

"Thank you," I whisper. Words I never thought I would say to her. They unsettle us both.

"You want to thank me, Barrow?" she mutters, kicking away the last of my bindings. "Then keep your word. And let this fucking place burn."

Before I can tell her I'll be of no use, that I'll need days, weeks, months to recover, Wren puts her hands to my neck. I realize now why Evangeline dragged a skin healer along. Not for herself. For me.

Warmth bleeds down my spine, into my veins and bones and marrow. It pounds through me so completely I almost expect the healing to hurt. I drop to a knee, overtaken. The aches vanish. The trembling fingers, weak legs, sluggish pulse—every last ghost of Silent Stone flees before the touch of a healer. My head will never forget what happened to me, but my body quickly does.

The electricity rushes back, thundering from the deepest part of me. Every nerve shrieks to life. All down the hallway, the lightbulbs shatter on their chandeliers. The hidden cameras explode into sparks and spitting wires. Wren jumps back, yelping.

I look down to see purple and white. Naked electricity jumps between my fingers, hissing in the air. The push and pull is achingly familiar. My ability, my strength, my power has returned.

Evangeline takes a measured step back. Her eyes reflect my sparks. They glow.

"Keep your promise, lightning girl."

Darkness walks with me.

Every light sizzles and blinks out as I pass. Glass shatters, electricity spits. The air buzzes like a live wire. It caresses my open palms, and I shiver at the feel of such power. I thought I had forgotten what this was like. But that's impossible. I can forget almost everything else in this world, but not my lightning. Not who and what I am.

The manacles made it exhausting to walk. Without them weighing me down, I fly. Toward the smoke, the danger, to what could finally be my salvation or my ending. I don't care which, so long as I'm not stuck in this hellish prison one second longer. My dress flutters in ruby tatters, ripped enough to let me run as fast as I can. The sleeves smolder, burning with every new burst of sparks. I don't hold myself back now. The lightning goes where it wants. It explodes through me with every heartbeat. The purple-white bolts and sparks dance along my fingers, blazing in and out of my palms. I shudder in pleasure. Nothing has ever felt so wonderful. I keep looking at the electricity, enamored with every vein. *It's been so long. It's been so long.*

This must be what hunters feel like. Every corner I turn, I hope to find some kind of prey. I run the shortest route I know, tearing through the council chamber, its empty seats haunting me as I sprint over the Nortan seal. If I had time, I would obliterate the symbol beneath my feet. Tear up every inch of the Burning Crown. But I have a real crown to kill. Because that's what I'm going to do. If Maven is still here, if the wretched boy hasn't gotten away. I'm going to watch his last breath and know he can never hold my leash again.

The Security officers retreat in my direction, their backs to me. Still doing as Evangeline commanded. All three have their long guns tucked into the crooks of their shoulders, fingers on triggers as they cover the passageway. I don't know their names, just their colors. House Greco, strongarms all. They don't need bullets to kill me. One of them could break my back, crush my rib cage, pop my skull like a grape. It's me or them.

The first hears my footsteps. He turns his chin, looking over his shoulder. My lightning shrieks up his spine and into his brain. I feel his branching nerves for a split second. Then darkness. The other two react, swinging around to face me. The lightning is quicker than they are, splitting them both.

I never break pace, vaulting over their smoking bodies.

The next hall runs alongside the square, its once-gleaming windows streaked with ash. A few chandeliers lie smashed against the floor in twisted heaps of gold and glass. There are bodies too. Security officers in their black uniforms, Scarlet Guard with their red scarves. The aftermath of a skirmish, one of many raging within the larger battle. I check the closest Guardsman to me, reaching down to feel her neck. No pulse. Her eyes are closed. I'm glad I don't recognize her.

Outside, another burst of blue lightning forks through the clouds. I can't help but grin, the corners of my mouth pulling sharply on my scars. Another newblood who can control lightning. I'm not alone.

Moving quickly, I take what I can off the bodies. A pistol and ammunition from an officer. A red scarf from the woman. She died for me. *Another time, Mare,* I chide myself, pushing aside the quicksand of such thoughts. Using my teeth, I tie the scarf to my wrist.

Bullets ping against the windows, a spray of them. I flinch, dropping to the floor, but the windows hold firm. Diamondglass. Bulletproof. I'm safe behind them, but also trapped.

Never again.

I slide up against the wall, trying not to be seen as I observe. The sight makes me gasp.

What was once a wedding celebration is now all-out war. I was in awe of the house rebellion, Iral and Haven and Laris against the rest of Maven's court, but this dwarfs it substantially. Hundreds of Nortan officers, Lakelander guards, deadly nobles of the court on one side, with Scarlet Guard soldiers on the other. There have to be newbloods among them. So many Red soldiers, more than I ever thought possible. They outnumber the Silvers at least five to one, and they are certainly, clearly soldiers. Trained to military precision, from their tactical gear to the way they move. I start to wonder how they even got here, but then I see the airships. Six of them, all landed directly on the Square itself. Each one spits soldiers, dozens of them. Hope and excitement roar through me.

"Hell of a rescue," I can't help but whisper.

And I'm going to make sure it succeeds.

I'm not Silver; I don't need to pull my ability from my surroundings. But it certainly doesn't hurt to have more electricity, more power, on hand. Closing my eyes, just for a second, I call to every wire, every pulse, every charge, down to the static cling of the curtains. It rises at my demand. It fuels me, heals me as much as Wren.

After six months of darkness, I finally feel the light.

Purple-white flares at the edges of my vision. My entire body buzzes, skin shivering beneath the delight of lightning. I keep sprinting. Adrenaline and electricity. I feel like I could run through a wall.

More than a dozen Security officers guard the entrance hall. One, a magnetron, busies himself boarding up the windows with cages of twisted chandelier and gilt paneling. Bodies and blood in both colors cover the floor. The smell of gunpowder overwhelms everything but the blasts outside. The officers secure the palace, maintaining their position. Their attention is on the battle outside, the Square. Not their backs.

Crouching, I put my hands to the marble beneath my feet. It feels cold beneath my fingers. I will my lightning against the stone, sending it out along the floor in a jagged ripple of electricity. It pulses, a wave, catching them all off guard. Some fall, some rocket backward. The strength of the blast echoes in my chest. If it's enough to kill, I don't know.

My only thought is the Square. When the open air hits my lungs, I almost laugh. It's poisoned with ash, blood, the electric buzz of the lightning storm, but it tastes sweeter than anything. Above me, the black clouds rumble. The sound lives in my bones.

I streak purple-white bolts across the sky. A sign. The lightning girl is free.

I don't linger. Standing on the steps, overlooking the turmoil, is a good way to get shot in the head. I plunge into the fray, looking for a single familiar face. Not friendly, but at least familiar. People collide all around me with no rhyme or reason. The Silvers were taken unawares, unable to form up into their practiced ranks. Only the Scarlet Guard soldiers have any kind of organization, but it's rapidly breaking down. I weave toward the Treasury, the last place I saw Maven and his Sentinel. It was only a few minutes ago. They could still be there, surrounded, making a stand. I will kill him. I have to.

Bullets whistle past my head. I'm shorter than most, but still, I hunch as I run.

The first Silver to challenge me head-on has Provos robes, gold and black. A thin man with thinner hair. He throws out an arm and I rocket backward, my head slamming against the tiled ground. I grin at him, about to laugh. When suddenly I can't breathe. My chest contracts, tightening. My ribs. I look up to find him standing over me, his hand clenching into a fist. The telky is going to collapse my rib cage.

Lightning rises to meet him, sparking angrily. He dodges, faster than I anticipated. My vision spots as the lack of oxygen hits my brain. Another bolt, another dodge.

Provos is so focused on me, he doesn't notice the barrel-chested Red soldier a few yards away. He shoots him through the head with an armor-piercing round. It isn't pretty. Silver spatters across my ruined gown.

"Mare!" he shouts, hurrying to my side. I recognize his voice, his dark brown face—and his electric-blue eyes. Four other Guardsmen move with him. They circle up, protective. With strong hands, he hoists me to my feet.

Forcing a breath, I shiver in relief. When my brother's smuggling friend became a true soldier, I don't know, and now isn't the time to ask. "Crance."

One hand still on his gun, he raises the radio clawed in his other fist. "This is Crance. I have Barrow in the Square." The hiss of empty feedback is not promising. "Repeat. I have Barrow." Cursing, he tucks the radio back into his belt. "Channels are a mess. Too much interference."

"From the storm?" I glance up again. Blue, white, green. I narrow my eyes and throw another bolt of purple into the crash of blinding color.

"Probably. Cal warned us—"

Air hisses through my teeth. I grab him tightly, making him flinch. "Cal. Where is he?"

"I have to get you out—"

"Where?"

He sighs, knowing I won't ask again.

"He's on the ground. I don't know where exactly! Your rendezvous point is the main gate," he shouts in my ear, making sure he can be heard. "Five minutes. Grab the woman in green. Take this," he adds, shrugging out of his heavy jacket. I pull it over my tattered dress without argument. It feels weighted. "Flak jacket. Semibulletproof. It'll give you some cover."

My feet carry me away before I can even say thank you, leaving Crance and his detail in my wake. Cal is here somewhere. He'll be hunting Maven, just like me. The crowd surges, a swiftly changing tide. If not for the Guardsmen pushing through the fray, I could force my way through. Blast everyone in front of me, clear a path across the Square. Instead I rely on my old instincts. Dancing steps, agility, predicting every pulsing wave of the chaos. Lightning trails in my wake, staving off any hands. A strongarm knocks me sideways, sending me careening through arms and legs, but I don't return to fight him. I keep moving, keep pushing, keep running. One name screams through my head. *Cal. Cal. Cal. If I can get to him, I'll be safe.* A lie maybe, but a good lie.

The smell of smoke gets stronger as I push on. Hope flares. Where there's smoke, there's a fire prince.

Ash and soot streak the white walls of the Treasury Hall. One of the airjet missiles took a chunk out of the corner, slicing through marble like butter. It lies in a pile of rubble around the entrance, forming good cover. The Sentinels make full use of it, their ranks bolstered by the Lakelanders and a few of the purple-uniformed Treasury guards. Some of them fire into the oncoming Guardsmen, using bullets to defend their king's escape, and many more utilize their abilities. I dart around a few bodies frozen solid on their feet, the violent work of a Gliacon shiver. Another few are alive but on their knees, bleeding from the ears. Marinos banshee. The evidence of so many deadly Silvers is all around. Corpses speared by metal, necks broken, skulls caved in, mouths dripping water, a particularly gruesome body that seems to have choked on the plants growing out of its mouth. As I watch, a greeny throws a handful of seeds at an attacking swath of Scarlet Guard. Before my eyes, the seeds burst like grenades, spitting vines and thorns in a verdant explosion.

I don't see Cal here, or any other faces I recognize. Maven is already in the Treasury, headed for the train.

Clenching a fist, I throw everything I can at the Sentinels. My lightning crackles along the rubble, sending them scurrying back. Dimly, I hear someone shout to push forward. The Guardsmen do, continuing to fire round after round. I keep up the pressure, sending another blaze of lightning across them like a cracking whip.

"Incoming!" a voice screams.

I look up, expecting a blow from the sky. Airjets dance through the stormy clouds, chasing one another. None of them seem concerned by us.

Then someone pushes me aside, throwing me out of the way. I turn in time to see a person I recognize barrel along a cleared pathway, his head lowered, body armored on the head, neck, and shoulders. He picks up speed, legs pumping.

"Darmian!"

He doesn't hear me, too busy crashing toward the marble blockade. Bullets ping off his armor and skin. A shiver sends a blast of icicles at his chest, but they shatter. If he's afraid, he doesn't show it. He never hesitates. Cal taught him that. Back at the Notch. When we were all together. I remember a different Darmian then, the one I knew. He was a quiet man compared to Nix, another newblood who shared his ability of impenetrable flesh. Nix is long dead now, but Darmian is very much alive. Roaring, he clambers over the marble blockade, careening into two Sentinels.

They fall on him with everything they have. *Stupid*. They might as well be shooting at bulletproof glass. Darmian responds in kind, dropping grenades with cold rhythm. They bloom in fire and smoke. Sentinels fall backward, few of them able to withstand a direct explosion.

Guardsmen vault over the rubble, following in Darmian's wake. Many overtake him. The Sentinels are not their mission. Maven is. They flood into the Treasury, hot on the king's trail.

As I run forward, I let my ability press on ahead. I feel the lights of the Treasury's main hall, spiraling down into the rock beneath us. My sense jumps along the wires, deeper and deeper. Something big idles below, its engine a rising purr. He's still here.

The marble beneath my feet is easy to scale. I scrabble over the rubble on all fours, my mind focused a hundred feet down. The next grenade blast catches me unawares. Its force blows me backward in a wave of heat. I land hard, flat on my back, gasping for breath, quietly thankful for Crance's jacket. The explosion blazes over me, close enough to burn my cheek.

Too big for a grenade. Too controlled for natural flame.

I scramble to my feet, forcing my legs to obey as I suck down air. *Maven*. I should have known. He wouldn't leave me up here. Wouldn't run away without his favorite pet. He's come to put the chains back on me himself.

Good luck.

Smoke follows the swirling fire, making the already dark Square hazy. It surrounds me, growing stronger and hotter with every passing second. Tensing, I send lightning through my nerves, letting it crackle over every inch. I take a step toward his silhouette, black and strange in the shifting firelight. The smoke curls, the fire shooting with raging hot blue flame. Sweat drips down my neck. My fists clench, ready to run him through with every drop of rage collected in his prison. I've been waiting for this moment. Maven is a cunning king, but no fighter. I'm going to rip him apart.

Lighting ripples over our heads, flashing brighter than the flame. It illuminates him as the wind picks up, blowing away the smoke to reveal—

Red-gold eyes. Broad shoulders. Callused hands, familiar lips, unruly black hair, and a face I have ached for.

Not Maven. All thoughts of the boy king disappear in an instant.

"Cal!"

The fireball hisses through the air, almost engulfing my head. I roll beneath it on instinct alone. Confusion rules my brain. He's unmistakable. Cal, standing there in tactical armor, a red sash tied across him from waist to hip. I fight the animal need to run toward him. It takes every fiber of control to step back.

"Cal, it's me! It's Mare!"

He doesn't speak, just pivots on his feet, keeping me in front of him. The fire around us churns and contracts, pulling inward with blinding speed. The heat crushes the air from my lungs, and I choke down smoke. Only lightning keeps me safe, crackling around me in a shield of electricity to keep me from burning alive.

I roll again, bursting through his inferno. My dress smolders, trailing smoke. I don't waste precious time or brainpower trying to figure out what's going on. I already know.

His eyes are shadowed, unfocused. No recognition in them. No indication that we've spent the last six months trying to get back to each other. And his movements are robotic, even compared to his military-trained precision.

A whisper has his mind. I don't have to guess which one.

"I'm sorry," I mumble, even though he can't hear me.

A blast of lightning throws him back, the sparks dancing over the plates of his armor. He seizes, twitching as the electricity pulls on his nerves. I bite my lip, trying harder than I ever have before to walk the narrow line between incapacitation and injury. I err on the weak side. A mistake.

Cal is stronger than I ever realized. And he has such an advantage. I'm trying to save him. He's trying to kill me.

He fights through the pain, charging. I dodge, my focus shifting from keeping him at bay to keeping out of his crushing grip. A fire-fueled punch arcs over my head. I smell burned hair. Another catches me in the stomach and I fall backward. I roll with the momentum and pop up again, my old tricks returning. With a twist of my hand, I send another bolt of sparks dancing up his leg and into his spine. He howls. The sound cuts my insides. But it gives me a head start.

My focus narrows to one thing, one person's devilish face. Samson Merandus.

He has to be close enough to bewitch Cal and send him after me.

I search the battle as I run, looking for his blue suit. If he's here, he's hiding well. Or he could be perched above, looking down from the Treasury roof or the many windows of the adjoining buildings. Frustration eats at my resolve. Cal's right here. We're back together. And he's trying to kill me.

The heat of his rage licks at my heels. Another blast rips along my left, sending needles of white-hot agony down my arm. Adrenaline drowns it out quickly. I can't afford pain right now.

At least I'm faster than he is. After the manacles, every step feels easier than the last. I let the storm above fuel me, feeding on the electric energy of the other lightning-wielding newblood somewhere. Her blue hair doesn't cross my vision again. Too bad. I could use her right now.

If Samson is hiding near the Treasury, I only have to get Cal out of his circle of influence. Skidding, I turn to look over my shoulder. Cal is still following me, a shadow of blue-tinged flame and anger.

"Come and get me, Calore!" I shout to him, sending a blast of lightning at his chest. Stronger than the last, enough to leave a mark.

He twists sideways, dodging, never breaking step. Hot on my trail.

I hope this works.

No one dares get in our way.

Red and blue and purple, fire and lightning, chase in our wake, splitting the battle like a knife. He pursues with the singular resolve of a hunting dog. And I certainly feel hunted across the Square.

I angle for the main gate, to whatever rendezvous Crance mentioned. My escape. Not that I'll take it yet. Not without Cal.

After a hundred yards, it's clear that Samson is running with us, just out of sight. No Merandus whisper has a bigger range than that, not even Elara. I twist back and forth, scanning the bloodbath. The longer the battle pushes on, the more time the Silvers have to organize.

Army soldiers in clouded gray uniforms flood the Square, systematically winning over pieces of it. Most of the nobles retreat behind the wall of military protection, though a few—the strongest, the bravest, the most bloodthirsty—continue fighting. I expect members of House Samos to be in the thick of it, but I see no magnetrons that I recognize. And still no other familiar members of the Scarlet Guard. No Farley, no Colonel, no Kilorn or Cameron or any of the newbloods I helped recruit. Just Darmian, probably blasting his way through the Treasury, and Cal, trying his best to put me in the ground.

I curse, wishing for Cameron above all of them. She could silence Cal, keep him contained long enough for me to find and destroy Samson. Instead, I have to do it myself. Keep him at bay, keep myself alive, and somehow root out the Merandus whisper plaguing us both.

Suddenly navy blue blurs by at the edge of my vision.

Long months in Silver captivity have made me attuned to house colors. Lady Blonos drilled her knowledge into me, and now, more than ever, I thank her for it.

I whirl, changing direction with a vengeance. Ash-blond hair darts through the Silver soldiers, attempting to blend into their ranks. Instead, he stands out, his formal suit in sharp contrast to their military uniforms. Everything narrows to him. All my focus, all my energy. I throw what I can in his direction, loosing jagged lightning upon Samson and the Silver shield between us.

His eyes lock on mine and the lightning arcs like a cracking whip. He has the same eyes as Elara, the same eyes as Maven. Blue as ice; blue as flame. Cold and unforgiving.

Somehow my electricity bends, curving around him. It slingshots away, rocketing in another direction. My hand swings with it, my body moving of its own accord as the lightning races at Cal. I try to shout out, even though warning a bewitched man will do nothing at all. But my lips don't move. Horror bleeds down my spine, the only sensation I can feel. Not the ground beneath my feet, not the bite of new burns, not even the smoky air in my nose. It all disappears, wiped away. Taken.

Inside, I scream because Samson has me now. I can't make a sound. There is no mistaking the jagged brush of his brain against my mind.

Cal blinks like someone waking up from a long sleep. He barely has time to react, lifting his arms to protect his head from the electric blow. Some of the jagged sparks turn to flame, manipulated by his ability. Most of them hit home, though, dropping him to his knees with a pained roar.

"Samson!" he screams through gritted teeth.

I realize my hand is moving, straying to my hip. It draws the pistol I took and puts steel to my temple.

Samson's whispers rise in my head, threatening to drown out everything else.

Do it. Do it. Do it.

I don't feel the trigger. I won't feel the bullet.

Cal rips my arm back, spinning me away. He breaks my grip on the gun and tosses it across the tile. I've never seen him so afraid.

Kill him. Kill him. Kill him.

My body obeys.

I am a spectator in my own head. A furious battle rages before my eyes and I can't do anything but watch. The tiled ground blurs as Samson makes me sprint, colliding head-on with Cal. I act as a human lightning rod, latching on to his armor, drawing electricity out of the sky to pour into him.

Pain and fear cloud his eyes. His flame can only shield so much.

I lunge, grabbing at his wrist. But the flamemaker bracelet holds firm.

Kill him. Kill him. Kill him.

Fire pushes me back. I tumble end over end, shoulders and skull bouncing. The world spins, and dizzy limbs try to make me stand.

Get up. Get up. Get up.

"Stay down, Mare!" I hear from Cal's direction. His figure dances before me, splitting into three. I might have a concussion. Red blood pulses across the white tile.

Get up. Get up. Get up.

My feet move beneath me, pushing hard. I stand too quickly, nearly falling over again as Samson forces me into drunken steps. He closes the distance between my body and Cal's. I've seen this before, a thousand years ago. Samson Merandus in the arena, forcing another Silver to cut up his own insides. He'll do the same to me too, once he uses me to kill Cal.

I try to fight, though I don't know where to start. Try to twitch a finger, a toe. Nothing responds.

Kill him. Kill him. Kill him.

Lightning erupts from my hand, spiraling toward Cal. It misses, off balance like my body. He sends an arc of fire in response, forcing me to dodge and stumble.

Get up. Kill him. Get up.

The whispers are sharp, cutting wounds across my mind. I must be bleeding in my brain.

KILL HIM. GET UP. KILL HIM.

Through the flames, I see navy blue again. Cal stalks after Samson and skids to a knee, taking aim with a pistol of his own.

GET UP—

Pain crashes through me like a wave and I fall backward just as a bullet tears overhead. Another follows, closer. On pure instinct, fighting the ringing in my bruised skull, I scramble to my toes. I move of my own volition.

Shrieking, I turn Cal's fire to lightning, the red curls becoming purple-white veins of electricity. It shields me as Cal empties bullet after bullet in my direction. Behind him, Samson grins.

Bastard. He's going to play us off each other for as long as it takes.

I push the lightning as fast as I can, letting it splinter toward Samson. If I can break his concentration, just for a second, it could be enough.

Cal reacts, a puppet on strings. He shields Samson with his broad body, taking the brunt of my attack.

"Someone help!" I shout to no one. We're only three people in a battle of hundreds. A battle turning one-sided. The Silver ranks grow, fed by reinforcements from the barracks and the rest of the Archeon garrison. My five minutes have long passed. Whatever escape Crance promised is long gone.

I have to break Samson. I have to.

Another bolt of lightning, this time across the ground in a flood. No dodging that.

KILL HIM. KILL HIM. KILL HIM.

The whispers return, pulling back the electricity with my own two hands. It arcs backward in a crashing wave.

Cal drops and spins, throwing out his leg in a sweeping kick. It connects, sending Samson sprawling.

His control of me drops and I push forward. Another electric wave.

This one washes through them both. Cal curses, biting back a yelp. Samson writhes and screams, a blood-curdling sound. He isn't used to pain.

Kill him—

The whisper is far away, weakening. I can fight it.

Cal grabs Samson by the neck, pulling him up only to smash his head back down.

Kill him—

I slice a hand through the air, pulling lightning with it. It splits a gash in Samson from hip to shoulder. The wound spurts Silver blood.

Help me—

Fire races down Samson's throat, charring his insides. His vocal cords shred. The only screaming I hear now is in my head.

I bring my lightning into his brain. Electricity fries the tissue in his skull like an egg in a pan. His eyes roll over white. I want to make it last longer, want to make him pay for what torture he gave to me and so many others. But he dies too quickly.

The whispers disappear.

"It's done," I gasp aloud.

Cal looks up, still kneeling over the body. His eyes widen as if seeing me for the first time. I feel the same. I've been dreaming of this moment, wanting it for months and months. If not for the battle, for our precarious position wedged in the middle, I would wrap my arms around his neck and bury myself in the fire prince.

Instead, I help him to his feet, throwing one of his arms over my shoulder. He limps, one leg a mess of muscle spasms. I'm hurt too, bleeding slowly from a tear in my side. I press my free hand to the wound. The pain sharpens.

"Maven is below the Treasury. He has a train," I say as we clamber away together.

His arm tightens around me. He steers us toward the main gate, quickening his pace with every step. "I'm not here for Maven."

The gate looms, wide enough to allow three transports to drive through side by side. On the other side, the Bridge of Archeon spans the Capital River to meet the eastern half of the city. Smoke rises all over, reaching into the storm-black sky. I fight the urge to turn around and sprint for the Treasury. Maven will be gone by now. He is beyond my reach.

More military transports speed toward us while airjets scream in our direction. Too many reinforcements to withstand.

"What's the plan, then?" I mumble. We're about to be surrounded. The thought wears through my shock and adrenaline, sobering me up. All this for me. Bodies everywhere, Red and Silver. What a waste.

Cal's hands find my face, making me turn to look at him. In spite of the destruction around us, he smiles.

"For once, we have one."

I see green out of the corner of my eye. Feel another hand grab my arm.

And the world squeezes to nothing.

NINETEEN
Evangeline

He's late, and my heartbeat guns into overdrive. I fight the surge of fear, twisting it into fuel. Using the new energy, I shred apart the gilded frames holding portraits all down the palace hallway. The flecks of gold leaf twist into brutal, glinting shards. Gold is a weak metal. Soft. Malleable. Useless in a true fight. I let them drop. I don't have the time or energy to waste on weak things.

The pearly rhodium plates along my arms and legs vibrate with adrenaline, their mirror-bright edges rippling like liquid mercury. Ready to become whatever I need to stay alive. A sword, a shield, a bullet. I'm not in direct danger, not right now. But if Tolly isn't here in one minute, I'm going out there after him, and then I certainly will be.

She promised, I tell myself.

It sounds idiotic, the wish of a particularly foolish child. I should know better. The only bond in my world is blood; the only promise is family. A Silver would smile and agree with another house and break their oath in the next heartbeat. Mare Barrow is not Silver—she should have less honor than any of us. And she owes my brother, owes me, less than nothing. She would be justified in slaughtering us all. House Samos has not been kind to the lightning girl.

"We have a schedule, Evangeline," Wren mutters next to me. She cradles one hand against her chest, doing her best not to antagonize an already-ugly burn. The skin healer wasn't fast enough to avoid all of Mare's returning ability. But she got the job done, and that's all that matters. Now the lightning girl is free to wreak as much havoc as she can.

"I'm giving him another minute."

The hallway seems to stretch before me, growing longer with every second. On this side of the palace, we can barely hear the battle in the Square. The windows look out on a still courtyard, with only dark storm clouds above. If I wanted to, I could pretend this was another day of my usual torment. Everyone smiling with their fangs, circling an increasingly lethal throne. I thought the end of the queen would mean the end of danger. It's not like me to underestimate a person's evils, but I certainly underestimated Maven. He has more of his mother in him than anyone realized, as well as his own kind of monster.

A monster I no longer have to suffer, thank my colors. Once we're back home, I'll send the Lakelander princess a gift for taking my place at his side.

He'll be far away by now, ferried to safety by his train. The new bride and groom were already in the Treasury when I left them. Unless Maven's disgusting obsession with Mare won out. The boy is impossible to predict where she is involved. For all I know, he could have turned around to find her. He could be dead. I certainly hope he is dead. It would make the next steps infinitely easier.

I know Mother and Father too well to worry about them. Woe to the person, Silver or Red, who might challenge my father in open combat. And Mother has her own contingencies in place. The attack on the wedding was not a surprise to any of us. House Samos is prepared. So long as Tolly sticks to the plan. My brother has a hard time backing down from a fight, and he is impulsive. Another man impossible to predict. We're not supposed to hurt the rebels or impede their progress in any way. Father's orders. I hope my brother follows them.

We'll be fine. I exhale slowly, holding on to those three words. They do little to calm my nerves. I want to be rid of this place. I want to go home. I want to see Elane again. I want Tolly to strut around the corner, safe and whole.

Instead, he can barely walk.

"Ptolemus!" I bark, forgetting every fear but one as he rounds the corner.

His blood stands out sharply against black steel armor, silver spattered down his chest like paint. I can taste the iron in it, a sharp tang of metal. Without thinking, I yank on his armor, pulling him through the air with it. Before he can collapse, I brace my torso against his, keeping him on his feet. He's almost too weak to stand, let alone run. Icy-cold terror trails fingers down my spine.

"You're late," I whisper, earning a pained grin. Still alive enough for a sense of humor.

Wren works swiftly, pulling off his plates of armor, but she's not faster than me. With another jerk of my hand, it falls from his body in a few clattering echoes. My eyes fly to his bare chest, expecting to see an ugly wound. Nothing there but a few shallow cuts, none of them serious enough to level someone like Ptolemus.

"Blood loss," Wren explains. The skin healer pushes my brother to his knees, holding his left arm aloft, and he whimpers from the pain of it. I keep steady at his shoulder, crouching with him. "I don't have time to heal this."

This. I trail my gaze along his arm, over white skin gray and black with fresh bruises. It ends in a bloody, blunt stump. His hand is gone. Cut clean through the wrist. Silver blood pulses sluggishly from the severed veins, despite his meager attempts to wrap the wound.

"You have to," Ptolemus grinds out, his voice hoarse with agony.

I nod fervently. "Wren, it'll only take a few minutes." No magnetron is a stranger to a lost finger. We've been playing with knives since we could walk. We know how quickly a digit can be regrown.

"If he ever wants to use that hand again, you'll do as I say," she replies. "It's too complicated to do quickly. I have to seal the wound for now." He makes another strangled noise, choking on the thought and the pain.

"Wren!" I plead.

She doesn't back down. "For now!" Her beautiful eyes, gray Skonos eyes, bore into mine with urgency. I see fear in her, and no wonder. A few minutes ago she watched me murder four guards and free a prisoner of the crown. She is also complicit in the treason of House Samos.

"Fine." I squeeze Tolly's shoulder, imploring him to listen. "For now. The second we're in the clear, she'll fix you."

He doesn't reply, only nodding as Wren gets to work. Tolly turns his head, unable to watch the skin grow over his wrist, sealing up the veins and bones. It happens quickly. Blue-black fingers dance across his pale flesh as she knits him together. Skin growth is easy, or so I'm told. Nerves, bones, those are more complex.

I do my best to distract him from the blunt end of his arm. "So who did it?"

"Another magnetron. Lakelander." He forces out each word. "Saw me breaking off to leave. Sliced me before I knew what was happening."

Lakelanders. Frozen fools. All stern in their hideous blue. To think Maven traded the might of House Samos for them. "I hope you repaid the favor."

"He no longer has a head."

"That'll do."

"There," Wren says, finishing up the wrist. She runs her hands along his arm and down his spine to the small of his back. "I'll stimulate your marrow and kidneys, raise your blood production as much as I can. You'll still be weak, though."

"That's fine. As long as I can walk." He already sounds stronger. "Help me up, Evie."

I oblige, bracing his good arm over my shoulder. He's heavy, almost deadweight. "Ease up on the desserts," I grumble. "Come on now, move with me."

Tolly does what he can, forcing one foot after the other. Nowhere near fast enough for my taste. "Very well," I mutter, reaching out to his discarded armor. It flattens and re-forms into a sheet of rippled steel. "Sorry, Tolly."

I push him down onto it, using my ability to hold up the sheet like a stretcher.

"I can walk . . . ," he protests, but weakly. "You need your focus."

"Then focus for both of us," I shoot back. "Men are useless when injured, aren't they?"

Keeping him elevated takes a corner of my ability, but not all of it. I sprint as fast as I can, one hand on the sheet. It follows on an invisible tether, flanked by Wren on the other side.

Metal sings on the edge of my perception. I note each piece as we press on, filing them away on instinct. Copper wiring—a garrote with which to strangle. Door locks and hinges—darts or bullets. Window frames—iron hilts with glass daggers. Father used to quiz me on such things, until it became second nature. Until I couldn't enter a room without marking its weapons. House Samos is never caught off guard.

Father devised our swift getaway from Archeon. Through the barracks and down the northern cliffs to boats waiting in the river. Steel boats, specially made, fluted for speed and silence. Between Father and me, they'll cut through the water like needles through flesh.

We're behind schedule, but only by a few minutes. In the chaos, it will take hours before anyone in Maven's court realizes House Samos has disappeared. I don't doubt other houses will take the same opportunity, like rats fleeing a sinking ship. Maven is not the only person with an escape plan. In fact, I wouldn't be surprised if every house has one of its own. The court is a powder keg with an increasingly short fuse and a spitfire king. You'd have to be an idiot not to expect an explosion.

Father felt the winds shift the moment Maven stopped listening to him, as soon as it became clear that allying to the Calore king would be our downfall. Without Elara, no one could hold Maven's leash. Not even my father. And then the Scarlet Guard rabble became more organized, a real threat rather than an inconvenience. They seemed to grow with each passing day. Operating in Piedmont and the Lakelands, whispers of an alliance with Montfort far to the west. They're much larger than anyone anticipated, better organized and more determined than any insurrection in memory. All the while, my wretched betrothed lost his grip. On the throne, on his sanity, on anything but Mare Barrow.

He tried to let her go, or so Elane told me. Maven knew as well as any of us what a danger his obsession would become. *Kill her. Be done. Be rid of her poison,* he used to mutter. Elane listened undetected, quiet in her corner of his private quarters. The words were only words. He could never part with her. So it was easy to push her into his path—and push him off course. The equivalent of waving a red flag in front of a bull. She was his hurricane, and every nudge pulled him deeper into the eye of the storm. I thought she was an easy tool to use. A distracted king makes for a more powerful queen.

But Maven shut me out of a place that was rightfully mine. He didn't know to look for Elane. My lovely, invisible shadow. Her reports came later, under the cover of night. They were very thorough. I feel them still, whispered against my skin with only the moon to listen. Elane Haven is the most beautiful girl I've ever seen in any capacity, but she looks best in moonlight.

After Queenstrial, I promised her a consort's crown. But that dream disappeared with Prince Tiberias, as most dreams do with the harsh break of day. *Whore.* That's what Maven called her after the attempt on his life. I almost killed him where he stood.

I shake my head, refocusing on the task at hand. Elane can wait. Elane is waiting, just as my parents promised. Safe in our home, tucked away in the Rift.

The back courtyards of Archeon open onto flourishing gardens, which in turn are bounded by the palace walls. A few wrought-iron fences ward the flowers and shrubbery. Good for spears. The wall and garden patrols used to be guards of many different house—Laris windweavers, silks of Iral, vigilant Eagrie eyes—but things have changed in recent months. Laris and Iral stand in opposition to Maven's rule, alongside House Haven. And with a battle raging, the king himself in danger, the other palace guards are scattered. I look up through the greenery, magnolia and cherry blossoms bright against the dark sky. Figures in black prowl the diamondglass ramparts.

Only House Samos remains to man the wall.

"Cousins of iron!"

They snap toward my voice, responding in kind.

"Cousins of steel!"

Sweat trickles down my neck as the wall looms closer. From fear, from exertion. Only a few more yards. In preparation, I thicken the pearly metal of my boots, hardening my last steps.

"Can you get yourself up?" I ask Ptolemus, reaching for Wren as I speak.

With a groan, he swings off the stretcher, forcing himself onto unsteady feet. "I'm not a child, Eve; I can cover thirty feet." To prove his point, the black steel re-forms to his body in sleek scales.

If we had more time, I would point out the weaknesses in his usually perfect armor. Holes at the sides, thinning across the back. Instead, I only nod. "You first."

He lifts a corner of his mouth, trying to smirk, trying to lessen my concern. I exhale in relief as he rises into the air, rocketing up to the ramparts of the wall. Our cousins above catch him deftly, drawing him in with their own ability.

"Our turn."

Wren clings to my side, safe beneath my arm. I haul in a breath, holding on to the feel of the rhodium metal curving beneath my toes, up my legs, over my shoulders. *Rise,* I tell my armor.

Pop.

The first sensation my father made me memorize was a bullet. I slept with one around my neck for two years. Until it became as familiar to me as my colors. I can name rounds from a hundred yards. Know their weight, their shape, their composition. Such a small piece of metal is the difference between another person's life and my death. It could be my killer, or my savior.

Pop, pop, pop. The bullets exploding in their chambers feel like needles, sharp, impossible to ignore. They're coming from behind. My toes hit the ground again as my focus narrows, my hands flying up to shield against the sudden onslaught.

Armor-piercing rounds, fat copper jackets with brutal tungsten cores and tapered tips, arc before my eyes, flying backward to land harmlessly in the grass. Another volley comes from at least a dozen guns, and I throw out an arm, protecting myself. The thunder of automatic gunfire drowns out Tolly shouting above me.

Each bullet ripples against my ability, taking another piece of it, of me. Some halt midair; some crumple. I throw everything I can to create a cocoon of safety. From the wall, Tolly and my cousins do the same. They lift the weight enough to actually let me figure out who is shooting at me.

Red rags, hard eyes. Scarlet Guard.

I grit my teeth. The bullets in the grass would be easy to toss back into their skulls. Instead, I rip apart the tungsten like wool, spinning it into glinting thread as fast as I can. Tungsten is incredibly heavy and strong. It takes more energy to work. Another bead of sweat rolls along my spine.

The threads splay out in a web, hitting the twelve rebels head-on. In the same motion, I wrench the guns from their hands, shredding them to pieces. Wren clings to me, holding tightly, and I feel myself pulled back and up, sliding along perfect diamondglass.

Tolly catches me, as he always does.

"And down again," he mutters. His grip on my arm is crushing.

Wren gulps, leaning to look. Her eyes widen. "Bit farther this time."

I know. It's a hundred feet down sheer cliff, and then another two hundred over sloping rock to twist around to the river's edge. *In the shadow of the bridge,* Father said.

In the garden, the rebels struggle, straining against my net. I feel them push and pull it, as the metal itself strains to break apart. It eats at my focus. *Tungsten,* I curse to myself. *I need more practice.*

"Let's go," I tell them all.

Behind me, the tungsten cracks apart into dust. A strong, heavy thing, but brittle. Without a magnetron's hand, it breaks before it bends.

House Samos is done with both.

We will not break, and we will no longer bend.

The boats cut soundlessly through the water, gliding across the surface. We make good time. Our only obstacle is the pollution of Gray Town. The stink of it clings to my hair, still foul in my body even as we break through the second ring of barrier trees. Wren senses my discomfort and puts a hand on my bare wrist. Her healing touch clears my lungs and chases away my exhaustion. Pushing steel through water becomes tiring after a while.

Mother leans over the sleek side of my boat, trailing one hand in the flowing Capital. A few catfish rise to her touch, their whiskers twining with her fingers. The slimy beasts don't bother her, but I shudder with disgust. She isn't concerned by whatever they tell her, meaning they can't sense anyone pursuing us. Her falcon overhead keeps watch as well. When the sun sets, Mother will replace him with bats. As expected, not a scratch on her, or Father. He stands at the prow of the lead boat, setting our path. A black silhouette against the blue river and green hills. His presence calms me more than the peaceful valley.

No one speaks for many miles. Not even the cousins, who I can usually count on for nonsense chatter. Instead, they focus on discarding their Security uniforms. Emblems of Norta float in our wake, while the jewel-bright medals and badges sink into darkness. Hard earned with Samos blood, marks of our allegiance and loyalty. Now lost to the depths of the river and the past.

We are not Nortans anymore.

"So it's decided," I murmur.

Behind me, Tolly straightens up. His ruined arm is still bandaged. Wren won't risk regrowing an entire hand on the river. "Was there ever any doubt?"

"Was there ever a choice?" Mother turns to look over her shoulder. She moves with the lean grace of a cat, stretching out in her bright green gown. The butterflies are long gone. "A weak king we could control, but there's no handling madness. As soon as Iral decided to oppose him outright, our play was decided for us. And choosing the Lakelander"—she rolls her eyes—"Maven cut the last bonds between our houses himself."

I almost scoff in her face. No one decides anything for my father. But laughing at Mother is not a mistake I'm stupid enough to make. "Will the other houses back us, then? I know Father was negotiating." Leaving his children alone, at the mercy of Maven's increasingly volatile court. More words I would never dare say aloud to either of my parents.

Mother senses them anyway. "You did well, Eve," she croons, putting a hand to my hair. She runs a few silver strands through her wet fingers. "And you, Ptolemus. Between that mess in Corvium and the house rebellions, no one doubted your allegiance. You bought us time, valuable time."

I keep my focus on steel and water, ignoring her cold touch. "I hope it was worth it."

Before today, Maven faced multiple rebellions. Without House

Samos, our resources, our lands, our soldiers, how could he stand to win? But before today, he didn't have the Lakelands. Now I have no idea what might unfold. I don't like the feeling at all. My life has been a study in planning and patience. An uncertain future frightens me.

In the west, the sun sinks red against the hills. Red as Elane's hair. *She's waiting,* I tell myself again. *She's safe.*

Her sister was not so fortunate. Mariella died poorly, hollowed out by the seething Merandus whisper. I avoided him as much as I could, glad I knew nothing of Father's plans.

I saw the depths of his punishment in Mare. After the interrogation, she flinched from him like a kicked dog. It was my fault. I forced Maven's hand. Without my interference, he might have never let the whisper have his way—but then he would have stayed away from Mare altogether. He would not have been so blinded by her. Instead, he did as I hoped, and drew her closer. I expected them to drown each other. How easy. Sink two enemies with one anchor. But she refused to break. The girl I remember, the masquerading, terrified servant who believed every lie, would have submitted to Maven months ago. Instead, she donned a different mask. Danced on his strings, sat by his side, lived a half-life without freedom or ability. And still held on to her pride, her fire, her anger. It was always there, burning in her eyes.

I have to respect her for that. Even though she took so much from me.

She was a constant reminder of what I was supposed to be. A princess. A queen. I was born ten months after Tiberias. I was made to marry him.

My first memories are of Mother's snakes hissing in my ears, breathing her whispers and promises. *You are a daughter of fangs and steel. What are you meant for, if not to rule?* Every lesson in the classroom or the arena was preparation. *Be the best, the strongest, the smartest, the most deadly and the most cunning. The most worthy.* And I was everything.

Kings are not known for their kindness or their compassion. Queenstrial is not meant to make happy marriages, but strong children. With Cal, I had both. He would not have begrudged me my own consort, or tried to control me. His eyes were soft and thoughtful. He was more than I had ever hoped for. And I had earned him with every drop of blood I'd spilled, all my sweat, all my tears of pain and frustration. Every sacrifice of who my heart wanted to be.

The night before Queenstrial, I dreamed what it would be like. My throne. My royal children. Subject to no one, not even Father. Tiberias would be my friend and Elane my lover. She would marry Tolly, as planned, ensuring none of us could ever be parted.

Then Mare fell into our lives and blew that dream away like sand.

Once, I thought the crown prince would do the unthinkable. Push me aside for the long-lost Titanos with strange ways and an even stranger ability. Instead, she was a deadly pawn, sweeping my king from the board. The paths of fate have strange twists. I wonder if that newblood seer knew about today. Does he laugh at what he sees? I wish I'd gotten my hands on him just once. I hate not knowing.

On the banks ahead, manicured lawns come into view. The edges of the grass tinge gold and red, giving the estates lining the river a lovely glow. Our own manor house is close, just one more mile. Then we turn west. Toward our true home.

Mother never answered my question.

"So, was Father able to convince the other houses?" I ask her.

She narrows her eyes, her entire body tightening. Coiling up, like one of her snakes. "House Laris was already with us."

That I knew. Along with controlling most of the Nortan Air Fleet, the Laris windweavers govern the Rift. In truth, they rule by our command. Eager puppets, willing to trade anything to maintain our iron and coal mines.

Elane. House Haven. If they aren't with us—

I lick lips that are suddenly dry. A fist clenches at my side. The boat groans beneath me. "And . . ."

"Iral has not agreed to the terms, and more than half of Haven won't either." Mother sniffs. She folds her arms across her chest, as if insulted. "Don't worry, Elane isn't one of them. Please stop crushing the boat. I don't feel like swimming the last mile."

Tolly nudges my arm, a slight touch. Exhaling, I realize my grip on the steel was a bit too strong. The bow smooths again, rippling back into shape.

"Apologies," I mutter quickly. "I'm just . . . confused. I thought the terms were already agreed upon. The Rift will rise in open defiance. Iral brings on House Lerolan and all of Delphie. An entire state will secede."

Mother glances past me, to Father. He angles his boat toward the shore, and I follow his lead. Our familiar estate peeks through the trees, backlit by dusk. "There was some debate over titles."

"Titles?" I sneer. "How stupid. What could their argument possibly be?"

Steel hits stone, bumping up to the low retaining wall running along the water. With a small burst of focus, I hold the metal firm against the current. Wren helps Tolly out first, stepping up onto the lush carpet of grass. Mother watches, her gaze lingering on his missing hand while the cousins follow.

A shadow falls over us both. Father. He stands over her shoulder. A light wind ripples his cloak, playing along the folds of void-black silk and silver thread. Hidden beneath is a suit of blue-tinged chromium so fine it could be liquid.

"'I will not kneel to another greedy king,'" he whispers. Father's voice is always soft as velvet, deadly as a predator. "That's what Salin Iral said."

He reaches down, offering my mother his hand. She takes it deftly and steps from the boat. It doesn't move under her, held by my ability.

Another king.

"Father . . . ?"

The word dies in my mouth.

"Cousins of iron!" he shouts, never breaking our stare.

Behind him, our Samos cousins drop to a knee. Ptolemus does not, looking on with as much confusion as I feel. Blood members of a house do not kneel to one another. Not like this.

They respond as one, their voices ringing. "Kings of steel!"

Quickly, Father extends his hand, catching my wrist before my shock ripples the boat beneath.

His whisper is almost too low to hear.

"To the Kingdom of the Rift."

TWENTY

Mare

The green-uniformed teleporter lands evenly, on steady feet. It's been a long time since the world squeezed and blurred for me. The last time was Shade. The split-second memory of him aches. Paired with my wound and the nauseating rush of pain, it's no wonder I collapse to my hands and knees. Spots dance before my eyes, threatening to spread and consume. I will myself to stay awake and not vomit all over . . . wherever I am.

Before I can look much farther than the metal beneath my fingers, someone pulls me up into a crushing embrace. I cling on as hard as I can.

"Cal," I whisper in his ear, lips brushing flesh. He smells like smoke and blood, heat and sweat. My head fits perfectly in the space between his neck and shoulder.

He trembles in my arms, shaking. Even his breath hitches. He's thinking the same thing I am.

This can't be real.

Slowly, he pulls back, bringing his hands to cup my face. He searches my eyes and glares over every inch of me. I do the same, looking for the trick, the lie, the betrayal. Maybe Maven has skin changers like Nanny. Maybe this is another Merandus hallucination. I could wake up on Maven's train, to his ice eyes and Evangeline's razor smile. The entire wedding, my escape, the battle—some horrific joke. But Cal feels real.

He's paler than I remember, with blunt, close-cut hair. It would curl like Maven's if given the chance. Rough stubble lines his cheeks, along with a few minor nicks and cuts along the sharp edges of his jaw. He is leaner than I remember, his muscles harder beneath my hands. Only his eyes remain the same. Bronze, red-gold, like iron brought to blazing heat.

I look different too. A skeleton, an echo. He runs a limp lock of hair through his fingers, watching the brown fade to brittle gray. And then he touches the scars. At my neck, my spine, ending with the brand below my ruined dress. His fingers are gentle, shockingly so after we almost ripped each other apart. I am glass to him, a fragile thing that might shatter or disappear at any moment.

"It's me," I tell him, whispering words we both need to hear. "I'm back."

I'm back.

"Is it you, Cal?" I sound like a child.

He nods, his gaze never wavering. "It's me."

I move because he won't, taking us both by surprise. My lips mold to his with ferocity, and I pull him in. His heat falls like a blanket around my shoulders. I fight to keep my sparks from doing the same. Still, the hairs on his neck rise, responding to the electric current jumping in the air. Neither of us closes our eyes. This might still be a dream.

He comes to his senses first, scooping me off my feet. A dozen faces pretend to look away in some semblance of propriety. I don't care. Let them look. No flush of shame rises. I've been forced to do far worse in front of a crowd.

We're on an airjet. The long fuselage, dull roar of engines, and clouds slipping past make it unmistakable. Not to mention the delicious purr of electricity pulsing through wires spanning every inch. I reach out, laying my palm flat against the cool, curved metal of the jet wall. It would be easy to drink the rhythmic pulse, pull it into me. Easy and stupid. As much as I want to gorge myself on the sensation, that would end very poorly.

Cal never removes his hand from the small of my back. He turns to look over his shoulder, addressing one of the dozen people harnessed in their seats.

"Healer Reese, her first," he says.

"Sure thing."

My grin disappears the second an unfamiliar man puts his hands on me. His fingers close around my wrist. The grip feels wrong, heavy. Like stone. Manacles. Without thought, I smack him away and jump back, as if burned. Terror mauls my insides as sparks spit from my fingers. Faces flash, clouding my vision. Maven, Samson, the Arven guards with their bruising hands and hard eyes. Overhead, the lights flicker.

The red-haired healer flinches back, yelping, as Cal smoothly angles between us.

"Mare, he's going to treat your wounds. He's a newblood, with us." He braces one hand against the wall by my face, shielding me. Boxing me in. Suddenly the decent-sized jet is too small, the air stale and suffocating. The weight of manacles is gone but not forgotten. I still feel them at my wrists and ankles.

The lights flicker again. I swallow hard, squeezing my eyes shut, trying to focus. Control. But my heartbeat rages on, my pulse a thunder. I suck down air through gritted teeth, willing myself to calm down. *You're safe. You're with Cal, the Guard. You're safe.*

Cal takes my face again, pleading. "Open your eyes, look at me."

No one else makes a sound.

"Mare, no one is going to hurt you here. It's all over. Look at me!" I hear the desperation in him. He knows as well as I do what could happen to the jet if I lose control entirely.

The jet shifts beneath my feet, angling down in a steady decline. Getting us close to the ground should the worst happen. Setting my jaw, I force my eyes open.

Look at me.

Maven said those words once. In Harbor Bay. When the sounder threatened to tear me apart. I hear him in Cal's voice, see him in Cal's face. *No, I escaped you. I got away.* But Maven is everywhere.

Cal sighs, exasperated and pained. "Cameron."

The name rips my eyes open and I slam both fists into Cal's chest. He stumbles back, surprised by the force. A silver flush colors his cheeks. He knits his brows in confusion.

Behind him, Cameron keeps one hand on her seat, steadily swaying with the motion of the jet. She looks strong, zipped into thick-weave tactical gear, with her fresh braids tightly wound to her head. Her deep brown eyes bore into mine.

"Not that." Begging comes too easily. "Anything but that. Please. I can't—I can't feel that again."

The smother of silence. The slow death. I spent six months beneath that weight and now, feeling myself again, I may not survive another moment with it. A gasp of freedom between two prisons is just another torture.

Cameron keeps her hands at her sides, long, dark fingers still. Waiting to strike. The months have changed her too. Her fire has not disappeared, but it has direction, focus. Purpose.

"Fine," she replies. With deliberate motions, she crosses her arms over her chest, folding away her lethal hands. I almost collapse in relief. "It's good to see you, Mare."

My heartbeat still thrums, enough to make me breathless, but the lights stop flickering. I dip my head in relief. "Thank you."

At my side, Cal looks on grimly. A muscle ripples in his cheek. What he's thinking, I can't say. But I can guess. I spent six months with monsters, and I haven't forgotten what it feels like to be a monster myself.

Slowly, I sink into an empty seat, putting my palms on my knees. Then I lace my fingers together. Then sit on my hands. I don't know which looks the least threatening. Furious with myself, I glare at the metal between my toes. Suddenly I'm very aware of my army jacket and battered dress, ripped at almost every seam, and how cold it is in here.

The healer notes my shiver and quickly drapes a blanket around my shoulders. He moves steadily, all business. When he catches my eye, he gives me a half smile.

"Happens all the time," he mutters.

I force a chuckle, a hollow sound.

"Let's see that side, okay?"

As I twist to show him the shallow but long gash along my ribs, Cal takes the seat next to me. He offers a smile of his own.

Sorry, he mouths to me.

Sorry, I mouth back.

Even though I have nothing to be truly sorry for. For once. I've come through horrendous things, done horrendous things to survive. It's easier this way. For now.

I don't know why I pretend to sleep. As the healer does his work, my eyes slip closed and they stay that way for hours. I've dreamed of this moment for so long it's almost overwhelming. The only thing I can do is lean back and breathe easy. I feel like a bomb. No sudden moves. Cal stays close to my side, his leg pressed up against mine. I hear him shift occasionally, but he doesn't speak with the others. Neither does Cameron. Their attention is reserved for me.

Part of me wants to talk. Ask them about my family. Kilorn. Farley. What happened before, what's happening now. Where the hell we're even going. I can't get past thinking the words. There's only enough energy in me to feel relief. Cool, soothing relief. Cal is alive; Cameron is alive. I'm alive.

The others mutter among themselves, their voices low out of respect. Or they just don't want to wake me up and risk another brush with fickle lightning.

Eavesdropping is second nature at this point. I catch a few words, enough to paint a hazy picture. Scarlet Guard, tactical success, Montfort. The last takes me a long moment of contemplation. I barely remember the newblood twins, envoys of another nation far away. Their faces blur in my memory. But I certainly remember their offer. Safe haven for newbloods, provided I accompany them. It unsettled me then and unsettles me now. If they've made an alliance with the Scarlet Guard—what was the price? My body tenses at the implication. Montfort wants me for something, that much is clear. And Montfort seems to have aided my rescue.

In my head, I brush against the electricity of the jet, letting it call to me the electricity inside me. Something tells me this battle isn't over yet.

★ ★ ★

The jet lands smoothly, touching down after sunset. I jump at the sensation and Cal reacts with catlike reflexes, his hand coming down on my wrist. I flinch away again with a spike of adrenaline.

"Sorry," he sputters. "I—"

Despite my churning stomach, I force myself to calm down. I take his wrist in my hand, fingers brushing along the steel of his flame-maker bracelet.

"He kept me chained up. Silent Stone manacles, night and day," I whisper. I tighten my grip, letting him feel a bit of what I remember. "I still can't get them out of my head."

His brow furrows over darkening eyes. I know pain intimately, but I can't find the strength to see it in Cal. I drop my gaze, running a thumb along his hot skin. Another reminder that he is here and I am here. No matter what happens, there is always this.

He shifts, moving with his lethal grace, until I'm holding his hand. Our fingers lace and tighten. "I wish I could make you forget," he says.

"That won't help anything."

"I know. But still."

Cameron watches from across the aisle, one tapping leg crossed over the other. She looks almost amused when I glance at her. "Amazing," she says.

I try not to bristle. My relationship with Cameron, though short, was not exactly smooth. In hindsight, my fault. Another in a long line of mistakes I desperately want to fix. "What?"

Grinning, she unstraps from her seat and stands as the jet slows. "You still haven't asked where we're going."

"Anywhere's better than where I was." I throw a pointed glance at Cal and pull my hand away to fool with the buckles of my harness.

"And I figured someone would fill me in."

He shrugs as he gets up. "Waiting for the right time. Didn't want to overload you."

For the first time in a long time, I truly laugh. "That is an absolutely horrific pun."

His wide smile matches mine. "Does the job."

"This is bleeding unbearable," Cameron mutters to herself.

Once I'm free from my seat, I approach her, tentative. She notes my apprehension and shoves her hands in her pockets. It's not like Cameron to back down or soften, but she does for me. I didn't see her in the battle and I'd be stupid not to realize her true purpose. She's on this jet to keep an eye on me, a bucket of water next to a campfire should it rage out of control.

Slowly, I put my arms around her shoulders, hugging her close. I tell myself not to flinch at the feel of her skin. *She can control it,* I tell myself. *She won't let her silence touch you.* "Thanks for being here," I tell her. I mean it.

She nods tightly, her chin brushing the top of my head. So damn tall. Either she's still growing or I've started shrinking. Even money on both.

"Now tell me where here is," I add, pulling back. "And what the hell I've been missing."

She ducks her chin, gesturing toward the tail of the plane. Like the old Blackrun, this airjet features a ramp entrance. It lowers with a pneumatic hiss. Healer Reese leads the others out, and we follow, a few paces behind. I tense as we go, not knowing what to expect outside.

"We're a lucky bunch," Cameron says. "We get to see what Piedmont looks like."

"Piedmont?" I glance at Cal, unable to hide my shock or my confusion.

He rolls his shoulders. Discomfort flashes across his face. "I wasn't aware until this was planned. They didn't tell us much."

"They never do." That's how the Guard works, how it keeps ahead of Silvers like Samson or Elara. People know exactly what they need to, and nothing more. It takes a lot of faith, or stupidity, to follow orders like that.

I walk down the ramp, each step lighter than the last. Without the deadweight of manacles, I feel like I could fly. The other Guardsmen keep on ahead of us and join in with a crowd of other soldiers.

"The Piedmont branch of the Scarlet Guard, right? Big branch, by the looks of it."

"What do you mean?" Cal mutters in my ear. Over his shoulder, Cameron eyes us both, equally puzzled. I glance between them, searching for the right thing to say. I choose the truth.

"That's why we're in Piedmont. The Guard has been operating here as in Norta and the Lakelands." The words of the Piedmont princes, Daraeus and Alexandret, echo in my mind.

Cal holds my gaze for a moment, before turning to look at Cameron. "You're close to Farley. You hear anything about this?"

Cameron taps her lip. "She never mentioned it. I doubt she knows. Or has clearance to tell me."

Their tones change. Sharper, all business. They don't like each other. On Cameron's end, I understand. On Cal's? He was raised a prince. Even the Scarlet Guard can't scrub away every inch of brat.

"Is my family here?" I sharpen too. "Do you know that, at least?"

"Of course," Cal replies. He's not a good liar, and I see no lie in him now. "I was assured of it. They came from Trial with the rest of the Colonel's team."

"Good. I'm going to see them as soon as possible."

The Piedmont air is hot, heavy, sticky. Like the deepest hole of summer, even though it's only spring. I've never started sweating so quickly. Even the breeze is warm, offering no respite as it rolls across the flat, hot concrete. The landing field is awash with floodlights, so bright it almost crowds out the stars. In the distance, more jets line up. Some are forest green, same as the ones I saw in Caesar's Square. Airjets like the Blackrun, as well as bigger cargo craft. *Montfort,* I realize as the dots connect in my brain. *The white triangle on their wings is their mark.* I saw it before, back at Tuck on crates of equipment and on the twins' uniforms. Peppered in with the Montfort crafts are deep blue jets, as well as yellow-and-white ones, their wings painted in stripes. The first are Lakelander, the second from Piedmont itself. Everything around us is well-organized and, judging by hangars and outbuildings, well funded.

Clearly, we're on a military base, and not the kind the Scarlet Guard is used to.

Both Cal and Cameron look just as surprised as I do.

"I just spent six months a prisoner, and you're telling me I know more about our operations than the both of you?" I scoff at them.

Cal looks sheepish. He's a general; he's Silver; he was born a prince. Being confused and helpless deeply unsettles him.

Cameron just bristles. "Took you just a few hours to regain your self-righteousness. Must be a new record."

She's right, and it stings. I hurry to catch her, Cal at my side. "I just—sorry. I thought this would be easier."

A hand at the small of my back bleeds warmth, soothing my muscles. "What do you know that we don't?" Cal asks, his voice achingly gentle. Part of me wants to shake him out of it. I'm not a doll—not Maven's doll, no one's—and I'm in control again. I don't need to be handled. But the rest relishes his tender treatment. It's better than anything I've experienced in so long.

I don't break my stride, but I keep my voice low. "On the day House Iral and the others tried to kill Maven, he was holding a feast for two princes from Piedmont. Daraeus and Alexandret. They questioned me beforehand, asking about the Scarlet Guard, their operations in their kingdom. Something about a prince and princess." The memory sharpens into focus. "Charlotta and Michael. They're missing."

A dark cloud crosses Cal's face. "We heard the princes were in Archeon. Alexandret died afterward. In the assassination attempt."

I blink, surprised. "How do you—"

"We kept tabs on you as best we could," he explains. "It was in the reports."

Reports. The word spirals. "Is that why Nanny was embedded in court? To keep an eye on me?"

"Nanny was my fault," Cal spits out. He glares at his feet. "No one else's."

Next to him, Cameron scowls. "Damn right."

"Miss Barrow!"

The voice isn't a shock. Where the Scarlet Guard goes, so does Colonel Farley. He looks almost the same as always: careworn, gruff, and brutish, close-cropped white-blond hair, his face lined with premature stress, and one eye clouded with a permanent film of scarlet blood. The only changes are the steady graying of his hair, as well as a sunburn across his nose and more freckles on his exposed forearms. The Lakelander isn't used to Piedmont sunshine, and he's been here long enough to feel it.

Lakelander soldiers of his own, their uniforms a split of red and blue, accompany him in flanking position. Two others in green trail along as well. I recognize Rash and Tahir at a distance, walking in even step. Farley isn't with them. And I don't see her on the concrete, leaving one of the airjets. It isn't like her to turn from a fight—unless she never made it out of Norta. I swallow the sobering thought and focus on her father.

"Colonel." I dip my head in greeting.

He surprises me when he puts out one incredibly callused hand.

"Good to see you whole," he says.

"Whole as can be expected."

That unsettles him. He coughs, looking between the three of us. A precarious place to be for a man who openly fears what we are.

"I'm going to see my family now, Colonel."

There's no reason to ask permission. I move to sidestep him, but his hand stops me cold. This time, I fight the gut urge to flinch away. No one else is going to see my fear. Not right now. Instead, I level my eyes on his, and let him realize exactly what he's doing.

"This isn't my decision," the Colonel says firmly. He raises his eyebrows, imploring me to listen. Then he tips his head to the side. Over his shoulder, Rash and Tahir nod at me.

"Miss Barrow—"

"We've been instructed—"

"—to escort you—"

"—to your debriefing."

The twins blink at me in unison, finishing their maddening tandem speech. Like the Colonel, they sweat in the humidity. It makes their matching black beards and ocher skin gleam.

Instead of punching them both, as I wish I could, I take a small step back. *Debriefing*. The thought of explaining all I've been through to some Guard strategist makes me want to scream or storm—or both.

Cal cuts between us, if only to cushion whatever blow I might send their way.

"You're really going to make her do this now?" His tone of disbelief is undercut with warning. "It can wait."

The Colonel exhales slowly, the picture of exasperation. "It may seem heartless"—he throws a cutting glare at the Montfort twins—"but you have vital information on our enemies. These are our orders, Barrow." His voice softens. "I wish they weren't."

With a light touch, I push Cal to the side. "I'm—going—to—see—my—family—now!" I shout, speaking back and forth between the insufferable twins. They just scowl.

"How rude," Rash mutters.

"Quite rude," Tahir mutters back.

Cameron conceals a low laugh as a cough. "Don't tempt her," she warns. "I'll look the other way if lightning strikes."

"The orders can wait," Cal adds, using all of his military training to seem commanding, even if he has little authority here. The Scarlet Guard sees him as a weapon, nothing more. I know because I used to see him the same way.

The twins don't budge. Rash blusters, drawing himself up like a bird fluffing its feathers. "Certainly you have as much motive as anyone to aid in King Maven's downfall?"

"Certainly you know the best ways to defeat him?" Tahir carries on.

They're not wrong. I've seen Maven's deepest wounds and darkest parts. Where to hit him to make him bleed most. But in this moment, with everyone I love so close, I can barely see straight. Right now, if someone chained Maven to the ground in front of me, I wouldn't stop to kick him in the teeth.

"I don't care who's holding your leash, any of you." I step neatly around them both. "Tell your master to wait."

The brothers trade glances. They speak in each other's thoughts, debating. I would walk away if I knew where to go, but I'm hopelessly adrift.

My mind already races ahead, to Mom, Dad, Gisa, Tramy, and Bree. I picture them holed up in another barracks, squeezed into a dormitory room smaller than our stilt house. Mom's bad cooking stinking up the space. Dad's chair, Gisa's scraps. It makes my heart ache.

"I'll find them myself," I hiss, intending to leave the twins behind for good.

Instead, Rash and Tahir bow back, waving me on. "Very well—"

"Your debriefing is in the morning, Miss Barrow."

"Colonel, if you would escort her to—"

"Yes," the Colonel says sharply, cutting them both off. I'm grateful for his hastiness. "Follow me, Mare."

The Piedmont base is much larger than Tuck, judging by the size of the landing field. In the dark it's hard to tell, but it reminds me more of Fort Patriot, the Nortan military headquarters in Harbor Bay. The hangars are larger, the aircraft numbering in the dozens. Instead of walking to wherever we're going, the Colonel's men drive us in an open-topped transport. Like some of the jets, its sides are striped yellow and white. Tuck I could understand. An abandoned base, out of sight, out of mind, was probably easy for the Scarlet Guard to take. But this is none of those things.

"Where's Kilorn?" I mumble under my breath, nudging Cal beside me.

"With your family, I assume. He bounced between them and the newbloods most of the time."

Because he has no family of his own.

I drop my voice lower, to save the Colonel any offense. "And Farley?"

Cameron leans around Cal, her eyes oddly kind. "She's in the hospital, but don't worry. She didn't go to Archeon; she isn't injured. You'll see her soon." She blinks rapidly, selecting her words with care. "You two will have . . . things to talk about."

"Good."

The warm air tugs at me with sticky fingers, tangling my hair. I can barely sit still in my seat, too excited and nervous. When I was taken, Shade had just died—because of me. I wouldn't blame anyone, including Farley, if they hated me for it. Time doesn't always heal wounds. Once in a while, it makes them worse.

Cal keeps a hand on my leg, a firm weight as a reminder of his presence. Next to me, his eyes whip back and forth, noting every turn of the transport. I should do the same. The Piedmont base is unfamiliar ground. But I can't bring myself to do much more than chew my lip and hope. My nerves buzz, but not from electricity. When we make a right, turning in to a network of cheery brick row houses, I feel like I might explode.

"Officers' quarters," Cal mutters under his breath. "This is a royal base. Government funded. There's only a few Piedmont bases of this size."

His tone tells me he wonders as I do. *Then how are we here?*

We slow in front of the only house with every window ablaze. Without thought, I vault over the side of the transport, almost tripping over the rags of my dress. My vision narrows to the path in front of me. Gravel walk, flagstone steps. The ripples of movement behind curtained windows. I hear only my heartbeat, and the creak of an opening door.

Mom reaches me first, outstripping both my long-limbed brothers. The collision almost knocks the air from my lungs, and her resulting hug actually does. I don't mind. She could break every bone in my body and I wouldn't mind.

Bree and Tramy half carry both of us up the steps and into the row house. They're shouting something while Mom whispers in my ear. I hear none of it. Happiness and joy overwhelm every sense. I've never felt anything like it.

My knees brush against a rug and Mom kneels with me in the middle of the large foyer. She keeps kissing my face, alternating cheeks so quickly I think they might bruise. Gisa worms in with us, her dark red hair ablaze in the corner of my eye. Like the Colonel, she has a dusting of new freckles, brown spots against golden skin. I tuck her close. She used to be smaller.

Tramy grins over us, sporting a dark, well-kept beard. He was always trying to grow one as a teenager. Never got further than patchy stubble. Bree used to tease him. Not now. He braces himself against my back, thick arms wrapping around Mom and me. His cheeks are wet. With a jolt, I realize mine are too.

"Where's . . . ?" I ask.

Thankfully, I don't have time to fear the worst. When he appears, I wonder if I'm hallucinating.

He leans heavy on Kilorn's arm and a cane. The months have been good to him. Regular meals filled him out. He walks slowly from an adjoining room. *Walks*. His pace is stilted, unnatural, unfamiliar. My father has not had two legs in years. Or more than one working lung. As he approaches, eyes bright, I listen. No rasp. No click of a machine to help him breathe. No squeak of a rusty old wheelchair. I don't know what to think or say. I forgot how tall he is.

Healers. Probably Sara herself. I thank her a thousand times silently inside my heart. Slowly, I stand, pulling the army jacket tight around me. It has bullet holes. Dad eyes them, still a soldier.

"You can hug me. I won't fall over," he says.

Liar. He almost topples when I wrap my arms around his middle, but Kilorn keeps him upright. We embrace in a way we haven't been able to since I was a little girl.

Mom's soft hands brush my hair away from my face, and she settles her head next to mine. They keep me between them, sheltered and safe. And for that moment, I forget. There is no Maven, no manacles, no brand, no scars. No war, no rebellion.

No Shade.

I wasn't the only one missing from our family. Nothing can change that.

He isn't here, and never will be again. My brother is alone on an abandoned island.

I refuse to let another Barrow share his fate.

TWENTY-ONE
Mare

The bathwater swirls brown and red. Dirt and blood. Mom drains the water twice, and still she keeps finding more in my hair. At least the healer on the jet took care of my fresh wounds, so I can enjoy the soapy heat without any more pain. Gisa perches on a stool by the edge of the tub, her spine straight in the stiff posture she perfected over the years. Either she's gotten prettier or six months dulled my memory of her face. Straight nose, full lips, and sparkling, dark eyes. Mom's eyes, my eyes. The eyes all the Barrows have, except Shade. He was the only one of us with eyes like honey or gold. From my dad's mother. Those eyes are gone forever.

I turn from thoughts of my brother and stare at Gisa's hand. The one I broke with my foolish mistakes.

The skin is smooth now, the bones reset. No evidence of her mangled body part, shattered by the butt of a Security officer's gun.

"Sara," Gisa explains gently, flexing her fingers.

"She did a good job," I tell her. "With Dad too."

"That took a whole week, you know. Regrowing everything from the thigh down. And he's still getting used to it. But it didn't hurt as much as this." She flexes her fingers, grinning. "You know she had to rebreak these two?" Her index and middle finger wiggle. "Used a hammer. Hurt like hell."

"Gisa Barrow, your language is appalling." I splash a little water at her feet. She swears again, drawing her toes away.

"Blame the Scarlet Guard. Seems they spend all their time cursing and asking for more flags." *Sounds about right.* Not one to be outdone, Gisa reaches into the tub and flicks water at me.

Mom tuts at both of us. She tries to look stern, and fails horribly. "None of that, you two."

A fuzzy white towel snaps between her hands, held out. As much as I want to spend another hour soaking in soothing hot water, I want to get back downstairs much more.

The water sloshes around me as I stand up and step out of the bath, curling into the towel. Gisa's smile falters a little. My scars are plain as day, pearly bits of white flesh against darker skin. Even Mom glances away, giving me a second to wrap the towel a bit better, hiding the brand on my collarbone.

I focus on the bathroom instead of their shamed faces. It isn't as fine as the one I had in Archeon, but the lack of Silent Stone more than makes up for it. Whatever officer lived here had very bright taste. The walls are garish orange trimmed in white to match the porcelain fixings, including a fluted sink, the deep bathtub, and a shower hidden behind a lime-green curtain. My reflection stares back from the mirror over the sink. I look like a drowned rat, albeit a very clean one. Next to my mother, I see our resemblance more closely. She's small-boned as I am, our skin the same golden shade. Though hers is more careworn and wrinkled, carved with the years.

Gisa leads us out and into the hall, while Mom follows, drying my hair with another soft towel. They show me into a powder-blue bedroom with two fluffy beds. It's small but more than suitable. I'd take a dirt floor over the most sumptuous chamber in Maven's palace. Mom is quick to pull me into a pair of cotton pajamas, not to mention socks and a soft shawl.

"Mom, I'm going to boil," I protest kindly, unwinding the shawl from my neck.

She takes it back with a smile. Then she kisses me again, swooping to brush both my cheeks. "Just making you comfortable."

"Trust me, I am," I tell her, giving her arm a squeeze.

In the corner, I notice my jeweled gown from the wedding, now reduced to scraps. Gisa follows my gaze and blushes.

"Thought I could save a bit of it," my sister admits, looking almost sheepish. "Those are rubies. I'm not going to waste rubies."

It seems she has more of my thief's instincts than I realized.

And, apparently, so does my mother.

She speaks before I even take a step toward the bedroom door.

"If you think I'm going to let you stay up to all hours talking war, you are absolutely incorrect." To cement her point, she folds her arms and settles directly in my path. My mother is shorter, like me, but she's a laborer of many years. She is far from weak. I've seen her manhandle all three of my brothers, and I know firsthand she'll wrestle me into bed if she needs to.

"Mom, there are things I need to say—"

"Your debriefing is at eight a.m. tomorrow. Say it then."

"—and I want to know what I missed—"

"The Guard overthrew Corvium. They're working on Piedmont.

That's all anyone downstairs knows." She speaks rapid-fire, herding me toward the bed.

I look to Gisa for help, but she backs away, hands raised.

"I haven't spoken to Kilorn—"

"He understands."

"Cal—"

"Is absolutely fine with your father and brothers. He can storm the capital; he can handle them."

With a smirk, I imagine Cal sandwiched between Bree and Tramy.

"Besides, he did everything he could to bring you back to us," she adds with a wink. "They won't give him any trouble, not tonight at least. Now get in that bed and shut your eyes, or I'll shut them for you."

The lights hiss in their bulbs; the wiring in the room snakes along electric lines of light. None of it compares to the strength of my mother's voice. I do as she says, clambering under the blankets of the closest bed. To my surprise, she gets in next to me, hugging me close.

For the thousandth time tonight, she kisses my cheek. "You're not going anywhere."

In my heart, I know that's not true.

This war is far from won.

But at least it can be true for tonight.

Birds in Piedmont make a horrible racket. They chirp and trill outside the windows, and I imagine droves of them perched in the trees. It's the only explanation for such noise. They are good for one thing, though: I never heard birds in Archeon. Even before I open my eyes, I know yesterday was not a dream. I know where I'm waking up, and what I'm waking up to.

Mom is an early riser by habit. Gisa isn't here either, but I'm not alone. I poke out the bedroom door to find a lanky boy sitting at the top of the stairs, his legs stretched out over the steps.

Kilorn gets to his feet with a grin, his arms spread wide. There's a decent chance I'll fall apart from all the hugging.

"Took you long enough," he says. Even after six months of capture and torment, he won't treat me with kid gloves. We fall back into our old ways with blinding speed.

I nudge him in the ribs. "No thanks to you."

"Yeah, military raids and tactical strikes aren't exactly my specialty."

"You have a specialty?"

"Well, besides being a nuisance?" he laughs, walking me downstairs. Pots and pans clatter somewhere, and I follow the smell of frying bacon. In the daylight, the row house seems friendly, and out of place for a military base. Butter-yellow walls and florid purple rugs warm the central hallway, but it is suspiciously bare of decorations. Nail holes dot the wallpaper. Maybe a dozen paintings have been removed. The rooms we pass—a salon and a study—are also sparsely furnished. Either the officer who lived here emptied his home, or someone else did it for him.

Stop it, I tell myself. I've earned the right not to think about betrayals or backstabbing for one damn day. *You're safe; you're safe; it's over.* I repeat the words in my head.

Kilorn puts an arm out, stopping me at the door to the kitchen. He leans forward into my space, until I can't avoid his eyes. Green as I remember. They narrow in concern. "You're okay?"

Usually, I would nod, smile away the insinuation. I've done it so many times before. I pushed away the people closest to me, thinking I could bleed alone. I won't do that anymore. It made me hateful, horrific. But the words I want to pour out of me won't come. Not for Kilorn. He wouldn't understand.

"Starting to think I need a word that means yes and no at the same time," I whisper, looking at my toes.

He puts a hand to my shoulder. It doesn't linger. Kilorn knows the lines I've drawn between us. He won't push past them. "I'm here when you need to talk." Not *if*, *when*. "I'll hound you until you do."

I offer a shaky grin. "Good." The sound of cooking fat crackles on the air. "I hope Bree hasn't eaten it all."

My brother certainly tries. While Tramy helps her cook, Bree hovers at Mom's shoulder, picking strips of bacon right out of the hot grease. She swats him away as Tramy gloats, smirking over a pan of eggs. They're both adults, but they seem like children, like I remember them. Gisa sits at the kitchen table, watching out of the corner of her eye. Doing her best to remain proper. She drums her fingers on the wooden tabletop.

Dad is more restrained, leaning against a wall of cabinets, his new leg angled out in front of him. He spots me before the others and offers a small, private smile. Despite the cheerful scene, sadness eats at his edges.

He feels our missing piece. The one that will never be found.

I swallow around the lump in my throat, pushing the ghost of Shade away.

Cal is also noticeably absent. Not that he will stay away long. He's probably sleeping, or perhaps planning the next stage of . . . whatever's going on.

"Other people need to eat," I scold as I pass Bree. Quickly, I snatch the bacon from his fingers. Six months have not dulled my reflexes or impulses. I grin at him as I take a seat next to Gisa, now twisting her long hair into a neat bun.

Bree makes a face as he sits, a plate in hand piled with buttered toast. He never ate this well in the army, or on Tuck. Like the rest of us, he's taking full advantage of the food. "Yeah, Tramy, save some for the rest of us."

"Like you really need it," Tramy retorts, pinching Bree's cheek. They end up slapping each other away. *Children,* I think again. *And soldiers too.*

Both of them were conscripted, and both of them survived longer than most. Some might call it luck, but they're strong, both of them. Smart in battle, if not at home. Warriors lie beneath their easy grins and boyish behavior. For now I'm glad I don't have to see it.

Mom serves me first. No one complains, not even Bree. I dig into eggs and bacon, as well as a cup of rich, hot coffee with cream and sugar. The food is fit for a Silver noble, and I should know. "Mom, how did you get this?" I ask around bites of egg. Gisa makes a face, wrinkling her nose at the food lolling about in my mouth as I speak.

"Daily delivery for the street," Mom replies, tossing a braid of gray-and-brown hair over her shoulder. "This row is all Guard officers, ranking officials, and significant individuals—and their families."

"'Significant individuals' meaning . . ." I try to read between the lines. "Newbloods?"

Kilorn answers instead. "If they're officers, yeah. But newblood recruits live in the barracks with the rest of the soldiers. Thought it was better that way. Less division, less fear. We're never going to have a proper army if most of the troops are afraid of the person next to them."

In spite of myself, I feel my eyebrows rise in surprise.

"Told you I had a specialty," he whispers with a wink.

My mother beams, putting the next plate of food in front of him. She ruffles his hair fondly, setting the tawny locks on end. He awkwardly tries to smooth them down. "Kilorn's been improving relations between the newbloods and the rest of the Scarlet Guard," she says proudly. He tries to hide the resulting blush with a hand.

"Warren, if you're not going to eat that——"

Dad reacts faster than any of us, rapping Tramy's outstretched hand with his cane. "Manners, boy," he growls. Then he snatches bacon from my own plate. "Good stuff."

"Best I've ever had," Gisa agrees. She daintily but eagerly picks at eggs sprinkled with cheese. "Montfort knows their food."

"Piedmont," Dad corrects. "Food and stores are from Piedmont."

I file the information away and wince at the instinct to do so. I'm so used to dissecting the words of everyone around me that I do it without thought, even to my family. *You're safe; you're safe; it's over.* The words repeat in my head. Their rhythm levels me out a bit.

Dad still refuses to sit.

"So how do you like the leg?" I ask.

He scratches his head, fidgeting. "Well, I won't be returning it anytime soon," he says with a rare smile. "Takes getting used to. Skin healer's helping when she can."

"That's good. That's really good."

I was never truly ashamed of Dad's injury. It meant he was alive and safe from conscription. So many other fathers, Kilorn's included, died for a nonsense war while mine lived. The missing leg made him sour, discontent, resentful of his chair. He scowled more than he smiled, a bitter hermit to most. But he was a living man. He told me once it was cruel to give hope where none should be. He had no hope of walking again, of being the man he was before. Now he stands as proof of the opposite and that hope, no matter how small, no matter how impossible, can still be answered.

In Maven's prison, I despaired. I wasted. I counted the days and wished for an ending, no matter the kind. But I had hope. Foolish, illogical hope. Sometimes a single flicker, sometimes a flame. It also seemed impossible. Just like the path ahead, through war and revolution. We could all die in the coming days. We could be betrayed. Or . . . we could win.

I don't even know what that looks like, or what exactly to hope for. I just know that I must keep my hope alive. It is the only shield I have against the darkness inside.

I look around at the kitchen table. Once I lamented that my family did not know me, didn't understand what I had become. I thought myself separate, alone, isolated.

I could not be more wrong. I know better now. I know who I am.

I am Mare Barrow. Not Mareena, not the lightning girl. Mare.

My parents quietly offer to accompany me to the debriefing. Gisa does too. I refuse. This is a military undertaking, all business, all for the cause. It will be easier for me to recall in detail if my mother isn't holding my hand. I can be strong in front of the Colonel and his officers, but not her. She makes it too tempting to break. Weakness is acceptable, forgivable, around family. But not when lives and wars hang in the balance.

The kitchen clock ticks eight a.m., and right on time an open-topped transport rolls up outside the row house. I go quietly. Only Kilorn follows me out, but not to join me. He knows he has no part in this.

"So what will you do with yourself for the day?" I ask as I wrench open the brass-knobbed door.

He shrugs. "I had a schedule up in Trial. Bit of training, rounds with the newbloods, lessons with Ada. After I came down here with your parents, I figured I'll keep it up."

"A schedule," I snort, stepping out into the sunshine. "You sound like a Silver lady."

"Well, when you're as good-looking as I am . . . ," he sighs.

It's already hot, the sun blazing above the eastern horizon, and I strip off the thin jacket Mom forced me into. Leafy trees line the street, disguising the military base as an upper-class neighborhood. Most of the brick row houses look empty, their windows dark and shuttered. At the bottom of the steps, my transport waits. The driver behind the wheel pushes down his sunglasses, eyeing me over the brim. I should have known. Cal gave me all the time I needed with my family, but he couldn't stay away long.

"Kilorn," he calls, waving a hand in greeting. Kilorn returns the gesture with ease and a smile. Six months has killed their rivalry at the root.

"I'll find you later," I tell him. "Compare notes."

He nods. "Sure thing."

Even though it's Cal in the driver's seat, drawing me in like a beacon, I walk slowly to the transport. In the distance, airjet engines roar. Every step is another inch closer to reliving six months of captivity. If I turned around, no one would blame me. But it would only prolong the inevitable.

Cal watches, his face grim in the daylight. He extends a hand, helping me into the front seat like I'm some kind of invalid. The engine purrs, its electric heart a comfort and a reminder. I may be scared, but I'm not weak.

With one last wave to Kilorn, Cal guns the engine and spins the wheel, driving us down the street. The breeze ruffles his roughly cut hair, highlighting uneven spots.

I run a hand down the back of his head. "Did you do this yourself?"

He flushes silver. "I tried." Leaving one hand on the wheel, he takes mine in the other. "Are you going to be all right for this?"

"I'll get through it. I suppose your reports have most of the important parts. I just have to fill in the holes." The trees thin on either side of us, where the officer street hits a larger avenue. To the left is the landing field. We turn right, the transport arcing smoothly over pavement. "And hopefully someone starts filling me in on all . . . this."

"With these people, you have to demand answers rather than wait for them."

"Have you been demanding, Your Highness?"

He chuckles low in his throat. "They certainly think so."

It's a five-minute drive to our destination, and Cal does his best to get me up to speed. There was a headquarters along the Lakelander border near Trial. All the Colonel's soldiers evacuated north in anticipation of a raid on the island. They spent months belowground, in freezing bunkers, while Farley and the Colonel traded communications with Command and prepared for their next target. Corvium. Cal's voice breaks a little when he describes the siege. He led the strike himself, taking the walls in a surprise raid and then the fortress city, block by block. It's possible he knew the soldiers he was fighting. It's possible he killed friends. I don't prod at either wound. In the end, they completed the siege, removing the last Silver officers by offering them surrender or execution.

"Most are held hostage now, some ransomed back to their families. And some chose death," he murmurs, his voice trailing off. He glances over at me, just for a moment, his eyes hidden behind lenses of darkened glass.

"I'm sorry," I murmur, and I mean it. Not just because Cal is in pain, but because I have long since learned how gray this world is. "Will Julian be at the debriefing?"

Cal sighs, grateful for the change in subject. "I don't know. This morning he said the Montfort brass have been very accommodating where he is concerned—giving him access to the base archives, a laboratory, all the time he wants to continue his newblood studies."

I can think of no better reward for Julian Jacos. Time and books.

"But they might not be too keen on letting a singer near their leader," Cal adds, thoughtful.

"Understandable," I reply. While our abilities are more destructive, Julian's ability to manipulate is just as deadly. "So, how long has Montfort been at this?"

"I don't know either," he says, his annoyance obvious. "But they took real notice after Corvium. And now, with Maven's alliance with the Lakelands? He's uniting too, on the rebellion," he explains. "Montfort and the Guard did the same. Instead of guns and food, Montfort started sending soldiers. Reds, newbloods. They already had a plan to spring you out of Archeon. Pincer move. Us from Trial, Montfort from Piedmont. They can organize, I'll give them that. They just needed the right moment."

I scoff. "They picked a hell of a moment." Gunfire and bloodshed cloud my thoughts. "All that for me. Seems stupid."

Cal's grip on my hand tightens. He was raised to be the perfect Silver soldier. I remember his manuals, his books on military tactics.

Victory at any cost, they said. And he used to believe it. Just as I used to think nothing on earth could make me go back to Maven.

"Either they had another target in Archeon, or Montfort really, really wants you," Cal mutters as the transport slows.

We stop in front of another brick building, its front decorated by white columns and a long, wrapping porch. Again I think of Fort Patriot, its gates decorated in foreboding bronze. Silvers like beautiful things, and this is no exception. Flowering vines crawl up the columns, blooming with purple bursts of wisteria and fragrant honeysuckle. Soldiers in uniform walk beneath the plants, keeping to the shade. I spot Scarlet Guard in their mismatched clothes and red scarves, Lakelanders in blue, and a crawling mess of official Montfort green. My stomach flips.

The Colonel marches out to meet us, blissfully alone.

He starts in before I manage to get down from the transport. "You'll be meeting with me, two Montfort generals, and one Command officer."

Both Cal and I jolt, eyes wide. "Command?" I balk.

"Yes." The Colonel's good eye flashes. He spins on his heel, forcing us to keep up. "Let's just say wheels are in motion."

I roll my eyes, already exasperated. "How about you just say what you mean?"

"Probably because he doesn't know," replies a familiar voice.

Farley leans in the shadow of one of the columns, arms crossed high over her chest. I gape, jaw dropping open. Because she is hugely, hilariously pregnant. Her belly strains against an altered uniform of a tied shift dress and baggy pants. I wouldn't be surprised if she gave birth in the next thirty seconds.

"Ah" is all I can think to say.

She looks almost amused. "Do the math, Barrow."

Nine months. Shade. Her reaction on the cargo jet when I told her what Jon said. *The answer to your question is yes.*

I didn't know what it meant, but she did. She had her suspicions. And she learned she was pregnant with my brother's child less than an hour after he was murdered. Each revelation is a kick in the gut. Equal parts joy and sorrow. Shade has a child—one he'll never get to see.

"Can't believe no one thought to tell you," Farley continues, throwing pointed glares at Cal, who shuffles awkwardly. "Certainly had the time."

In my shock, all I can do is agree. Not just Cal, but my mother, the rest of the family. "Everyone knew about this?"

"Well, no use arguing about it now," Farley pushes on, heaving herself off the column. Even in the Stilts, most women take to bed at this stage of pregnancy, but not her. She keeps a gun at her hip, holstered in open warning. A pregnant Farley is still a dangerous Farley. Probably more so. "I have a feeling you want to get this over as quickly as possible."

When she turns her back, leading us in, I hit Cal in the ribs. Twice for good measure.

He grits his teeth, breathing through the blow. "Sorry," he grumbles.

The interior of what must be the base command building seems more like a mansion. Staircases spiral on either side of the entrance hall, connecting to a gallery above lined by windows. Crown molding lines the ceiling, which is painted to look like the wisteria outside. The floor is parquet wood, alternating planks of mahogany, cherry, and oak in intricate designs. But like in the row houses, anything that can't be bolted down is gone. Blank spaces line the walls, while alcoves meant for sculptures or busts hold guards instead. Montfort guards.

Up close, their uniforms are better made than anything the Scarlet Guard or the Colonel's Lakelanders wear. More like the uniforms of Silver officers. They're mass-produced—sturdy—with badges, insignia, and the white triangle emblazoned on their arms.

Cal observes as closely as I do. He nudges me, nodding up the stairs. In the gallery, no fewer than six Montfort officers watch us go. They are gray-haired, battle-worn, with enough medals to sink a ship. Generals.

"Cameras too," I whisper to him. In my head I pick them out, noting each electric signature while we pass through the entrance hall.

Despite the empty walls and sparse decorations, the fine passages make my skin crawl. I keep telling myself the person next to me isn't one of the Arvens. This isn't Whitefire. My ability is proof of that. No one is keeping me prisoner. I wish I could drop my guard. It's second nature at this point.

The meeting room reminds me of Maven's council chamber. It has a long, polished table and finely upholstered chairs, and it's illuminated by a bank of windows looking out over another garden. Again the walls are empty, except for a seal painted directly on the wall. Yellow and white stripes, with a purple star in the center. Piedmont.

We're the first to arrive. I expect the Colonel to take a seat at the head of the table, but he doesn't, electing for the chair on its right instead. The rest of us file in next to him, facing the empty side we leave open for the Montfort officers and Command.

The Colonel looks on, perplexed. He watches as Farley sits, his good eye cold and steely. "Captain, you don't have clearance for this."

Cal and I exchange glances, eyebrows raised. Farley and the Colonel clash often. At least that hasn't changed.

"Oh, were you not informed?" she replies, pulling a folded strip of paper from her pocket. "So sad how that happens." With a flick of her hand, she slides the paper over to the Colonel.

He unfolds it greedily, eyes scanning a page of harsh-typed letters. It isn't long, but he stares at it for a while, not believing the words. Finally he smooths the message against the table. "This can't be right."

"Command wants a representative at the table." Farley grins. She splays her hands wide. "Here I am."

"Then Command made a mistake."

"I'm Command now, Colonel. There is no mistake."

Command rules the Scarlet Guard, the hub of a very secretive wheel. I have only heard whispers of their existence, but enough to know they control the entirety of a vast, complicated operation. If they made Farley one of them, does this mean that the Guard is truly coming out of the shadows—or is it just Farley they want?

"Diana, you can't—"

She bristles, flushing red. "Because I'm pregnant? I assure you, I can handle two tasks at once." If not for their uncanny resemblance, both in appearance and attitude, it would be easy to forget that Farley is the Colonel's daughter. "Do you want to press the matter further, Willis?"

He clenches a fist on the message, knuckles turning bone white. But he shakes his head.

"Good. And it's General now. Act accordingly."

A retort dies in the Colonel's throat, giving him a strangled look. With a satisfied smirk, Farley retrieves the message and tucks it away. She notes Cal watching, just as confused as I am.

"You're not the only ranking officer in the room now, Calore."

"I suppose not. Congratulations," he adds, offering a tight smile.

It takes her off guard. After her father's open hostility, she didn't expect support from anyone, least of all the begrudging Silver prince.

The Montfort generals enter from another door, resplendent in their dark green uniforms. One I saw in the gallery. She has an even bob of white hair, watery brown eyes, and long, fluttering lashes. She blinks rapidly. The other, a dark-haired woman, brown-skinned, looks to be about forty and built like an ox. She tips her head at me, as if greeting a friend.

"I know you," I say, trying to place her face. "How do I know you?"

She doesn't answer, turning her head over her shoulder to wait for one more person, a gray-haired man in plain clothing. But I barely notice him at all, distracted by his companion. Even without his house colors, dressed in simple grays instead of his usual faded gold, Julian is hard to miss. I feel a burst of warmth at the sight of my old teacher. Julian inclines his head, offering a small smile in greeting. He looks better than I've ever seen him, even when I first met him at the summer palace. Then he was worn, wearied by a court of enemies, haunted by a dead sister, a broken Sara Skonos, and his own doubt. Though his hair is now more gray than brown, his wrinkles deeper, he seems vibrant, alive, unburdened. Whole. The Scarlet Guard has given him purpose. And Sara too, I bet.

His presence soothes Cal even more than me. He relaxes a bit at my side, giving his uncle the slightest nod. Both of us see what this is, what kind of message Montfort is trying to send. They do not hate Silvers— and they do not fear them.

The other man shuts the door behind him as Julian takes a seat, firmly planting himself on our side of the table. Even though he's six feet tall, he seems small without a uniform of his own. Instead, he wears civilian clothing. A simple buttoned shirt, pants, shoes. No weapons that I can see. He has red blood, that's certain, judging by the pink undertones in his sandy skin. Newblood or Red, I don't know. Everything about him is decidedly neutral, pleasantly average, and unassuming. He seems a blank page, either by nature or design. There's nothing else to indicate who or what he might be.

But Farley knows. She moves to get to her feet, and he waves her down.

"No need for that, General," he says. In a way, he reminds me of Julian. They have the same wild eyes, the only thing remarkable about him. His are angled, darting back and forth, taking in everything for observation and understanding. "It's a pleasure to finally meet you all," he adds, nodding to each of us in turn. "Colonel, Miss Barrow, Your Highness."

Under the table, Cal's fingers twitch against his leg. No one calls him that anymore. Not people who mean it.

"And who are you, exactly?" the Colonel asks.

"Of course," the man replies. "I'm sorry I could not come sooner. My name is Dane Davidson, sir. I serve as premier to the Free Republic of Montfort."

Cal's fingers twitch again.

"Thank you all for coming. I've wanted this meeting for some time now," Davidson continues, "and I think that together, we can achieve magnificent things."

This man is the leader of the entire country. He's the one who asked for me, who wanted me to join him. Has he done all this to get his way? Like his general's face, his name rings a distant bell.

"This is General Torkins." Davidson gestures between them. "And General Salida."

Salida. I don't know her name. But now I'm certain I've seen her before.

The sturdily built general notes my confusion. "I did some reconnaissance, Miss Barrow. I presented myself to King Maven when he was interviewing Ardent—I mean newbloods. You may remember." To demonstrate she sweeps her hand at the table. No, not *at*. *Through*. Like it's made of nothing—or she is.

The memory snaps into focus. She displayed her abilities and was accepted into Maven's "protection," along with many other newbloods. One of them, in her fear, exposed Nanny to the entire court.

I stare at her. "You were there the day Nanny—the newblood who could change her face—died."

Salida looks truly sorry. She dips her head. "If I had known, if I could have done something, truly I would have. But Montfort and the Scarlet Guard did not communicate openly, not then. We didn't know all your operations, and they did not know ours."

"No longer." Davidson remains standing, his fists braced against the table. "The Scarlet Guard has need for secrecy, yes, but I'm afraid it will only do more harm than good from here onward. Too many moving parts not to get in each other's way."

Farley shifts in her seat. Either she wants to disagree or the chair is uncomfortable. But she holds her tongue, letting Davidson carry on.

"So, in the interest of transparency, I felt it best for Miss Barrow to detail her captivity, as much as she can, to all parties. And afterward, I will answer any and all questions you may have about myself, my country, and our road ahead."

In Julian's histories, there were records of rulers who were elected, rather than born. They earned their crowns with an array of attributes—some strength, some intelligence, some empty promises and intimidation. Davidson rules the so-called Free Republic, and his people chose him to lead. Based on what, I can't say yet. He has a firm way of speaking, a natural conviction. And he's obviously very smart. Not to mention he is the kind of man who gets more attractive with the years. I could easily see how people wanted him to rule.

"Miss Barrow, whenever you're ready."

To my surprise, the first hand to hold mine is not Cal's, but Farley's. She gives me a reassuring squeeze.

I start at the beginning. The only place I can think to start.

My voice breaks when I detail how I was forced to remember Shade. Farley lowers her eyes, her pain just as deep as mine. I soldier through, to Maven's growing obsession, the boy king who twisted lies into weapons, using my face and his words to turn as many newbloods as possible against the Scarlet Guard. All the while his fraying edges becoming more apparent.

"He says she left holes," I tell them. "The queen. She toyed in his head, taking pieces away, putting pieces in, jumbling him up. He knows that he is wrong, but he believes himself on a path, and he won't turn from it."

A current of heat ripples. At my side, Cal keeps his face still, eyes boring holes in the table. I tread carefully.

His mother took away his love for you, Cal. He loved you. He knows he did. It just isn't there anymore, and it never will be. But those words are not for Davidson or the Colonel or even Farley to hear.

The Montfort people seem most interested in the Piedmont visit. They perk up at the mention of Daraeus and Alexandret, and I walk them through their visit step by step. Their questioning, their manner, down to what kind of clothes they wore. When I mention Michael and Charlotta, the missing prince and princess, Davidson purses his lips.

As I speak, spilling more and more of my ordeal, a numbness washes over me. I detach from the words. My voice drones. The house rebellion.

Jon's escape. Maven's near death. The sight of silver blood gushing from his neck. Another interrogation, mine and the Haven woman's. That was the first time I saw Maven truly rattled, when Elane's sister pledged her allegiance to a different king. To Cal. It resulted in the exile of many members of court, possible allies.

"I tried to separate him from House Samos. I knew they were his strongest remaining ally, so I played on his weakness for me. If he married Evangeline, I told him, she would kill me." Pieces move into place as I speak them. I flush at the implication that I am the reason for such a deadly alliance. "I think it may have convinced him to look to the Lakelands for a different bride—"

Julian cuts me off. "Volo Samos was already searching for an excuse to detach from Maven. Ending the betrothal was just the final straw. And I assume the Lakelander negotiations were in play much longer than you think." He quirks a thin smile. Even if he's lying, it makes me feel a bit better.

I race through my memories of the coronation tour, a glorified parade to hide his dealings with the Lakelanders. Maven's revocation of the Measures, the end of the Lakelander War, his betrothal to Iris. Careful moves to buy goodwill from his kingdom, to get credit for stopping a war without stopping its destruction.

"Silver nobles came back to court before the wedding, and Maven kept me alone for most of the time. Then there was the wedding itself. The Lakelander alliance was sealed. The storm—your storm—followed. Maven and Iris fled to his escape train, but we were separated."

It was only yesterday. Still, this feels like recalling a dream. Adrenaline fogs the battle, reducing my memories to color and pain and fear. "My guards dragged me back into the palace."

I pause, hesitating. Even now, I can't believe what Evangeline did.

"Mare?" Cal prods, his voice and the brush of his hand gentle. He's just as curious as the rest.

It's easier to face him than the others. He alone understands how strange my escape was. "Evangeline Samos cut us off. She killed the Arven guards and she . . . she freed me. She set me loose. I still don't know why."

A silence descends over the table. My greatest rival, a girl who threatened to kill me, a person with cold steel instead of a heart, is the reason I'm here. Julian doesn't try to hide his surprise, his thin eyebrows almost disappearing into his hairline. But Cal doesn't look surprised at all. Instead, he draws a deep breath, his chest rising with the motion. Could that be—pride?

I don't have the energy to guess. Or to detail the way Samson Merandus died, playing Cal and me off each other until we both burned him alive.

"You know the rest," I finish, exhausted. I feel like I've been talking for decades.

Premier Davidson stands, stretching. I expect more questions, but instead he opens a cabinet and pours me a glass of water. I don't touch it. I'm in an unfamiliar place run by unfamiliar people. I have very little trust left in me, and I won't waste it on someone I just met.

"Our turn?" Cal asks. He leans forward, eager to begin his own interrogation.

Davidson inclines his head, lips tugged into flat, neutral line. "Of course. I assume you're wondering what we're doing here in Piedmont, and on a royal fleet base to boot?"

When no one stops him, Davidson launches ahead.

"As you know, the Scarlet Guard began in the Lakelands, and

filtered down into Norta this past year. Colonel Farley and General Farley were integral to both endeavors, and I thank them for their hard work." He nods at them in turn. "At the orders of your Command, other operatives undertook a similar campaign in Piedmont. Infiltrate, control, overthrow. Here, in fact, is where agents of Montfort first encountered agents of the Scarlet Guard, which, up until last year, seemed a fiction to us. But the Scarlet Guard was very real, and we certainly shared a goal. Like your compatriots, we seek to overthrow oppressive Silver rulers and expand our democratic republic."

"It seems you've done so already." Farley indicates the room.

Cal narrows his eyes. "How?"

"We concentrated our efforts on Piedmont due to its precarious structure. Princes and princesses rule their territories in shaky peace beneath a high prince elected from their ranks. Some control large tracts of land, others a city or simply a few miles of farms. Power is fluid, always changing. Currently, Prince Bracken of the Lowcountry is the high prince, the strongest Silver in Piedmont, with the largest territory and the greatest resources." With a sweep of his hand, Davidson brushes his fingers against the seal on the wall. He traces the purple star. "This is the grandest of the three military fortresses in his possession. It is now ceded to our personal use."

Cal sucks in a breath. "You're working with Bracken?"

"He's working for us," Davidson replies proudly.

My mind spins out. A Silver royal, operating on behalf of a country looking to take everything away from him? For a moment, it sounds ludicrous. Then I remember exactly who's sitting next to me.

"The princes visited Maven on Bracken's behalf. They questioned me for him." I narrow my eyes at the premier. "You told them to do that?"

General Torkins shifts in her seat and clears her throat. "Daraeus and Alexandret are sworn allies to Bracken. We had no knowledge of their contact with King Maven until one of them turned up dead in the middle of an assassination attempt."

"Thanks to you, we know why," Salida adds.

"What about the survivor? Daraeus. He's working against you—"

Davidson blinks slowly, his eyes blank and unreadable. "He was working against us."

"Oh," I murmur, thinking of all the ways the Piedmont prince could have been killed.

"And the others?" The Colonel presses on. "Michael and Charlotta. The missing prince and princess."

"Bracken's children," Julian says, his voice tight.

A sick feeling washes over me. "You took his children? To make him cooperate?"

"A boy and girl for control of coastal Piedmont? For all these resources?" Torkins scoffs, her white hair rippling as she shakes her head. "An easy trade. Think of the lives we would lose fighting for every mile. Instead, Montfort and the Scarlet Guard have real progress."

My heart clenches at the thought of two children, Silver or not, being held captive to make their father kneel. Davidson reads the sentiment on my face.

"They're well taken care of. Provided for."

Overhead, the lights flicker like the beating of moth's wings. "A cell is still a cell, no matter how you dress it up," I sneer.

He doesn't flinch. "And a war is a war, Mare Barrow. No matter how good your intentions may be."

I shake my head. "Well, it's too bad. Save all those soldiers here, but waste them on rescuing one person. Was that an easy trade too? Their lives for mine?"

"General Salida, what was the last count?" the premier asks.

She nods, reciting from memory. "Of the one hundred and two Ardents recruited to the Nortan army in the last few months, sixty were present as special guards to the wedding. All sixty were rescued, and debriefed last night."

"Due in large part to the efforts of General Salida, who was embedded with them." Davidson claps a hand on her meaty shoulder. "Including you, we saved sixty-one Ardents from your king. Each will be given food, shelter, and a choice of resettlement or service. In addition, we were able to raid a large amount of the Nortan Treasury. Wars are not cheap. Ransoming worthless or weak prisoners only gets us so far." He pauses. "Does that answer your question?"

Relief mixes with the undercurrent of dread I can never seem to shake. The attack on Archeon was not just for me. I have not been freed from one dictator only to be taken by another. None of us knows what Davidson might do, but he isn't Maven. His blood is red.

"One more question for you, I'm afraid," Davidson pushes on. "Miss Barrow, would you say the king of Norta is in love with you?"

In Whitefire, I smashed too many glasses of water to count. I feel the urge to do it again. "I don't know." A lie. An easy lie.

Davidson is not so easily swayed. His wild eyes flicker, amused. Catching the light, they seem gold then brown then gold again. Shifting as the sun on a field of swaying wheat. "You can take a well-educated guess."

Hot anger licks up inside me like a flame.

"What Maven considers love is not love at all." I yank aside the collar of my shirt, revealing my brand. The *M* is plain as day. So many eyes brush my skin, taking in the raised edges of pearly scar tissue and burned flesh. Davidson's gaze traces the lines of fire, and I feel Maven's touch in his stare.

"Enough," I breathe, pushing the shirt back in place.

The premier nods. "Fine. I will ask you to—"

"No, I mean I've had enough of this. I need . . . time." Heaving a shaky breath, I push back from the table. My chair scrapes against the floor, echoing in the sudden silence. No one stops me. They just watch, eyes full of pity. For once, I'm glad of it. Their pity lets me go.

Another chair follows mine. I don't need to look back to know it's Cal.

As on the airjet, I feel the world start to close and suffocate, expand and overwhelm. The halls, so like Whitefire, stretch into an endless line. Lights pulse overhead. I lean into the sensation, hoping it will ground me. *You're safe; you're safe; it's over.* My thoughts spiral out of control, and my feet move of their own volition. Down the stairs, through another door, out into a garden choked by fragrant flowers. The clear sky above is a torment. I want it to rain. I want to be washed clean.

Cal's hands find the back of my neck. The scars ache beneath his touch. His warmth bleeds into my muscles, trying to soothe away the pain. I press the heels of my hands to my eyes. It helps a little. I can't see anything in the darkness, including Maven, his palace, or the bounds of that horrible room.

You're safe; you're safe; it's over.

It would be easy to stay in the dark, to drown. Slowly, I lower my hands and force myself to look at the sunlight. It takes more effort than I thought possible. I refuse to let Maven keep me prisoner one second longer than he already has. I refuse to live this way.

"Can I take you back to your house?" Cal asks, his voice low. His thumbs work steady circles at the space between neck and shoulders. "We can walk, give you some time."

"I'm not giving him any more of my time." Angry, I turn around and raise my chin, forcing myself to look Cal in the eye. He doesn't move, patient and unassuming. All reaction, adjusting to my emotions, letting me set the pace. After so long at the mercy of others, it feels good to know someone will allow me my own choices. "I don't want to go back yet."

"Fine."

"I don't want to stay here."

"Me neither."

"I don't want to talk about Maven or politics or war."

My voice echoes in the leaves. I sound like a child, but Cal just nods along. For once, he seems a child too, with a ragged haircut and simple clothing. No uniform, no military gear. Only a thin shirt, pants, boots, and his bracelets. In another life, he might look normal. I stare at him, waiting for his features to shift into Maven's. They never do. I realize he isn't quite Cal either. He has more worry than I thought possible. The last six months have ruined him too.

"Are you okay?" I ask him.

His shoulders droop, the slightest release of steel tension. He blinks. Cal is not one to be taken off guard. I wonder if anyone has bothered to ask him that question since the day I was taken.

After a long pause, he heaves a breath. "I will be. I hope."

"So do I."

This garden was tended by greenwardens once, its many flower beds spiraling in the overgrown remnants of intricate designs. Nature takes over now, different blossoms and colors spilling into one another. Blending, decaying, dying, blooming as they wish.

"Remind me to trouble both of you for some blood at a more opportune moment."

I laugh out loud at Julian's graceless request. He idles at the edge of the garden, kindly intruding. Not that I mind. I grin and cross the garden quickly, embracing him. He returns the action happily.

"That would sound strange coming from anyone else," I tell him as I pull back. Cal chuckles in agreement at my side. "But sure, Julian. Feel free. Besides, I owe you."

Julian tips his head in confusion. "Oh?"

"I found some books of yours in Whitefire." I don't lie, but I'm careful with my words. No use hurting Cal more than he's already been. He doesn't need to know that Maven gave me the books. I won't give him any more false hope for his brother. "Helped pass the . . . time."

While the mention of my imprisonment sobers Cal, Julian doesn't let us linger in the pain. "Then you understand what I'm trying to do," he says quickly. His smile doesn't reach his darkening eyes. "Don't you, Mare?"

"'Not a god's chosen, but a god's cursed,'" I murmur, recalling the words he scrawled in a forgotten book. "You're going to figure out where we came from, and why."

Julian folds his arms. "I'm certainly going to try."

TWENTY-TWO
Mare

Every morning starts the same way. I can't stay in the bedroom; the birds always wake me up early. Good that they do. It's too hot to run later in the day. The Piedmont base makes for a good track, though. It is well protected, the boundaries guarded by both Montfort and Piedmont soldiers. The latter are all Reds, of course. Davidson knows that Bracken, the puppet prince, is likely quietly scheming and won't let any of his Silvers past the gates. In fact, I haven't seen any Silvers at all, except the ones I already know. All of the abilitied are newbloods or Ardents, depending on who you speak to. If Davidson has Silvers with him, serving equally in his Free Republic as he says they are, I haven't seen any.

I lace my shoes tightly. Mist curls in the street outside, hanging low along the brick canyon. Unlatching the front door, I grin when the cool air hits my skin. It smells like rain and thunder.

As expected, Cal sits on the bottom step, legs stretched out on the narrow sidewalk. Still, my heart lurches in my chest at the sight of him. He yawns loudly in greeting, almost unhinging his jaw.

"Come on," I chide him, "this is sleeping in for a soldier."

"That doesn't mean I don't prefer to sleep in when I can." He stands with exaggerated annoyance, all but sticking his tongue out.

"Feel free to go back to that little bunk room you insist on staying in at the barracks. You know, you'd get a bit more time if you moved to Officers Row—or stopped running with me altogether." I shrug with a sly grin.

Matching my smile, he tugs on the hem of my shirt, pulling me toward him. "Don't insult my bunk room," he mutters, before dropping a kiss on my lips. Then my jaw. Then my neck. Each touch blooms, a burst of fire beneath my skin.

Reluctantly, I push his face away. "There is a real possibility my dad shoots you from the window if you keep this up here."

"Right, right." He recovers quickly, paling. If I didn't know any better, I'd say Cal was actually scared of my father. The thought is comical. A Silver prince, a general who can raise infernos with a flick of his fingers, afraid of a limping old Red. "Let's stretch."

We go through the motions, Cal more thoroughly than I. He scolds me gently, finding something wrong with every move. "Don't lunge into it. Don't rock back and forth. Easy, slow." But I'm eager, thirsty to run. Eventually, he relents. With a nod of his head, he lets us begin.

At first the pace is easy. I almost dance on my toes, exhilarated by the steps. They feel like freedom. The fresh air, the birds, the mist brushing past with damp fingers. My even, steady breath and steadily rising heartbeat. The first time we ran here, I had to stop and cry, too happy to stop the tears. Cal sets a good clip, keeping me from sprinting until my lungs give out. The first mile passes well enough, getting us to the perimeter wall. Half stone, half chain link topped with razor wire, and a few soldiers patrol the far side. Montfort men. They nod to each of us, used to our route after two weeks. Other soldiers jog in the distance, running their usual training exercises, but we don't join them. They drill in rows with shouting sergeants. It's not for me. Cal is demanding enough. And thankfully, Davidson hasn't pressed me on the whole "resettlement or service" choice. In fact, I haven't seen him since my debriefing, even though he now lives on base with the rest of us.

The next two miles are more difficult. Cal pushes a harder pace. It's hotter today, even this early, with clouds gathering overhead. As the mist burns off, I sweat hard and salt collects on my lips. Legs pumping, I wipe my face on the hem of my shirt. Cal feels the heat too. At my side, he just pulls his shirt off entirely, tucking it into the waistband of tight training pants. My first instinct is to warn him against sunburn. The second is to stop and stare at the well-defined muscles of his bare abdomen. Instead, I focus on the path before me, forcing another mile. Another. Another. His breathing beside me is suddenly very distracting.

We round the shallow forest separating the barracks and Officers Row from the airfield, when thunder rumbles somewhere. A few miles away, certainly. Cal puts out an arm at the noise, slowing me down. He snaps to face me, both hands gripping my shoulders as he leans down to my eye level. Bronze eyes bore into mine, looking for something. The thunder rolls again, closer.

"What's wrong?" he asks, all concern. One hand strays to my neck to soothe the scars burning red hot with exertion. "Calm down."

"That's not me." I tip my head toward the darkening storm clouds with a smile. "That's just weather. Sometimes, when it gets too hot and humid, thunderstorms can—"

He laughs. "Okay, I get it. Thank you."

"Ruining a perfectly good run," I tut, moving my hand to take his. He grins crookedly, smiling so wide it crinkles his eyes. As the storm moves closer, I feel its electric heart thrumming. My pulse steadies to match it, but I push away the seductive purr of lightning. Can't let loose a storm so close.

I have no control of rain, and it falls in a sudden curtain, making us both yelp. Whatever bits of my clothes weren't covered in sweat quickly soak through. The sudden cold is a shock to us both, Cal in particular.

His bare skin steams, wrapping his torso and arms in a thin layer of gray mist. Raindrops hiss when they make contact, flash-boiling. As he calms, it stops, but he still pulses with warmth. Without thought, I tuck into him, shivering down my spine.

"We should go back," he mutters to the top of my head. I feel his voice reverberate in his chest, my palm flat to where his heart rips a fast tempo. It thunders under my touch, in stark contrast to his calm face.

Something stops me from agreeing. Another tug, deeper inside. Somewhere I can't name.

"Should we?" I whisper, expecting the rain to swallow my voice.

His arms tighten around me. He didn't miss a word.

The trees are new growth, their leaves and branches not splayed wide enough to offer total cover from the sky. But enough from the street. My shirt goes first, landing in mud. I toss his into the muck too, just so we're even. Rain pelts down in fat drops, each one a cold surprise to run down my nose or spine or my arms wrapped around his neck. Warm hands do battle across my back, a delightful opposite to the water. His fingers walk the length of my spine, pressing into each vertebra. I do the same, counting his ribs. He shivers, and not from the rain, as my nails scrape along his side. Cal responds with teeth. They graze the length of my jaw before finding my ear. I shut my eyes for a second, unable to do anything but feel. Every sensation is a firework, a thunderbolt, an explosion.

The thunder gets closer. As if drawn to us.

I run my fingers through his hair, using it to pull him closer. Closer. Closer. Closer. He tastes like salt and smoke. Closer. I can't seem to get close enough. "Have you done this before?" I should be afraid, but only the cold makes me shiver.

He tips his head back, and I almost whine in protest. "No," he whispers, looking away. Dark lashes drip rain. His jaw tightens, as if ashamed.

So like Cal, to feel embarrassment for something like this. He likes to know the end of a path, the answer to a question before asking. I almost laugh.

This is a different kind of battle. There's no training. And instead of donning armor, we throw the rest of our clothes away.

After six months of sitting by his brother's side, lending my entire being to an evil cause, I have no fear of giving my body to a person I love. Even in the mud. Lightning flashes overhead and behind my eyes. Every nerve sparks to life. It takes all my concentration to keep Cal from feeling the wrong end of such things.

His chest flushes beneath my palms, rising with reckless heat. His skin looks even paler next to mine. Using his teeth, he unlatches his flamemaker bracelets and tosses them into the undergrowth.

"Thank my colors for the rain," he murmurs.

I feel the opposite. I want to burn.

I refuse to go back to the row house covered in mud, and due to Cal's oh-so-inconvenient living quarters, I can't clean off at his barracks unless I feel like sharing the showers with a dozen other soldiers. He picks leaves out of my hair as we walk toward the base hospital, a squat building overgrown with ivy.

"You look like a shrub," he says, sporting an almost-manic smile.

"That's exactly what you're supposed to say."

Cal nearly giggles. "How would you know?"

"I—ugh," I deflect, ducking into the entrance.

The hospital is nearly deserted at this hour, staffed with a few nurses and doctors to oversee next to no patients. Healers make them mostly irrelevant, needed only for lengthy diseases or extremely complicated injuries. We walk the cinder-block halls alone, under harsh fluorescent lights and easy silence. My cheeks still burn as my mind does war with itself. Instinct makes me want to shove Cal into the nearest room and lock the door behind us. Sense tells me I cannot.

I thought it would be different. I thought I would feel different. Cal's touch has not erased Maven's. My memories are still there, still just as painful as they were yesterday. And as much as I try, I have not forgotten the canyon that will always stretch between us. No kind of love can erase his faults, just like none can erase mine.

A nurse with an armful of blankets rounds the corner ahead, her feet a blur over the tiled floor. She stops at the sight of us, almost dropping the linens. "Oh!" she says. "You're fast, Miss Barrow!"

My flush intensifies as Cal quickly turns a laugh into a cough. "Excuse me?"

She grins. "We just sent a message to your home."

"Uh . . . ?"

"Follow me, sweetie; I'll take you to her." The nurse beckons, shifting the linens to her hip. Cal and I trade confused glances. He shrugs and trots after her, oddly carefree. His army-trained caution seems far away.

The nurse chatters excitedly as we walk in her wake. Her accent is Piedmontese, making the words slower and sweeter. "Shouldn't take long. She's progressing quickly. Soldier to the bone, I suppose. Doesn't want to waste any time."

Our hallway dead-ends into a larger ward, much busier than the rest of the hospital. Wide windows look out on yet another garden, now dark and lashed with rain. Piedmont certainly has a thing for flowers. Several doors branch off on either side, leading to empty rooms and empty beds. One of them is open, and more nurses flit in and out. An armed Scarlet Guard soldier keeps watch, although he doesn't look very alert. It's still early, and he blinks slowly, numbed by the quiet efficiency of the ward.

Sara Skonos looks awake enough for the two of them. Before I can call to her, she raises her head, eyes gray as the storm clouds outside.

Julian was right. She has a lovely voice.

"Good morning," she says. It's the first time I've ever heard her speak.

I don't know her very well, but we embrace anyway. Her hands graze my bare arms, sending shooting stars of relief into overworked muscles. When she leans back, she pulls another leaf out of my hair, then demurely brushes mud from the back of my shoulder. Her eyes flicker, noting the mud streaking Cal's limbs. Next to the sterile atmosphere of the hospital, with its gleaming surfaces and bright lights, we stick out like a pair of very sore and dirty thumbs.

Her lips twist into the slightest smirk. "I hope you enjoyed your morning run."

Cal clears his throat and his face flushes. He wipes a hand on his pants, but only succeeds in spreading the incriminating mud even more. "Yeah."

"Each of these rooms is equipped with a bathroom, including a shower. I can arrange for changes of clothes as well." Sara points with her chin. "If you like."

The prince ducks his face to hide his flush as it deepens. He slinks away, leaving a trail of wet footprints in his wake.

I remain, letting him go on ahead. Even though she can speak again, her tongue returned by another skin healer, I assume, Sara doesn't talk much. She has more meaningful ways to communicate.

She touches my arm again, gently pushing me toward the open door. With Cal out of sight, I can think a little more clearly. The dots connect, one by one. Something tightens in my chest, an equal twist of sadness and excitement. I wish Shade were here.

Farley sits up in the bed, her face red and swollen, a sheen of sweat across her brow. The thunder outside is gone, melting to a downpour of endless rain weeping down the windows. She barks out a laugh at the sight of me, then winces at the sudden action. Sara moves quickly to her side, putting soothing hands to Farley's cheeks. Another nurse idles against the wall, waiting to be useful.

"Did you run here or crawl through a sewer?" Farley asks over Sara's fussing.

I move deeper into the room, careful not to get anything else dirty. "Got caught in the storm."

"Right." She sounds entirely unconvinced. "Was that Cal outside?"

My blush suddenly matches hers. "Yes."

"Right," she says again, drawing out the word.

Her eyes tick over me, as if she can read the last half hour on my skin. I fight the urge to check myself for any suspicious handprints. Then she reaches out, gesturing for the nurse. She leans down and Farley whispers in her ear, her words too fast and low for me to catch. The nurse nods, scurrying off to procure whatever Farley wants. She gives me a tight smile as she goes.

"You can come closer. I'm not going to explode." She glances up at Sara. "Yet."

The skin healer offers a well-practiced, obliging smile. "It won't be long now."

Tentative, I take a few steps forward, until I can reach out and take Farley's hand if I want to. A few machines blink at the side of her bed, pulsing slowly and quietly. They pull me in, hypnotic in their even rhythm. The ache for Shade multiplies. We're going to get a piece of him soon, but he's never coming back. Not even in a baby with his eyes, his name, his smile. A baby he will never get to love.

"I thought about Madeline."

Her voice snaps me out of the spiral. "What?"

Farley picks at her white bedspread. "That was my sister's name."

"Oh."

Last year, I found a photo of her family in the Colonel's office. It was taken years ago, but Farley and her father were unmistakable, posing next to her equally blond mother and sister. All of them had a similar look. Broad-shouldered, athletic, their eyes blue and steely. Farley's sister was the smallest of them all, still growing into her features.

"Or Clara. After my mother."

If she wants to keep talking, I'm here to listen. But I won't pry. So I keep quiet, waiting, letting her lead the conversation. "They died a few years ago. Back in the Lakelands, at home. The Scarlet Guard wasn't so careful then, and one of our operatives was caught knowing too much." Pain flickers across her face now and then, both from the memory and her current state. "Our village was small, overlooked, unimportant. The perfect place for something like the Guard to grow.

Until one man breathed its name under torture. The king of the Lake-lands punished us himself."

The memory of him flashes through my mind. A small man, still and foreboding as the surface of undisturbed water. Orrec Cygnet. "My father and I were away when he raised the shores of the Hud, pulling water out of the bay to flood our village and wipe it from the face of his kingdom."

"They drowned," I murmur.

Her voice never wavers. "Reds across the country were inflamed by the Drowning of the Northlands. My father told our story up and down the lakes, in too many villages and towns to count, and the Guard flourished." Farley's empty expression becomes a scowl. "'At least they died for something,' he used to say. 'We could only be so lucky.'"

"Better to live for something." I agree, a lesson I learned the hard way.

"Yes, exactly. Exactly . . ." She trails off, but she takes my hand without flinching. "So how are you adjusting?"

"Slowly."

"That's not a bad thing."

"The family stays around the house most days. Julian visits when he isn't holed up in the base lab. Kilorn is always around too. Nurses come to work with my dad, get him readjusted to the leg—he's progressing beautifully by the way," I add, looking back to Sara, quiet in her corner. She beams, pleased. "He's good at hiding what he feels, but I can tell he's happy. Happy as he can be."

"I didn't ask about your family. I asked about you." Farley taps a finger against the inside of my wrist. In spite of myself, I flinch, remembering the weight of manacles. "For once, I'm giving you per-mission to whine about yourself, lightning girl."

I sigh.

"I—I can't be alone in rooms with locked doors. I can't . . ." Slowly, I pull my wrist from her grasp. "I don't like things on my wrists. It feels too much like the manacles Maven used to keep me a prisoner. And I can't see anything for what it is. I look for deceit everywhere, in everyone."

Her eyes darken. "That's not necessarily a terrible instinct."

"I know," I mutter.

"What about Cal?"

"What about him?"

"The last time I saw you two together before—all that, you were inches from ripping each other to shreds." *And inches away from Shade's corpse.* "I assume that's all settled."

I remember the moment. We haven't spoken of it. My relief, our relief at my escape pushed it far into the background, forgotten. But as Farley speaks, I feel the old wound reopen. I try to rationalize. "He is still here. He helped the Guard raid Archeon; he led the takeover of Corvium. I only wanted him to choose a side, and he clearly has."

Words whisper in my ear, tugging on the back of a memory. *Choose me. Choose the dawn.* "He chose me."

"Took him long enough."

I have to agree. But at least there's no turning him from this path now. Cal is the Scarlet Guard's. Maven made sure the country knew that.

"I have to go clean up. If my brothers see me like this . . ."

"Go ahead." Farley shifts against her raised pillows, trying to adjust into a more comfortable position. "You might have a niece or nephew by the time you get back."

Again the thought is bittersweet. I force a smile, for her sake.

"I wonder if the baby will be . . . like Shade." My meaning is obvious. Not in appearance, but ability. Will their child be a newblood like he was and I am? Is that how this even works?

Farley just shrugs, understanding. "Well, it hasn't teleported out of me yet. So who knows?"

At the door, her nurse returns, holding a shallow cup. I move back to let her pass, but she approaches me, not Farley. "The general asked me to get you this," she says, holding out the cup. In it is a single pill. White, unassuming.

"Your choice," Farley says from the bed. Her eyes are grave as her hands cradle her stomach. "I thought you should have that, at least."

I don't hesitate. The pill goes down easily.

Some time later, I have a niece. Mom refuses to let anyone else hold Clara. She claims to see Shade in the newborn, even though that's practically impossible. The little girl looks more like a wrinkled red tomato than any brother of mine.

Out in the ward, the rest of the Barrows congregate in their excitement. Cal is gone, returning to his training schedule. He didn't want to intrude on a private family moment. Giving me space as much as anyone else.

Kilorn sits with me, cramped into a little chair against the windows. The rain weakens with every passing second.

"Good time to fish," he says, glancing at the gray sky.

"Oh, don't you start mumbling about the weather too."

"Touchy, touchy."

"You're living on borrowed time, Warren."

He laughs, rising to the joke. "I think we all are at this point."

From anyone else it would sound foreboding, but I know Kilorn too well for that. I nudge his shoulder. "So, how's training going?"

"Well. Montfort has dozens of newblood soldiers, all trained. Some abilities overlap—Darmian, Harrick, Farrah, a few more—and they're improving by leaps and bounds with their mentors. I drill with Ada, and the kids when Cal doesn't. They need a familiar face."

"No time for fishing, then?"

He chuckles, leaning forward to brace his elbows on his knees. "No, not really. It's funny—I used to hate getting up to work the river. Hated every second of sunburns and rope burns and stuck hooks and fish guts all over my clothes." He gnaws on his nails. "Now I miss it."

I miss that boy too.

"The smell made it really hard to be friends with you."

"Probably why we stuck together. No one else could handle my stink or your attitude."

I smile and tip my head back, leaning my skull against the window glass. Raindrops roll past, fat and steady. I count them in my head. It's easier than thinking about anything else around me or ahead of me.

Forty-one, forty-two . . .

"I didn't know you could sit still for this long."

Kilorn watches me, thoughtful. He's a thief too, and he has thief's instincts. Lying to him won't accomplish anything, only push him farther away. And that's not something I can bear right now.

"I don't know what to do," I whisper. "Even in Whitefire, as a prisoner, I tried to escape, tried to scheme, spy, survive. But now . . . I don't know. I'm not sure I can continue."

"You don't have to. No one on earth would blame you if you walked away from all of this and never came back."

I keep staring at the raindrops. In the pit of my belly, I feel sick. "I know." Guilt eats through me. "But even if I could disappear right now, with everyone I care about, I wouldn't do it."

There's too much anger in me. Too much hate.

Kilorn nods in understanding. "But you don't want to fight either."

"I don't want to become . . ." My voice trails away.

I don't want to become a monster. A shell with nothing but ghosts. Like Maven.

"You won't. I won't let you. And don't even get me started on Gisa."

In spite of myself, I bite back a laugh. "Right."

"You're not alone in this. In all my work with the newbloods, I found that's what they most fear." He leans his own head back against the window. "You should talk to them."

"I should," I murmur, and I mean it. A tiny bit of relief blooms in my chest. Those words comfort me like nothing else.

"And in the end, you need to figure out what you want," he prods gently.

Bathwater swirls, boiling lazily in fat, white bubbles. A pale boy looks up at me, his eyes wide and his neck bared. In reality I just stood. I was weak and stupid and scared. But in the daydream I put my hands around his neck and squeeze. He flails in the scalding water, dipping under. Never to resurface. Never to haunt me again.

"I want to kill him."

Kilorn's eyes narrow as a muscle twinges in his cheek. "Then you have to train, and you have to win."

Slowly, I nod.

At the edge of the ward, almost entirely in shadow, the Colonel keeps vigil. He stares at his feet, not moving. He doesn't go in to see his daughter and new grandchild. But he doesn't leave either.

TWENTY-THREE
Evangeline

She laughs against my neck, her touch a brush of lips and cold steel. My crown perches precariously on her red curls, steel and diamond glinting between ruby locks. With her ability, she makes the diamonds wink like luminous stars.

Reluctant, I sit up and leave my bed, the silky sheets, and Elane behind. She yelps when I throw open the curtains, letting the sunlight stream in. With a flick of her hand the window shadows, blooming with shade until the light reduces to her liking.

I dress in the dimness, donning small black undergarments and a pair of laced sandals. Today is special, and I take my time molding an outfit to my form from the metal sheets in my closet. Titanium and darkened steel ripple across my limbs. Black and silver, it reflects light in an array of brilliant colors. I don't need a maid to complete my appearance, nor do I want one floating around in my room. I do it myself, matching sparkling blue-black lipstick to coal-dark eyeliner dotted with specially made crystals. Elane dozes through it all, until I pull the crown from her head. It fits me perfectly.

"Mine," I tell her, leaning down to kiss her once more. She smiles lazily, her lips curving against my own. "Don't forget, you're supposed to be present today."

She bows playfully. "As Your Highness commands."

The title is so delicious I want to lick the words right out of her mouth. But at the risk of ruining my makeup, I refrain. And I don't look back, lest I lose my grip on whatever self-control I have left these days.

Ridge House has belonged to my family for generations, sprawling across the cresting edge of the many rifts that give our region its name. All steel and glass, it's easily my favorite of the family estates. My personal chambers face east, toward the dawn. I like rising with the sun, as much as Elane disagrees. The passage connecting my rooms to the main halls of the estate are magnetron designed, made of steel walkways with open sides. Some run along the ground, but many arch over the leafy treetops, jagged rocks, and springs dotting the property. Should battle ever come to our door, an invading force would have a difficult time fighting their way through a structure set against them.

Despite the manicured forest and luxurious grounds of the Ridge, few birds come here. They know better. As children, Ptolemus and I used many for target practice. The rest fell to my mother's whims.

More than three hundred years ago, before the Calore kings rose, the Ridge did not exist, and neither did Norta. This corner of land was ruled by a Samos warlord, my direct ancestor. Ours is the blood of conquerors, and our fortunes have risen again. Maven is not the only king in Norta anymore.

Servants are good at making themselves scarce here, appearing only when needed or called upon. In recent weeks, they seem almost too good at their job. It isn't hard to guess why. Many Reds are fleeing, either to the cities for safety against civil war, or to join the Scarlet Guard's rebellion. Father says the Guard itself has escaped to Piedmont, which is all but a puppet, dancing on Montfort's strings. He maintains channels of communication with the Montfort and Guard leaders, albeit begrudgingly. But for now, the enemy of our enemy is our friend, making us all tentative allies where Maven is concerned.

Tolly waits in the gallery, the wide, open hall running the length of the main house. Windows on all sides offer a view in every direction, over miles of the Rift. On the clearest of days, I might be able to see Pitarus to the west, but clouds hang low in the distance as spring rains race the length of the sprawling river valley. In the east, valleys and hills roll off in increasingly high slopes, ending in blue-green mountains. The Rift region is, in my correct opinion, the most beautiful piece of Norta. And it is mine. My family's. House Samos rules this heaven.

My brother certainly looks like a prince, the heir to the throne of the Rift. Instead of armor, Tolly wears a new uniform. Silver gray instead of black, with gleaming onyx-and-steel buttons and an oil-dark sash crossing him from shoulder to hip. No medals yet, at least none that he can wear. The rest were earned in service to another king. His silvery hair is wet, plastered back against his head. Fresh from a shower. He keeps his new hand tucked in close, protective of the appendage. It took Wren the better part of a day to regrow it properly, and even then she needed an immense amount of help from two of her kin.

"Where's my wife?" he asks, looking down the open passage behind me.

"She'll be along eventually. Lazy thing." Tolly married Elane a week ago. I don't know if he's seen her since the wedding night, but he hardly minds. The arrangement is mutually agreed upon.

He links his good arm in mine. "Not everyone can operate on as little sleep as you."

"Well, what about you? I've heard all that work on your hand has led to some late nights with Lady Wren," I reply, leering. "Or am I misinformed?"

Tolly grins, sheepish. "Is it that even possible?"

"Not here." In Ridge House, it's near impossible to keep secrets. Especially from Mother. Her eyes are everywhere, in mice and cats and the occasional daring sparrow. Sunlight angles through the gallery, playing across many sculptures of fluid metal. As we pass, Ptolemus twists his new hand in the air, and the sculptures twist with it. They re-form, each one more complex than the last.

"Don't dawdle, Tolly. If the ambassadors arrive before we do, Father might spike our heads to the gate," I scold him. He laughs at the common threat and old joke. Neither of us has ever seen such a thing. Father has killed before, certainly, but never so crudely or so close to home. *Don't bleed in your own garden,* he would say.

We wind our way down from the gallery, keeping to the outer walkways so as to better enjoy the spring weather. Most of the interior salons look out on the walkway, their windows polished plate glass or their doors thrown open to catch the spring breeze. Samos guards line one, and they nod their heads when we approach, paying deference to their prince and princess. I smile at the gesture, but their presence unsettles me.

The Samos guards oversee a violent operation: the making of Silent Stone. Even Ptolemus pales as we pass. The smell of blood overpowers us both for a moment, filling the air with sharp iron. Two Arvens sit inside the salon, chained to their seats. Neither is here willingly. Their house is allied to Maven, but we have need for Silent Stone, and so they are here. Wren hovers between them, noting their progress. Both their wrists have been slit open, and they bleed freely into large buckets. When the Arvens reach their limit, Wren will heal them up and stimulate their blood production, all to begin again. Meanwhile, the blood will be mixed with cement, hardened into the deadly blocks of ability-suppressing stone. For what, I don't know, but Father certainly has plans for it. A prison, maybe, like the one Maven built for Silvers and newbloods both.

Our grandest receiving chamber, the aptly named Sunset Stretch, is on the western slope. I suppose now it's technically our throne room as well. As we approach, courtiers of my father's newly created nobility dot the way, thickening with every forward step. Most are Samos cousins, elevated by our declaration of independence. A few of closer blood, my father's siblings and their children, claim princely titles for themselves, but the rest remain lords and ladies, content as always to live off my father's name and my father's ambitions.

Bright colors stand out among the usual black and silver, an obvious indication of today's assembly. Ambassadors from the other houses in open revolt have come to treat with the kingdom of the Rift. To kneel. House Iral will argue. Attempt to bargain. The silks think their secrets can buy them a crown, but power is the only currency here. Strength the only coin. And they surrendered both by entering our territory.

Haven has come as well, the shadows basking in sunlight, while the Laris windweavers in yellow keep close to each other. The latter have already given their allegiance to my father, and they bring with them the might of the Air Fleet, having seized control of most air bases. I care more about House Haven, though. Elane won't say it, but she misses her family. Some have pledged loyalty to Samos already, but not all, including her own father, and it tears at her to see her house splinter. In truth, I think it's why she didn't come down here with me. She can't bear the sight of her house divided. I wish I could make them kneel for her.

In the morning light, the Sunset Stretch is still impressive with its smooth river-rock flooring and sweeping views of the valley. The Allegiant River winds like a blue ribbon over green silk, lazily curving back and forth into the distant rainstorm.

The coalition has not arrived yet, allowing Tolly and me time to take our seats—thrones. His on Father's right, mine on Mother's left. All are made of the finest steel, polished to a mirror sheen. It's cold to the touch, and I tell myself not to shiver as I sit. Goose bumps rise on my skin anyway, mostly in anticipation. I am a princess, Evangeline of the Rift, of the royal house of Samos. I thought my fate was to be someone else's queen, subject to someone else's crown. This is so much better. This is what we should have been planning for all along. I almost regret the years of my life wasted training only to be someone's wife.

Father enters the hall with a crowd of advisers, his head dipped to listen. He doesn't speak much by nature. His thoughts are his own, but he listens well, taking all into consideration before making decisions. Not like Maven, the foolish king who only followed his own flawed compass.

Mother follows alone, in her usual green, without ladies or advisers. Most give her a wide berth. Probably because of the two-hundred-pound black panther padding at her heels. It keeps pace with her, breaking from her side only when she reaches her throne. Then it weaves around me, nuzzling its massive head against my ankle. I keep still out of habit. Mother's control of her creatures is well practiced, but not perfect. I've seen her pets take bites out of many servants, whether she willed it or not. The panther shakes its head once before returning to Mother, taking a seat on her left, between us. She rests a single hand blazing with emeralds on its head, strokes its silky black fur. The gigantic cat blinks slowly, its yellow eyes round.

I meet Mother's gaze over the animal, raising a single brow. "Hell of an entrance."

"It was the panther or the python," she replies. Emeralds flash across the crown of her head, expertly set into silver. Her hair falls in a thick, black sheet, perfectly straight and smooth. "I couldn't find a gown to match the snake." She gestures down at the jade folds of her chiffon dress. I doubt that's the reason, but I don't say so out loud. Her machinations will become apparent soon enough. Smart as she is, Mother has little talent for subterfuge. Her threats come openly. Father is a good match for her in this way. His maneuvers take years, always moving in the shadows.

But for now, he stands in bright sunlight. His advisers fall back at a wave of his hand, and he ascends to sit with us. A powerful sight. Like Ptolemus, he wears clothes of brocaded silver, his old black robes abandoned. I can feel the suit of armor beneath his regalia. Chromium. Just like the simple band across his brow. No gems for Father. He has little use for them.

"Cousins of iron," he says quietly to the Sunset Stretch, looking out on the many Samos faces dotting the receiving crowd.

"Kings of steel!" they shout back, putting fists to the air. The force of it thrums in my chest.

In Norta, in the throne rooms of Whitefire or Summerton, someone always crowed the name of the king, announcing his presence. As with gems, Father doesn't care about such needless displays. Everyone here knows our name. To repeat it would only show weakness, a thirst for reassurance. Father has neither.

"Begin," he says. His fingers drum on the arm of his throne, and the heavy iron doors at the far end of the hall swing open.

The ambassadors are few but high-ranking, leaders of their houses. Lord Salin of Iral seems to be wearing all the jewels my father lacks, his broad collar of rubies and sapphires stretching from shoulder to shoulder. The rest of his clothes are equally patterned in red and blue, and his robes billow around his ankles. Another might trip, but an Iral silk has no such fear. He moves with lethal grace, eyes hard and dark. He does his best to measure up to the memory of his predecessor, Ara Iral. His escorts are silks as well, just as flamboyant. They are a beautiful house, with skin like cold bronze and lush black hair. Sonya is not with him. I considered her a friend at court, as much as I consider anyone a friend. I don't miss her, and it's probably for the best she isn't here.

Salin's eyes narrow at the sight of my mother's panther, now purring beneath her touch. *Ah.* I had forgotten. His mother, the murdered lady of Iral, was called the Panther in her youth. *Subtle, Mother.*

Half a dozen Haven shadows ripple into being, their faces decidedly less hostile. In the back of the room, I notice Elane appear as well. But her face stays in shadow, hiding her pain from everyone else in the crowded room. I wish I could seat her next to me. But even though my family has been more than obliging where she is concerned, that can never happen. She'll sit behind Tolly one day. Not me.

Lord Jerald, Elane's father, is the leading member of the Haven delegation. Like her, he has vibrant red hair and glowing skin. He seems younger than his years, softened by his natural ability to manipulate light. If he knows his daughter is in the back of the room, he doesn't show it.

"Your Majesty." Salin Iral inclines his head just enough to be polite.

Father does not bend. Only his eyes move, flickering between the ambassadors. "My lords. My ladies. Welcome to the kingdom of the Rift."

"We thank you for your hospitality," Jerald offers.

I can almost hear my father grind his teeth. He despises wasted time, and such pleasantries are certainly that. "Well, you traveled all this way. I hope it is to uphold your pledge."

"We pledged to support you in coalition, to supplant Maven," Salin says. "Not this."

Father sighs. "Maven has been supplanted in the Rift. And with your allegiance, that can spread."

"With you as king. One dictator for another." Mutters break out among the crowd, but we remain silent as Salin spits his nonsense.

Next to me, Mother leans forward. "It's hardly fair to compare my husband to that addled prince who has no business sitting his father's throne."

"I won't stand by and let you seize a crown that is not yours," Salin growls back.

Mother clucks her tongue. "You mean a crown you didn't think to seize yourself? Pity the Panther was murdered. She would have planned for this, at least." She continues stroking the glossy predator at her side. It growls low in its throat, baring fangs.

"The fact remains, my lord," Father cuts in, "while Maven is floundering, his armies and resources vastly outnumber our own. Especially now that the Lakelanders have bound themselves to him. But together, we can defend. Strike out in force. Wait for more of his kingdom to crumble. Wait for the Scarlet Guard—"

"The Scarlet Guard." Jerald spits on our beautiful floor. His face colors with a gray flush. "You mean Montfort. The true power behind those wretched terrorists. Another kingdom."

"Technically—" Tolly begins, but Jerald presses on.

"I'm beginning to think you care not for Norta, but only for your title and your crown. On keeping whatever you piece you can while greater beasts devour our nation," Jerald snaps. In the crowd, Elane flinches and shuts her eyes. No one speaks to my father this way.

The panther snarls again, matching Mother's rising temper. Father just sits back against his throne, watching the open threat ripple through the Sunset Stretch.

After a long, trembling moment, Jerald sinks to a knee. "My apologies, Your Majesty. I misspoke. I did not intend . . ." He trails off under the king's watchful eye, the words dying on his fleshy lips.

"The Scarlet Guard will never take hold here. No matter what radicals may be backing them." Father speaks resolutely. "Reds are inferior, beneath us. That is the work of biology. Life itself knows we are their masters. Why else are we Silver? Why else are we their gods, if not to rule them?"

The Samos cousins cheer. "Kings of steel!" echoes through the chamber again.

"If newbloods want to throw their lot in with insects, let them. If they want to turn their backs on our way of life, let them. And when they return to fight us, to fight nature, kill them."

The cheer grows, spreading from our house to Laris. Even a few in the delegations clap or nod along. I doubt they've ever heard Volo Samos speak this much—he's been saving his voice and his words for the moments that matter. This is certainly that.

Only Salin remains still. His dark eyes, rimmed with black liner, stand out sharply. "Is that why your daughter let a terrorist go free? Why she slaughtered four Silvers of a noble house to do so?"

"Four Arvens sworn to Maven." My voice snaps like a whip crack.

The Iral lord turns his gaze on me and I feel electrified, almost rising in my seat. These are my first words as a princess, my first words spoken with a voice that is truly my own. "Four soldiers who would take everything you are if their wretched king asked. Do you mourn them, my lord?"

Salin scowls in disgust. "I mourn the loss of a valuable hostage, nothing more. And obviously I question your decision, Princess."

Another drop of derision in your voice and I'll cut out your tongue.

"The decision was mine," Father says evenly. "Like you said, the Barrow girl was a valuable hostage. We took her from Maven." *And loosed her on the Square, like a beast from its cage.* I wonder how many of Maven's soldiers she took with her that day. Enough to fulfill Father's plan at least, to cover our own escape.

"And now she's in the wind!" Salin implores. His temper slips, inch by inch.

Father shows no signs of interest and states the obvious. "She is in Piedmont, of course. And I assure you, Barrow was more dangerous under Maven's command than she'll ever be under theirs. Our concern should be eliminating Maven, not radicals destined to fail."

Salin blanches. "Fail? They hold Corvium. They control a vast amount of Piedmont, using a Silver prince as a puppet. If that is failure—"

"They seek to make equal that which is not fundamentally equal." My mother speaks coldly, and her words ring true. "It is foolish, like balancing an impossible equation. And it will end in bloodshed. But it will end. Piedmont will rise up. Norta will throw back Red devils. The world will keep turning."

All argument seems to die with Mother's voice. Like Father, she sits back, satisfied. For once, she is without her familiar hiss of snakes. Just the great panther, purring under her touch.

Father forges on, eager to land the killing strike. "Our objective is Maven. The Lakelands. Cleaving the king from his new ally will leave him vulnerable, mortally so. Will you support us in our quest to rid this poison from our country?"

Slowly, Salin and Jerald exchange glances, their eyes meeting across the empty space between them. Adrenaline surges in my veins. They will kneel. They must kneel.

"Will you support House Samos, House Laris, House Lerolan—"

A voice cuts him off. The voice of a woman. It echoes—from nowhere. "You presume to speak for me?"

Jerald twists his wrist, his fingers moving in a rapid circle. Everyone in the chamber gasps, including me, when a third ambassador blinks into existence between Iral and Haven. Her house appears behind her, a dozen of them in clothes of red and orange, like the setting sun. Like an explosion.

Mother jolts beside me, surprised for the first time in many, many years. My adrenaline becomes spikes of ice, chilling my blood.

The leader of House Lerolan takes a daring step forward. Her appearance is severe. Gray hair tied into a neat bun, her eyes burning like heated bronze. The older woman does not know the name of fear. "I will not support a Samos king while a Calore heir lives."

"I knew I smelled smoke," Mother mutters, pulling her hand back from the panther. It immediately tenses, shifting to stand as its claws slide into place.

She just shrugs, smirking. "Easy to say, Larentia, now that you see me standing here." Her fingers drum at her side. I watch them closely.

She is an oblivion, able to explode things with a touch. If she got close enough, she could obliterate my heart in my chest or my brain in my skull.

"I am a queen—"

"So am I." Anabel Lerolan grins wider. Though her clothes are fine, she wears no jewelry that I can see, no crown. No metal. My fist claws at my side. "We will not turn our backs on my grandson. The throne of Norta belongs to Tiberias the Seventh. Ours is a crown of flames, not steel."

Father's anger gathers like thunder and breaks like lightning. He stands from his throne, one fist clenching. The metal reinforcements of the chamber itself twist, groaning under the strain of his fury.

"We had a deal, Anabel!" he snarls. "The Barrow girl for your support."

She just blinks.

Even from the far side, I can hear my brother hiss. "Have you forgotten the reason the Guard has Corvium? Did you not see your grandson fighting his own in Archeon? How can the kingdom stand behind him now?"

Anabel doesn't flinch. Her lined face remains still, her expression open and patient. A kindly old woman in everything but the waves of ferocity emanating from her. She waits for my brother to push on, but he doesn't, and she inclines her head. "Thank you, Prince Ptolemus, for at least not furthering the outrageous falsity of my son's murder and my grandson's exile. Both committed at the hands of Elara Merandus, both spread through the kingdom in the worst propaganda I have ever seen. Yes, Tiberias has done terrible things to survive. But they were to survive. After every one of us turned on him, abandoned him, after his own poisoned brother tried to kill him in the arena like a base criminal.

A crown is the least we can give him in apology."

Behind her, Iral and Haven stand firm. A curtain of tension falls over the hall. Everyone feels it. We're Silvers, born to strength and power. All of us train to fight, to kill. We hear the tick of a clock in every heart, counting down to bloodshed. I glance at Elane, lock eyes with her. She presses her lips into a grim line.

"The Rift is mine," Father growls, sounding like one of Mother's beasts. The noise shudders in my bones, and I am instantly a child.

It has no such effect on the old queen. Anabel just tips her head to the side. Sunlight glints down the straight, iron strands of her hair gathered at the nape of her neck.

"Then keep it," she replies with a shrug. "As you said, we had a deal."

And just like that, the coiling turmoil threatening to engulf the room sweeps away. A few of the cousins, as well as Lord Jerald, visibly exhale.

Anabel spreads her hands wide, an open gesture. "You are the king of the Rift, and may you reign for many prosperous years. But my grandson is the rightful king of Norta. And he will need every ally we can muster to take his kingdom back."

Even Father did not foresee this turn. Anabel Lerolan has not been to court in many years, electing to remain in Delphie, her house's seat. She despised Elara Merandus and could not be near her—that, or she feared her. I suppose now, with the whisper queen gone, the oblivion queen can return. And return she has.

I tell myself not to panic. Blindsided as Father may be, this is not surrender. We keep the Rift. We keep our home. We keep our crowns. It's only been a few weeks, but I'm loath to give away what we've planned for. What I deserve.

"I wonder how you intend to restore a king who wants no part in a throne," Father muses. He steeples his fingers and surveys Anabel over them. "Your grandson is in Piedmont—"

"My grandson is an unwilling operative of the Scarlet Guard, which in turn is controlled by the Free Republic of Montfort. You'll find that their leader, the one calling himself premier, is quite a reasonable man," she adds with the air of someone discussing the weather.

My stomach twists, and I feel vaguely sick. Something in me, a deep instinct, screams for me to kill her before she can continue.

Father raises an eyebrow. "You've made contact with him?"

The Lerolan queen smiles tightly. "Enough to negotiate. But I speak to my grandson more often these days. He's a talented boy, very good with machines. He reached out in his desperation, asking for only one thing. And thanks to you, I delivered."

Mare.

Father narrows his eyes. "Does he know of your plans, then?"

"He will."

"And Montfort?"

"Is eager to ally themselves with a king. They will support a war of restoration in the name of Tiberias the Seventh."

"As they have in Piedmont?" If no one else will point out her folly, I certainly must. "Prince Bracken dances on their strings, controlled. Reports indicate they have taken his children. You would so willingly let your grandson become their puppet too?"

I came here eager to see others kneel. I remain seated, but I feel bare before Anabel as she grins. "As your mother said so eloquently, they seek to make equal that which is not fundamentally equal. Victory is impossible. Silver blood cannot be overthrown."

Even the panther is quiet, watching the exchange with ticking eyes.

Its tail flicks slowly. I focus on its fur, dark as the night sky. An abyss, just like the one we edge toward. My heart drums a harried rhythm, pumping both fear and adrenaline throughout my body. I don't know which way Father will lean. I don't know what will become of this path. It makes my skin crawl.

"Of course," Anabel adds, "the kingdom of Norta and the kingdom of the Rift would be tightly bound by their alliance. And by marriage."

The floor seems to tip beneath me. It takes every ounce of will and pride to remain on my cold and vicious throne. *You are steel,* I whisper in my head. *Steel does not break or bend.* But I can already feel myself bowing, giving way to my father's will. He'll trade me in a heartbeat, if it means keeping the crown. The kingdom of the Rift, the kingdom of Norta—Volo Samos will take whatever he can grasp. If the latter is out of reach, he will do whatever he can to maintain the first. Even if it means breaking his promise. Selling me off one more time. My skin prickles. I thought all this was behind us. I am a princess now, my father a king. I don't need to marry anyone for a crown. The crown is in my blood, in me.

No, that isn't true. You still need Father. You need his name. You are never your own.

Blood thunders in my ears, the roar of a hurricane. I can't bring myself to look up at Elane. I promised her. She married my brother so we would never be parted. She upheld her side of the bargain, but now? They'll send me to Archeon. She'll stay here with Tolly as his wife and, one day, his queen. I want to scream. I want to rip the infernal chair under me to shreds and tear everyone in this room apart. Including myself. I can't do this. I can't live like this.

A few weeks of the closest thing to freedom I've ever known—and I can't let it go. I can't go back to living for someone else's ambitions.

I breathe through my nose, trying to keep my rage in check. I have no gods, but I certainly pray.

Say no. Say no. Say no. Please, Father, say no.

No one looks at me, my only relief. No one watches my slow unraveling. They only have eyes for my father and his decision. I try to detach. Try to put my pain in a box and tuck it away. It's easy to do in Training, in a fight. But it's almost impossible now.

Of course. The voice in my head laughs sadly. *Your path always led here, no matter what.* I was made to marry the Calore heir. Physically made. Mentally made. Constructed. Like a castle, or a tomb. My life has never been my own, and it never will be.

My father's words drive nails into my heart, each one another burst of bloody sorrow.

"To the kingdom of Norta. And the kingdom of the Rift."

TWENTY-FOUR
Cameron

It takes Morrey longer than the other hostages.

Some believed within minutes. Others held out for days, stubbornly clinging to the lies they'd been spoon-fed. *The Scarlet Guard is a collection of terrorists, the Scarlet Guard is evil. The Scarlet Guard will make life worse for you. King Maven freed you from war and will free you from more still.* Twisted half-truths spun into propaganda. I can understand how they and so many others were taken in. Maven exploited a thirst in Reds who didn't know what it was to be manipulated. They saw a Silver pledging to listen when his predecessors would not, to hear the voices of people who had never been heard. An easy hope to buy into.

And the Scarlet Guard are far from innocent heroes. They are flawed at best, combating oppression with violence. The children of the Dagger Legion remain wary. They're all just teenagers bouncing from the trenches of one army to another. I don't blame them for keeping their eyes open.

Morrey still clings to his misgivings. Because of me, what I am. Maven accused the Guard of murdering people like me. No matter how much my brother tries, he can't shake the words.

As we sit down to breakfast, our bowls of oatmeal hot to the touch, I brace myself for the usual questions. We like to eat outside on the grass, beneath the open sky, with the training fields stretched out. After fifteen years in our slum, every fresh breeze feels like a miracle. I sit cross-legged, my dark green coveralls soft from wear and too much washing to count.

"Why don't you leave?" Morrey asks, jumping right in. He stirs the oatmeal three times, counterclockwise. "You haven't pledged your oath to the Guard. You don't have any reason to stay here."

"Why do you do that?" I tap his spoon with mine. A stupid question, but an easy dodge. I never have a good answer for him, and I hate that he makes me wonder.

He shrugs his narrow shoulders. "I like the routine," he mumbles. "At home . . . well, you know home was bleeding awful, but . . ." He stirs again, the metal scraping. "You remember the schedules, the whistles."

"I do." I still hear them in my dreams. "And you miss that?"

He scoffs. "Of course not. I just . . . Not knowing what's going to happen. I don't understand it. It's—it's scary."

I spoon up some oatmeal. It's thick and tasty. Morrey gave me his sugar ration, and the extra sweetness undercuts whatever discomfort I feel. "I think that's how everyone feels. I think it's why I stay."

Morrey turns to look at me, narrowing his eyes against the glare of the still-rising sun. It illuminates his face, throwing into harsh contrast how much he's changed. Steady rations have filled him out. And the cleaner air clearly agrees with him. I haven't heard the scraping cough that used to punctuate his sentences.

One thing hasn't changed, though. He still has the tattoo, just as

I do. Black ink like a brand around his neck. Our letters and numbers match almost exactly.

NT-ARSM-188908, his reads. *New Town, Assembly and Repair, Small Manufacturing*. I'm 188907. I was born first. My neck itches at the memory of the day when we were marked, permanently bound to our indentured jobs.

"I don't know where to go." I say the words out loud for the first time, even though I've been thinking them every day since I escaped Corros. "We can't go home."

"I guess not," he mumbles. "So what do we do here? You're going to stay and let these people—"

"I told you before, they don't want to kill newbloods. That was a lie, Maven's lie—"

"I'm not talking about that. So the Scarlet Guard isn't going to kill you—but they're still putting you in danger. You spend every minute you're not with me training to fight, to kill. And in Corvium I saw . . . when you led us out . . ."

Don't say what I did. I remember it well enough without him describing the way I killed two Silvers. Faster than I've ever killed before. Blood pouring from their eyes and mouths, their insides dying organ by organ as my silence destroyed everything in them. I felt it then. I feel it still. The sensation of death pulses through my body.

"I know you can help." He puts his oatmeal down and takes my hand. In the factories, I used to hold on to him. Our roles reverse. "I don't want to see them turn you into a weapon. You're my sister, Cameron. You did everything you could to save me. Let me do the same."

With a huff, I fall back against the soft grass, leaving the bowl at my side.

He lets me think, and instead turns his eyes on the horizon. He waves a dark hand at the fields in front of us. "It's so bleeding green here. Do you think the rest of the world is like this?"

"I don't know."

"We could find out." His voice is so soft I pretend not to hear him, and we lapse into an easy silence. I watch spring winds chase clouds across the sky while he eats, his motions quick and efficient. "Or we could go home. Mama and Dad—"

"Impossible." I focus on the blue above, blue like we never saw in that hellhole we were born in.

"You saved me."

"And we almost died. Better odds, and we almost died." I exhale slowly. "There's nothing we can do for them right now. I thought maybe once but—all we can do is hope."

Sorrow tugs at his face, souring his expression. But he nods. "And stay alive. Stay ourselves. You hear me, Cam?" He grabs my hand. "Don't let this change you."

He's right. Even though I'm angry, even though I feel so much hatred for everything that threatens my family—is feeding that rage worth the cost?

"So what should I do?" I finally force myself to ask.

"I don't know what having an ability's like. You have friends who do." His eyes twinkle as he pauses for effect. "You do have friends, right?" He quirks a smirk at me over the rim of his bowl. I smack his arm for the implication.

My mind jumps to Farley first, but she's still in the hospital, adjusting to a new baby, and she doesn't have an ability. Doesn't know what it's like to be so lethal, in control of something so deadly.

"I'm scared, Morrey. When you throw a tantrum, you just yell and cry. With me, with what I can do . . ." I reach a hand to the sky, flexing my fingers against the clouds. "I'm scared of it."

"Maybe that's good."

"What do you mean?"

"At home, you remember how they use the kids? To fix the big gears, the deep wires?" Morrey widens his dark eyes, trying to make me understand.

The memory echoes. Iron on iron, the screech and twist of constantly whirring machinery across endless factory floors. I can almost smell the oil, almost feel the wrench in my hand. It was a relief when Morrey and I got too big to be spiders—what the overseers called the little kids in our division. Small enough to go where adult workers couldn't, too young to be afraid of being crushed.

"Fear can be a good thing, Cam," he pushes on. "Fear doesn't let you forget. And the fear you have, the respect you have for this deadly thing inside of you, I think that's an ability too."

My oatmeal is cold now, but I force a mouthful so I don't have to talk. Now the sugary taste is overpowering, and the glop sticks to my teeth.

"Your braids are a mess," Morrey mutters to himself. He turns to another routine, an old one familiar to us both. Our parents worked earlier than we did, and we had to help each other get ready at dawn. He's long since known how to fix my hair, and it takes no time at all for him to untangle it. It feels good to have him back, and I'm overcome with emotion as he plaits my curly black hair into two braids.

He doesn't push me to make a decision, but the conversation is enough to let questions I already had rise to the surface. *Who do I want to be? What choice am I going to make?*

In the distance, around the edge of the training fields, I spot two familiar figures. One tall, one short, both of them jogging the boundary. They do this every day, their exercises familiar to most of us. Despite Cal's much longer legs, Mare doesn't have a problem keeping up. As they get closer, I can see her smiling. I don't understand a lot of things about the lightning girl, and smiling during a run is one of them.

"Thanks, Morrey," I say, getting to my feet when he finishes.

My brother doesn't stand with me. He follows my gaze, laying eyes on Mare as she gets closer. She doesn't make him tense up, but Cal does. Morrey quickly busies himself with the bowls, ducking his head to hide his scowl. No love lost between the Coles and the prince of Norta.

Mare raises her chin as she jogs, acknowledging us both.

The prince tries to hide his annoyance when she slows her pace, easing into a walk to approach me and Morrey. Cal doesn't do it well, but he nods at both of us in an attempt at a polite greeting.

"Morning," Mare says, shifting from foot to foot as she catches her breath. Her complexion has improved more than anything; a golden warmth is returning to her brown skin. "Cameron, Morrey," she says, her eyes ticking between us with catlike speed. Her brain is always spinning, looking for cracks. After what she's been through, how could she be any other way?

She must sense the hesitation in me, because she stays put, waiting for me to say something. I almost lose my nerve, but Morrey brushes against my leg. *Just bite the bullet,* I tell myself. *She might even understand.*

"Would you mind taking a walk with me?"

Before her capture, she would have scoffed, told me to train, brushed me away like an annoying fly. She barely tolerated me. Now she bobs her head. With a single gesture, Mare waves off Cal like only she can.

Prison changed her, like it changed us all.

"Sure, Cameron."

★ ★ ★

It feels like I talk for hours, spilling everything I've been keeping inside. The fear, the anger, the sick sensation I get every time I think about what I can do and what I've done. How it used to thrill me. How such power made me feel invincible, indestructible—and now it makes me feel ashamed. It feels like stabbing myself in the stomach and letting my guts fall out. I avoid her eyes as I speak, keeping my gaze firmly on my feet as we pace the training grounds. As we press on, more and more soldiers flood the field. Newbloods and Reds, all going through their morning exercises. In their uniforms, green coveralls provided by Montfort, it's hard to tell which is which. We all look the same, united. "I want to protect my brother. He tells me we should go, leave . . ." My voice weakens, trailing off until there are no more words.

Mare is forceful in her reply. "My sister says the same thing. Every day. She wants to take up Davidson's offer. Relocate. Let other people fight." Her eyes darken with intensity. They wobble over the landscape full of green uniforms. She is mechanical in her observations, whether she knows it or not, reading risks and threats. "She said we've given enough."

"So what will you do?"

"I can't turn my back." She bites her lip, thoughtful. "There's too much anger in me. If I don't find a way to get rid of it, it might poison me for the rest of my life. But that probably isn't what you want to hear." It would be an accusation from anyone else. From Cal, or Farley. From who Mare was six months ago. Instead her words are softer.

"Holding on will eat me alive," I admit. "Continuing on this way, using my ability to kill . . . it will make me a monster."

Monster. She shivers when I say it, withdrawing inside herself. Mare Barrow has had her fair share of monsters. She looks away, idly tugging on a braid of hair curling with sweat and humidity.

"Monsters are so easily made, especially in people like us," she mumbles. But she recovers quickly. "You didn't fight in Archeon. Or if you did, I didn't see you."

"No, I was just there to . . ." *Keep you in check.* In the moment, a good plan. But now that I know what she went through, I feel terrible.

She doesn't push.

"Kilorn's idea back in Trial," I say. "He works well branching the newbloods and Reds, and he knew I wanted to take a step back. So I went along—but not to fight, not to kill, unless absolutely necessary."

"And you want to continue on that path." Not a question.

Slowly, I nod. I shouldn't feel embarrassed. "I think it's better this way. Defend, not destroy." At my side, my fingers flex. Silence pools beneath my flesh. I don't hate my ability, but I can hate what it does.

Mare fixes me with a grin. "I'm not your commander. I can't tell you what to do, or how to fight. But I think it's a good idea. And if anyone tries to tell you otherwise, point them my way."

I smile. Somehow I feel a weight lift. "Thanks."

"I'm sorry, by the way," she adds, coming closer. "I'm the reason you're here. I know now, what I did to you, forcing you to join up—it was wrong. And I'm sorry."

"You're absolutely right. You did wrong, that's for bleeding sure. But I got what I wanted, in the end."

"Morrey." She sighs. "I'm glad you got him back." Her smile doesn't disappear, but it certainly fades, weakened by all mention of brothers.

On the low rise ahead, Morrey waits, now standing in silhouette against the base buildings spread out behind him. Cal is gone. Good.

Even though he's been with us for months, Cal is awkward without purpose, bad at conversation, and always on edge when he doesn't have a strategy to mull over. Part of me still thinks he sees us all as disposable—cards to picked up and thrown away as strategy dictates. *But he loves Mare,* I remind myself. *He loves a girl with Red blood.*

That must count for something.

Before we make it back to my brother, one last fear bubbles up in my throat.

"Am I abandoning you all? The newbloods."

My ability is silent death. I am a weapon, like it or not. I can be used. I can be useful. Is it selfish to walk away?

I get the feeling it's a question Mare has asked herself many times. But her answer is for me, and me alone.

"Of course not," she mutters. "You're still here. And you're one less monster for us to worry about. One less ghost."

TWENTY-FIVE
Mare

Even though my time at the Notch was fraught with exhaustion and heartbreak, it still holds a corner of my heart. For once, I remember the good more vividly than the bad. Days when we returned with living newbloods, snatched from the jaws of execution. It felt like progress. Every face was proof that I was not alone—and that I could save people as easily as kill them. Some days, it felt simple. Right. I've been chasing that sensation ever since.

The Piedmont base has its own training facilities, both indoor and outdoor. Some are equipped for Silvers, the rest for Red soldiers to learn war. The Colonel and his men, now numbering in the thousands and growing every day, claim the shooting range. Newbloods like Ada, those with less-devastating abilities, train with him, perfecting their aim and combat skills. Kilorn shuttles between their ranks and the newbloods on the Silver training grounds. He belongs with neither group, yet his presence soothes many. The fish boy is the opposite of a threat, not to mention a familiar face. And he doesn't fear them, like so many of the "true" Red soldiers. No, Kilorn has seen enough from me to never be afraid of a newblood ever again.

He accompanies me now, escorting me around the edge of a building about the size of an airjet hangar. But it has no runway. "Silver gymnasium," he says, pointing at the structure. "All sorts of stuff in there. Weights, an obstacle course, an arena—"

"I get it." I learned my skills in a place like that, surrounded by leering Silvers who would kill me if they saw one drop of my blood. At least I don't have to worry about that anymore. "Probably shouldn't train anywhere with a roof or lightbulbs."

Kilorn snorts. "Probably not."

One of the gymnasium doors bangs open and a figure steps out, a towel around his neck. Cal scrubs sweat off his face, still silver-flushed with exertion. Weight lifting, I assume.

He narrows his eyes and closes the distance between us as quickly as he can. Still panting, he puts a hand out. Kilorn takes it with an open grin. "Kilorn." Cal nods. "Taking her on a tour?"

"Ye—"

"Nah, she's going to start up with some of the others today." Kilorn speaks over me, and I resist the urge to elbow him in the gut.

"What?"

Cal darkens. He heaves a deep breath. "I thought you were going to give yourself more time."

Kilorn surprised me in the hospital, but he's right. I can't sit around anymore. It feels useless. And I am restless, with anger boiling beneath my skin. I'm not Cameron. I'm not strong enough to step back. Even lightbulbs have started sparking when I enter a room. I need release.

"It's been a few days. I thought it over." I put my hands on my hips, bracing myself against his inevitable counter. Without even realizing it, Cal settles into his patented arguing-with-Mare stance. Arms crossed, brow furrowed, feet firmly planted. With the sun behind me, he has to squint, and after his workout, he reeks of sweat.

Kilorn, the rotten coward, backs away a few steps. "I'll see you when you finish having a moment." He tosses a shit-eating grin over his shoulder, leaving me to fend for myself.

"Just a minute," I call at his retreating form. He only waves, disappearing around the corner of the gymnasium. "Some backup he is. Not that I need it," I add quickly, "since it's my decision and this is just training. I'll be perfectly fine."

"Well, half my worry is for the people in the blast zone. And the rest . . ." He takes my hand, using it to pull me closer. I wrinkle my nose, digging in my heels. Not that it matters much. I slide along the pavement anyway.

"You're all sweaty."

He grins wrapping one arm around my back. No escape. "Yep."

The scent isn't entirely unpleasant, even though it should be. "So you're not going to fight me on this?"

"Like you said. Your decision."

"Good. I don't have the energy to bicker twice in one morning."

He shifts and pushes me back gently, to better see my face. His thumbs graze the underside of my jaw. "Gisa?"

"Gisa." I huff, brushing a wisp of hair out of my face. Without the Silent Stone, my health has vastly improved, down to my nails and hair growing at a normal rate again. Still gray ends, though. That's never going away. "She keeps bothering me about relocation. Go to Montfort. Leave everything behind."

"And you told her go ahead, didn't you?"

I blush scarlet. "It just slipped out! Sometimes . . . I don't think before I speak."

He laughs. "What? You?"

"And then Mom took her side, of course, and Dad didn't take a side at all, playing peacemaker, of course. It's like"—my breath hitches—"it's like nothing ever changed. We could have been back in the Stilts, in the kitchen. I guess that shouldn't bother me so much. In the scheme of things." Embarrassed, I force myself to look up at Cal. It feels horrible complaining about family to him. But he asked. And it spilled out. He just studies me like I'm battlefield terrain. "This isn't something you want to think about. It's nothing."

His grip on my hand tightens before I can even think to pull away. He knows the way I run. "Actually, I was thinking about all the soldiers I trained with. At the front, especially. I've seen soldiers come back whole in body, but missing something else. They can't sleep or maybe they can't eat. Sometimes they slide right back into the past—into a memory of battle, triggered by a sound or a smell or any other sensation."

I gulp and circle my wrist with shaking fingers. Squeezing, I remember the manacles. The touch makes me sick. "Sounds familiar."

"You know what helps?"

Of course I don't, or else I'd do it. I shake my head.

"Normalcy. Routine. Talking. I know you don't exactly like the last one," he adds, smirking slowly. "But your family just wants you to be safe. They went through hell when you were . . . gone." He still hasn't figured out the proper word for what happened to me. *Captured* or *imprisoned* doesn't exactly carry the right weight. "And now that you're back, they're doing what anyone would do. They're protecting you. Not the lightning girl, not Mareena Titanos, but you. Mare Barrow. The girl they know and remember. That's all."

"Right." I nod slowly. "Thanks."

"So about that talking thing."

"Oh, come on, right now?"

His grin splits and he laughs, his stomach muscles tensing against me. "Fine, later. After training."

"You should go shower."

"Are you kidding? I'm going to be two steps behind you the whole time. You want to train? Then you're going to train properly." He pokes me in the small of my back, making me stumble forward. "Come on."

The prince is incessant, jogging backward until I match his pace. We pass the track, the outdoor obstacle course, a wide field of close-cut grass, not to mention several circles of dirt for sparring and a target range more than a quarter mile long. Some newbloods run the obstacle course and the track, while a few practice alone in the field. I don't recognize them, but the abilities I see are familiar enough. A newblood akin to a nymph forms columns of clear water before letting them drop to the grass, creating spreading puddles of mud. A teleporter navigates the course with ease. She appears and disappears all over the equipment, laughing at others having a more difficult time. Every time she jumps, my stomach twists, remembering Shade.

The sparring circles unsettle me most of all. I haven't fought someone for training, for sport, since Evangeline so many months ago. It was not an experience I care to repeat. But I'll certainly have to.

Cal's voice keeps me level, drawing my focus back to the task at hand. "I'll get you on your weights routine starting tomorrow, but today we can jump into target and theory."

Target I understand. "Theory?"

We stop at the edge of the long range, staring at the mist burning off in the distance.

"You came into Training about a decade late for that. But before our abilities are in fighting form, we spend a lot of time studying our advantages and disadvantages, how to use them."

"Like nymphs beating burners, water over fire."

"Sort of. That's an easy one. But what if you're the burner?" I just shake my head, and he grins. "See, tricky. Takes a lot of memorization and comprehension. Testing. But you're going to do this on the fly."

I forgot how suited to this Cal is. He is a fish in water, at ease, grinning. Eager. This is what he's good at, what he understands, where he excels. It's a lifeline in a world that never seems to make any sense.

"Is it too late to say I don't want to train anymore?"

Cal just laughs, tipping his head back. A bead of sweat rolls down his neck. "You're stuck with me, Barrow. Now, hit the first target." He stretches out a hand, indicating a square granite block ten yards away, painted like a bull's-eye. "One bolt. Dead center."

Smirking, I do as asked. I can't miss at this range. A single purple-white bolt streaks through the air and hits home. With a resounding crack, the lightning leaves a black mark in the center of the bull's-eye.

Before I have time to feel proud, Cal bodily shoves me aside. Off guard, I stumble, almost falling into the dirt. "Hey!"

He just steps away and points. "Next target. Twenty yards."

"Fine," I huff, turning my eyes on the second block. I raise my arm again, ready to aim—and Cal shoves me again. This time my feet react more quickly, but not enough, and my bolt goes wild, crackling into the dirt.

"This feels very unprofessional."

"I used to do this with someone firing blanks next to my head. Would you prefer that?" he asks. I shake my head quickly. "Then hit—the—target."

Normally, I'd be annoyed, but his smile spreads, making me blush.

It's training, I think. *Get a hold of yourself.*

This time, when he goes to push me, I sidestep and fire, clipping the granite marker. Another dodge, another shot. Cal starts to change up his tactic, going for my legs or even burning a fireball across my vision. The first time he does that, I hit the ground so fast I end up spitting dirt. "Hit the target" becomes his anthem, followed by a yard marker anywhere between fifty and ten. He shouts the targets at random, all while forcing me to dance on my toes. It's harder than running, much harder, and the sun turns brutal as the day wears on.

"The target is a swift. What do you do?" he asks.

I grit my teeth, panting. "Spread the bolt. Catch him as he dodges—"

"Don't tell me, do it."

With a grunt, I swing my arm in a chopping, horizontal motion, sending a spray of voltage in the target's direction. The sparks are weaker, less concentrated, but enough to slow a swift down. Next to me, Cal just nods his head, the only indication that I did something right. It feels good anyway.

"Thirty yards. Banshee."

Clapping my hands to my ears, I squint at the target, willing lightning without use of my fingers. A bolt vaults from my body, arcing like a rainbow. It misses, but I splash the electricity, making the sparks burst in different directions.

"Five yards. Silence."

The thought of an Arven floods me with panic. I try to focus. My hand strays for a gun that isn't there, and I pretend to shoot the target. "Bang."

Cal snorts a bit. "That doesn't count, but okay. Five yards, magnetron."

That one I know intimately. With all the force I can muster, I rocket a blast of lightning at the target. It cracks in two, sliding apart at dead center.

"Theory?" a soft voice says behind us.

I was so focused on the range that I didn't notice Julian standing by to watch, with Kilorn at his side. My old teacher offers a tight smile, his hands folded behind his back in his usual way. I've never seen him so casually dressed, with a light cotton shirt and shorts revealing thin chicken legs. Cal should get him on a weights routine too.

"Theory," Cal confirms. "After a fashion." He waves me down, giving me a brief respite. Immediately I sit in the dirt, stretching out my legs. Despite the constant dodging, it's the lightning that makes me tired. Without the adrenaline of battle or the threat of death hanging over my head, my stamina is decidedly lessened. Not to mention the fact that I'm about six months out of practice. With even motions, Kilorn stoops and puts a frosty water bottle down at my side.

"Thought you might need this," he says with a wink.

I grin up at him. "Thanks," I manage, before gulping down a few cold mouthfuls. "What are you doing down here, Julian?"

"Just on my way to the archives. Then I decided to see what all the fuss was about." He gestures over his shoulder. I jolt at the sight of a dozen or so assembled on the edge of the range, all of them staring at us. At me. "Seems you have a bit of an audience."

I grit my teeth. *Great.*

Cal shifts, just a bit, to hide me from view. "Sorry. Didn't want to break your concentration."

"It's fine," I tell him, forcing myself to stand. My limbs groan in protest.

"Well, I'll see you both later," Julian says, looking between me and Cal.

I answer quickly. "We can go with you—"

But he cuts me off with a knowing smirk, gesturing toward the crowd of bystanders. "Oh, I think you have introductions to make. Kilorn, would you mind?"

"Not at all," Kilorn replies. I want to smack the grin right off his face, and he knows it. "After you, Mare."

"Fine," I force through a clenched jaw.

Fighting my natural instinct to slink away from attention, I take a few steps toward the newbloods. A few more. A few more. Until I reach them, Cal and Kilorn alongside. In the Notch, I didn't want friends. Friends are harder to say good-bye to. That hasn't changed, but I see what Kilorn and Julian are doing. I can't close myself off from others anymore. I try to force a winning smile at the people around me.

"Hi. I'm Mare." It sounds stupid and I feel stupid.

One of the newbloods, the teleporter, bobs her head. She has a forest-green Montfort uniform, long limbs, and closely cropped brown hair. "Yeah, we know. I'm Arezzo," she says, sticking out a hand. "I jumped you and Calore out of Archeon."

No wonder I didn't recognize her. The minutes after my escape are still a blur of fear, adrenaline, and overpowering relief. "Right, of course. Thank you for that." I blink, trying to remember her.

The others are just as friendly and open, as pleased to meet another newblood as I am. Everyone in this group is Montfort-born or Montfort-allied, in green uniforms with white triangles on the breast and insignia on each bicep. Some are easy to decipher—two wavy lines for the nymph-like newblood, three arrows for the swift. No one has badges or medals, though. There's no telling who might be an officer. But all are military-trained, if not military-raised.

They use last names and have firm handshakes, each one a born or made soldier. Most know Cal on sight and nod at him in a very official manner. Kilorn they greet like an old friend.

"Where's Ella?" Kilorn asks, directing his question at a man with black skin and shockingly green hair. Dyed, clearly. His name is Rafe. "I sent her a message to come down and meet Mare. Tyton too."

"Last I saw, they were practicing on top of Storm Hill. Which, technically"—he glances at me, almost apologetic—"is where electricons are supposed to train."

"What's an electricon?" I ask, and immediately feel foolish.

"You."

I sigh, sheepish. "Right. I figured that about as soon as I asked."

Rafe floats a spark over his hand, letting it weave between his fingers. I feel it, but not like my own lightning. The green sparks answer to him and him alone. "It's an odd word, but we're odd things, aren't we?"

I stare at him, almost breathless with excitement. "You're . . . like me?"

He nods, indicating the lightning bolts on his sleeves. "Yes, *we* are."

Storm Hill is just like it sounds. It rises at a gentle incline in the middle of another field at the opposite end of the base, as far from the airfield as possible. Less chance of hitting a jet with a stray bolt of lightning. I get the sense the hill is a new addition, judging by the loose earth beneath my feet as we approach the summit. The grass is new growth too, the work of a greeny or newblood equivalent. It's more lush than the training fields. But the crown of the slope is a mess, charred earth packed flat, crisscrossed by cracks and the smell of a distant thunderstorm. While the rest of the base enjoys bright blue skies, a black cloud revolves over Storm Hill. A thunderhead, rising thousands of feet into the sky like a column of dark smoke. I've never seen anything like it, so controlled and contained.

The blue-haired woman from Archeon stands beneath the cloud, her arms outstretched, palms up to the thunder. A straight-backed man with swooping white hair like a wave's crest stands back from her, thin and lean in his green uniform. Both have lightning-bolt insignia.

Blue sparks dance over the woman's hands, small as worms.

Rafe leads us, Cal close at my side. Even though he deals with his fair share of lightning, the black cloud puts him on edge. He keeps glancing up, as if expecting it to explode. Some blue flashes weakly in the darkness, illuminating it from within. Thunder rumbles with it, low and thrumming like a cat's purr. It shivers my bones.

"Ella, Tyton," Cal calls. He waves a hand.

They turn at their names, and the flashing in the clouds abruptly stops. The woman lowers her hands, tucking away her palms, and the thunderhead starts to dissolve before our eyes. She bounds over in leaps of energy, trailed by the more stoic man.

"I was wondering when we would meet," she says, her voice high and breathy to match her dainty stature. Without warning, she takes my hands and kisses me on both cheeks. Her touch shocks, sparks leaping from her skin to mine. It doesn't hurt, but it certainly perks me up. "I'm Ella, and you're Mare, of course. And this tall drink of water is Tyton."

The man in question is certainly tall, with tawny skin, a sprinkling of freckles, and a jaw sharper than the edge of a cliff. With a flick of his head, he tosses his white hair to one side, letting it fall over his left eye. He winks with the right. I expected him to be old, with hair like that, but he can't be more than twenty-five. "Hello" is all he says, his voice deep and certain.

"Hi." I nod at them, overwhelmed both by their presence and my own inability to act anywhere close to normal. "Sorry, this is a bit of a shock."

Tyton rolls his eyes, but Ella bursts out laughing. A half second later, I understand and cringe.

Cal chuckles at my side. "That was pretty horrible, Mare." He nudges my shoulder as discreetly as he can, a brush of warmth emanating from him. A very small comfort in the Piedmont heat.

"We understand," Ella offers quickly, stealing the words away. "It's always overwhelming to meet another Ardent, let alone three who share your ability. Right, boys?" She elbows Tyton in the chest and he barely reacts, annoyed. Rafe just nods. I get the feeling Ella does most of the talking and, based on what I remember from the blue lightning storm in Archeon, most of the fighting. "I despair of you both," Ella mutters, shaking her head at them. "But I have you now, don't I, Mare?"

Her eager nature and open smile take me severely off guard. People this nice are always hiding something. I swallow my suspicion enough to give her what I hope is a genuine smile.

"Thank you for bringing her," she adds to Cal, her tone shifting. The cheery, blue-haired pixie draws up her spine and hardens her voice, becoming a soldier before my eyes. "I think we can take her training from here."

Cal barks out a low laugh. "Alone? Are you serious?"

"Were you?" she shoots back, narrowing her eyes. "I saw your 'practice.' Little bursts on a target range is hardly sufficient to maximize her abilities. Or do you know how to coax a storm out of her?"

Based on the way his lips twist, I can tell he wants to say something decidedly inappropriate. I stop him before he can, grabbing his wrist. "Cal's military background—"

"—is fine for conditioning." Ella cuts me off. "And perfect for training you to fight Silvers the way he does. But your abilities stretch beyond his understanding. There are things he can't teach you, things you must learn either the hard way—by yourself—or the easy way . . . with us."

Her logic is sound, albeit unsettling. *There are things Cal can't teach me, things he doesn't understand.* I remember when I tried to train Cameron—I didn't know her ability the same way I knew mine. It was like speaking a different language. I was still able to communicate, but not truly.

"I'll watch, then," Cal says with stony resolve. "Is that acceptable?"

Ella grins, her mood bouncing back to cheerful. "Of course. I would, however, advise you to stand back and stay alert. Lightning is a bit of a wild filly. No matter how much you rein her in, she'll always try to run wild."

He gives me one last look and the tiniest quirk of a supportive smile before heading to the edge of the hilltop, well beyond the ring of blast marks. When he gets there, he flops down and leans back on his arms, eyes trained on me.

"He's nice. For a prince," Ella offers.

"And a Silver," Rafe pipes in.

I glance at him, confused. "There aren't nice Silvers in Montfort?"

"I wouldn't know. I've never been," he replies. "I'm Piedmont-born, from down in the Floridians." He dots his fingers in the air, illustrating the chain of swampy islands. "Montfort recruited me a few months ago."

"And you two?" I look between Ella and Tyton.

She's quick to reply. "Prairie. The Sandhills. That's raider country, and my family lived on the move. Eventually we kept west into the mountains. Montfort took us in near ten years ago. That's where I met Tyton."

"Montfort-born," he says, as if that's any explanation. Not very talkative, probably because Ella has enough words for all of us. She steers me toward the center of what can only be called a blast zone, until I'm directly beneath the still-dissipating storm cloud.

"Well, let's see what we're working with," Ella says, nudging me into place. The breeze rustles her hair, sending bright blue locks over one shoulder. Moving in tandem, the other two take up spots around me, until we're clustered in the four corners of a square. "Start small."

"Why? I can—"

Tyton looks up. "She wants to check your control."

Ella nods.

I heave a breath. Excited as I am with fellow electricons, I feel a bit like an overnannied child. "Fine." Cupping my hands, I call forth the lightning, letting jagged sparks of purple and white splay around the bowl of my fingers.

"Purple sparks?" Rafe says, grinning. "Nice."

I flicker between the unnatural colors on their heads, smirking. Green, blue, white locks.

"I have no plans to dye my hair."

Summer hits Piedmont with a boiling vengeance, and Cal is the only person who can stand it. Gasping from exertion and heat, I smack him in the ribs until he rolls away. He does so slowly, lazily, almost drifting off to sleep. Instead, he goes too far and falls right off the narrow bed onto the hard, laminated floor. That wakes him up. He vaults forward, black hair sticking up at angles, naked as a newborn.

"My colors," he curses, rubbing his skull.

I have little pity for his pain. "If you didn't insist on sleeping in a glorified broom closet, this wouldn't be an issue." Even the ceiling, blocks of speckled plaster, is depressing. And the single open window does nothing for the heat, especially in the middle of the day. I don't want to think about the walls or how thin they might be. At least he doesn't have to bunk with other soldiers.

Still on the floor, Cal grumbles. "I like the barracks." He fumbles for a pair of shorts before pulling them on. Then go the bracelets, snapping back into place on his wrists. The latches are complicated, but he slips them on like it's second nature. "And you don't have to share a room with your sister."

I shift and throw a shirt over my head. Our midday break will be over in a few minutes, and I'm expected up on Storm Hill soon. "You're right. I'll just get over that little thing I have about sleeping alone." Of course, by *thing* I mean still-debilitating trauma. I have terrible nightmares if there isn't someone in the room with me.

Cal stills, shirt half over his head. He sucks in a breath, wincing. "That's not what I meant."

It's my turn to grumble. I pick at Cal's sheets. Military-issue, washed so many times they're almost worn through. "I know."

The bed shifts, springs groaning, as he leans toward me. His lips brush the crown of my head. "Any more nightmares?"

"No." I answer so quickly he raises an eyebrow in suspicion, but it's the truth. "As long as Gisa's there. She says I don't make a sound. Her, on the other hand . . . I forgot so much noise could come from such a small person." I laugh to myself, and find the courage to look him in the eye. "What about you?"

Back in the Notch, we slept side by side. Most nights he tossed and turned, muttering in his sleep. Sometimes he cried.

A muscle ripples in his jaw. "Just a few. Maybe twice a week, that I can remember."

"Of?"

"My father, mostly. You. What it felt like to be fighting you, watching myself try to kill you, and not being able to do a thing to stop it." He flexes his hands in memory of the dream. "And Maven. When he was little. Six or seven."

The name still feels like acid in my bones, even though it's been so long since I last saw him. He has given several broadcasts and declarations since, but I refuse to watch them. My memories of him are terrorizing enough. Cal knows that, and out of respect for me, he absolutely does not talk about his brother. Until now. *You asked,* I scold myself. I grit my teeth, mostly to stop from vomiting up all the words I haven't told him. Too painful for him. It won't help to know what kind of monster his brother was forced into becoming.

He pushes on, eyes far away in the memory. "He used to be afraid of the dark, until one day he just wasn't. In my dreams, he's playing in my room, sort of walking around. Looking at my books. And darkness follows him. I try to tell him. Try to warn him. He doesn't care. He doesn't mind. And I can't stop it. It swallows him whole." Slowly, Cal runs a hand down his face. "Don't need to be a whisper to know what that means."

"Elara is dead," I murmur, moving so we're side by side. As if that's any comfort.

"And he still took you. He still did horrible things." Cal stares at the floor, unable to hold my gaze. "I just can't understand why."

I could keep quiet. Or distract him. But the words boil furiously in my throat. He deserves the truth. Reluctant, I take his hand.

"He remembers loving you, loving your father. But she took that love away, he said. Cut it out of him like a tumor. She tried to do the same with his feelings for me"—and Thomas before—"but it didn't work. Certain kinds of love . . ." My breath hitches. "He said they're harder to remove. I think the attempt twisted him, more than he already was. She made it impossible for him to let go of me. Everything he felt for both of us was corrupted, made into something worse. With you, hatred. With me, obsession. And there is nothing either of us could do to change him. I don't even think she could undo her own work."

His only reply is silence, letting the revelation hang in the air. My heart breaks for the exiled prince. I give him what I think he needs. My hand, my presence, and my patience. After a long, long time, he opens his eyes.

"As far as I know, there are no newblood whispers," he says. "Not one that I've found or been told about. And I've done my fair share of searching."

This I did not expect. I blink, confused.

"Newbloods are stronger than Silvers. And Elara was just Silver. If someone can . . . can fix him, isn't it worth it to try?"

"I don't know" is all I can say. Just the idea numbs me, and I don't know how to feel. If Maven could be healed, so to speak, would that be enough to redeem him? Certainly it won't change what he's done. Not only to me and Cal, to his father, but to hundreds of other people. "I really don't know."

But it gives Cal hope. I see it there, like a tiny light in the distance of his eyes. I sigh, smoothing his hair. He needs another cut with a steadier hand than his own. "I guess if Evangeline can change, maybe anyone can."

His sudden laugh echoes low in his chest. "Oh, Evangeline is the same as always. She just had more incentive to let you go than to let you stay."

"How do you know?"

"Because I know who told her to do it."

"What?" I ask sharply.

With a sigh, Cal gets up and crosses the room. The opposite wall is all cabinetry, and mostly empty. He doesn't have many possessions beyond his clothes and a few bits of tactical gear. To my surprise, he paces. It sets my teeth on edge.

"The Guard blocked every attempt I made to get you back," he says, hands moving rapidly as he speaks. "No messages, no support for infiltration. No spies of any kind. I wasn't going to sit in that freezing base and wait for someone to tell me what to do. So I made contact with someone I trust."

Realization punches me in the gut. "Evangeline?"

"My colors, no," he gasps. "But Nanabel, my grandmother—my father's mother—"

Anabel Lerolan. The old queen. "You call her . . . Nanabel?"

He flushes silver and my heart skips a beat. "Force of habit," he grumbles. "Anyway, she never came to court while Elara was there, but I thought she might once she died. She knew what Elara was, and she knows me. She would have seen through the queen's lie. She would have understood Maven's role in our father's death."

Communicating with the enemy. There's no way Farley knew about this, or the Colonel. Nortan prince or not, either of them would have shot him if they did.

"I was desperate. And in hindsight, it was really, really stupid," he adds. "But it worked. She promised to get you free when the opportunity presented itself. The wedding was that opportunity. She must have given support to Volo Samos to ensure your escape, and it was worth it. You're here now because of her."

I speak slowly. I must understand. "So you let her know the raid on Archeon was coming?"

He moves back to me with blinding speed, kneeling to take both my hands. His fingers are blazing hot, but I force myself not to pull away. "Yes. She's more open to channeling with Montfort than I realized."

"She *communicated* with them?"

He blinks. "She still does."

For a second, I wish I had colors to curse with. "How? How is this possible?"

"I assume you don't want an explanation of how radios and broadcasters work." He smiles. I don't laugh at the joke. "Montfort is obviously open to working with Silvers, in whatever capacity, to reach their goals. This is an"—he searches for the right words—"even partnership. They want the same thing."

I almost scoff in disbelief. Royal Silvers working with Montfort . . . and the Guard? It sounds positively ludicrous. "And what do they want?"

"Maven off the throne."

A chill goes through me despite the summer heat and the closeness of Cal's body. Tears I can't control spring to my eyes.

"But they still want a throne."

"No—"

"A Silver king for Montfort to control, but a Silver king all the same. Reds in the dirt, as always."

"I promise you, that's not what this is."

"Long live Tiberias the Seventh," I whisper. He flinches. "When the houses rebelled, Maven interrogated them. And every one of them died saying those words."

His face falls in sadness. "I never asked for that," he murmurs. "Never wanted that."

The young man kneeling in front of me was born to a crown. Want had nothing to do with his upbringing. Want was stamped out of him at a young age, replaced with duty, with what his wretched father told him a king should be.

"Then what do you want?" When Kilorn asked me that same question, it gave me focus, purpose, a clear path in darkness. "What do you want, Cal?"

He answers quickly, eyes blazing. "You." His fingers tighten on mine, hot but steady in temperature. He's holding himself back as much as he can. "I am in love with you, and I want you more than anything else in the world."

Love is not a word we use. We feel it, we mean it, but we don't say it. It feels so final, a declaration from which there is no easy return. I'm a thief. I know my exits. And I was a prisoner. I hate locked doors. But his eyes are so close, so eager. And it's what I feel. Even though the words terrify me, they are the truth. Didn't I say I would start telling the truth?

"I love you," I whisper, leaning forward to brace my forehead against his. Eyelashes that are not my own flutter close to my skin.

"Promise me. Promise you won't leave. Promise you won't go back. Promise you won't undo everything my brother died for."

His low sigh washes across my face.

"I promise."

"Remember when we told each other no distractions?"

"Yes." He runs a blazing finger over my earrings, touching each one in turn.

"Distract me."

TWENTY-SIX
Mare

My training continues twofold, leaving me exhausted. It's for the best. Exhaustion makes it easy to sleep and hard to worry. Every time doubt tugs at my brain, over Cal or Piedmont or whatever comes next, I'm too tired to entertain the thoughts. I run and weight train with Cal in the mornings, taking advantage of the lasting effects of Silent Stone. After their heaviness, nothing physical seems difficult. He also slips in a bit of theory between laps, even though I assure him Ella has it covered. He just shrugs and keeps on. I don't mention that her training is more brutal, designed to kill. Cal was raised to fight, but with a skin healer in the wings. His version of sparring is very different from hers, which focuses on total annihilation. Cal is more oriented on defense. His unwillingness to kill Silvers unless absolutely necessary is thrown into harsh relief by my hours with the electricons.

Ella is a brawler. Her storms gather with blinding speed, spinning black clouds out of clear skies to fuel a merciless fusillade of lightning. I remember her in Archeon, wielding a gun with one hand and lightning in the other. Only Iris Cygnet's quick thinking kept her from turning

Maven to a pile of smoking ash. I don't think my lightning will ever be as destructive as hers, not without years of training, but her tutelage is invaluable. From her I learn that storm lightning is more powerful than any other kind, hotter than the surface of the sun, with the strength to split even diamondglass. Just one bolt like hers drains me so fully I can barely stand, but she does it for fun and target practice. Once she made me run through a minefield of her storm lightning to test my footwork.

Web lightning, as Rafe calls it, is more familiar. He uses bolts and sparks thrown from his hands and feet, usually in splaying webs of green, to protect his body. While he can call storms too, he prefers more accurate methods, and he fights with precision. His lightning can take form. He's best at the shield, a weaving crackle of electric energy that can stop a bullet, and a whip to cut through rock and bone. The latter is striking to behold: a fraying arc of electricity that moves like deadly rope, able to burn through anything in its path. I feel the force of it every time we spar. It doesn't hurt me as much as it would anyone else, but any lightning I can't wrench control of strikes deep. Usually I end the day with my hair on end, and when Cal kisses me, he always gets a shock or two.

The quiet Tyton doesn't spar with any of us, or with anyone, for that matter. He has given no name to his specialty, but Ella calls it pulse lightning. His control of electricity is astounding. The pure white sparks are small but concentrated, containing the strength of a storm bolt. Like a live-wire bullet.

"I'd show you brain lightning," he mutters to me one day, "but I doubt anyone would volunteer to help the demonstration."

We pass the sparring circles together, beginning the long walk across the base to Storm Hill. Now that I've been with them awhile,

Tyton actually speaks more than a few words to me. Still, it's a surprise to hear his slow, methodic voice.

"What's brain lightning?" I ask, intrigued.

"What it sounds like."

"Helpful," Ella sneers at my side. She continues braiding her vivid hair back from her face. It hasn't been dyed in a few weeks, as evidenced by the dirty-blond hair showing at the root. "He means that a human body runs on a pulse of electrical signals. Very small, ridiculously fast. Difficult to detect and almost impossible to control. They're most concentrated in the brain, and easiest to harness there."

My eyes widen as I look at Tyton. He just keeps walking, white hair over one eye, hands shoved into his pockets. Unassuming. As if what Ella just said isn't terrifying. "You can control someone's brain?" Cold fear rips me like a knife to the gut.

"Not the way you're thinking."

"How do you know—"

"Because you're very easy to predict, Mare. I'm not a mind reader, but I know six months at the mercy of a whisper would make anyone suspicious." With an annoyed sigh, he raises a hand. A spark brighter than the sun and more blinding weaves through his fingers. One touch from it could turn a man inside out with its force. "Ella's trying to say I can look at a person and drop them like a sack of hammers. Affect the electricity in their body. Give them a seizure if I'm feeling merciful. Kill them outright if not."

I look back at Ella and Rafe, blinking between them. "Have either of you learned that?"

Both scoff. "Neither of us has anywhere near the control required," Ella says.

"Tyton can kill someone discreetly, without anyone else knowing,"

Rafe explains. "We could be having dinner in the mess hall and the premier drops on the other side of the room. Seizure. He dies. Tyton doesn't blink and keeps on eating. Of course," he adds, clapping Tyton on the back, "not that we think you would ever do that."

Tyton barely reacts. "Comforting."

What a monstrous—and useful—way to use our ability.

In the sparring circles, someone yells in frustration. The sound draws my attention, and I turn to see a pair of newbloods grappling. Kilorn oversees the spar and waves at us.

"Going to give the rings a try today?" he says, gesturing at the circles of dirt marking the sparring grounds. "Haven't seen the lightning girl spark up in a long while."

I feel a surprisingly eager tug. Sparring with Ella or Rafe is exciting, but matching lightning to lightning isn't exactly helpful. There's no reason to practice fighting something we won't encounter for a long time.

Ella answers before I can, stepping forward. "We spar on Storm Hill. And we're already late."

Kilorn just raises an eyebrow. He wants my answer, not hers.

"Actually, I wouldn't mind. We should be practicing against what Maven has in his arsenal." I try to keep my tone diplomatic. I like Ella; I like Rafe. I even like what I know of Tyton, which is very little. But I have a voice too. And I think we can only go so far fighting each other. "I'd like to spar here today."

Ella opens her mouth to argue, but it's Tyton who speaks first. "Fine," he says. "Who?"

The closest thing to Maven we have.

★ ★ ★

"You know, I'm a lot better at this than he is."

Cal stretches an arm over his head, the bicep straining against thin cotton. He grins as I watch, enjoying the attention. I just glower and cross my arms over my chest. He hasn't agreed to my request, but he hasn't said no either. And the fact that Cal cut short his own training routine to come to the sparring circles says enough.

"Good. That will make fighting him easier." I'm careful with my words. *Fight*, not *kill*. Ever since Cal mentioned his search for someone who can "fix" his brother, I have to tread lightly. As much as I want to kill Maven for what he did to me, I can't voice those thoughts. "If I train against you, he won't be difficult at all."

He scuffs the dirt beneath his feet. Testing the terrain. "We already fought."

"Under the influence of a whisper. Someone else pulled the strings. That's not the same."

At the edge of the circle, a bit of a crowd gathers to watch. When Cal and I step onto the same sparring ground, word travels quickly. I think Kilorn might even be taking bets, weaving through the dozen or so newbloods with a shifty grin. One of them is Reese, the healer I struck when I was first rescued. He lies in wait like the skin healers used to when I trained with Silvers. Ready to fix whatever we break.

My fingers drum against my arms, each one ticking. In my bones, I call to lightning. It rises at my command, and I feel the clouds gather overhead. "Are you going to keep wasting my time so you can strategize, or can we get started?"

He just winks and continues his stretches. "Almost done."

"Fine." Stooping, I brush the finely ground dirt over my hands, wiping away any sweat. Cal taught me that. He grins and does the same. Then, to the surprise and delight of more than a few people, he pulls his shirt clean off and tosses it to the side.

Better food and hard training have made us both more muscular, but where I am lean and agile, smoothly curved, he is all hard angles and cut lines of definition. I've seen him undressed many times and still it gives me pause, sending a flush from my cheeks all the way down to my toes. I swallow forcibly. At the edge of my vision, both Ella and Rafe look him over with interest.

"Trying to distract me?" I pretend to shrug it off, ignoring the heat all over my face.

He cocks his head to side, a picture of innocence. He even claps his hand to his chest, forcing a false gasp as if to say *Who, me?* "You'll just fry the shirt anyway. I'm saving supplies. But," he adds, beginning to circle, "a good soldier uses every advantage at his disposal."

Above me, the sky continues to darken. Now I can definitely hear Kilorn taking bets. "Oh, you think you have the advantage? That's cute." I match his movements, circling in the opposite direction. My feet move of their own accord. I trust them. The adrenaline feels familiar, born of the Stilts, the training arena, every battle I've ever been in. It takes hold in my nerves.

I hear Cal's voice in my head, even as he tenses, settling into an all-too-familiar stance. *Burner. Ten yards.* My hands fall to my sides, fingers swirling as purple-white sparks jump in and out of my skin. Across the circle, he flicks his wrists—and searing heat blazes across my palms.

I yelp, jumping back to see my sparks are red flame. He took them from me. With a burst of energy, I thrust them back into lightning. They ripple, wanting to become fire, but I hold my concentration, keeping the sparks from bursting out of control.

"First blow to Calore!" Kilorn yells at the edge of the circle. A mix of groans and cheers runs through the still-growing crowd. He claps and thumps his feet. It reminds me of the arena, the Stilts, when he yelled for Silver champions. "Let's go, Mare, pick it up!"

A good lesson, I realize. Cal didn't have to open our spar by revealing something I wasn't prepared for. He could have held it back. Waited to use that unseen advantage. Instead, he played that piece first. He's going easy on me.

First mistake.

Ten yards away, Cal beckons, indicating for me to continue. A taunt as much as anything. He's best on the defense. He wants me to come to him. Fine.

At the edge of the circle, Ella mutters a warning to the crowd. "I'd step back if I were you."

My fist clenches, and lightning strikes. It rips down with blinding force, hitting the circle dead center, like an arrow to a bull's-eye. But it doesn't dig into the ground, cracking the earth as it should. Instead, I use a combination of storm and web. The purple-white bolt flares across the sparring circle, racing over the dirt at knee height. Cal throws up an arm to protect his eyes from the bright flash, using the other hand to ripple the sparks around him, morphing them to blazing blue flame. I sprint and burst from the lightning he can't bear to look at. With a roar, I slide into his legs, knocking him down. He hits the sparks and flops, seizing from the shock as I pop back to my feet.

Red-hot heat brushes my face, but I push it back with a shield of electricity. Then I'm on the ground too, legs swept out from under me. My face hits the ground hard and I taste dirt. A hand grabs my shoulder, a hand that burns, and I swing out with an elbow, catching his jaw. That burns too. His entire body is aflame. Red and orange, yellow and blue. Waves of heat distortion pulse from him, making the entire world sway and undulate.

Scrambling, I scoop my arm against the dirt and haul, chucking as much as I can into his face. He flinches, and it smothers some of his fire, giving me enough time to get to my feet. With another swing of my arms, I pull a whip of lightning into form, sparking and hissing in the air. He dodges each blow, rolling and ducking, light as a dancer on his feet. Fireballs spit from my electricity, the pieces I can't entirely control. Cal pulls them into churning whips of his own, surrounding the circle in an inferno. Purple and red clash, spark and burn, until the packed dirt beneath us churns like a stormy sea, and the sky goes black, raining thunderbolts.

He dances close enough for a blow. I feel the force of his fist ripple as I drop beneath it, and I smell burned hair. I get in a strike of my own, landing a brutal elbow to a kidney. He grunts in pain but responds in kind, ripping flaming fingers down my back. My flesh ripples with fresh blisters, and I bite my lip to keep from screaming. Cal would stop the fight if he knew how much this hurt. And it hurts. Pain shrieks up my spine and my knees buckle. Scrambling, I throw out my arms to stop a fall, and the lightning pushes me to my feet. I push through the searing pain because I have to know what it feels like. Maven will probably do worse when the time comes.

I use web again, a defensive maneuver to keep his hands off me. A strong bolt races up his leg, into his muscles, nerves, and bones. The skeleton of a prince flashes in my head. I pull back the blow enough to avoid permanent damage. He twitches, falling onto his side. I'm on him without thinking, working the bracelets I've seen him latch and unlatch a dozen times. Beneath me, his eyes roll and he tries to fight me off. The bracelets go flying, glinting purple against my sparks.

An arm wraps around my middle, flipping me over. The ground

against my back is like a tongue of white-hot fire. I scream this time, losing control. Sparks burst from my hands, and Cal flies back of his own accord, scrambling from the fury of lightning.

Fighting tears, I push up, fingers digging into the dirt. A few yards away, Cal does the same. His hair is wild with static energy. We're both wounded, both too proud to stop. We stagger to our feet like old men, swaying on uneasy limbs. Without his bracelets, he calls to the grass burning on the edge of the circle, forming flame from embers. It rockets at me as my lightning bursts again.

Both collide—with a tingling blue wall. It hisses, absorbing the force of both strikes. Then it disappears like a window wiped clean.

"Perhaps next time you two should spar in the range field," Davidson calls. Today the premier looks like everyone else in his plain green uniform, standing on the edge of the circle. At least, it was a circle. Now the dirt and grass are a charred mess, completely torn up, a battleground ripped apart by our abilities.

Hissing, I sit back down, quietly grateful for the end. Even breathing hurts my back. I have to lean forward on my knees, clenching my fists against the pain.

Cal takes a step toward me, then collapses as well, falling back on his elbows. He pants heavily, chest rising and falling with exertion. Not even enough strength to offer a smile. Sweat coats him from head to toe.

"Without an audience, if possible," Davidson adds. Behind him, as the smoke clears, another blue wall of something divides the spectators from our spar. With a wave of Davidson's hand, it blinks out of existence. He gives a tight, bland smile and indicates the symbol on his arm, his designation. A white hexagon. "Shield. Quite useful."

"I'll say," Kilorn barks, charging toward me. He crouches at my side. "Reese," he adds over his shoulder.

But the red-haired skin healer stops a few yards away. He holds his ground. "You know that's not how it works."

"Reese, stop it!" Kilorn hisses. He clenches his teeth in exasperation. "She's burned all down the back and he can barely walk."

Cal blinks at me, still panting. His face pulls in concern and regret, but also pain. I'm in agony and so is he. The prince does his best to look strong and tries to sit up. He just hisses, immediately falling back down.

Reese holds firm. "Sparring has consequences. We're not Silver. We need to know what our abilities do to each other." The words sound rehearsed. If I weren't in so much pain, I would agree. I remember the arenas where Silvers battled for sport, without fear. I remember my Training at the Hall of the Sun. A skin healer was always waiting, ready to patch up every scrape. Silvers don't care about hurting another person because the effects don't last. Reese looks us both over and all but wags a scolding finger. "It's not life-threatening. They spend twenty-four hours this way. That's protocol, Warren."

"Normally, I would agree," Davidson says. With sure footing, he crosses to the healer's side and fixes him with an empty stare. "But unfortunately I need these two sharp, and I need it now. Get it done."

"Sir—"

"Get it done."

The dirt squeezes through my fingers, the smallest relief as I claw my hands in the ground. If it means ending this torture, I'll listen to whatever the premier wants, and I'll do it with a smile.

My coverall uniform is itchy and it smells like disinfecting chemicals. I would complain, but I don't have the brain capacity. Not after

Davidson's operatives' latest briefing. Even the premier looks shaky, pacing back and forth in front of the long table of military advisers, including Cal and me. Davidson balls his fist beneath his chin and stares at the floor with his unreadable eyes.

Farley watches him for a long moment before glancing down to read Ada's meticulous handwriting. The newblood woman with perfect intelligence is an officer now, working closely with Farley and the Scarlet Guard. I wouldn't be surprised if baby Clara were made an officer too. She dozes against her mother's chest, wrapped tightly in a cloth sling. A crown of dark brown fuzz spots over her head. She really does look like Shade.

"Five thousand Red soldiers of the Scarlet Guard and five hundred newbloods of Montfort currently hold the Corvium garrison," Farley recites from Ada's notes. "Reports put Maven's forces in the thousands, all Silver. Massing at Fort Patriot in Harbor Bay, and outside Detraon in the Lakelands. We don't have exact numbers, or an ability count."

My hands tremble on the flat of the table, and I quickly shove them under my legs. In my head, I tick off who could possibly be aiding Maven's attempt to retake the fortress city. Samos is gone; Laris, Iral, Haven too. Lerolan, if Cal's grandmother can be believed. As much as I want to disappear, I force myself to speak. "He has strong support in Rhambos and Welle. Strongarms, greenwardens. Arvens too. They'll be able to neutralize any newblood attack." I don't explain further. I know what Arvens can do firsthand. "I don't know the Lakelanders, beyond the nymph royals."

The Colonel leans forward, bracing his palms on the table. "I do. They fight hard, and they endure. And their loyalty to their king is unyielding. If he throws his support to the wretch—" He stops himself and glances sidelong at Cal, who doesn't react. "To Maven, they won't hesitate to follow. Their nymphs are deadliest of course, followed by storms, shivers, and windweavers. Stoneskin berserkers are a nasty bunch too."

I flinch as he names each one.

Davidson spins on his heel to face Tahir in his seat. The newblood looks incomplete without his twin, and leans oddly, as if to compensate for his absence. "Any update on the time frame?" the premier barks. "Within the week isn't narrow enough."

Squinting his eyes, Tahir focuses elsewhere, far beyond the room. To wherever his twin might be. Like many of the operations here, Rash's location is classified, but I can guess. Salida was once embedded in Maven's newblood army. Rash is a perfect replacement for her, probably working as a Red servant somewhere in the court. It's quite brilliant. Using his link to Tahir, he can ferry information as quickly as any radio or communication link, without any of the evidence or possibility of interception.

"Still confirming," he says slowly. "Whispers of . . ." The newblood stills, and his mouth drops into an O of surprise. "Within the day. An attack from both sides of the border."

I bite my lip, drawing blood. How could this happen so quickly? Without warning?

Cal shares my sentiment. "I thought you were keeping watch on troop movements. Armies don't mass overnight." A low current of heat ripples from him, baking along my right side.

"We know the bulk of the force is in the Lakelands. Maven's new bride and her alliance put us in a bit of a bind," Farley explains. "We don't have nearly enough resources there, now that most of the Guard is here. We can't monitor three separate countries—"

"But you're sure it's Corvium? You're absolutely sure?" Cal snaps.

Ada nods without hesitation. "All intelligence points to yes."

"Maven likes traps." I hate saying his name. "It could be a ploy to draw us out in force, catch us in transit." I remember the scream of our jet torn apart midflight, sheering into jagged edges against the stars. "Or a feint. We go to Corvium. He hits the Lowcountry. Takes our foundation out from under us."

"Which is why we wait." Davidson clenches a fist in resolve. "Let them move first so we can make our counter. If they hold, we'll know it was a trick."

The Colonel flushes, skin red as his eye. "And if it's an offensive, plain and simple?"

"We'll move quickly once intentions are known—"

"And how many of my soldiers die while you move quickly?"

"As many as mine," Davidson sneers. "Don't act like your people are the only ones who will bleed for this."

"My people . . . ?"

"Enough!" Farley shouts them both down, loud enough to wake Clara. The infant is better tempered than anyone I know, and just blinks sleepily at the interruption of her nap. "If we can't get more intelligence, then waiting is our only option. We've made enough mistakes charging in headfirst."

Too many times to count.

"It's a sacrifice, I admit." The premier looks as sober as his generals, all stoic and stone-faced at the news. If there were another way, he would take it. But none of us see one. Not even Cal, who remains silent. "But a sacrifice of inches. Inches for miles."

The Colonel sputters in anger, slamming a fist on the council table. A glass pitcher full of water wobbles, and Davidson calmly rights it with quick, even reflexes.

"Calore, I'll need you to coordinate."

With his grandmother. With Silvers. People who stared at me and my chains and did nothing until it was convenient. People who still think my family should be their slaves. I bite my tongue. *People we need to win.*

Cal dips his head. "The Kingdom of the Rift has pledged support. We'll have Samos soldiers, Iral, Laris, and Lerolan."

"The Kingdom of the Rift," I say under my breath, almost spitting. Evangeline got her crown after all.

"What about you, Barrow?"

I look up to see Davidson staring, still with that blank expression. He is impossible to read.

"Do we have you as well?"

My family flickers before my eyes, but only for a moment. I should feel ashamed that my own anger, the rage I keep burning in the pit of my stomach and the corners of my brain, outweighs them all. Mom and Dad will kill me for leaving again. But I'm willing to join a war to find some semblance of peace.

"Yes."

TWENTY-SEVEN
Mare

It is not a trap and it is not a trick.

Gisa shakes me awake sometime after midnight, her brown eyes wide and worried. I told my family what was going to happen over dinner. As expected, they weren't exactly happy about my decision. Mom twisted the knife as much as she could. She wept over Shade, still a fresh wound, and my capture. Told me how selfish I was. Taking myself from them again.

Later, her reproaches turned into apologies and whispers of how brave I am. Too brave and stubborn and precious for her to let me go.

Dad just shut down, his knuckles white on his cane. We're the same, he and I. We make choices and follow through, even if the choice is wrong.

At least Bree and Tramy understood. They weren't called for this mission. That's comfort enough.

"Cal is downstairs," Gisa whispers, her keen hands on my shoulders. "You have to go."

As I sit up, already dressed in my uniform, I pull her into one last embrace.

"You do this too much," she mutters, trying to sound playful around the choking sobs in her throat. "Come back this time."

I nod, but I don't promise.

Kilorn meets us in the hall, bleary-eyed in his pajamas. He isn't coming either. Corvium is far past his limits. Another bitter comfort. As much as I used to complain about dragging him along, worrying about the fish boy good at knots and nothing else, I'll miss him dearly. Especially because none of that is true. He protected and helped me more than I ever did him.

I open my mouth to say all this, but he shuts me up with a quick kiss on the cheek. "You even try to say good-bye and I'll throw you down the stairs."

"Fine," I force out. My chest tightens, though, and it becomes harder to breathe with every step down to the first floor.

Everyone waits in congregation, looking grim as a firing squad. Mom's eyes are red and puffy, as are Bree's. He hugs me first, lifting me clean off the floor. The giant lets loose one sob into the crook of my neck. Tramy is more reserved. Farley is in the hallway too. She holds Clara tightly, rocking her back and forth. Mom is going to take her, of course.

Everything blurs, as much as I want to hold on to every inch of this moment. Time passes far too quickly. My head spins, and before I know what's happening, I'm out the door, down the steps, and tucked safely into a transport. Did Dad shake Cal's hand or did I imagine that? Am I still asleep? Am I dreaming? The lights of the base stream through the dark like shooting stars. The headlights cut the shadows, illuminating the road to the airfield. Already I hear the roar of engines and the scream of jets taking to the skies.

Most are dropjets, designed to transport large numbers of troops at speed. They land vertically, without runways, and can be piloted directly into Corvium. I'm seized by a terrible sense of familiarity as we board ours. The last time I did this, I spent six months as a prisoner, and came back a ghost.

Cal senses my unease. He takes over buckling me into my jet seat, fingers moving swiftly as I stare at the metal grating beneath my feet. "It won't happen again," he murmurs, low enough so only I can hear. "This time is different."

I take his face in my hands, making him stop and look at me. "So why does it feel the same?"

Bronze eyes search mine. Searching for an answer. He finds none. Instead, he kisses me, as if that can solve anything. His lips burn against my own. It lasts longer than it should, especially with so many people around, but no one makes a fuss.

When he pulls back, he pushes something into my hand.

"Don't forget who you are," he whispers.

I don't need to look to know it's an earring, a tiny bit of colored stone set in metal. Something to say farewell, to say stay safe, to say remember me if we are parted. Another tradition from my old life. I keep it tight in my fist, almost letting the sharp sting pierce my skin. Only when he sits down across from me do I look.

Red. Of course. Red as blood, red as fire. Red as the anger eating us both alive.

Unable to punch it through my ear right now, I tuck it away, careful to keep the tiny stone safe. It will join the others soon.

Farley moves with a vengeance, taking her seat near the Montfort pilots. Cameron follows closely, offering a tight smile as she sits down.

She finally has an official green uniform, as does Farley, though Farley's is different. Not green, but dark red, with a white *C* on her arm. *Command.* She shaved her head again in preparation, shedding inches of blond hair in favor of her old style. She looks severe, with her twisting facial scar and blue eyes to pierce any armor. It suits. I understand why Shade loved her.

She has a reason to stop fighting, more than any of us. But she keeps on. A bit of her determination floods into me. If she can do this, so can I.

Davidson boards our jet last, rounding out the forty of us aboard the drop. He follows a troop of gravitrons marked by downward lines of insignia. He's still wearing the same battered uniform, and his normally smooth hair is unkempt. I doubt he slept. It makes me like him a bit more.

He nods at us as he passes, stomping the length of the jet to sit with Farley. They duck their heads together in thought almost immediately.

My electrical sense has improved since my work with the electricons. I can feel the jet down to its wiring. Every spark, every pulse. Ella, Rafe, and Tyton are coming of course, but no one dares put us all on a single dropjet. If the worst should happen, at least we won't all die together.

Cal fidgets in his seat. Nervous energy. I do the opposite. I try to feel numb, to ignore the hungry fury begging to be set loose. I still haven't seen Maven since my escape, and I imagine his face as it was then. Shouting for me through the crowd, trying to turn around. He didn't want to let me go. And when I wrap my hands around his throat, I won't let him go. I won't be scared. Only a battle stands in my way.

"My grandmother is bringing as many with her as she can," Cal mutters. "Davidson already knows, but I don't think anyone filled you in."

"Oh."

"She has Lerolan, the other rebelling houses. Samos too."

"Princess Evangeline," I mutter, still laughing at the thought. Cal sneers with me.

"At least now she has her own crown, and doesn't have to steal her way to someone else's," he says.

"You two would've been married by now. If . . ." *If*, meaning so many things.

He nods. "Married long enough to go absolutely crazy. She'd make a good queen, but not for me." He takes my hand without looking. "And she would be a terrible wife."

I don't have the energy to follow that thread of implication, but a burst of warmth blooms in my chest.

The jet lurches, spooling into high gear. Rotors and engines whir, drowning out all conversation. With another lurch we're airborne, rising into the hot summer night. I shut my eyes for a moment and imagine what is to come. I know Corvium from pictures and broadcasts. Black granite walls, gold and iron reinforcements. A spiraling fortress that used to be the last stop for any soldier heading into the Choke. In another life, I would have passed through. And now it's under siege for the second time this year. Maven's forces set out a few hours ago, landing at their controlled strip in Rocasta before heading overland. They should be at the walls soon. Before us.

Inches for miles, Davidson said.

I hope he's right.

Cameron tosses her cards into my lap. Four queens smolder up at me, all of them teasing. "Four ladies, Barrow," she snickers. "What next? Going to bet your bleeding boots?"

I grin and swipe the cards into my pile, discarding my useless hand of red numbers and a single black prince. "They wouldn't fit you," I answer. "My feet aren't canoes."

She cackles loudly, tossing her head back as she kicks her toes out. Indeed, her feet are very long and thin. I hope, for the sake of resources, Cameron is all done growing. "Another round," she goads, and holds out a hand for the cards. "I bet a week of laundry."

Across from us, Cal stops his preparatory stretching to snort. "You think Mare does laundry?"

"Do you, Your Highness?" I snap back, grinning. He just pretends not to hear me.

The easy banter is both a balm and a distraction. I don't have to dwell on the battle facing us if I'm being robbed blind by Cameron's card skills. She learned in the factories, of course. I barely even understand how to play this game, but it helps me stay focused in the moment.

Beneath us, the dropjet sways, bouncing on a bubble of air turbulence. After many hours in flight, it doesn't faze me, and I continue shuffling cards. The second bump is deeper, but no cause for alarm. The third sends the cards flying out of my hands, fanning out in midair. I slam back against my seat and fumble for my harness. Cameron does the same while Cal snaps himself back, his eyes flashing to the cockpit. I follow his gaze to see both pilots working furiously to keep the jet level.

More concerning is the view. It should be sunrise by now, but the sky ahead of us is black.

"Storms," Cal breathes, meaning both the weather and the Silvers. "We have to climb."

The words barely leave his lips before I feel the jet tip beneath me, angling upward to higher altitudes. Lightning flashes deep within the clouds. Real lightning, born of the thunderheads and not a newblood's ability. I feel it thumping like a faraway heart.

I tighten my grip on the straps crossing over my chest. "We can't land in that."

"We can't land at all," Cal snarls.

"Maybe I can do something, stop the lightning—"

"It won't just be lightning down there!" Even over the roar of the climbing plane, his voice rumbles. More than a few heads turn in his direction. Davidson's is one of them. "Windweavers and storms are going to blow us off course the second we drop through the clouds. They'll make us crash."

Cal's eyes flutter up and down jet, taking stock of us. The wheels turn in his head, working on overdrive. My fear gives way to faith. "What's your plan?"

The jet bucks again, bouncing us all in our seats. It doesn't faze Cal.

"I need gravitrons, and I need you," he adds, pointing at Cameron.

Her gaze turns steely. She nods. "I think I know where you're going with this."

"Radio the other jets. We're going to need a teleporter in here, and I need to know where the rest of the gravitrons are. They have to distribute."

Davidson ducks his chin in a sharp nod. "You heard him."

My stomach swoops at the implication as the jet bursts into activity. Soldiers double-check their weapons and zip into tactical gear, their faces full of determination. Cal most of all.

He forces himself out of his seat, clutching the supports to keep steady. "Get us directly over Corvium. Where's that teleporter?"

Arezzo blinks into existence, dropping to a knee to stop her momentum. "I do not enjoy that," she spits.

"Unfortunately you and the other 'porters are going to be doing it a lot," Cal replies. "Can you handle jumping between the jets?"

"Of course," she says, like it's the most obvious thing in the world.

"Good. Once we're down, take Cameron to the next jet in line."

Down.

"Cal," I almost whimper. I can do a lot of things, but this?

Arezzo cracks her knuckles, speaking over me. "Affirmative."

"Gravitrons, use your cables. Six to a body. Keep it tight."

The newbloods in question spring to their feet, pulling wound cords from special slots on their tactical vests. Each one has a mess of clips, allowing them to transport multiple people with their ability to manipulate gravity. Back at the Notch, I recruited a man named Gareth. He used his ability to fly or jump great distances.

But not to jump out of jets.

Suddenly I feel very sick, and sweat breaks out on my forehead.

"Cal?" I say again, my voice climbing higher.

He ignores me. "Cam, your job is to protect the jet. Put out as much silence as you can—picture a sphere; it'll help keep us level in the storm."

"Cal?" I yelp. Am I the only one thinking this is suicide? Am I the only sane person here? Even Farley seems nonplussed, her lips pursed into a grim line as she cables herself to one of the six gravitrons. She feels my eyes and looks up. Her face flickers for an instant, reflecting one ounce of the terror I feel. Then she winks. *For Shade,* she mouths.

Cal forces me up, either ignoring my fear or not noticing it. He personally straps me to the tallest gravitron, a lanky woman. He cables in next to me, one arm heavy across my shoulders while the rest of me is crushed against the newblood. All down the jet, the others do the same, flanking their gravitron lifelines.

"Pilot, what's our position?" Cal shouts over my head.

"Five seconds to center," comes a responding bark.

"Plan all passed on?"

"Affirmative, sir! Center, sir!"

Cal grits his teeth. "Arezzo?"

She salutes. "Ready, sir."

There's a very good chance I will throw up all over the poor gravitron in the middle of this honeycomb of people. "Easy," Cal breathes in my ear. "Just hold on; you'll be fine. Close your eyes."

I definitely want to. I fidget now, tapping my legs, shuddering. All nerves, all movement.

"This isn't crazy," Cal whispers. "People do this. Soldiers train to do stuff like this."

I tighten my grip on him, enough to make it hurt. "Have you?"

He just gulps.

"Cam, you can start. Pilot, begin drop."

The wave of silence hits me like a sledgehammer. It isn't enough to hurt, but the memory of it makes my knees buckle. I grit my teeth to keep from screaming and squeeze my eyes shut so tightly I see stars. Cal's natural warmth acts as an anchor, but a shaky one. I tighten my grip around his back, as if I can bury myself inside him. He murmurs to me but I can't hear him. Not past the feel of slow, smothering darkness and an even worse death. My heartbeat triples, ramming in my chest until I think it might explode out of me. I can't believe it, but I actually want to jump out of the plane now. Anything to get away from

Cameron's silence. Anything to stop remembering.

I barely feel the plane drop or rock against the storm. Cameron exhales in steady puffs, trying to keep her breathing even. If the rest of the plane feels the pain of her ability, they don't show it. We descend in quiet. Or maybe my body is simply refusing to hear anymore.

When we shuffle backward, crowding onto the drop platform, I realize this is it. The jet rumbles, buffeted by winds Cameron cannot deflect. She shouts something I can't decipher over the pound of blood in my ears.

Then the world opens beneath me. And we fall.

At least when House Samos ripped my last jet out of the sky, they had the decency to leave us in a cage of metal. We have nothing but the wind and freezing rain and swirling darkness pulling us every which way. Our momentum must be enough to keep us on target, as well as the fact that no sane person would expect us to be leaping out of planes a few thousand feet in the air in the middle of a storm. The wind whistles like a woman's scream, clawing at every inch of me. At least the pressure of Cameron's silence is gone. The veins of lightning in the clouds call to me, as if saying good-bye before I'm turned into a crater.

Everyone yells on the way down. Even Cal.

I'm still yelling when we start slowing about fifty feet above the jagged tips of Corvium, spiraling out in a hexagon of buildings and inner walls. And I'm hoarse when we bump gently against the smoothly paved ground, slick with at least two inches of rainwater.

Our newblood hastily unclips us all, and I fall backward, not caring about the bitterly cold puddle I'm lying in. Cal jumps to his feet.

I lie there for a second, thinking of nothing. Just staring up at the sky I plummeted through—and somehow survived. Then Cal grabs my arm and hoists me up, literally pulling me back to reality.

"The rest are going to be landing here, so we have to move." He shoves me ahead of him, and I stumble a bit through the sloshing water. "Gravitrons, Arezzo will come down with the next batch to teleport you back up. Stay sharp."

"Yes, sir," they echo, bracing themselves for another round. I'm almost sick at the thought.

Farley actually is sick. She heaves up her guts in an alleyway, dumping whatever her quick breakfast was. I forgot she hates flying, not to mention teleporting. The drop was the worst of both.

I make for her, looping my arm to help her stand up straight. "You okay?"

"Fine," she replies. "Just giving the wall a fresh coat of paint."

I glance at the sky, still lashing us with cold rain. Oddly cold for this time of year, even in the north. "Let's get moving. They aren't on the walls yet, but they will be."

Cal steams slightly and zips up the neck of his vest to keep the water out. "Shivers," he calls. "I have a feeling we're about to be snowed in."

"Should we go to the gates?"

"No. They're warded with Silent Stone. Silvers can't pummel their way in. They have to go over." He gestures for us and the rest of our dropjet to follow him. "We have to be on the ramparts, ready to push back whatever they throw. The storm is just the vanguard. Block us in, reduce our vision. Keep us blind until they're on top of us."

His pace is hard to match, especially through the rain, but I forge to his side anyway. Water soaks through my boots, and it isn't long before I lose sensation in my toes. Cal stares ahead, as if his eyes alone can set the entire world on fire. I think he wants to. That would make this easier.

Once again he must fight—and probably kill—the people he was raised to protect. I take his hand, because there are no words I can say right now. He squeezes my fingers, but lets them go just as quickly.

"Your grandmother's troops can't get in the same way." As I speak, more gravitrons and soldiers plummet out of the sky. All screaming, all safe when they touch down. We turn a corner, moving from one ring of walls to the next, leaving them behind. "How do we join our forces?"

"They're coming from the Rift. That's southwest. Ideally, we'll keep Maven's force occupied long enough for them to take the rear. Pin them between us."

I gulp. So much of the plan relies on the work of Silvers. I know better than to trust such things. House Samos could simply not arrive and let us all be captured or killed. Then they would be free to challenge Maven outright. Cal isn't stupid. He knows all this. And he knows Corvium and its garrison are too valuable to lose. This is our flag, our rebellion, our promise. We stand against the might of Maven Calore, and his twisted throne.

Newbloods man the ramparts, joined by Red soldiers with arms and ammunition. They don't fire, only stare out into the distance. One of them, a tall string bean of a man with a uniform like Farley's and a *C* on his shoulder, steps forward. He clasps arms with her first, nodding his head.

"General Farley," he says.

She dips her chin. "General Townsend." Then she nods to another ranking officer in green, probably the commander of the Montfort newbloods. The short, squat woman with bronze skin and a long, white braid coiled around her head returns the action. "General Akkadi."

"What are we looking at?" Farley asks them both.

Another soldier approaches in red instead of green. Her hair is different, dyed scarlet, but I recognize her.

"Good to see you, Lory," Farley says, all business. I would greet the newblood too if we had the time. I'm quietly happy to see another one of the Notch recruits not just alive but thriving. Like Farley, her red hair is closely cut. Lory belongs to the cause.

She nods at us all before throwing an arm out over the metal-edged ramparts. Her ability is extremely heightened senses, allowing her to see much farther than we can. "Their force is to the west, with their backs to the Choke. They have storms and shivers just inside the first ring of cloud cover, out of your sight."

Cal leans forward, squinting at the thick black clouds and pelting rain. They make it impossible for him to see farther than a quarter mile from the walls. "Do you have snipers?"

"We tried," General Townsend sighs.

Akkadi concurs. "Waste of ammunition. The wind just eats the bullet."

"Windweavers too, then." Cal sets his jaw. "They have the aim for that."

The meaning is clear. The windweavers of Norta, House Laris, rebelled against Maven. So this force is Lakelander. Another person might miss the twitch of a smile or the release of tension in Cal's shoulders, but I don't. And I know why. He was raised to fight Lakelanders. This is an enemy that won't break his heart.

"We need Ella. She's best at storm lightning." I point up at the looming towers overlooking this section of wall. "If we get her up high, she can turn the storm against them. Not control it, but use it to fuel herself."

"Good, get it done," Cal says with a clipped tone. I've seen him in a fight, in battle, but never something like this. He becomes another person entirely. Laser-focused, inhumanly so, without even a flicker of the gentle, torn prince. Whatever warmth he has left is an inferno, meant to destroy. Meant to win. "When the gravitrons finish the drops, put them here, evenly spaced. The Lakelanders are going to charge the walls. Let's make it hard for them to move. General Akkadi, who else do you have on hand?"

"Good mix of defensive and offensive," she responds. "Enough bombers to turn the Choke road into a minefield." With a proud smirk, she indicates the nearby newbloods who have what look like sunbursts on their shoulders. Bombers. Better than oblivions, able to explode something or someone on sight instead of just touch.

"Sounds like a plan," Cal says. "You keep your newbloods ready. Strike at your discretion."

If Townsend minds being dictated to, and by a Silver at that, he doesn't show it. Like the rest of us, he feels the thrum of death in the air. There's no room for politics now. "And my soldiers? I've got a thousand Reds on the walls."

"Keep them there. Bullets are just as good as abilities, sometimes more so. But conserve ammunition. Target only those who slip through the first wave of defenses. They want us to overexert, and we're not going to do that." He glances at me. "Are we?"

I grin, blinking away the rain. "No, sir."

At first, I wonder if the Lakelanders are very slow to move, or very stupid. It takes the better part of the hour, but between Cameron, the gravitrons, and the teleporters, we manage to get everyone into Corvium from the thirty or so dropjets. About a thousand soldiers, all trained and deadly. Our advantage, Cal says, lies in uncertainty. Silvers still don't know how to fight people like me. They don't know what we're truly capable of. I think that's why Cal mostly leaves Akkadi to her own devices. He doesn't know her troops well enough to command them properly. But Reds he knows. It leaves a bitter taste in my mouth, one I try to swallow away. In the stretch of time, I try not to wonder how many Reds the person I love sacrificed for an empty war.

The storm never changes. Always churning, dumping rain. If they're trying to flood us, it's going to take a long time. Most of the water drains, but some of the lower streets and alleys are six inches deep in murky water. It makes Cal uneasy. He keeps wiping off his face or pushing back his hair, skin slightly steaming in the cold.

Farley has no shame. She propped her jacket up over her head a long time ago, and looks like some kind of maroon ghost. I don't think she moves for twenty minutes, her head resting on folded arms as she stares out at the landscape. Like the rest of us, she waits for a strike that may come at any second. It sets my teeth on edge, and the constant rage of adrenaline drains me almost as badly as Silent Stone.

I jump when Farley speaks.

"Lory, are you thinking what I'm thinking?"

At another perch, Lory also has a jacket over her head. She doesn't turn, unable to wrench her senses away. "I really hope not."

"What?" I ask, looking between them. The movement sends fresh rainwater down my shirt collar, and I shiver. Cal sees it happen and moves closer to my back, extending some of his warmth to me.

Slowly, Farley turns, trying not to get drenched. "The storm is moving. Closing in. A few feet every minute, and getting faster."

"Shit," Cal breathes behind me. Then he springs into action, taking his warmth with him. "Gravitrons, be ready! When I say, you tighten your grip on that field." *Tighten.* I've never seen a gravitron use their ability to strengthen gravity, only loosen it. "Drop whatever's coming."

As I watch, the storm picks up speed, enough to note at a glance. It continues swirling, but spirals closer and closer with every rotation, clouds bleeding over open ground. Lightning cracks deep within, a pale, empty color. I narrow my eyes, and for a moment, it flashes purple, veining with strength and rage. But I have nothing to aim at yet. Lightning, no matter how powerful, is useless without a target.

"The force is marching behind the storm, closing the distance," Lory calls, confirming our worst fears. "They're coming."

TWENTY-EIGHT
Mare

The wind howls. It buffets the walls and ramparts, blowing more than a few back from their position. Rain freezes on the stonework, making our footing precarious. The first casualty is a fall. A Red soldier, one of Townsend's. The wind catches his jacket, blowing him backward along the slick walkway. He shouts as he goes over the edge, plunging thirty feet—before sailing skyward, born of a gravitron's concentration. He lands hard on the wall, colliding with a sickening crack. The gravitron didn't have enough control. But the soldier is alive. Injured, but alive.

"Brace yourself!" echoes down the lines of soldiers, passing between green uniforms and red. When the wind roars again, we buckle down. I tuck myself against the icy metal of a rampart, safe from the worst of it. A windweavers' strike is unpredictable, unlike normal weather. It splits and curves, clawing like fingers. All while the storm tightens around us.

Cameron shoves in next to me. I glance at her, surprised. She's supposed to be back with the healers, to form a last wall against any siege. If anyone can defend them from Silvers, give them the time and space to treat our soldiers, it's her. The rain makes her shiver, her teeth chattering. She seems smaller, younger, in the cold and closing darkness. I wonder if she's even turned sixteen yet.

"All right, lightning girl?" she says with some difficulty. Water drips over her face.

"All right," I murmur back. "What are you doing up here?"

"Wanted to see," she says, lying. The young girl is here because she believes she has to be. *Am I abandoning you?* she asked before. I see the question in her eyes now. And my answer is the same. If she doesn't want to be a killer, she shouldn't have to be.

I shake my head. "You protect the healers, Cameron. Get back to them. They're defenseless, and if they go down—"

She bites her lip. "We all do."

We stare at each other, trying to be strong, trying to find strength in each other. Like me, she's soaked through. Her dark lashes clump together, and every time she blinks it looks like she's crying. The raindrops land hard, making us both squint as they pelt down our faces. Until they don't. Until the raindrops start rolling in the opposite direction, flowing up. Her eyes widen as mine do, watching with horror.

"Nymph strike!" I scream in warning.

Above us, the rain shimmers, dancing on the air, joining together into larger and larger droplets. And the puddles, the inches of water in the streets and alleys—they become rivers.

"Brace!" echoes again. This time the blow is freezing water instead of wind, foaming white as it breaks like a wave, curving up and over the walls and buildings of Corvium. A spray catches me hard, dashing my head against the rampart, and the world spins. A few bodies go over the wall, spinning into the storm. Their silhouettes disappear quickly, as do their screams. The gravitrons save a few, but not all.

Cameron slides away, on hands and knees, to get back to the stairs. She uses her ability to make a cocoon of safety as she sprints back to her post well inside the second wall.

Cal skids next to me, almost losing his footing. In my daze, I grab at him, pulling him close. If he goes over the wall, I know I'll just go after him. He watches, terrified, as the water assaults our ranks like the waves of a churning sea. It makes him useless. Flame has no place here. His fire cannot burn. And my lightning is just the same. One spark and I'll shock who knows how many of our own troops. I can't risk it.

Akkadi and Davidson have no such restriction. While the premier throws up a glowing blue shield at the edge of the wall, protecting anyone else from going over the edge, Akkadi roars to her newblood troops, barking orders I can't hear over the crashing waves.

The water spikes, shuddering. Suddenly at war with itself. We have nymphs too.

But no storms. No newbloods who can seize control of the hurricane around us. Its darkness closes in, so absolute it seems like midnight. We'll be fighting blind. And it hasn't even started yet. I still haven't seen a single one of Maven's soldiers, or the Lakelander army. Not one red banner or blue. But they're coming. They're certainly coming.

I grit my teeth. "Get up."

The prince is heavy, slowed by his fear. Putting a hand to his neck, I give him the smallest shock. The gentle kind Tyton showed me. He rockets to his feet, alive and alert. "Right, thanks," he mutters. With a glance, he takes stock. "The temperature's dropping."

"Genius," I hiss back. Every part of me feels frozen.

Above us, the water rages, splitting and re-forming. It wants to crash down, it wants to dissipate. Some of it peels off and vaults over Davidson's shield, racing away into the storm like a strange bird. After a moment, the rest crashes down, drenching us all anew. A cheer goes up anyway. The newblood nymphs, while outnumbered and off guard, just won their first bout.

Cal doesn't join in the celebrations. Instead, he rakes his wrists together, igniting his hands into weak flame. They sputter in the downpour, fighting to burn. Until, suddenly, the rain turns to bitter, blizzard snow. In the utter darkness it winks red, gleaming in the weak lights of Corvium and Cal's flame.

I feel my hair start to freeze on my head and shake my ponytail. Splinters of ice go flying in every direction.

A roar rises out of the storm, different from the wind. With many voices. A dozen, a hundred, a thousand. The blackout blizzard presses in. Briefly, Cal's eyes flutter shut, and he sighs aloud.

"Prepare for attack," he says hoarsely.

The first ice bridge spikes through the rampart two feet away from me and I vault back, yelping. Another splits the stone twenty feet away, spearing soldiers with its jagged edges. Arezzo and the other teleporters spring into action, collecting the wounded to jump them back to our healers. Almost instantly, Lakelander soldiers, their shadows like monsters, vault off the bridges—they ran up the ice as it grew. Ready to strike.

I've seen Silver battles before. They are chaos.

This is worse.

Cal lunges forward, his fires jumping hot and high. The ice is thick, not so easily melted, and he carves pieces from the nearest bridge like a lumberjack with a chainsaw. It makes him vulnerable. I slice through the first Lakelander to get near him, and my sparks send the armored man spinning into darkness. Another quickly follows, until my skin crawls with purple-white veins of hissing lightning. Gunfire drowns out whatever orders anyone might be shouting. I focus on myself, on Cal. Our survival. Farley stays close, gun tucked up. Like Cal, she puts me to her back, letting me defend her blind spot. She doesn't flinch as she fires her gun, pummeling the nearest bridge with bullets. She centers on the ice, not the warriors bursting out of the blizzard. It cracks and splinters beneath the berserkers, crumbling into darkness.

Thunder rumbles, closer by the second. Bolts of blue-white electricity explode through the clouds, crashing down around Corvium. From the towers, Ella's aim is deadly, striking just outside the walls. An ice bridge falls to her wrath, cracking in two—but it regrows, re-forming in midair at the will of a shiver hiding somewhere. Bombers do the same, obliterating glassy hunks of ice with bursts of explosive force. They just creep back, skittering through another rampart. Green lightning crackles somewhere to my left as Rafe arcs his whips into a stampeding horde of Lakelanders. His blow meets a shield of water, which absorbs the current as they advance. Water doesn't stop bullets, though. Farley peppers them with gunfire, dropping a few Silvers where they stand. Their bodies slide off into darkness.

I turn my attentions to the closest bridge of soldiers. Instead of the ice, I focus on the figures charging from the darkness. Their blue armor is thick, scaled, and with their helmets they look inhuman. It makes them easier to kill. They force one another forward, pressing on to the walls. A snaking line of faceless monsters. Purple lightning explodes from my clawed hands and races through their hearts, jumping from one suit of armor to the other. The metal superheats, fading from blue to red, and many fall off the bridge in their agony. More replace them, vaulting out of the storm. It is a killing ground, a funnel of death. Tears freeze on my cheeks as I lose count of how many skeletons I rip through.

Then the city wall cracks between my feet, one side sliding from the other. A concussive blow shudders through my bones. Then another. The crack widens. Quickly, I pick an edge, jumping to Cal's side before the crack swallows me whole. Roots worm up through the fissure, thick as my arm, and growing. They pry apart the stone like massive fingers, sending spider cracks past my feet like bolts of stone lightning. The wall bucks under the strain.

Greenwardens.

"The wall is going to break," Cal breathes. "They'll crack it right open and get behind us."

I clench a fist. "Unless?" He just stares blankly, at a loss. "There has to be something we can do!"

"It's the storm. If we can get rid of the storm, get visibility, we can use our range. . . ." As he speaks, he sets fire to the roots, now creeping closer. Flame races its length, charring the plant. It just grows back. "We need windweavers. Blow the clouds away."

"House Laris. So we hold until they get here?"

"Hold and hope they're enough."

"Fine. As for this . . ." I nod at the gap widening by the second. Soon a Silver army will burst right through. "Let's give them an explosive welcome."

Cal nods, understanding. "Bombers!" he roars over the howling wind and snow. "Get down there and be ready!" Pointing, he indicates the street running just inside the outer wall. The first place Lakelanders will overrun us.

A dozen or so bombers hear him and obey, peeling off their posts to man the street. My feet move of their own accord, intending to follow. Cal grabs my wrist and I almost skid. "I didn't say you," he growls. "You stay right here."

Quickly, I peel his fingers away. The grip is too tight, heavy as a manacle. Even in the heat of battle, I find myself thrown back through time, to a palace where I was a prisoner. "Cal, I'm going to help the bombers hold. I can do that." His bronze eyes flicker in the darkness, the red flames of two blazing candles. "If they breach the wall, you're going to be surrounded. And then the storm will be the least of our worries."

His decision is quick—and stupid. "Fine, I'll come."

"They need you up here." I put a palm to his chest, pushing him away from me. "Farley, Townsend, Akkadi—the soldiers need generals on the line. They need *you* on the line."

If not for the battle, Cal would argue. He just grazes my hand. There's no time for anything. Especially when I'm right.

"I'll be fine," I tell him as I jump away, sliding over frozen stones. The storm eats his response. I spare one heartbeat to worry for him, to wonder if we might never see each other again. The next heartbeat erases the thought. I have no time for it. I have to stay focused. I have to stay alive.

I pick up my feet up and slide down the stairs, the frozen rails slipping through my curled hands. On the street, out of the wind, the air is much warmer and the puddles are gone. Either frozen or the water was used above to assault the defenders of the Corvium wall.

Bombers face the crack in the wall, spreading farther with each second. Up on the ramparts it widens to several feet, but here the crack is just inches—and growing. Another shudder runs through the stone and below my feet, like an explosion or an earthquake in the ground. I swallow hard, imagining a strongarm on the other side of the wall, her fists raining blow after blow upon our foundations.

"Wait to strike," I tell the bombers. They look to me for orders, even though I'm not an officer. "No explosions until it's clear they're coming through. We don't need to help them along."

"I'll shield the breach as long as possible," a voice says behind me.

I whirl to see Davidson, his face streaked in gray blood steadily turning black. He looks pale beneath the blood, stunned by it. "Premier," I mutter, dipping my head. He responds after a long moment. Dazed by the battle. So different on the field than it is in the war room.

Instead, I turn my electricity on our attackers. Using the roots as a map, I run lightning along the plant matter, letting it curl and spiral with the path of the root. I can't see the greenwarden at the far side, but I feel him. Though dulled by the dense root, my sparks ripple through his body. A distant shriek echoes through the cracks in the stone, somehow audible over the chaos above and around.

The greenwarden isn't the only Silver able to bring down stone. Another takes his place, a strongarm judging by the way the stone shudders and cracks. Blow after blow sends rubble and dust through the widening gap.

Davidson stands on my left, mouth slightly agape. Numb.

"First battle?" I mutter as another thunderous strike hits home.

"Hardly," he says, to my surprise. "I was a soldier once too. I'm told I was on a list of yours?"

Dane Davidson. The name flutters in my mind, a butterfly brushing wings against the bars of a bone cage. It comes back as if through mud, slowly, with great effort. "Julian's list."

He nods. "Smart man, Jacos. Connecting dots no one else even sees. Yes, I was one of the Nortan Reds to be executed by their legion. For crimes of blood, not body. When I escaped, the officers marked me as dead anyway. So they didn't have to explain another lost criminal." He licks lips cracked by the cold. "I fled to Montfort, collecting others like me along the way."

Another crack. The gap before us widens as feeling returns to my toes. I wiggle them in my boots, preparing to fight. "Sounds familiar."

Davidson's voice gains strength and momentum as he speaks. As he remembers what we are fighting for. "Montfort was in ruin. A thousand Silvers claiming their own crowns, every mountain its own kingdom, the country splintered beyond recognition. Only Reds stood united. And Ardents were in the shadows, waiting to be unleashed. Divide and conquer, Miss Barrow. It's the only way to beat them."

The Kingdom of Norta, the Kingdom of the Rift, Piedmont, the Lakelands. Silvers at one another's throats, squabbling for smaller and smaller pieces while we wait to take the whole lot. Though Davidson looks overwhelmed, I can almost smell the steel in his bones. A genius, perhaps, and dangerous certainly.

A gust of snow brings me back. The only thing I need to be concerned with is what happens now. *Survive. Win.*

Blue-tinged energy bursts through the splintering wall, pulsing across the foot-wide expanse of emptiness. Davidson holds the shield in place with an outstretched hand. A drop of blood drips off his chin, steaming in the cold.

A silhouette on the other side pummels the shield, fists raining knuckled hell down on the rippling field. Another strongarm joins the shadow and works to widen the gap, attacking stone instead. The shield grows with their efforts.

"Be ready," Davidson says. "When I split the shield, fire with everything."

We obey, preparing to strike.

"Three."

Purple sparks web between my fingers and weave into a pulsing ball of destructive light.

"Two."

The bombers kneel in formation, like snipers. Instead of guns, they just have their fingers and eyes.

"One."

With a twitch, the blue shield cuts in two and slams the pair of strongarms into the walls with sickening cracks of bone. We fire through the opening, my lightning a blaze. It illuminates the darkness beyond, showing a dozen berserker soldiers ready to rush the breach. Many drop to their knees, spitting fire and blood as the bombers explode their insides. Before any can recover, Davidson seals the shield again, catching a returning volley of bullets.

He looks surprised by our success.

On the wall above us, a fireball churns in the black storm, a torch against the false night. Cal's fire spreads and strikes in a snake of flame. The red heat turns the sky to scarlet hell.

I just clench a fist and gesture at Davidson.

"Again," I tell him.

It's impossible to mark the passage of time. Without the sun, I have no idea how long we spend battling the breach. Even though we push back the assault again and again, every attempt widens the gap bit by bit. *Inches for miles,* I tell myself. On the wall, the wave of soldiers has not won the ramparts. The ice bridges keep coming back, and we keep fighting them. A few corpses land in the street, beyond even a healer's touch. Between strikes, we drag the bodies into the alleyways, out of sight. I search each dead face, holding my breath every time. Not Cal, not Farley. The only one I recognize is Townsend, his neck snapped clean. I expect a wash of guilt or pity, but I feel nothing. Just the knowledge that strongarms are up on the walls as well, tearing our soldiers apart.

Davidson's shield stretches across the gap in the wall, now at least ten feet wide, yawning open like stone jaws. Bodies lie in the open mouth. Smoking corpses felled by lightning, or brutally ripped open by a bomber's merciless stare. Through the quivering field of blue, shadows gather in the darkness, waiting to try our wall again. Hammers of water and ice batter against Davidson's ability. A banshee scream reverberates off its expanse, and even the echo is painful to our ears. Davidson winces. Now the blood on his face streaks with sweat dripping down his forehead, nose, and cheeks. He sprints toward his limit, and we are running out of time.

"Someone get me Rafe!" I shout. "And Tyton."

A runner sprints off as soon as the words are out of my mouth, vaulting up the steps to find them. I watch the wall above, searching for a familiar silhouette.

Cal works a manic rhythm, perfect as a machine. Step, turn, strike. Step, turn, strike. Like me, he finds an empty place where survival is the only thought. At every break in the oncoming rush of enemies, he re-forms his soldiers, directing the Reds in their fire, or working with Akkadi and Lory to eliminate another target in the darkness. How many are dead, I can't say.

Another corpse tumbles from the ramparts, end over end. I grab his arms to drag him off before I realize his armor is not armor at all, but scaled pieces of stony flesh, smoldering with the heat of a fire prince's anger. I draw back surprised, as if burned myself. A stoneskin. The few clothes on his dead body are blue and gray. House Macanthos. Norta. One of Maven's.

I swallow hard against the implication. Maven's forces have reached the walls. We aren't just fighting Lakelanders anymore. A roar of fury rises in my chest and I almost wish I could storm through the breach myself. Tear through everything on the other side. Hunt him down. Kill him between his army and mine.

Then the corpse grabs me.

He twists, and my wrist breaks with a snap. I shriek against the sudden bleeding pain racing up my arm.

Lightning ripples from my flesh, escaping me like a scream. It covers his body in purple sparks and lethal, dancing light. But either his stony flesh is too thick or his resolve is too strong. The stoneskin does not let go, his pincerlike fingers now clawing at my neck. Explosions blossom along his back, the work of bombers. Bits of stone slough off him like dead skin and he howls. His grip only tightens with the pain. I make the mistake of trying to pry off his hands, now locked around my throat. His rocky flesh cuts my skin, and blood wells up between my fingers, red and hot in the frozen air.

Spots dance before my eyes, and I loose another blast of lightning, letting it pour from my agony. The blow rockets him off me and back into a building. He crashes through headfirst, body hanging out into the street. The bombers finish him off, exploding through the exposed skin on his back.

Davidson trembles on his feet, still holding the thinning shield. He saw it all, and could do nothing unless he wanted the invading force to overrun us. A corner of his mouth quivers, as if to apologize for making the right decision.

"How much longer can you hold?" I ask, gasping out the words. I spit blood on the street.

He grits his teeth. "A little while."

That's not helpful, I want to snap. "A minute? Two?"

"One," he forces out.

"One will do."

I glare through the shield as it weakens, the vivid shade of blue fading with Davidson's strength. As it clears, so do the figures on the other side. Blue armor and black cut with red. Lakelands and Norta. No crown, no king. Just shock troops meant to overwhelm us. Maven won't set foot in Corvium unless the city is his. While the Calore brother on the wall will fight to the death, Maven is not foolish enough to risk himself in a fight. He knows his strength is behind the lines, on a throne rather than a battlefield.

Rafe and Tyton approach from opposite sides, having held their stretch of wall. While Rafe looks meticulous, green hair still slicked back from his face, Tyton is positively painted in blood. All silver. He isn't wounded. His eyes glow with a strange kind of anger, burning red in the churning firelight over our heads.

I note Darmian along with a number of other wreckers, all of them gifted with invulnerable flesh. They carry wicked axes, their edges worked to razor sharpness. Good to combat strongarms. At close range, they're our best chance.

"Form up," Tyton says, taciturn to a fault.

We follow, organizing into hasty lines at Davidson's back. His arm shakes as we move, holding on as long as he can. Rafe takes my left, Tyton my right. I glance between them, wondering if I should say something. I can feel the static energy blooming from them both, familiar but strange. Their electricity, not mine.

In the storm, the blue thunder continues to rage. Ella fuels us, and we leech to her lightning.

"Three," Davidson says.

Green on my left, white on my right. The colors flicker on the edge of my vision, each spark a tiny heartbeat.

"Two."

I suck in one more breath. My throat aches, bruised by the stone-skin. But I'm still breathing.

"One."

Again the shield collapses, opening our insides to the oncoming storm.

"BREACH!" echoes along the ramparts as the forces turn their attention on the gap in the wall. The Silver army responds in kind, surging toward us with a deafening yell. Green and purple lightning shudders through the killing ground, leaping along the first wave of soldiers. Tyton moves like a man throwing darts, his minuscule needles of lightning exploding into blinding bolts that toss Silver troops into the air. Many seize and twitch. He has no mercy.

The bombers follow our lead, moving with us as we close the breach. They only need an open line of sight to work, and their destruction churns stone, flesh, and earth in equal measure. Dirt falls with the snow, and the air tastes like ash. Is this what war is? Is this what it feels like to fight in the Choke? Tyton tosses me back, throwing out an arm to move my body. Darmian and the other wreckers surge before us, a human shield. Their axes cut in and out, spraying blood until the ruined walls on either side are coated in mirrored swaths of liquid silver.

No. I remember the Choke. The trenches. The horizon stretched in every direction, reaching down to meet a land cratered by decades of bloodshed. Each side knew the other. That war was evil, but defined. This is just a nightmare.

Soldier after soldier, Lakelander and Nortan, pulses into the breach.

Each pushed by the man or woman behind. As on the bridges, they funnel into a killing ground. The crowd moves like the pull of the ocean, one wave drawing us back before the other goes forward. We have the advantage, but only slightly. More strongarms pummel at the walls, hoping to widen the gap. Telkies lob rubble into our line, pulverizing one of the bombers, while another freezes solid, mouth fixed open in a silent scream.

Tyton dances with fluid movements, each palm blazing with white lightning. I use web on the ground, spreading a puddle of electric energy beneath the pounding feet of the advancing army. Their bodies pile up, threatening to form another wall across the breach. But the telkies just wave them away, sending corpses spinning into the black storm.

I taste blood, but my broken wrist is just a buzz of pain now. It hangs limp at my side, and I'm grateful for the adrenaline that won't let me feel the snapped bone.

The street and earth turn to liquid beneath my feet, running with red and silver. The swampy ground claims more than a few. When a newblood falls, a nymph jumps on him, pouring water down his nose and throat. He drowns before my eyes. Another corpse lies on her side, roots curling from her eyeballs. All I know is lightning. I can't remember my name, my purpose, what I'm fighting for—beyond the air in my lungs. Beyond one more second of life.

A telky splits us apart, sending Rafe flying backward. Then me in the opposite direction. I spiral forward, over the top of the force pushing through the wall breach. To the other side. To the killing fields of Corvium.

I land hard, rolling end over end until I come to an abrupt stop, half buried in freezing mud. A bolt of pain spikes through my adrenaline shield, reminding me of a very broken bone and perhaps a few more. The storm winds tear at my clothes as I try to sit up, shards of ice scraping at my eyes and cheeks. Even though the wind howls, it isn't so dark out here. Not black, but gray. A blizzard at dusk rather than midnight. I squint back and forth, too winded to do anything but lie in pain.

What were open fields, green lawns sloping off either side of the Iron Road, are now frozen tundra, each blade of grass like a razor of icicle. From this angle, Corvium is impossible to make out. Just like we couldn't see through the pitch black of the storm, neither can the assaulting forces. It hinders them as much as us. Several battalions cluster like shadows, cutting silhouettes against the storm. Some attempt the ice bridges still forming and re-forming, but now most surge toward the breach. The rest lie in wait behind me, a smudge outside the worst of the storm. Maybe hundreds held in reserve, maybe thousands. Blue and red flags snap in the wind, just bright enough to make out. *Caught between a rock and a hard place,* I sigh to myself. And I'm stuck in the mud, surrounded by corpses and the walking wounded. At least most are focused on themselves, on missing limbs or split bellies, rather than a single Red girl in their midst.

Lakelander soldiers dart around me, and I brace myself for the worst. But they march on, stomping for the thundering clouds and the rest of the army slouching toward destruction. "Get to the healers!" one of them shouts over their shoulder, not even looking back. I look down, realizing I'm covered in silver blood. Some red, but mostly silver.

Quickly, I rub mud over my bleeding wounds and the bits of my uniform that are still green. The cuts sear with pain, making me hiss through my teeth. I look back at the clouds, watching lightning pulse within. Blue at the crown, green at the base, where the breach is. Where I have to get back to.

The mud sucks at my limbs, trying to freeze solid around me. With my broken wrist tucked against my chest, I push off with one arm, fighting to be free. I pull away with a loud pop and start sprinting, heaving breath after breath. Each one burns.

I make it ten yards, almost to the back of the Silver army, before I realize this isn't going to work. They're packed too tightly to slip through, even for me. And they'll probably stop me if I try. My face is well known, even covered in mud. I can't chance it. Or the ice bridges. One might crumble beneath me, or the Red soldiers might shoot me dead as I try to get back over the wall. Each choice ends badly. But so does standing here. Maven's forces will push another assault and send another wave of troops. I see no way forward and no way back. For one terrifying, empty moment, I stare at the blackness of Corvium. Lightning flickers within the storm, weaker than before. It seems a towering hurricane topped with a thunderhead, layered with a blizzard and gale-force winds. I feel small against it, a single star in a sky of violent constellations.

How can we defeat this?

The first scream of a jet sends me to my knees, covering my head with my good hand. It ripples in my chest, a burst of electricity hammering like a heart. A dozen follow at low altitude, their engines spiraling the snow and ash as they scream between the two halves of the army.

More jets spiral on the outer edge of the storm, around and around, carving through it. The clouds drift with the jets, as if magnetized to the wings. Then I hear another roar. Another wind, stronger than the first, blowing with the fury of a hundred hurricanes. The wind works to clear the storm, tearing it apart with force. The clouds part enough to show the towers of Corvium, where blue lightning reigns. The wind follows the jets, pooling beneath their freshly painted wings.

Painted bright yellow.

House Laris.

My lips tug into a smile. They're here. Anabel Lerolan kept her word.

I look for the other houses, but a falcon screams around me, its blue-black wings beating the air. Talons gleam, sharp as a blade, and I jump back to cover my face from the bird. It just screeches keenly before flapping away, gliding over the battleground toward—oh no.

Maven's reserves are coming. Battalions, legions. Black armor, blue armor, red armor. I'm going to be smashed between both halves of his army.

Not without a fight.

I let loose, purple bolts rocketing down around me. Pushing back soldiers, making them question every step. They know what my abilities look like. They've seen what the lightning girl can do. They pause, but only for a moment. Enough to let me set my feet and turn, angling my body. Smaller target, larger chance of survival. My good fist clenches, ready to take them all down with me.

Many of the Silvers assaulting the breach turn in my direction. The distraction is their downfall. Green lightning and white pulse through them, clearing the way for red flame as it charges toward me.

The swifts close the distance first and catch a web of lightning. Some zip backward but others fall, unable to outrun sparks. Storm bolts, crackling out of the sky, keep the worst at bay, forming a protective circle around me. From the outside, it looks like a cage of electricity, but it's a cage of my own making. A cage I control.

I dare any king to put me in a cage now.

I expect my lightning to draw him, like a moth to a candle flame.

I search the oncoming horde for Maven. A red cape, a crown of iron flames. A white face in the sea, his eyes blue enough to pierce mountains.

Instead, the Laris jets move in for another pass, swooping low over both armies. They split around me, making soldiers scramble for cover as screaming metal rushes overhead. A dozen or so figures tumble from the backs of the larger jets, somersaulting on the air before plummeting to the ground at a speed that would pancake most humans. Instead, they throw out their arms, stopping themselves abruptly, churning up dirt, ash, and snow. And iron. Lots of iron.

Evangeline and her family, brother and father included, turn to face the oncoming army. The falcon keens around them, screaming as it darts on the harsh wind. Evangeline spares a glance over her shoulder, her eyes finding mine.

"Don't make this a habit!" she shouts.

Exhaustion hits me because, strangely, I feel safe.

Evangeline Samos has my back.

Fire blazes at the edge of my vision on either side. It hems me in, almost blinding. I stumble back and hit a wall of muscle and tactical armor. Cal cradles my broken wrist, holding it gently.

For once, I don't remember the manacles.

TWENTY-NINE
Evangeline

The doors of Corvium's administrative tower are solid oak, but their hinges and trimmings are iron. They glide open in front of us, bowing before the Royal House of Samos. We enter the council chamber gracefully, in front of the eyes of our patchwork excuse for an alliance. Montfort and the Scarlet Guard sit on the left, simple in their green uniforms, our Silvers on the right in their varying house colors. Their respective leaders, Premier Davidson and Queen Anabel, watch us enter in silence. Anabel wears her crown now, marking herself as a queen, albeit to a long-dead king. It's a beaten ring of rose gold, set with tiny black gems. Simple. But it stands out all the same. She drums her deadly fingers on the flat of the table, eagerly displaying her wedding ring. A fiery red jewel, also set in rose gold. Like Davidson, she has the look of a predator, never blinking, never distracted. Prince Tiberias and Mare Barrow are not here, or else I can't see them. I wonder if they'll split to their respective sides and colors.

Windows on every side of the tower room open on the land, where the air still smolders with ash and the western fields are choked in mud, flooded and swamped by the extraseasonal catastrophe. Even this high up, everything smells like blood. I scrubbed my hands for what seemed like hours, washing every inch, and still I can't get rid of the scent. It clings like a ghost, harder to forget than the faces of the people I killed on the field. The metallic tang infects everything.

Despite the commanding view, all eyes focus on the more commanding person leading our family. Father has no black robes, just his chromium armor shimmering like a mirror melded to his trim form. A warrior king in every inch. Mother does not disappoint either. Her crown of green stones matches the emerald boa constrictor draped around her neck and shoulders like a shawl. It slithers slowly, scales reflecting the afternoon light. Ptolemus looks similar to Father, though the armor painted to his broad chest, narrow waist, and lean legs is black as oil. Mine is a mix of both, striped in skintight layers of chromium and black steel. It isn't the armor I wore on the field, but the armor I need now. Terrible, threatening, showing every ounce of Samos pride and power.

Four chairs like thrones are set against the windows, and we sit as one, presenting a united front. No matter how much I want to scream.

I feel like a traitor to myself, having let days, weeks pass without opposition. Without so much as a whisper of how much Father's plan terrifies me. I don't want to be queen of Norta. I don't want to belong to anyone. But what I want doesn't matter. Nothing will threaten my father's machinations. King Volo is not one to be denied. Not by his own daughter, his flesh and blood. His possession.

An all-too-familiar ache rises in my chest as I settle onto my throne. I do my best to keep composed, quiet, and dutiful. Loyal to my blood. It's all I know.

I haven't spoken to my father in weeks. I can only nod to his commands. Words are beyond my ability. If I open my mouth, I fear my temper will get the best of me. It was Tolly's idea to stay quiet. *Give it time, Eve. Give it time.* But time for what, I have no idea. Father doesn't change his mind. And Queen Anabel is hell-bent on pushing her grandson back to the throne. My brother is just as disappointed as I am. Everything we did—marrying him to Elane, betraying Maven, supporting Father's kingly ambitions—was so we could stay together. All for nothing. He'll rule in the Rift, married to the girl I love, while I'm shipped off like a crate of ammunition, once more a gift to a king.

I'm grateful for the distraction when Mare Barrow decides to grace the council with her presence, Prince Tiberias trailing at her heels. I forgot what a tragic puppy he became in her presence, all wide eyes begging for attention. His keen soldier sense trains on her instead of the task at hand. Both of them are still vibrating with adrenaline from the siege, and no wonder. It was a brutal thing. Barrow still has blood on her uniform.

Both trek down the central aisle splitting the council. If they feel the weight of their action, they don't show it. Most conversation reduces to a murmur or stops altogether to watch the pair, waiting to see which side of the room they choose.

Mare is quick, stalking past the front row of green uniforms to lean against the far wall. Out of the spotlight.

The prince, the rightful king of Norta, doesn't follow. He approaches his grandmother instead, one hand outstretched to embrace her. Anabel is much smaller than him, reduced to an old woman in his presence. But her arms encircle him easily. They have the same eyes, burning like heated bronze. She grins up at him.

Tiberias lingers in her embrace, just for a moment, holding on to the last piece of his family. The seat beside his grandmother is empty, but he doesn't take it. He elects to join Mare at the wall. He crosses his arms over his broad chest, fixing Father with a heated stare. I wonder if he knows what she has planned for the two of us.

No one takes the seat he left behind. No one dares take the place of the rightful heir to Norta. *My beloved betrothed* echoes in my head. The words taunt me worse than my mother's snakes.

Suddenly, with a flick of his hand, Father drags Salin Iral by his belt buckle, pulling him up from his seat, over his table, and across the oak floor. No one protests, or makes a sound.

"You're supposed to be hunters."

Father's voice rumbles low in his throat.

Iral didn't bother to wash off after the battle, evidenced by the sweat matting his black hair. Or maybe he's just petrified. I wouldn't blame him. "Your Majesty—"

"You ensured Maven would not escape. I believe your exact words, my lord, were 'no snake can escape a silk fist.'" Father doesn't condescend to look at this failure of a lord, an embarrassment to his house and his name. Mother watches enough for both of them, seeing with her own eyes as well as the eyes of the green snake. It notices me staring and flicks its forked pink tongue in my direction.

Others watch Salin's humiliation. The Reds look dirtier than Salin, some of them still caked in mud and blue with cold. At least they aren't drunk. Lord General Laris sways in his chair, sipping conspicuously from a flask larger than anything one should have in polite company. Not that Father or Mother or anyone else will begrudge him the liquor. Laris and his house did their job beautifully, bringing airjets to the cause while dissipating that infernal storm threatening to snow Corvium under. They proved their worth.

As did the newbloods. Silly as their chosen name sounds, they held off the attack for hours. Without their blood and sacrifice, Corvium would be back in Maven's hands. Instead, he failed a second time. He has been defeated twice. Once by rabble, and now at the hands of a proper army and a proper king. My gut twists. Even though we won, the victory feels like defeat to me.

Mare glowers at the exchange, her entire body tensing like a twisting wire. Her eyes tick between Salin and my father, before straying to Tolly. I feel a tremor of fear for my brother, even though she promised not to kill him. In Caesar's Square she unleashed a wrath like I've never seen. And on the Corvium battlefield she held her own, even surrounded by an army of Silvers. Her lightning is far deadlier than I remember. If she chose to murder Tolly right now, I doubt anyone could stop her. Punish her, of course, but not stop her.

I have a feeling she won't be terribly pleased by Anabel's plan. Any Silver woman in love with a king would be content to be a consort, bound though not married—but I don't believe Reds think that way. They have no idea how important the house bonds are, or how deeply vital heirs of strong blood have always been. They think love matters when wedding vows are spoken. I suppose that is a small blessing in their lives. Without power, without strength, they have nothing to protect and no legacy to uphold. Their lives are inconsequential, but still, their lives are their own.

As I thought mine was, for a few brief, foolish weeks.

On the battlefield, I told Mare Barrow not to make a habit of letting me save her. Ironic. Now I hope she saves me from a queen's gilded prison, and a king's bridal cage. I hope her storm destroys the alliance before it even takes root.

". . . prepares for escape as well as attack. Swifts were in place, transports, airjets. We never even saw Maven." Salin keeps up his protest, hands raised above his head. Father lets him. Father always gives a person enough rope to hang themselves. "The Lakelander king was there. He commanded his troops himself."

Father's eyes flash and darken, the only indication of his sudden discomfort. "And?"

"And now he lies in a grave with them." Salin glances up at his steel king, a child searching for approval. He trembles down to his fingertips. I think of Iris left behind in Archeon, a new queen on a poisoned throne. And now without her father, cut off from the only family who came south at her side. She was formidable, to say the least, but this will weaken her immensely. If she weren't my enemy, I might feel pity.

Slowly, Father rises from his throne. He looks thoughtful. "Who killed the king of the Lakelands?"

The noose tightens.

Salin grins. "I did."

The noose snaps, and so does Father. With a clenched fist, in the blink of an eye, he twists Salin's buttons off his jacket, rolling them into thin spindles of iron. Each one wraps around his neck, pulling, forcing Salin to stand. They keep rising, until his toes scrabble against the floor, searching for purchase.

At the tables, the Montfort leader leans back in his chair. The woman next to him, a very severe blonde with facial scars, curls her lips into a scowl. I remember her from the attack on Summerton, the one that almost took my brother's life. Cal tortured her himself and now they're practically side by side. She's Scarlet Guard, highly ranked, and, if I'm not mistaken, one of Mare's closest allies.

"Your orders—" Salin chokes out. He claws at the iron threads around his neck, digging into his flesh. His face grays as blood pools beneath his flesh.

"My orders were to kill Maven Calore or prevent his escape. You did neither."

"I—"

"Killed a king of sovereign nation. An ally of Norta who had no reason to do anything but defend the new Lakelander queen. But now?" Father scoffs, using his ability to draw Salin closer. "You've given them a rather wonderful incentive to drown us all. The ruling queen of the Lakelands will not stand for this." He slaps Salin across the face with a resounding crack. The blow is meant to shame, not hurt. It works well. "I strip you of your titles and responsibilities. House Iral, redistribute them as you see fit. And get this worm out of my sight."

Salin's family is quick to drag him from the chamber before he can dig a deeper hole. When the iron threads spring free, all he does is cough and perhaps cry. His sobs echo in the hall but are quickly cut off by the slamming of the doors. A pathetic man. Though I'm glad he didn't kill Maven. If the Calore brat died today, there would be no obstacle between Cal and the throne. Cal and me. This way, at least, there is some dark hope.

"Does anyone have anything useful to contribute?" Father sits back down smoothly and runs a finger down the spine of Mother's snake. Its eyes slide shut in pleasure. Disgusting.

Jerald Haven looks like he wants to disappear in his chair, and he just might. He stares at his folded hands, willing my father not to humiliate him next. Luckily, he's saved by the scowling Scarlet Guard commander. She stands, scraping back her seat.

"Our intelligence indicates that Maven Calore now relies on eyes to keep him safe. They can see the immediate future—"

Mother clucks her tongue. "We know what an eye is, Red."

"Good for you," the commander replies without hesitation.

If not for Father and our precarious position, I expect Mother would ram her emerald snake down the Red's throat. She just purses her lips. "Control your people, Premier, or I will."

"I'm a Command general of the Scarlet Guard, Silver," the woman spits back. I catch Mare smirking behind her. "If you want our help, you're going to show some respect."

"Of course," Mother concedes graciously. Her gems sparkle as she dips her head. "Respect where respect is due."

The commander still glowers, her rage boiling. She eyes my mother's crown with disgust.

Thinking quickly, I clap my hands together. A familiar sound. A summons. Quietly, a Red maid of House Samos scampers into the chamber, a glass of wine in hand. She knows her orders and darts to my side, offering me the drink. With slow, exaggerated movements, I take the cup. I never break eye contact with the Red commander as I drink. My fingers drum along the etched glass to hide my nerves. At worst, I'll make Father angry. At best . . .

I smash the glass goblet on the floor. Even I flinch at the sound and the implication. Father tries not to react, but his mouth tightens. *You should know me better than this. I'm not giving up without a fight.*

Without hesitation, the maid kneels to clean it up, sweeping shards of glass into her bare hands. And without hesitation, the fierce Red woman vaults over her table, setting off a flurry of motion. Silvers jump to their feet, as do Reds, and Mare herself pushes off the wall, angling herself across her friend's path.

The Red commander towers over her, but Barrow holds her back all the same.

"How can we accept this?" the woman shouts at me, thrusting a fist at the maid on the floor. The tang of blood increases tenfold as she slices her hands. "How?"

Everyone in the room seems to be wondering the same thing. Shouts rise between more volatile members of each side. We are Silver houses of noble and ancient blood, allied with rebels, criminals, servants, and thieves. Abilities or not, our ways of life stand in direct opposition. Our goals are not the same. The council chamber is a powder keg. If I'm lucky it will explode. Blow apart any threat of marriage. Destroy the cage they want to put me back in.

Over Mare's shoulder, the commander sneers at me, her eyes like two blue daggers. If this room and my own clothes weren't dripping with metal, I might be afraid. I stare back at her, looking every inch the Silver princess she was raised to hate. At my feet, the maid finishes her work and shuffles away, her hands pincushioned with pieces of glass. I make a mental note to send Wren to heal her later.

"Poorly done," Mother whispers in my ear. She pats my arm and the snake slithers along her hand, curling over my skin. Its flesh is clammy and cold.

I grit my teeth against the sensation.

"How can we accept this?"

The prince's voice cuts the chaos. It stuns many into silence, including the sneering Red commander. Mare bodily removes her, escorting her back to her chair with some difficulty. The rest turn to the exiled prince, watching him as he straightens. The months have been good to Tiberias Calore. A life of war suits him. He seems vibrant and alive, even after narrowly escaping death on the walls. In her seat, his grandmother allows herself the smallest smile. I feel my heart sink in my chest. I don't like that look. My hands claw the arms of my throne, nails digging into wood instead of flesh.

"Every single person in this room knows we have reached a tipping point." His eyes wander to find Mare. He draws his strength from her. If I were a sentimental person, I might be moved. Instead, I think of Elane, left safely behind at Ridge House. Ptolemus has need of an heir, and neither of us wanted her in the battle. Even so, I wish she were here to sit beside me. I wish I didn't have to suffer this alone.

Cal was trained to statecraft, and he is no stranger to speeches. Still, he's not as talented as his brother, and he trips up more than a few times as he prowls the floor. Unfortunately, no one seems to mind. "Reds have lived their lives as glorified slaves, bonded to their lots. Be it in a slum town, in one of our palaces—or in the mud of a river village." A flush spreads across Mare's cheeks. "I used to think as I was taught. That our ways were set. Reds were inferior. Changing their place would never come to pass, not without bloodshed. Not without great sacrifice. Once, I thought those things were too high a cost to pay. But I was wrong.

"To those of you who disagree"—he glares at me, and I tremble—"who believe yourself better, who believe yourself gods, you are wrong. And not because people like the lightning girl exist. Not because we suddenly find ourselves in need of allies to defeat my brother. Because you are simply wrong.

"I was born a prince. I knew more privilege than almost anyone here. I was raised with servants at my beck and call, and I was taught that their blood, because of a color, meant less than mine. 'Reds are stupid; Reds are rats; Reds are incapable of controlling their own lives; Reds are meant to serve.' These are words we've all heard. And they are lies. Convenient ones that make our lives easier, our shame nonexistent, and their lives unbearable."

He stops next to his grandmother, tall at her side. "It can't be tolerated anymore. It simply can't be. Difference is not division."

Poor, naive Calore. His grandmother nods in approval, but I remember her in my own house, and what she said. She wants her grandson on the throne, and she wants the old world.

"Premier," Tiberias says, gesturing to the Montfort leader.

With a clearing of his throat, the man stands. Taller than most, but weedy. He has the look of a pale fish with an equally empty expression. "King Volo, we thank you for your aid in the defense of Corvium. And here, now, before the eyes of our leadership and your own, I would like to know your sentiments on what Prince Tiberias has just said."

"If you have a question, Premier, ask it," Father rumbles.

The man keeps his face still, unreadable. I get the sense he hides as many secrets and ambitions as the rest of us. Would that I could put the screws to him. "Red and Silver, Your Majesty. Which color rises in this rebellion?"

A muscle quivers in one pale cheek as my father exhales. He runs a hand through his pointed beard. "Both, Premier. This is a war for us both. On this you have my word, sworn on the heads of my children."

Thank you so much, Father. The Red commander would collect that price with a smile if given the opportunity.

"Prince Tiberias speaks truthfully," Father continues, lying though his teeth. "Our world has changed. We must change with it. Common enemies make strange allies, but we are allies all the same."

As with Salin, I sense a noose tightening. It loops around my neck, threatening to hang me above the abyss. Is this what the rest of my life will feel like? I want to be strong. This is what I trained and suffered for. This is what I thought I wanted. But freedom was too sweet. One gasp of it and I can't let go. *I'm sorry, Elane. I'm so sorry.*

"Do you have other questions about the terms, Premier Davidson?" Father pushes on. "Or shall we continue planning the overthrow of a tyrant?"

"And what terms would those be?" Mare's voice sounds different, and no wonder. I knew her last as a prisoner, smothered almost beyond recognition. Her sparks have returned with a vengeance. She glances between Father and her premier, looking to them for answers.

Father is almost gleeful as he explains, and I hold my breath. *Save me, Mare Barrow. Loose the storm I know you have. Bewitch the prince as you always do.*

"The Kingdom of the Rift will stand in sovereignty after Maven is removed. The kings of steel will reign for generations. With allowances made for my Red citizens, of course. I have no intention of creating a slave state like the one Norta is."

Mare looks far from convinced, but holds her tongue.

"Of course, Norta will need a king of her own."

Her eyes widen. Horror bleeds through her, and she whips her head to Cal, looking for answers. He seems just as taken aback as she fumes. The lightning girl is easier to read than the pages of a children's book.

Anabel rises from her seat to stand proudly. Her lined face beams as she turns to Cal, putting a hand to his cheek. He's too shocked to react to her touch. "My grandson is the rightful king of Norta, and the throne belongs to him."

"Premier . . . ," Mare whispers, now looking at the Montfort leader. She is almost begging. A flicker of sadness pierces his mask.

"Montfort pledges to back the installment of Ca—" He stops himself. The man looks anywhere but at Mare Barrow. "King Tiberias."

A current of heat ripples on the air. The prince is angry, violently so. And the worst is yet to come, for all of us. If I'm lucky, he'll burn the tower down.

"We will cement the alliance between the Rift and the rightful king in the usual way," Mother says, twisting the knife. She enjoys this. It takes everything to keep my tears inside, where no one else can see.

The implication of her words is not lost on anyone. Cal gives a strangled sort of yelp, a gasp very unbecoming of a prince, let alone a king.

"Even after all this, Queenstrial still brought forth a royal bride." Mother runs a hand over mine, her fingers crossing where my wedding ring will be.

Suddenly the high chamber feels stifling, and the smell of blood crashes through my senses. It's all I can think about, and I lean into the distraction, letting the sharp iron bite overwhelm me. My jaw clenches, teeth tight against all the things I want to say. They rattle in my throat, begging to be loose. *I don't want this anymore. Let me go home.* Each word is a betrayal to my house, my family, my blood. My teeth grate against one another, bone on bone. A locked cage for my heart.

I feel trapped inside myself.

Make him choose, Mare. Make him turn me aside.

She breathes heavily, her chest rising and falling at rapid speed. Like me, she has too many words she wants to scream. I hope she sees how much I want to refuse.

"No one thought to consult me," the prince hisses, pushing his grandmother away. His eyes burn. He has perfected the art of glaring at a dozen people at once. "You mean to make me a king—without my consent?"

Anabel has no fear of flame and seizes his face again. "We're not making you anything. We're simply helping you be what you are. Your father died for your crown, and you want to throw it away? For who? Abandon your country? For what?"

He has no answer. *Say no. Say no. Say no.*

But already I see the tug. The lure. Power seduces all, and it makes us blind. Cal is not immune to it. If anything, he is particularly vulnerable. All his life he watched a throne, preparing for a day it would be his. I know firsthand that's not a habit a person can easily break. And I know firsthand that few things taste sweeter than a crown. I think of Elane again. Does he think of Mare?

"I need some air," he whispers.

Of course, Mare follows him out, sparks trembling in her wake.

On instinct, I almost call for another cup of wine. But I refrain. Mare isn't here to stop the commander if she snaps again, and more alcohol will just make me sicker than I already am.

"Long live Tiberias the Seventh," Anabel says.

The chamber echoes the sentiment. I only mouth the words. I feel poisoned.

EPILOGUE

He scrapes his bracelets together angrily, letting his wrists spit sparks. None of them catch or burst into flame. Spark after spark, each one cold and weak compared to mine. Useless. Futile. I follow him down a spiraling stair to a balcony. If it has a lovely view, I don't know. I don't have the capacity to see much farther than Cal. Everything inside me quivers.

Hope and fear battle through me in equal measure. I see it in Cal too, flashing behind his eyes. A storm rages in the bronze, two kinds of fire.

"You promised," I whisper, trying to tear him apart without moving a muscle.

Cal paces wildly before putting his back to the rails of the balcony. His mouth flops open and closed, searching for something to say. For any explanation. *He's not Maven. He's not a liar,* I have to remind myself. *He doesn't want to do this to you.* But will that stop him?

"I didn't think—what logical person could want me to be king after what I've done? Tell me if you truly thought anyone would let me near a throne," he says. "I've killed Silvers, Mare, my own people." He buries his face in his blazing hands, scrubbing them over his features. Like he wants to pull himself inside out.

"You killed Reds too. I thought you said there was no difference."

"Difference not division."

I snarl. "You make a wonderful speech about equality but let that Samos bastard sit there and claim a kingdom just like the one we want to end. Don't lie and say you didn't know about his terms, his new crown. . . ." My voice trails away before I can speak the rest aloud. And make it real.

"You know I had no idea."

"Not one?" I raise an eyebrow. "Not a whisper from your grandmother. Not even a dream of this?"

He swallows hard, unable to deny his deepest desires. So he doesn't even try. "There's nothing we can do to stop Samos. Not yet—"

I slap him across the face. His head moves with the momentum of the blow and stays that way, looking out to the horizon I refuse to see.

My voice cracks. "I'm not talking about Samos."

"I didn't know," he says, the words soft on the ash wind. Sadly, I believe him. It makes it harder to stay angry, and without anger I have only fear and sorrow. "I really didn't know."

Tears burn salty tracks down my cheeks, and I hate myself for crying. I just watched who knows how many people die, and killed many of them myself. How can I shed tears over this? Over one person still breathing right before my eyes?

My voice hitches. "Is this the part where I ask you to choose me?"

Because it is a choice. He need only say no. Or yes. One word holds both our fates.

Choose me. Choose the dawn. He didn't before. He has to now.

Shaking, I take his face in my hands and turn him to look at me. When he can't, when his bronze eyes focus on my lips or my shoulder or the brand exposed to the warm air, something inside me breaks.

"I don't have to marry her," he murmurs. "That can be negotiated."

"No, it can't. You know it can't." I laugh coldly at his absurd posturing.

His eyes darken. "And you know what marriage is to us—to Silvers. It doesn't mean anything. It has no bearing on what we feel, and who we feel for."

"Do you really think it's the marriage I'm angry about?" Rage boils in me, hot and wild and impossible to ignore. "Do you really think I have any ambition to be your—or anyone's—queen?"

Warm fingers tremble against mine, their grip tightening as I start to slip away. "Mare, think of what I can do. What kind of king I can be."

"Why does anyone need to be king at all?" I ask slowly, sharpening every word.

He has no answer.

In the palace, during my imprisonment, I learned that Maven had been made by his mother, formed into the monster he became. There is nothing on earth that can change him or what she did. But Cal was made too. All of us were made by someone else, and all of us have some thread of steel that nothing and no one can cut.

I thought Cal was immune to the corruptive temptation of power. How wrong I was.

He was born to be a king. It's what he was made for. It's what he was made to want.

"Tiberias." I've never said his real name before. It doesn't suit him. It doesn't suit us. But that's who he is. "Choose me."

His hands smooth over mine, his fingers splaying to match my own. As he does, I shut my eyes. I allow myself one long second to memorize what he feels like. Like that day in Piedmont, when the rainstorm caught us both, I want to burn. I want to burn.

"Mare," he whispers. "Choose me."

Choose a crown. Choose another king's cage. Choose a betrayal to everything you've bled for.

I find my thread of steel too. Thin but unbreakable.

"I am in love with you, and I want you more than anything else in the world." His words sound hollow coming from me. "Anything else in this world."

Slowly, my eyelids flutter open. He finds the spine to match my gaze.

"Think what we could do together," he murmurs, trying to pull me closer. My feet hold firm. "You know what you are to me. Without you, I have no one. I am alone. I have nothing left. Don't leave me alone."

My breathing turns ragged.

I kiss him for what could be, what might be, what will be—the last time. His lips feel strangely cold as we both turn to ice.

"You aren't alone." The hope in his eyes cuts deeply. "You have your crown."

I thought I knew what heartbreak was. I thought that was what Maven did to me. When he stood and left me kneeling. When he told me everything I ever thought him to be was a lie. But then, I believed I loved him.

I know now, I didn't know what love was. Or what even the echo of heartbreak felt like.

To stand in front of a person who is your whole world and be told you are not enough. You are not the choice. You are a shadow to the person who is your sun.

"Mare, please." He begs like a child in his desperation. "How did you think this was going to end? What did you really think would happen next?" I feel the heat of him even as every part of me goes cold. "You don't have to do this."

But I do.

I turn away, deaf to his protests. But he doesn't try to stop me. He lets me walk away.

Blood drowns out everything but my screaming thoughts. Terrible ideas, hateful words, broken and twisted like a bird without wings. They limp by, each one worse than the last. *Not a god's chosen, but a god's cursed.* That's what we all are.

It's a wonder I don't fall down the spiraling steps of the tower—a miracle I make it outside without collapsing. The sun overhead is hatefully bright, a harsh contrast to the abyss inside me. I shove a hand deep into my uniform pocket and barely register the sharp sting of something. It doesn't take long to realize—the earring. The one Cal gave me. I almost laugh at the thought of it. Another broken promise. Another Calore betrayal.

A burning need to run tugs at my heart. I want Kilorn, I want Gisa. I want Shade to appear and tell me this is another dream. I imagine them beside me, their words and open arms a comfort.

Another voice drowns them out. It burns my insides.

Cal follows orders, but he can't make choices.

I sigh at the thought of Maven's words. Cal did make a choice. And in the deepest parts of myself, I'm not surprised. The prince is as he has always been. A good person at his core, but unwilling to act. Unwilling to truly change himself. The crown is in his heart, and hearts do not change.

Farley finds me in an alley, staring at a wall with blank eyes, my tears long since dried. She hesitates for once, her boldness long gone. Instead, she approaches with almost tender slowness, a hand outstretched to touch my shoulder.

"I didn't know until you did," she murmurs. "I swear it."

The person she loved is dead, stolen by someone else. Mine chose to walk away. Chose everything I hate over everything I am. I wonder which hurts more.

Before I let myself relax into her, allow her to comfort me, I notice someone else standing nearby.

"I knew," Premier Davidson says. It sounds like an apology. At first I feel another surge of anger, but it isn't his fault. Cal didn't have to agree. Cal didn't have to let me go.

Cal didn't have to eagerly leap into a well-baited trap.

"Divide and conquer," I whisper, remembering his own words. The fog of heartbreak clears enough for me to understand. Montfort and the Scarlet Guard would never support a Silver king, not truly. Not without other motives in play.

Davidson nods his head. "It's the only way to beat them."

Samos, Calore, Cygnet. The Rift, Norta, the Lakelands. All driven by greed, all ready to break one another for an already-broken crown. All part of Montfort's own plan. I force another breath, and try to recover. Try to forget Cal, forget Maven, focus on the road ahead. Where it leads, I don't know.

Somewhere in the distance, somewhere in my bones, thunder rolls.

We're going to let them kill each other.

ACKNOWLEDGMENTS

Thank you to the armies of people who made and continue to make my books a possibility. To my editor Kristen and the entire editorial team, the HarperTeen and HarperCollins family, Gina, the Elizabeths (both Ward and Lynch), Margot, the best cover designer in the world, Sarah Kaufman, and the design team. To our foreign publishers and agents, the Universal film team, Sara, Elizabeth, Jay, Gennifer, and of course, the powerhouse that is New Leaf Literary. Suzie, always in my corner. Pouya, Kathleen, Mia, Jo, Jackie, Jaida, Hilary, Chris, Danielle, and Sara keeping my head on straight and coming through with some amazing notes to shape *King's Cage*. New Leaf is always pushing forward. And once more, to Suzie, because I can never thank her enough.

Thank you to the just as formidable army that is my friends and family. My parents, Lou and Heather, still the reason for all this and the drive behind everything I am. My brother, Andy, who is now a better adult than me. My grandparents, aunts and uncles, and cousins, with great love to Kim and Michelle, the closest things I have to sisters. Thank you to friends from my old home, Natalie, Alex, Katrina, Kim,

Lauren, and more. Thank you to friends from my new home, Bayan, Angela, Erin, Jenn, Ginger, Jordan, what seems like most of Culver City, and whoever ends up in the rocking chairs for PMCC Sunday. Thank you to my bunkmates in Slytherin Common Room, Jen and Morgan, and the missing bunkmate, Tori, who always has bedcouch waiting.

This might be a bragging paragraph, but I've made so many real friends and grown so much through meeting other authors over the past year. We have a weird job that I could not do without you guys. I would be remiss not to name, shame, and thank a few of you. First, Emma Theriault. Remember that name. Her support has been invaluable over the years. Thank you, in no particular order, to Adam Silvera, Renee Ahdieh, Leigh Bardugo, Jenny Han, Veronica Roth, Soman Chainani, Brendan Reichs, Dhonielle Clayton, Maurene Goo, Sarah Enni, Kara Thomas, Danielle Paige, and the entire YALL family. Warrior mother Margie Stohl. The first friend I ever made in this industry, Sabaa Tahir, who continues to be a torch against the night falling around us. My deepest love and admiration to Susan Dennard, who is not only an exemplary human, but a deeply talented writer with unparalleled insight into our craft. And of course, Alex Bracken, who tolerates too many text message rants to count, is both equally versed in *Star Wars* and American history, has the cutest child-emperor dog in the world, and is a truly steadfast, lovely, determined, intelligent friend who happens to be a crackerjack writer as well. I think I ran out of adjectives.

I'm blessed enough to have readers, and it goes without saying, I extend my deepest gratitude to each and every one of you. To quote JK, "no story lives unless someone wants to listen." Thank you for listening. And thank you to the entire YA community. You've been a light through the dark waves of 2016.

Last time around I thanked pizza, and that stands. Thank you to the National Parks and the National Parks Service, who continue to maintain and protect the natural beauty of the country I love. Happy 100th birthday! To learn more, volunteer, or donate, go to www.nps.gov/getinvolved. Our natural treasures must be protected for generations to come.

Thank you to Hillary Rodham Clinton, Bernie Sanders, Elizabeth Warren, President Barack Obama, First Lady Michelle Obama, and all those working to defend the rights of women, minorities, Muslim Americans, refugees, and LGBTQ+ Americans. Thank you to Mitt Romney for his unwavering opposition to demagoguery, and his patriotic duty to the United States. Thank you to John McCain for his continued fight against torture, as well as his years of service and his defense of military families. Thank you to Charlie Baker, Governor of Massachusetts, for his support of common sense gun reform, women's rights, and marriage equality. And just in case any of the above has an about-face by the time we publish, these acknowledgments were written in November 2016.

Thank you to the Khans, and to every Gold Star family in our nation. Thank you to every member of our military, every veteran, and every military family serving the United States with sacrifices most of us cannot fathom. And thank you to every educator in our country. You are the hands shaping the future.

Thank you to the people of Scotland, who voted against division and fear. Thank you to the elected representatives of California, who will continue to defend their constituents. Thank you to Lin-Manuel Miranda and the cast of *Hamilton*, who have performed a true service to our country through their lasting art. You guys are nonstop.

Thank you to everyone in positions of power who speak and stand against injustice, tyranny, and hatred in the United States, and across the globe. Thank you to everyone listening, and watching, and keeping your eyes open.

Turn the page to read an excerpt from

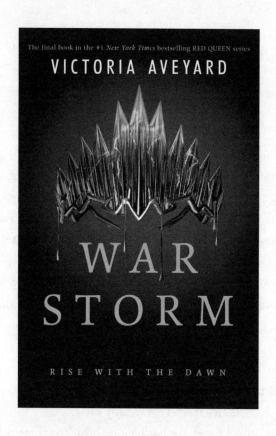

The final book in the #1 *New York Times* bestselling RED QUEEN series

VICTORIA AVEYARD

WAR STORM

RISE WITH THE DAWN

ONE
Mare

We drown in silence for a long moment.

Corvium yawns around us, full of people, but it feels empty.

Divide and conquer.

The implications are clear, the lines sharply drawn. Farley and Davidson regard me with equal intensity, and I stare back at them.

I suppose Cal has no idea, no inkling, that the Scarlet Guard and Montfort have absolutely no intention of letting him keep whatever throne he wins. I suppose he cares more about the crown than about whatever any Red thinks. And I suppose I shouldn't call him Cal anymore.

Tiberias Calore. King Tiberias. Tiberias the Seventh.

It's the name he was born with, the name he wore when I met him. *Thief*, he called me then. That was my name.

I wish I could forget the last hour. Fall backward just a little bit. Falter. Stumble. Enjoy one more second of that strangely blissful place where the only thing I felt was the ache of tired muscles and repaired bones. The emptiness after battle's adrenaline. The certainty of his love and support. And even through the heartbreak, I can't find it in myself to hate him for his choice. The rage will come later.

Concern crosses Farley's face. It seems strange on her. I'm more accustomed to cold determination or red anger from Diana Farley. She notes my stare with a twitch of her scarred mouth.

"I'll relay Cal's decision to the rest of Command," she says, breaking the silent tension. Her words are low and measured. "*Just* Command. Ada will carry the message."

The Montfort premier ducks his chin in agreement. "Good. I think Generals Drummer and Swan may have an idea of these developments already. They've been keeping tabs on the Lerolan queen since she came into play."

"Anabel Lerolan was in Maven's court long enough, at least a few weeks," I reply. Somehow, my voice doesn't tremble. The words come out evenly, full of force. I have to look strong, even if I don't feel it right now. It's a lie, but a good lie. "She probably has more information than I ever gave you."

"Probably," Davidson says with a thoughtful bob of the head. He narrows his eyes on the ground. Not searching, but focusing. A plan spirals out in front of him. The road ahead won't be easy. A child would know that. "Which is why I have to get back up there," he adds, almost in apology. As if I could be angry with him for doing what he must. "Ears and eyes open, yeah?"

"Ears and eyes open," Farley and I respond in unison, surprising each other.

He steps away from us, backing out of the alleyway. The sun flashes in his glossy gray hair. He was careful to clean up after the battle, washing away the sweat and ash, replacing his bloodstained uniform with a fresh one. All to present his usual calm, collected, and strangely ordinary demeanor. A wise decision. Silvers devote so much energy to their appearance, to the false pride of visible strength and power. And none so much as the Samos king and his family in the tower above us. Next to Volo, Evangeline, Ptolemus, and the hissing Viper queen, Davidson barely registers. He could blend into the walls if he wanted to. *They won't see him coming. They won't see us coming.*

I take a shaky breath and swallow, forcing the next thought. *And Cal won't either.*

Tiberias, I snap at myself. One fist clenches, digging nails into flesh with a satisfying sting. *Call him Tiberias.*

The black walls of Corvium feel strangely silent and bare without the siege. I turn away from Davidson's retreating form to eye the parapets ringing the inner ward of the fortress city. The shiver attacking snowstorm is long gone, the darkness lifted, and everything here seems smaller now. Less imposing. Red soldiers used to be herded through this city, most on the march to inevitable death in a trench. Now Reds patrol the walls, the streets, the gates. Reds sit alongside Silver kings and speak of war. A few soldiers with crimson scarves walk back and forth, their eyes darting, well-used guns ready in hand. The Scarlet Guard will not be caught unawares, though they have little reason to be so on edge. For now, anyway. Maven's armies have retreated. And not even Volo Samos is bold enough to attempt an attack from the inside of Corvium. Not when he needs the Guard, needs Montfort, needs us. And especially not with Cal—*Tiberias, you fool*—and all his empty talk of equality. Like us, Volo needs him. Needs his name, needs his crown, and needs his damn hand in that damn marriage to his damn daughter.

My face burns hot. I feel embarrassed by the plume of jealousy rising up inside me. Losing him should be the least of my worries. Losing him shouldn't hurt as much as the possibility of dying, of losing our war, of letting everything we've worked for be in vain. But it does. All I can do is try to bear it.

Why didn't I say yes?

I walked away from his offer. From him. I was torn apart by another betrayal—Cal's betrayal, but also mine. *I love you* is a promise we both made, and we both broke. It should mean *I choose you above all else. I want you more. I need you always. I cannot live without you. I will do anything to keep our lives from parting.*

But he wouldn't. And I won't.

I am less than his crown, and he is less than my cause.

And less, far less, than my fear of another cage. *Consort,* he said, offering me an impossible crown. He would make me a queen, if Evangeline could be pushed aside *again.* I already know what the world looks like from a king's right hand. I don't care to live that life again. Even though Cal is not Maven, the throne is still the same. It changes people, corrupts them.

What a strange fate that would have been. Cal with his crown and his Samos queen and me. In spite of myself, a small part of me wishes I'd said yes. It would have been easy. A chance to let go, step back, *win*—and enjoy a world I never could have dreamed of. Give my family the best life possible. Keep us all safe. And stay with him. Stand at Cal's side, a Red girl with a Silver king on her arm. With the power to change the world. To kill Maven. To sleep without nightmares, and live without fear.

I bite my lip sharply to drive away the want. It seduces, and I almost understand his choice. Even ripped apart, we suit each other.

Farley shifts loudly, drawing my attention. She sighs as she puts her back to the alley wall, arms folded across her chest. Unlike Davidson, she hasn't bothered to change out of her bloody uniform. Hers isn't as disgusting as mine, free of mud and muck. There's silver blood on her, of course, now dried black. It's only been a few months since Clara was born, and she wears the lingering weight around her hips proudly. Whatever sympathy she had disappears, replaced by a rage sparking in her blue eyes. Not directed at me, though. She looks skyward, at the tower above us. Where the strange council of Silvers and Reds now tries to decide our fates.

"That was him in there." She doesn't wait for me to ask who. "Silver hair, thick neck, ridiculous armor. And somehow still breathing, even though he put a blade through Shade's heart."

My nails dig deeper at the thought of Ptolemus Samos. Prince of the Rift. My brother's killer. Like Farley, I feel a sudden rage too. And an equal burst of shame.

"Yes."

"Because you made a bargain with his sister. Your freedom for his life."

"For my vengeance," I mumble in admission. "And yes, I gave Evangeline my word."

Farley bares her teeth, her disgust evident. "You gave a Silver your word. That promise is less than ash."

"But a promise still."

She makes a guttural sound deep in her throat, like a growl. Her broad shoulders square and she turns her body to face the tower fully. I wonder how much restraint it's taking to stop her from marching back up there to rip Ptolemus's eyes out of his skull. I wouldn't stop her if she could. In fact, I'd pull up a chair and watch.

I let my fist open a bit, putting away the slice of pain. Quietly, I take a step forward, closing the space between us. After a split second of hesitation, I put a hand on her arm. "A promise *I* made. Not you. Not anyone else."

Farley stills a bit, and her snarl becomes a smirk. She turns to look at me head-on, her eyes brightly blue as they catch a shaft of sunlight. "I think you might be better suited to politics than war, Mare Barrow."

I offer a pained smile. "They're the same thing." A hard lesson I think I've finally learned. "Do you think you can do it? Kill him?"

Once, I would have expected her to scoff and boldly sneer at the implication she couldn't. Farley is a hard woman with a harder shell. She's what she needs to be. But something—Shade probably, Clara definitely, the bond we now share—affords me a glimpse past the general's stony and sure exterior. She falters, her smirk fading a little.

"I don't know," she murmurs. "But I'll never be able to look at myself, look at Clara, if I don't try."

"And neither will I, if I let you die in the attempt." My grip tightens on her arm. "Please, don't be stupid about this."

Like the flip of a switch, her smirk returns in full force. She even winks. "Since when am I stupid, Mare Barrow?"

Looking up at her sends a twinge through the scars at the back of my neck, scars I almost forgot about. The pain of them seems small compared to everything else. "I just wonder where it will end," I murmur, hoping to make her understand.

She shakes her head. "I can't respond to a question with too many answers."

"I mean . . . with Shade. Ptolemus. You kill him, and then what? Evangeline kills you? Kills Clara? I kill Evangeline? On and on, with no end?" I'm no stranger to death, but this feels oddly different. Calculated endings. It feels like something Maven would do, not us. Even though Farley marked Ptolemus for death long before, when I masqueraded as

Mareena Titanos, that was for the Guard. For a cause, for something other than blind and bloody revenge.

Her eyes widen, vibrant and impossible. "You want me to let him live?"

"Of course not," I almost snap. "I don't know what I want. I don't know what I'm talking about." The words tumble over one another. "But I can still wonder, Farley. I know what vengeance and rage can do to a person, to the people around you. And of course I don't want Clara to grow up without her mother."

She turns away sharply, hiding her face. But not quickly enough to hide a sudden surge of tears. They never fall. With a jerk of her shoulder, she shrugs me away.

I push on. I have to. She needs to hear this. "She already lost Shade, and if given the choice between revenge for her father and a living mother—I know what she would choose."

Read on to discover the thrilling world of

1

THE SMUGGLER'S DAUGHTER
Corayne

There was clear sight for miles. A good day for the end of a voyage.

And a good day to begin one.

Corayne loved the coast of Siscaria this time of year, in the mornings of early summer. No spring storms, no crackling thunderheads, no winter fog. No splendor of color, no beauty. No illusions. Nothing but the empty blue horizon of the Long Sea.

Her leather satchel bounced at her hip, her ledger safe inside. The book of charts and lists was worth its weight in gold, especially today. She eagerly walked the ancient Cor road along the cliffs, following the flat, paved stones into Lemarta. She knew the way like she knew her mother's own face. Sand-colored and wind-carved, not worn by the sun but gilded by it. The Long Sea crashed fifty feet below, kicking up spray in rhythm with the tide. Olive and cypress trees grew over the hills, and the wind blew kindly, smelling of salt and oranges.

A good day, she thought again, turning her face to the sun.

Her guardian, Kastio, walked at her side, his body weathered by decades on the waves. Gray-haired with furious black eyebrows, the old Siscarian sailor was darkly tanned from fingertips to toes. He walked at an odd pace, suffering from old knees and permanent sea legs.

"Any more dreams?" he asked, glancing at his charge sidelong. His vivid blue eyes searched her face with the focus of an eagle.

Corayne shook her head, blinking tired eyes. "Just excited," she offered, forcing a thin smile to placate him. "You know I barely sleep before the ship returns."

The old sailor was easily thrown off.

He doesn't need to know about my dreams, nor does anyone. He would certainly tell Mother, who would make it all the more unbearable with her concern.

But they still come every night. And, somehow, they're getting worse.

White hands, shadowed faces. Something moving in the dark.

The memory of the dream chilled her even in broad daylight, and she sped up, as if she could outrun her own mind.

Ships made their way along the Empress Coast toward the Lemartan port. They had to sail up the gullet of the city's natural harbor, in full sight of the road and the watchtowers of Siscaria. Most of the towers were relics of Old Cor, near ruins of storm-washed stone, named for emperors and empresses long gone. They stood out like teeth in a half-empty jaw. The towers still standing were manned by old soldiers or land-bound sailors, men in their twilight.

"What's the count this morning, Reo?" Corayne asked as she passed the Tower of Balliscor. In the window stood its single keeper, a decaying old man.

He waggled a set of wrinkled fingers, his skin worn as old leather. "Only two in beyond the point. Blue-green sails."

Aquamarine sails, she corrected in her head, *marked with the golden mermaid of Tyriot.* "You don't miss a trick, do you?" she said, not breaking stride.

He chuckled weakly. "My hearing might be going, but my eye's sharp as ever."

"Sharp as ever!" Corayne echoed, fighting a smirk.

Indeed two Tyri galleys were past Antero Point, but a third ship crawled through the shallows, in the shadow of the cliffs. Difficult to spot, for those who did not know where to look. Or those paid to look elsewhere.

Corayne left no coin behind for the half-blind watchman of Balliscor, but she dropped the usual bribes at the towers of Macorras and Alcora. *An alliance bought is still an alliance made,* she thought, hearing her mother's voice in her head.

She gave the same to the gatekeeper at the Lemarta walls, though the port city was small, the gate already open, Corayne and Kastio well known. *Or at least my mother is well known, well liked, and well feared in equal measure.*

The gatekeeper took the coin, waving them onto familiar streets overgrown with lilac and orange blossoms. They perfumed the air, hiding the smells of a crowded port, somewhere between small city and bustling town. Lemarta was a bright place, the stone buildings painted in the radiant colors of sunrise and sunset. On a summer morning, the market streets crowded with tradespeople and townsfolk alike.

Corayne offered smiles like her coin: an item to trade. Like always, she felt a barrier between herself and the throng of people, as if she were watching them through glass. Farmers drove their mules in from the cliffs, carting vegetables, fruits, and grain. Merchants shouted their wares in every language of the Long Sea. Dedicant priests walked in lines, their robes dyed in varying shades to note their orders. The blue-cloaked priests of Meira were always most numerous, praying to the goddess of the waters. Sailors waiting for a tide or a wind already idled in seden courtyards, drinking wine in the sunshine.

A port city was many things, but above all a crossroads. While Lemarta was insignificant in the scheme of the world, she was nothing to sneer at. She was a good place to drop anchor.

But not for me, Corayne thought as she quickened her pace. *Not one second longer.*

A maze of steps took them down to the docks, spitting Corayne and Kastio out onto the stone walkway edging the water. The climbing sun flashed brilliantly off the turquoise shallows. Lemarta stared down at the harbor, hunched against the cliffs like an audience in an amphitheater.

The ships from Tyriot were newly docked, anchored on either side of a longer pier jutting out into deeper water. A mess of crew crowded the galleys and the pier, spilling over the planks. Corayne caught snatches of Tyri and Kasan passed from deck to dock, but most spoke Paramount, the shared language of trade on both sides of the Long Sea. The crews unloaded crates and live animals for a pair of Siscarian harbor officers, who made a great show of taking notes for their tax records and dock duties. Half a dozen soldiers accompanied them, clad in rich purple tunics.

Nothing of spectacular quality or particular interest, Corayne noted, eyeing the haul.

Kastio followed her gaze, squinting out beneath his eyebrows. "Where from?" he asked.

Her smirk bloomed as quickly as an answer. "Salt from the Aegir mines," Corayne said, all confidence. "And I bet you a cup of wine the olive oil is from the Orisi groves."

The old sailor chuckled. "No bet—I've learned my lesson more than once," he replied. "You've a head for this business, none can deny that."

She faltered in her steps, her voice sharpening. "Let's hope so."

Another harbor officer waited at the end of the next pier, though the berth was empty. The soldiers with him looked half-asleep, wholly uninterested. Corayne fixed her lips into her best smile, one hand in her satchel with her fingers closed around the final and heaviest pouch. The weight was a comfort, as good as a knight's shield.

Though she'd done this a dozen times, still her fingers trembled. *A good day to begin a voyage,* she told herself again. *A good day to begin.*

Over the officer's shoulder, a ship came into harbor, sailing out of the cliff shadow. There was no mistaking the galley, its deep purple flag a beacon. Corayne's heartbeat drummed.

"Officer Galeri," she called, Kastio close behind her. Though neither wore fine clothes, clad in light summer tunics, leather leggings, and boots, they walked the pier like royalty. "Always a pleasure to see you."

Galeri inclined his head. The officer was almost three times her age— nearing fifty years old—and spectacularly ugly. Still, Galeri was popular with the women of Lemarta, mostly because his pockets were well lined with bribes.

"*Domiana* Corayne, you know the pleasure is mine," he replied, taking her outstretched hand with a flourish. The pouch passed from her fingers to his, disappearing into his coat. "And good morning to you, *Domo* Kastio," he added, nodding at the old man. Kastio glowered in reply "More of the usual this morning? How fares the *Tempestborn*?"

"She fares well." Corayne grinned truly, looking over the galley as she glided in.

The *Tempestborn* was bigger than the Tyri galleys, longer by half and twice as fine, with a ram better suited to battle than trade just below the waterline. She was a beautiful ship, her hull darkly painted for voyages in colder seas. With the turn of the season, warm-water camouflage would come: sea-green and sand stripes. But for now she was as shadow, flying the wine-dark purple of a Siscarian ship returning home. The crew was in good shape, Corayne knew, watching their oars move in perfect motion as they maneuvered the long, flat ship to the dock.

A silhouette stood at the stern, and warmth spread in Corayne's chest.

She turned back to Galeri sharply, pulling a paper from her ledger, already stamped with the seal of a noble family. "The cargo listing, more of the usual." *For cargo not yet unloaded.* "You'll find accurate counts. Salt and honey, taken on in Aegironos."

Galeri eyed the paper without interest. "Bound for?" he asked, opening his own ledger of notes. Behind him, one of the soldiers took to pissing off the dock.

Corayne wisely ignored him. "Lecorra," she said. The Siscarian capital. Once the center of the known realm, now a shadow of its imperial glory. "To His Excellency, Duke Reccio—"

"That will suffice," Galeri muttered. Noble shipments could not be taxed, and their seals were easy to replicate or steal, for those with the inclination, skill, and daring.

At the end of the pier, ropes were thrown, men leaping with them. Their voices were a tangle of languages: Paramount and Kasan and Treckish and even the lilting Rhashiran tongue. The patchwork of noise wove with the hiss of rope on wood, the splash of an anchor, the slap of a sail. Corayne could barely stand it, ready to jump out of her skin with excitement.

Galeri dropped into a shallow bow, grinning. Two of his teeth were brighter than the rest. *Ivory, bought or bribed.* "Very well, this is settled. We'll stand watch, of course, to observe your shipment for His Excellency."

It was the only invitation Corayne needed. She trotted by the officer and his soldiers, doing her best not to break into a run. In her younger years, she would have, sprinting to the *Tempestborn* with arms outstretched. *But I am seventeen years old, nearly a woman, and the ship's agent besides,* she told herself. *I must act like crew and not a child clutching at skirts.*

Not that I've ever seen my mother wear a skirt.

"Welcome back!" Corayne called, first in Paramount, then in the half-dozen other languages she knew, and the two more she could attempt. Rhashiran was still beyond her grasp, while the Jydi tongue was famously impossible for outsiders.

"You've been practicing," said Ehjer, the first crew member to meet her. He was near seven feet tall, his white skin covered in tattoos and scars hard-won in the snows of the Jyd. She knew the stories of the worst of them—a bear, a skirmish, a lover, a particularly angry moose. *Or perhaps the last two were the same?* she wondered before he embraced her.

"Don't patronize me, Ehjer; I sound *haarblød*," she gasped, struggling to breathe in his grip. He laughed heartily.

The pier crowded with reunion, the planks a mess of crew and crates. Corayne passed through, careful to note any new recruits picked up on the voyage. There were always a few, easy to spot. Most had blistered hands and sunburns, unaccustomed to life on deck. The *Tempestborn* liked to train their own from the waves up.

Mother's rule, like so many others.

Corayne found her where she always did, half perched on the railing.

Meliz an-Amarat was neither tall nor short, but her presence was vast and commanded attention. A good quality for any ship's captain to have. She scanned the dock with a hawk's eye and a dragon's pride, her task yet unfinished though the ship was safely in port. She was not a captain to laze in her cabin or flit off to the nearest seden to drink while the crew did the hard work. Every crate and burlap sack passed beneath her gaze, to be checked off on a mental tally.

"How fare the winds?" Corayne called, watching her mother rule over her galley kingdom.

From the deck, Meliz beamed, her hair free about her shoulders, black as a storm cloud. The faint smile lines around her mouth were well earned.

"Fine, for they bring me home," she said, her voice like honey.

They were words spoken since Corayne was a child, barely old enough to know where her mother was going, when all she could do was wave with one hand and clutch at Kastio with the other. *Not so anymore.*